DEADLY FAE DUOLOGY

BOOK 2

POISON
AMIDST
BLOOMS

CASSANDRA ASTON

For those who go weak in the knees at the "my wife" trope, brace yourself: this isn't that kind of love story.

CONTENT AND TRIGGER WARNINGS

This book contains themes and scenes that may be disturbing to some readers, including:

Violence, Torture, and Gore

- Graphic and non-graphic violence (guns, axes, knives, swords, and other weapons)
- Explicit torture (including magical and medical torture)
- Forced self-harm
- Body horror, blood, and injury detail
- On-page character deaths (including major and minor characters)
- Self-sacrifice and non-consensual deaths
- Child loss and child endangerment
- Child slavery
- War, raids, and mass casualties

Mental Health and Trauma

- PTSD, flashbacks, and panic attacks
- Grief and loss of family members
- Depression and other mental health themes
- Hallucinations and altered states of consciousness

Sexual Content and Consent

- Sexual content
- Sexual assault, attempted sexual assault, and coercion
- Allusions to non-consensual sexual acts
- Loss of bodily autonomy

Power, Coercion, and Discrimination

- Mental manipulation and mind control
- Loss of autonomy and captivity/imprisonment
- Bigotry, speciesism, and hate-motivated violence
- References to cults and cult mentality

Substances

- Alcohol and drug use
- Use of medical and magical drugs, including poisoning

Fantasy and Body Content Notes

- Fantastical mythical creatures
- Unusual anatomy (including male characters who appear to have two penises)
- Unrealistic smells and scents especially after days without showering

Whispers Among Thorns Recap

Reports from Foxglove (WHISPER) to General Creig (THORN)

WHISPER:THORN

General, as you know, Mab's been gone six years. Since the last sweep, sections of Spring continue to vanish; fae with them. Two streams through Winter are sealed restricting access even from their prince. Plan as if the board is shrinking under your feet—because it is.

WHISPER:THORN

Night smoke over Central Park. Dane lit the building to flush our folk. Several folk detained below AFF headquarters. Sav captured, but escaped with the help of a human. Dane's son.

WHISPER:THORN

Prince Kaspar stood beside Sav in Winter. Vouched for the impending marriage. She and the human are enroute to Spring. Winter declined her request for aid. She plans to request it from her sister. Other intel: Jack planned a rescue attempt on AFF headquarters with assistance from two other human companions prior to his initial interaction with Sav. Will report when I learn more about them.

WHISPER:THORN

Sav, Jack and Hazel arrived in Ferndell in search of Ivy, Spring Court healer. Sav was unaware she'd relocated to the castle when much of the Ashwood disappeared. Hazel was injured by a snowbird. They go to Spring in hopes of finding someone to aid her there. I will install myself in court to keep an eye on the trio. Still no sign of Sav's magic since it was bound by her sister three years ago.

WHISPER:THORN

Hazel has made a full recovery. Sage denied Sav's request to free the folk held at AFF. Jack was imprisoned by the princess of Spring when his heritage was revealed. Prince Kaspar arrived just in time to aid in their escape. The group made for Spring's portal to Earth, but only Sav and Jack went to Earth. Move to intercept on Earth. They are unaware of the bounty on their heads. There's something odd about the human. He's showing signs of fae magic. Proceed with caution. Recommend taking Murz.

WHISPER:THORN

The Prince of Summer has leverage over Sav. As yet, unsure what it is. His proposal three years ago may have been about more than a court alliance. Will investigate.

WHISPER:THORN

It is as you feared. Sav and the human are entangled. Do NOT recommend proceeding with the original plan. Buy-in from Sav will be required. Recommend outing her plan to ensure Jack goes willingly.

THORN:WHISPER

Understood. Casualties are not an option. We've lost too many to the sadist cult leader at AFF. We depart at nightfall.

WHISPER:THORN

Extraction was a success, but the cost was Sav's human. Jack is in ISHFA custody now. They're leaning on Mab's law: Never fall in love with a human. Expect retaliation from Sav. I'll stay close to ensure she does not get herself captured.

WHISPER:THORN

Sav and the Prince of Lakes and Streams have wed. She returned to Spring only to find Sage and most of the castle taken by whatever is eating Faerie. Silv, the Spring Court's satyr clan leader, unbound some of her magic, but not all. She's headed to you.

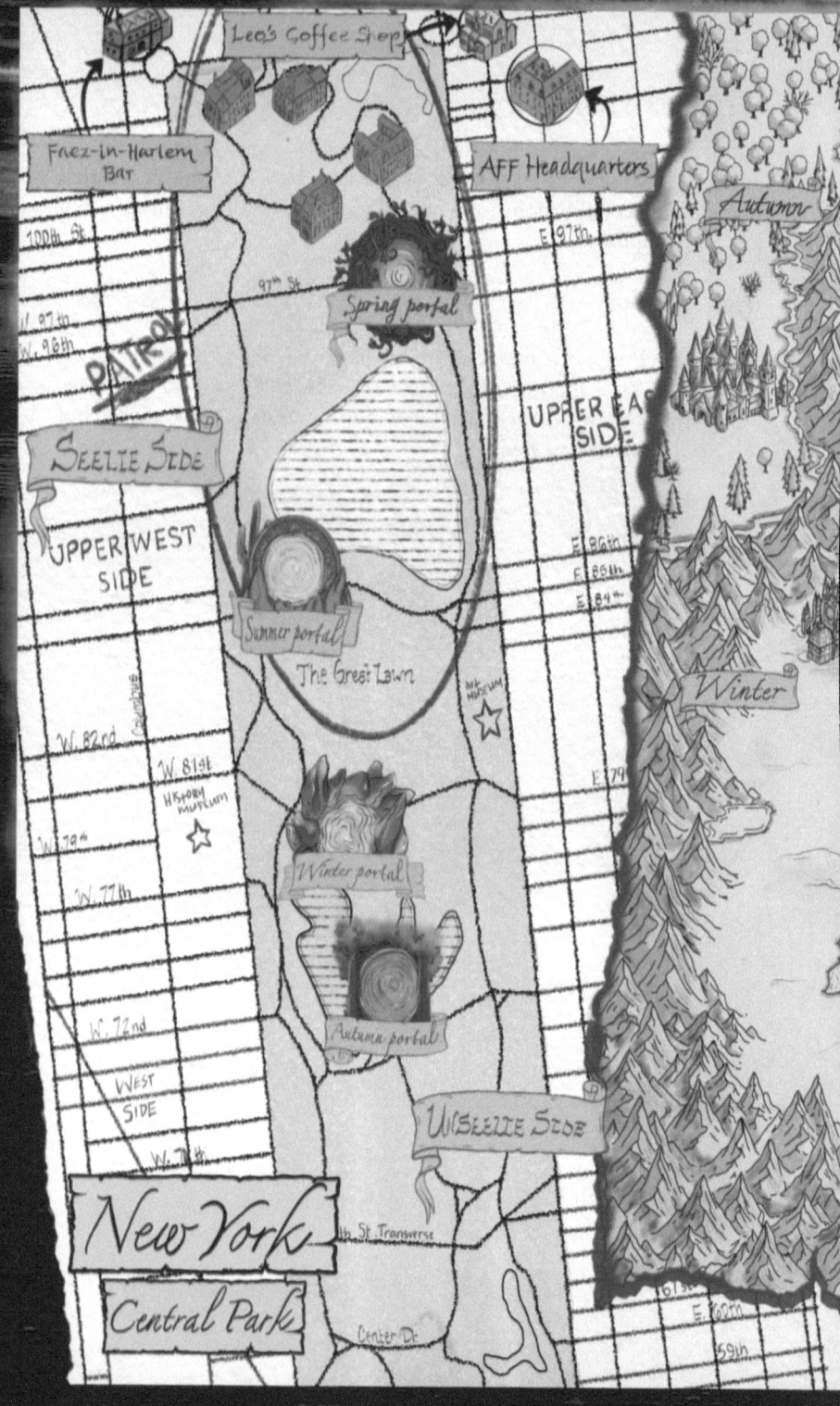

PROLOGUE

FERO

TWO HUNDRED AND SIXTY-FOUR YEARS AGO

I ran a hand over the stubble at my jaw as I paced the sandy beach outside my castle, eyes scanning the glittering sea. The salt air did nothing to calm the tightness in my chest. If this went badly, it could mean war for my people. After six months of Prince Kaspar choking off access to fresh water, the one resource my court could not survive without, desperation had become our constant companion.

All signs pointed to me, and I wasn't fool enough to assume he would allow me the opportunity to explain.

Whoever had killed the prince's sister wanted war between our two courts, and would soon have their wish. In a climate where water was a finite resource, he need only wait for us to die and the more time that passed, the more convinced I was that he intended to do just that.

My plan was reckless, but I had to make things right with the Prince of Lakes and Streams.

"Fero."

I stiffened. Only a master spy could have approached in broad daylight without me catching a hint of his scent or movement. I turned slowly, gaze locking on the aquamarine eyes of the prince who was barely more than a boy.

In Summer, all fae had their magic tested at age twenty-five. The most powerful was handed the principality and forced to lead. It was a flawed system that often turned out to be incorrect. Although all high fae came into their magic at that age, it was a taste of what they would become.

1

While most accurately displayed their potential, others, like me, were less obvious in their early years.

Had my innate gifts—the ones whose secret I guarded with my life—not been that of both magic sensor *and* siphon, I would have displayed nearly no magic at all. But, as I'd learned on that day, I could sense the most powerful creature nearby and borrow their ability. On my day of testing, I'd reached for the strongest water wielder and lent my fledgling gift aid.

In a court where such a precious resource determined our fate, having a powerful water wielder on the throne was an omen of great prosperity for my folk.

Now, I sensed the wild magic coursing through the prince's veins. It was similar, yet so unlike mine. It was nearly limitless, but I also sensed that he wasn't fully aware of how to harness it yet. In time, he would rival the legends of the great kelpie princes of old. Should he survive his uncle.

"Prince Kaspar."

The kelpie, in land fae form, raised his chin. A show of utter disrespect. I let it pass.

"I have come. Where is your evidence?"

I rolled the silver ball piercing my tongue over my teeth, my tongue like sandpaper against the roof of my mouth. I had one chance. If it went poorly, I would be the first summer prince in the history of Faerie forced to take his folk and abandon their court. What legacy would I leave? Spring was the closest in temperature, but with their alliance to Lakes and Streams they would not offer aid. That meant I was dependent on Winter or Autumn.

While Mab was our sovereign, I was under no illusion that she would deign to open Winter's doors to Summer. That left Autumn... A bitter prospect indeed.

None of those were viable options. This had to go well. Everything rode on this conversation.

"I did not kill Mira."

Kaspar's eyes narrowed and had he not left his water behind, I suspected he would have razed my court as he had the day he'd found her dead on my beach.

"Do not speak her name." His voice was deceptively soft.

I swallowed. My reputation had been built on the power I wielded. Showing weakness now was counter to every move I had made in my one hundred twenty years as ruler. And the prince would not have listened to my plea had I made one.

Straightening to my full height, I met his gaze, unblinking. "I did not kill your sister."

The kelpie's gaze darkened, but he said nothing. He was too aware of the state of my court. It was the reason he hadn't brought any water with him. He would give us none, even if it was his greatest weapon. He would rather die than see my folk survive his fury.

"Consider all that happened the night she was taken. I was with her, yes, but Lady Briar was also there. I tried to save her from the poison. When you attacked us in the gardens, your sister was already gone. How could I have taken her? When?"

The prince quirked a brow and, for a moment, I believed he might see reason. I hoped this meant I did not need to use my backup plan.

"It means nothing. You handed them the poisoned glasses—"

"They were given to me."

"By whom."

"I don't know. A server. A Spring Court server. I did not look closer than that. I never expected to be poisoned at a ball for the new princess of Spring. I was a guest in their court."

The cold, sharp eyes of the sea creature appraised me. I could see the doubt creeping in. It wasn't enough to convince him, but doubt was all I needed.

"Where were you the day my army attacked your castle? The day we found—" The words were choked at the end, a strange hint of emotion in them and it was my turn to raise a brow. As quickly as it arrived, it was gone. "The day my sister was found with her heart torn out on your beach."

"We were invited to the princess's ceremony in Autumn. None in our court had ever been. It was a high honor, one I could not refuse." I raised my arm, the only proof I had of that strange night, and showed him the black circle on the underside of my forearm. Though I remembered little of my time in Autumn's court, the bite had never healed properly, blackening with time and leaving a permanent scar.

There was no denying its origin. Only an Autumn Court fae with considerable blood magic, could leave such a mark. I could only hope it was enough to convince him of my innocence.

I had been certain we were gone no more than a night, but Ence, head of my guard, reported she'd waited outside the Autumn border for more than a week. By the time I returned home to a court littered with Kaspar's sparkling silver fish army scorched by Summer's unforgiving sun, it was too late to save them.

Prince Kaspar's posture relaxed, shoulders going soft and his brows smoothed out. He was the indifferent ruler of Lakes and Streams once more, and the hairs on the back of my neck rose. Whether it was from the emotion I'd thought charged the air moments before, or the reminder that his kind were cold and uncaring, I couldn't say.

Silence hung between us, heavy and humid. I stood perfectly still, prodding his gift. If he'd been preparing to call on the might of his water, I would have felt it, could have turned it against him. But the air was void of the ions that buzzed around him when water was nearby. He wasn't preparing, he was considering.

Behind him, some of my folk peeked their heads out from behind the trees lining the forest he'd come through. Their large round eyes moved from him to me and back. A reminder I could not fail them.

"I swear to you, I am not behind your sister's murder, and I will make a bargain with you to further prove it."

He pursed his lips and after a moment, nodded.

"I will aid you in your search for her killer and when the time comes, I will assist you in ending them."

Kaspar raised a brow. "One more question. What did you want with Lady Briar?"

I tipped my head, surprised by the question. Though I'd seen the way he watched her, he'd showed no interest beyond that of any court creature attempting to forge alliances. As sister to the princess of his closest ally, I would have expected nothing less. I could confess, I'd come seeking a similar alliance.

Our courts had been at odds too long. With Alder's new bride on the throne, I'd hoped we could begin again, set aside the differences of our predecessors. But Sav's innate gift, accessible to her six months before her twenty-fifth birthday, had taken me by surprise and my guard had been brought low by her disarming character.

She was a mystery and whether it was due to my innate gifts or simply because she charmed me, I very much wanted to puzzle her out. I didn't delude myself into believing there could ever be more than a friendship between myself and the princess's sister, but she would be a powerful ally to have when her magic was fully awakened.

"Only to forge new relationships with my neighbor."

Kaspar dipped his chin and I knew—with that one gesture—we were no longer at war.

ONE

JACK

My awareness kept slipping, the harsh light in Janet Glassdon's office flaring and fading. Time had unraveled; I couldn't tell if I'd been here for hours or days, a prisoner in her cell. When she —and I—realized I couldn't feel pain, it became a game to her.

She spent hours on me. Blood thrilled her most. I could see it in the way her eyes glazed over, her tongue sliding along her lips. Then she'd disappear to find her lover before coming back for another round.

But even without pain, blood loss had me swaying, and one thing was clear: I wasn't immune to dying.

By the third round of electric shocks, my thoughts slid out of order, my vision went soft, and I could swear life was draining from me.

I sagged forward, head heavy, and held onto thoughts of Sav, our kiss, and the fae I was certain she saved the night I drew Dane away. Anything to take my mind off the creeping numbness in my fingers and toes.

I was down to underwear now. Janet was as intent on watching me heal as she was on making me bleed.

We watched together in sick fascination as she sliced a finger open, peeling back layers of tiny muscle and ligament until the bone was all that remained, only for it to regrow. If it hadn't been my finger, I might have liked to study all the tiny details of human anatomy that made up such a unique body part. At times the blood blurred everything; an endless tide I couldn't seem to empty.

It slid across the floor and chased every crack.

No one had brought me so much as a sip of water since I'd arrived. Gnawing emptiness ate me from the inside, stealing my focus almost as often as the terror I couldn't quite overcome. At what point would my body stop knitting itself back together?

A chilling thought crept in: if I couldn't feel pain, could I break my wrists and ankles to slip free? They'd heal, but how far would elbows and knees carry me until they did?

The gleam in Janet's eye shifted, boredom edging in. Escalation was next, and the last question would be whether I came back from death. A new fear accompanied the litany of thoughts racing through my mind as I considered all I hadn't yet accomplished in my short life. My own mortality wasn't something I'd ever considered, but now, faced with the question.

My eyes sank closed, the hollow ache of an empty stomach chasing me into my dreams. A dark image rose behind my lids. I tried to blink, but they were too heavy. In the dark, emerald eyes flashed. The same eyes I'd seen on the path.

"Mom?" I couldn't tell if I spoke or only thought it. They blinked, searching the dark. Maybe it was delirium. A vision of the one person I wanted at the end. "I'll see you soon," I said. Or thought.

"Jack?"

My eyes flew open to the stark white office, my blood the only color left.

It had felt real. Her voice. My mother's.

TWO

SAV

"My sister is missing."

Kaspar's brows dipped low. "And if we don't leave Spring now, we will be too." Though his words held a warning, he appeared perfectly at ease in his navy suit. He rarely wore a shirt, let alone a jacket, but he'd made an exception on our wedding day.

I glanced to Hazel helplessly, but if I hoped to find an ally there, I had been wrong. Her eyes were wide and she glanced around at the expansive walls of Spring's throne room as if she expected our wing to vanish too. She looked out of place in the garb I'd grabbed for us. I wasn't sure I'd ever seen Hazel in pants before.

Foxglove scooted to my side. I bristled, but held my tongue. In truth, the pain slicing through my middle from ribbons of my sister's binding magic unwinding one by one, and the thought of running made me sick.

In six years, none of the fae who had disappeared ever returned. When we found the hidden pocket of Spring where Creig's free army hid, I'd nearly wept, but none of the lost folk were there, and although Creig had found many of the missing parts of Faerie, they were always empty.

My heart ached from something deeper than the pain of having my magic unbound. I was torn between racing to Creig, begging him to assist me in searching for my sister, and doing what I'd come here to do. Save Jack. I'd promised Creig I'd keep the Inter Species Human Fae Alliance off his plate, and I hadn't moved on them. Yet. Perhaps I could kill two birds with one stone.

"We're going to Creig."

Hazel's emerald eyes lifted. Hope.

Foxglove cut a look to Kaspar. "Princess." The word was sharp as a blade.

I spun to face my husband. Husband... The title scraped at my composure. "Kaspar—"

Kaspar's aquamarine eyes were darker than I'd ever seen them. "Go. I must check on our court. I will search for news of your sister. You know where to find me."

I grimaced. I did. In our court. In my new home. What I'd done only hours ago still had my stomach in knots. A little time apart would do us both some good. I nodded, turning to Foxglove.

"We're bringing Hazel."

Foxglove's brow furrowed, but he didn't argue.

I grabbed Hazel's hand.

Kaspar's jaw tightened. "Come through my court."

I glanced to Foxglove. "Are there no portals to Spring's hidden pocket of Faerie apart from the one on Earth?"

His frown deepened. He didn't like me sharing information about his and Creig's hideout with Kaspar. Had he already forgotten which court my allegiance was now promised to? Whether I wanted to share the details with Kaspar or not, he could demand them.

"There are not," he finally said, fingers drumming the side of his leg.

It was all he would say and all we needed to know. I dipped my chin to Kaspar. "We're coming with you it seems."

Once, Kaspar would've winked. Now, there was ice in that aquamarine gaze. The ache was mine to carry; I didn't have a stone heart to hide behind. But even as I thought it, I remembered the small touches laid out for me in my new room in Lakes and Streams. Thoughtful gestures a heartless prince wouldn't have seen to.

We reached the bottom of the lake and a tightness in my chest, one made of magic, loosened, knowing my court was safe from whatever was destroying Faerie.

The three of us gripped Kaspar's seaweed mane as he dove for the portal between realms and Hazel's eyes went round as the bright sparkling water was quickly replaced by murky, soot filled liquid that burned.

On the other side, Kaspar kicked off the sludge and we broke the surface gasping. I blinked several times, clearing away the grime and exhaled a shallow breath. Earth smelled worse every time. Smog and the heavy scent of iron filled my nostrils.

Kaspar trudged out of the lake, dragging us with him. Hazel's tail vanished; she wobbled on unsteady legs. Her glamour blurred her most telling features, but the white sheet of hair and those bright eyes would still turn heads.

Foxglove's glamour passed at a glance. He'd worn it often—long enough to walk among humans while feeding Creig intel on Jack's father and the other Anti Fae Faction members.

I turned to reach for Kaspar's turquoise neck, but he'd already eased back, sinking until only his head was visible in its murky depths.

"I'm sorry," I mouthed. Inadequate words for my oldest friend, but I had nothing else to give him. I would be back to search for Sage and find the other members of her court, to help Kaspar, if he needed it, but I couldn't abandon Jack.

Still, seeing Kaspar in my favorite kelpie form evoked memories of our early friendship and all he'd done for me. I hoped he understood.

Hazel clung to my arm, and I squeezed. New York was overwhelming, especially for one's first time. Sirens, iron, and trash were amplified tenfold with my senses no longer muffled. The late afternoon sun burned my already tender skin and I tugged at the sleeve of my top, trying and failing to cover my arms from its malicious gaze.

Dane's patrol ran this grid, but we were headed away from HQ, south, through Central Park, toward the old zoo. Something in my chest tugged me north, toward the building I knew Jack was being held in, but I wouldn't drag Hazel into ISHFA headquarters. I wouldn't trade anyone's life for my mistake but my own.

I'm coming Jack, I promised. *Hang on.*

THREE

KASPAR

The words to our vows repeated in my mind on a loop. We swore the court came before all else, especially our own desires. Yet the moment Sav had her magic back, most of it, she'd left to save Jack. Did she care so little for the creatures of our court that she would choose one man over them all?

I stepped through the air shield into my office, legs forming as I went, and reached for the book my father gave me when I was nine. *Study it every day. A kelpie who does not know his court has already lost it.* The words were burned into my brain, driving me to check and recheck the borders of my territory. Had he known he would be taken from me so young, perhaps he would have imparted more wisdom, prepared me better. But nothing he could have said would have prepared me to rule at eleven.

I ran the pad of my finger over a row of silver tubes, each more precious to me than any treasure.

Memphe cleared his throat outside my door, and I looked up, motioning him in. "Bring everyone into the great hall. I need a headcount. That means spies in the field, the elderly, and the children. Everyone attends."

"Yes, Sire."

"Get me the latest patrol reports. I want to know if anyone saw anything or if any of my lakes and streams have diverted paths."

"Yes, Sire."

"Are the access points to Winter reopened?"

"No, Sire."

A muscle in my jaw jumped as I clenched.

Memphe's long tongue darted out, sliding over one bulbous eye. His nervous tick. "Lady Elm lacks the authority. With Regent Goodfellow in power, only he can grant your request."

I slammed my fist onto the table; several inkpots tipped and spilled. Memphe rushed forward, attempting to right them. "Leave it."

Gravel and too much magic edged my voice; I grimaced when my advisor flinched. I needed to relax, or more than my wife would suspect my feelings this day.

My wife. Bitterness coated my tongue. Never had I imagined the day I'd envisioned for so long would go like this. My bride, pale faced and terrified, promising eternity with me while plotting her lover's escape. And after learning our court may be in danger, she left without a backward glance.

I couldn't worry about that now. As Prince of Lakes and Streams, I relied on more than spies. Water ran through every court; it saw what I could not. The bigger picture that none of us had yet grasped.

In the great hall, all were crowded shoulder to shoulder. After two centuries of putting my folk first, I'd rebuilt what my early mistakes broke. My spies, all shifters, could move on land or sea and most could tolerate salt. The other creatures, non-shifters and those who were not fae, stayed in my lake, close to the castle to ensure no act of war or error in judgement on the part of their prince might be the cause of their death.

"Kila, Twila, report."

My spy twins swam forward, fins fanning as they stopped before me. They bowed low, hovering in place. Long, navy strands of seaweed hair clouded around their heads—too like the dream that plagued me. My sister's inky blood slipping into the ocean as Summer's merciless waves crashed over her limp form.

My patience was thin, but I worked to check it. "Report."

They straightened.

"Only a thin strip of land around Lakes and Streams remains of Spring," Twila said.

"If it goes, the ocean will overtake us," Kila added.

Shouts of dismay echoed around the space. In my court, where secrets were our currency, we reported everything in the open. Better they know what may be coming for us. I nodded. "Anything else?"

Twila and Kila exchanged a glance. I fisted my hands, nails biting my palms.

Kila's gaze dropped to the floor. "With Autumn and Winter closed to us, our only hope is to divert to Summer."

"But Summer's stream can't hold the whole court." Twila finished.

I waved a hand, dismissing them. Looking out over the court, I beckoned Eras, my commander, forward. "What news from Summer's stream, Eras?"

He swam toward me, bowing low before rising. "Although our access has been sealed, the water has not been diverted. If anything, Summer's stream is shallower than ever."

Shouts rose; I lifted a hand as the pieces aligned in my head. I had suspected it, but I needed confirmation.

"Be at ease, folk of Lakes and Streams. Just as we made a home for ourselves here, I will carve a space for us in Summer."

"And when Summer disappears?" Someone called.

"It has been six years and they are with us yet. I am searching for a solution. One that will withstand this blight."

Faces were pale, eyes wide, and I thanked Oceanus that the folk of my court were not burdened by crushing fear. For if they felt the weight pressing on my chest—the old failure, an entire legion lost—they would flee in terror.

FOUR

DANE

Blue eyes blinked from the alley. Connor's signal. Across from Anti Fae Faction HQ, the coffee shop's back door banged open. Leo stepped out with a trash bag slung over a shoulder. I pocketed my phone.

Connor moved, slipping up behind Leo and wrapping an arm around his neck. His forearm cinched; Leo went boneless in seconds. I'd known Leo was former military, but whatever training he'd gone through had not stuck.

He slumped in Connor's arms and my second—now that Grif was gone—dragged him across the dark gap to a side entrance of our building. I scanned the street. Empty. I nodded. He hauled Leo inside. I jogged toward them and slipped in, closing it behind me.

"You want me to put him in a cage?" Connor's gaze skated over the cells and stuck on the locks. His jaw flexed, breath held. He never went near the latches if he could help it. His was the sharpest tactical mind I had, but cages made him flinch. I'd never asked for details, and he'd never shared them.

Grif would have shared the whole story, even if he knew it made me uncomfortable. I rubbed the ache in my chest that seemed to rise every time something reminded me of my fallen soldier.

"No. Put him in a room upstairs. I can't spare anyone to guard him down here."

"Want me to put him with Alice?"

I tugged my phone out. A picture of Jack and me outside Barclays

15

Center glowed to life. He was taller than me, even then. I stared at the photo for a moment before swiping to my text history with her.

"She's still out. He'll have to stay with you until we have a better place for him."

Connor's hold on Leo slipped and he dipped, grabbing him tightly. "Why don't we put him in the interrogation room? We still have hand and foot cuffs in there from the satyr."

I nodded. Connor always thought ahead. "Do it."

I stepped around him, climbed to the main floor, and held the door wide.

Once he disappeared, I texted Alice:

ME

Anything?

I waited, my grip going slick.

ALICE

Not yet.

Fuck. No proof of life soon and I'd raid ISHFA headquarters without backup.

Coming back now.

Three dots.

Unless you want me to stay.

I wasn't sure what I'd expected Alice to find. From the first floor, nothing could be seen inside ISHFA headquarters. I knew he was in there, though. When they'd come the night Jack brought the general's two sons, Morgan, ISHFA's face on the fae side, had frozen me in place while they dragged Jack away.

They were taking the allegation about his fairy lover seriously. Any interference from me would land me in their custody as well. Morgan's magic would be tough to beat. I needed a plan.

Leo could track her. He could buy me ten minutes. Keeping Jack safe from her long term was another issue, but I'd worry about that when he was back at the AFF safe and sound.

ME

No. Come back. New plan.

I shot the message to Alice and stuffed my phone back in my pocket. If I'd known what was coming, I never would have let the general take my new fairy army the night of the raid. Though I'd never be sorry for laying that trap.

"Dane."

I looked up. William barreled in, sweat bright under the fluorescents, and thumped a tome on the reception desk. My shoulders loosened; the mask slid into place. Lately every time I saw the man, I thought of the day he'd named Grif a spy and my fists clenched.

"Yes?"

He held up a hand, breathing hard. When he'd recovered enough to speak, he wiped an arm across his forehead. "I found something."

I raised a brow.

Flipping pages until he reached one with *The Lady of The Lake* printed in bold letters above a picture of a creature who looked very much like a human woman, draped in sheer white robes, long silver hair trailing down her back into a lake, he pointed.

"What am I looking at?"

William jabbed a meaty finger at an underlined passage halfway down the page. "It says here the Lady of the Lake was a land nixie, but she'd fallen in love with the lake prince and moved into his court to be close to him." He pushed his glasses up his nose. "When her only child died, heart ripped out by her lover in a jealous rage, she transformed, becoming—"

"The Bitter Wraith," I said, sliding the book closer to continue reading.

The Bitter Wraith guards access to the lake, stealing children who wander too near in retribution for the loss of her beloved daughter. Though once a land creature, and great seer, she never leaves the lake now, hoping to one day be reunited with her only child.

I rubbed my chin. "How accurate do you think this legend is?"

"We know she's real and that she lives in the lake. This book was written over sixty years ago. Before we knew fairies were real. What are the chances of whoever wrote this knowing so much?"

A seer was just what we needed and if the story was true, she had no love for the prince of Lakes and Streams. Maybe she was the weak link we needed to get into Faerie.

⟶⟨⟶♦♠♦♦⟶

The ice groaned beneath my boots as I inhaled a frigid breath, wrapping my coat tightly around myself. I should have brought a thicker jacket to the frozen lake.

Onyx eyes fixed on me, then dipped to my fists. No flower in my grasp. No offering. Just me, daring to meet her gaze.

The Bitter Wraith rushed toward me, lips stretching to expose needle-sharp teeth.

I lifted my hands, breath fogging the air. "Firethorn." If William's story was right, it was the one word that might stop her. Proof I wasn't just a dumb human.

She froze mid-strike, black nails inches from my throat. Her voice was a crack in the silence, scratchy from disuse. "That name is not for mortal mouths."

I lowered my hands slowly. "I know more. About your daughter. About the one who took her from you."

Her form flickered, between the dark creature she was now and something ethereal and glowing, rage and grief causing her glamour to slip.

The heavy thud of my heart sped. "I know what it is to have your child taken from you. What it is to want retribution."

Ice cracked under her bare feet, sending a fissure along the lake, but her hand fell to her side.

I had gambled with my life and this time, I'd won. Pressing the moment, I held up my hand. "I have a bargain for you, Wraith. Grant me and mine access through your portal when we ask, and I will give you the name of your daughter's killer after we return."

Even in this frozen place, a trickle of sweat ran down my back. If she wasn't as lost to her grief as I suspected, any number of things could go wrong, but I was counting on a mother's love and loss to muddle her thoughts. My wife's soft voice whispered beside my ear. *A fae bargain is a tricky thing. Choose your words wisely for their meaning is often literal.*

I didn't know who killed the child, but the bargain's wording bought me time. If all went according to plan, I'd get Jack back. Then we'd go to Faerie. We would take care of the Wraith when nothing else was left.

The wind stilled. For a heartbeat, I thought I'd miscalculated.

Then she spoke in a voice I hardly heard. "Swear it on your life, and the bargain is struck."

FIVE

SAV

Hazel stared around the map room in Creig's rebel hideout, cataloging intertwined mahogany vines interspersed with tiny green, orange and gold leaves, encircling us. Her gaze landed on the massive table at its center, covered in stacks of drawings that detailed every fractured pocket of Faerie, Central Park, and countless other places Creig was monitoring. She hadn't said a word in hours. I had to check to be sure my friend hadn't been swapped for a chameleon fae.

Creig slapped a hand on Foxglove's back but eyed me warily. "It's done then?"

I swallowed and lifted my chin. "It is."

He shifted an axe at his hip, black eyes meeting mine. "If you've come back here hoping to change my mind, Princess—"

"I haven't," I cut him off. "I want you to look after Hazel." My grip tightened in hers. "I'm not risking anyone else. Only myself. But Faerie isn't safe anymore. There's next to nothing left of Spring. Winter could be next."

Hazel tore her hand from mine, crossing her arms over her chest. "I can speak for myself." Her bright emerald gaze narrowed on me, reminding me painfully of Jack's green eyes. "I'm coming."

Larek slid to a stop in the door but was shoved through when Yolmar tumbled in after. The twins stood slack jawed, eyes never leaving Hazel. The corners of my lips threatened to tip up. I couldn't wait to see how this went.

"We heard we had company," Yolmar said, subtly flexing his biceps.

"We knew it would be Sav." Larek grinned.

They still weren't looking at me when they said in unison. "Who's your friend?"

I had to bite the inside of my cheek to stop the first laugh that threatened to break through in days as Hazel preened under the attention of two males. The weight pressing on my chest eased just a fraction. Not nearly enough.

"I'm Hazel." Her glamour fell away like silk, and a fluffy, white spotted tail with black rings at the ends, unfurled from her lower back as she strode toward them, hips swaying. Her ears twitched, making the shock of white hair at her back shine in the faelight. "What are your big strong friends' names, Sav?"

I opened my mouth. I don't know why, because the twins had no intention of letting me speak.

Yolmar puffed out his chest, scarred fingers sliding over the daggers at his hip. "I'm Yolmar. The handsome one."

Larek elbowed his twin aside, releasing the axe handle he had been gripping, and lifted Hazel's hand to his lips. "I'm Larek, the debonair one."

I snorted, another bit of ice cracking in my chest. Hazel glanced between the males, lashes lowered, full lips curved up at the corners.

Foxglove, dressed impeccably in a tailored tweed suit that was out of place among so much leather and metal, ignored the trio, moving around the table, and said, "I must attend to a few matters." Without a backward glance, he was gone.

"Boys. Get over here and leave the lady be."

Hazel winked at Larek and Yolmar as they scrambled to stand beside their father. Though they were more than two centuries old, orcs didn't truly fill out until somewhere near their fourth century. Creig looked every bit the father to his two young boys. I was surprised Hazel hadn't chosen Creig to flirt with first, but I knew my friend, and it was the attention she loved, not the males.

Creig eyed his sons. "I need you both in Faerie. Take Murz. We need to get a handle on how much of Spring is gone."

I rounded the table to stand beside them, my chest tight and my fingers clenching the edge of the map. Staring down at all the X's drawn through my court, my vision blurred. How much of my home was left? I pointed to the parts of the castle that were still intact when I left, willing my trembling fingers to still.

"This bit was still there, but everything disappeared so fast, I'm not sure what's left now." Glancing up, I discreetly wiped my cheek.

Creig nodded to his boys and they dipped their chins.

Murz appeared in the doorframe. "Lord Hawthorn said you needed me."

Creig motioned him in. Murz's skin was a darker shade of green and smoother than the others; his features softer, his braids ending in curls where Creig and the boys had coarse, blunt-cut hair and sharp bones. *Not all orc clans look alike*, I reminded myself. His mother's line could be from elsewhere—or something older might be at work.

Primrose, my oldest friend in Spring, was born into a cursed bloodline. It thinned their elemental magic and passed itself along, generation after generation. Some swore it stamped out daughters entirely; Prim's existence proved it wasn't as absolute as so many believed.

I'd hoped to see her when I returned. Prim taught me to use my voice when I was a lost girl in a garden of snakes. I could only hope she was on an emissary mission and not among the lost.

I looked up, finding Creig already watching me. "What is it, Love?"

"Could Faerie be collapsing because Mab is gone? If she made this place... would her end pull the threads loose?"

Creig frowned, glancing at Hazel. He didn't know her and that meant he didn't trust her. But he hadn't said anything about me bringing her to his hideout or to his map room. It was clear he didn't share Foxglove's reservations about letting those outside the rebellion in. I waited.

Hazel moved to stand beside me and the twins crowded closer. A look passed between him and his sons, some silent discussion playing between them.

The pregnant pause was broken when Creig said, "I want to tell ya a story," and the air shifted the way it does when low-fae lore wakes.

Murz hissed, "General—"

"No more secrets," Creig said.

Murz frowned, raven brows bunching between his unusual brown eyes, but after a moment he nodded and Creig went on.

"Before Mab, land had its queen and sea had its king." He stabbed a pointed nail into the map near Winter's castle. "She came to our world some ten-thousand years ago with one purpose. To rule. When the sea refused her, she dragged a star from the sky and boiled the ocean to brine."

The words slid behind my ribs and began to drum, the way old truths do. Something I'd carry whether I wanted to or not.

I frowned. If what he said was true, that meant I wasn't a native of Faerie. My stomach twisted.

He nudged a carved token toward Autumn. "My great, great grand-da said he was there the day she arrived heavy with child, and it was the orc clan who offered her refuge. The boy, Firethorn, had magic different to

21

ours. Molten hot and dangerous. But he wasn't cruel the way his mother was, and the low folk loved him."

Yolmar straightened, nudging his twin who was staring openly at Hazel. She winked at the pair and they grinned back dumbly.

"Mab left to fetch more of her kind," Creig went on, "and came back with an entire court." He searched my face, seeming to make up his mind and continued. "The low fae rebelled against their cruelty and their desire to rule. The result? Mass casualties on both sides."

Hazel reached for my hand, squeezing, and I met her eyes. All her usual confidence was gone, replaced by sadness. I squeezed back, offering what silent sympathy I could. Hazel's ancestors on her mother's side all died in the great war. Her only living relative was Mab, and she was a distant relative at best.

"As punishment, Mab separated the land into four seasonal courts. We, the low fae, were forced to work for the high fae who held the magic that controlled the land.

"But none suffered so much as the sea. Where all the water of Faerie was once fresh and pristine, the greatest body–the ocean–was now poisoned to sea folk. Many centuries passed before some evolved enough to live in the tainted water. Only kelpies and a rare few others could go between fresh and salt-water."

Bile rose in my throat. Was Mab responsible for so much suffering?

"So you see, Sav, Faerie would not be destroyed by her departure. It would be freed."

SIX

JACK

In the silent space after the last round, the room felt too bright, my nerves frayed to live wires ready to spark. Metal clicked and my eyes flew open as Janet rolled a tray close enough for me to smell the disinfectant. Morgan stood at my shoulder, arms folded.

"We're done guessing," Janet said, voice cold. "We're going to learn what you are."

On the tray, a thick needle, twice the normal size, lay beside three vials. Each was a different color, one shimmered gold in the harsh light. I leaned my head back. There was no use fighting. I was too weak. So... we would find out together.

Janet lifted the syringe, fitting a vial of blue liquid.

Morgan smiled, crimson lips twisting into points at the corners of her mouth. "We're not evil, you know." She licked her lips. "We owe Puck a great debt and you were payment. I didn't understand what Puck could want with a human." Her gaze dropped, tracing the scars across my chest. "But I see now, the wise creature always knows more than the rest of us."

Janet's mouth twitched, but she said nothing, continuing her work.

Morgan was always the chatty one.

"Mab used me for centuries," Morgan went on, examining her nails. Her fingers shook and she curled them into a fist. "She used Autumn's seers to predict strong bloodlines and then dismantled them." She looked up, meeting my eyes once more. "I was forced to use my gift. To convince mothers to drown their children. Lovers to throw themselves off cliffs. Anything to ensure none ever grew too powerful."

A shudder rolled through Morgan. "Puck freed me. And sent me to Earth as the price of that freedom."

"And when she got here," Janet said, as the needle pierced skin, "she found me." She didn't bother to disguise the warmth in her words. "We weren't allowed to exist together under Mab. Puck promised us a life where we wouldn't have to hide." Her gaze settled on the rapidly shrinking liquid filtering into my veins. "If we learn what you are."

I wanted to shout at them, to rage at the ridiculousness of their words. Not evil? Did she believe anything done to her justified doing it to others? I wanted that answer, too. But at what cost?

"You keep saying that," I said, my voice scratchy. "What I am."

"We know what you're not," Morgan said. "You're not just human. And now that Mab's dead..."

Fire raced up my arm; her words blurred together.

"Mab," I mumbled and the room tilted. "Dead?"

"Puck won't like this," Morgan said, gaze dropping to my arm. Then the room went dark.

-●→)(∪●▲◆●●-

Snow. Soft midday light. My breath fogged as I laughed.

I was small enough that Dad's mittens swallowed my hands. The park had been transformed into a winter wonderland, white blanketing every surface. I ran until my lungs burned, past the bench with the wrought-iron arms, past the low fence where the dog walkers always stopped to talk. My sled bumped over footprints and old snow ridges and landed in a drift that swallowed it whole.

"Coat zipped, bud," Dane said, hands shoved deep in his pockets, shoulders hunched against the cold. He kept half an eye on me and half an eye on the path, like danger might be lurking around the next corner.

Mom didn't wear a coat. She never did. Snow collected on her hair and melted. She reached to help me tug the sled free and, when the plastic refused to cooperate, she twirled her fingers in the air and the snow parted, revealing my sled. Her fingers brushed my cheek. Warm, even out here.

They stood, watching me as I climbed the small slope and turned to wave. I shouldn't have been able to hear them from this distance, but sometimes, I could.

"You're both safer here on Earth," Mom said. "She can't ever know about Jack."

"You promised me you had a plan. Sitting around doing nothing isn't a plan." Dane's mouth barely moved. "She'll come looking for you eventually."

"Time moves slowly for our kind. We have years. Decades maybe. Time enough to strengthen them."

"Then we do it your way," he said, voice rough and low. "But I won't let her take him. Ever."

Mom's hand rested on Dad's shoulder. "But... If I should disappear suddenly. Know that she's found me. Don't come looking for me. Promise me."

"I can't promise that."

Mom's eyes narrowed, brightening in the soft light. "You will. Dane Patrick Clyde, if I disappear, you will accept that I'm dead and do what you must to keep our son safe."

I slid down the hill, shouting with glee and threw my hands up.

Climbing off of my sled, I marched back to the top of the hill.

Dad was at the top and I reached it as he sank down, straightening my hat so it covered my ears. Mom joined us. "He doesn't feel the cold the way you do, Dane." She glanced at me and the corners of her mouth softened. "We're made of tougher stuff than that, aren't we my little prince?"

A dog barked. Somewhere, a car's horn blared. The streetlight flickered, the scene before me going dark. Suddenly, it wasn't midday, but the middle of the night.

Mom kissed my cheek. "Rest now, Jacaranda. I will see you soon."

The dream, or memory, soothed some of my terror. But each swallow scraped my too-dry throat, and the blast from the AC pebbled my abused skin. I wished desperately to return to that time and place where I'd believed two people would keep me safe.

"Dane's doing it for me." The words slurred together and drool slid over my chin.

Janet's sharp eyes stared down at me as the fluorescents came into focus, momentarily blinding me. "What?"

I pressed my lips together, desperate to keep my secrets. There was no telling what I'd said in my delirium, but I wouldn't willingly give them any more.

Morgan closed a folder and glared down at me. "Name."

I set my jaw. "You already have it."

"Your real name." Her eyes, blood-red, were violent in the bright light.

The word: Jacaranda begged to spill from my lips, but just as before, Morgan could make my body obey, but not my mind. Drugged or not, she couldn't pry it from me.

A weight lifted. My mother's name for me, the one even Dane didn't know, was sacred. Keeping it was all that mattered.

SEVEN

SAV

"Blasphemy." I bit my lower lip until I tasted blood, as if pain could anchor me. "If that's true, what does it mean for me—for all the high fae? That I'm not from Faerie?"

I wrapped my arms over my chest and took a step away from the group, needing distance from their eyes, from the words hanging between us. I had bled for this land. Killed for it. Every lesson, every story about our sacred birthright twisted in my mind, sour and wrong. If we weren't born of Faerie, then we were invaders wearing crowns that didn't belong to us. What did that make me? A usurper? A lie in a pretty dress?

It couldn't be true. If it was, everything I'd built myself on, duty, loyalty, the right to stand here, crumbled to ash.

"Sav," Yolmar said. I kept pacing.

Creig's tale had piled old stories together in my mind, slotting pieces into place. Our magic wasn't like the low fae's. We didn't conform to the world the way they did, living among nature and feeding it.

Sage's earth magic was supposed to feed Spring.

I turned to the group. Hazel hadn't said a word. Whether she believed it or just wouldn't cross the general, I couldn't worry about it now. If what Creig said was true, the long-standing secret in Faerie was that *we* didn't belong there.

The lore lodged under my ribs and wouldn't budge. I wanted to refute him, but it sat in my chest like a stone, heavy and undeniable. Their silence stoked my anger. Tiny sparks danced along my fingertips as the last pieces became clear. I went still.

"Sage's magic doesn't feed Spring. It keeps the seasons frozen in place."

My throat was dry, the words sticky. "The high fae aren't caring for Faerie. They're ensuring Mab's control over it never wanes."

I caught myself on the table as the revelation landed, my knees threatening to give out.

Yolmar and Larek moved to stand beside me, each placing a hand on my shoulder. But there was something else. Something Creig was still waiting for me to understand. I looked down at the tips of my fingers and grimaced. I was out of practice at holding back my magic. Dark marks scorched the surface of the long wooden table where I'd rested them.

"Wait."

I stared at my fingers, willing the magic to recede so I could mend the burns I'd left in his table. We didn't kill living things to build our homes. A table was meant to be shaped from what the land shed, not ruined by what I couldn't control.

"But..."

Creig nodded.

"My magic *does* feed the land."

Creig's grin went wide, pride bright as any father's.

I exhaled a shaky breath. "What does that mean?"

Yolmar squeezed my shoulder. "It means you're something different."

My stomach hollowed; the edges of my vision went dark. I swayed and Larek steadied me. I managed a wan smile. It was the best I could muster in appreciation as the world felt as though it had just been tilted on its axis. Different. What did that mean? How? Why? "But Sage," I breathed. "We're twins."

"My guess," he said, glancing at his sons. "Is that you're a step in your kind's evolution."

"What?"

"If your kind adapts, and it must, to survive different realms, it would shift to the world it lives in."

"You said Mab only had innate magic when she came. Wouldn't that mean all my kind only had it too? But we don't. We have elemental magic, based on the day of our birth."

"Any creature born in Faerie manifests the elemental gift for the month they're born in. It only took one generation for your kind to begin manifesting elemental magic."

"What's my second option?"

"The great Gaia blessed you herself," Hazel said at last.

I turned, eyes widening. "Hazel?"

"Winter has its own legends." She squeezed between the orcs towering above us. "There's a book."

My heart sped up. "What book?"

"It catalogs the realms Mab explored. Winter's treasure room holds it. We were bound not to speak of it. On pain of death."

"Were?"

"When Mab vanished, her bargains unraveled. That's why you survived stealing her crystal."

"What crystal?" Creig barked, and my cheeks flamed.

I craned my neck up to look at him. "I took her scrying crystal."

I winced. "We needed to find her. Things were bad. Faerie was disappearing. I thought she could put it right."

Creig shook his head, Murz grumbled something indiscernible under his breath and Larek and Yolmar gave me disapproving scowls. Had I never known how much contempt they held for our queen? Had I been the only fool blindly placing faith in her all this time?

"Mab treated me kindly in Winter. She even blessed my marriage. She was not the terrible monarch you've painted her to be."

"Love." The single word slid a frostbitten finger down my spine. "Mates aren't fated. Mab creates them."

"No," I breathed.

Creig's eyes were soft. "That's her gift... true name sensor. With it, she can compel anyone in any way she chooses."

Foxglove appeared in the door and I looked up, pressing a hand to the weight forcing the air from my chest. My eyes narrowed. "You knew." I stalked forward. "That's why you told my sister."

Three years of pent-up magic snapped loose and shot from my palms. Foxglove had known about Bracken. Known Mab was responsible. The memory of what he'd done slammed into me, bright and brutal, as if I were standing in that moment all over again.

My veins hummed, my skin too tight to hold the power roaring under it. The air warped with heat; the nearest vines popped and hissed, curling in on themselves and blackening at the edges. Foxglove leaped back, eyes wide, narrowly escaping the burst of flame that tore past his shoulder.

Part of me thrilled at the release, at finally letting my magic breathe. The rest of me was terrified of how good it felt. I couldn't drag it back. I didn't even try. I marched down the hall after him, each furious step kicking sparks across the floor as he fled.

"I told you I was trying to keep you safe!" he called over his shoulder.

"You could have told me the truth!" An arrow of flame leaped with my rage. Another. "You could have told me instead of running to my sister."

He disappeared through a doorway, and I slid to a stop as Juniper stood from a low table facing the window in a room piled to the ceiling with books, papers and maps. It could only be Foxglove's room.

She turned to me and I froze, staring at the ghost of my confident, independent friend. Her gaze was distant, looking at nothing.

The fire in my veins died. *My fault.* It was my fault she'd been transformed by Dane into a creature trapped in her own mind. I should have gone after her. Instead, I'd let them take her and hid in the alley with Jack like a coward.

"Juniper," I breathed.

Something cleared in her gaze and she lunged for me. I stepped back and Foxglove wrapped strong hands around hers, tugging her against his chest. There was a familiarity in his possessive hold that made my veins heat once more. She was *my* friend.

"You can't hide behind her forever."

"I only wanted you to listen for a moment."

I crossed my arms over my chest, saying nothing. I would give him one chance to explain. One opportunity for all the years I'd never let him until now.

"I, like the members of the Winter court, made a bargain that forbade me from ever speaking of Mab's gifts. When I learned what she was planning, I tried to break your engagement any way I could. My one loophole was my position. As Spring's spymaster, I could report it to my ruler."

Juniper's blank stare chilled my veins, cooling my temper as I considered his words. He knew and he couldn't tell me. Hadn't I thought we were friends all those years? It was, after all, Foxglove who showed me how to escape the castle when I needed a break from it all. He showed me the secret paths through the garden and the rooms with hidden doors.

When Primrose was gone for long stretches, it was Foxglove who had led me to the library and showed me the room of pixies who loved to regale me with songs.

Sage had imprisoned me for months when she learned of my engagement. "Thank Mab we have one loyal subject," she'd said. "You'd have saddled yourself to that soldier and tarnished our family name." Her words and my broken heart were my only companion.

"I'm sorry."

Foxglove's hold on Juniper loosened a fraction, his shoulders lowering. He had been trying to tell me for more than a decade and for that long, I hadn't been willing to listen. I thought perhaps he wasn't the only one I'd made hasty decisions about. There were others I owed apologies to.

The Prince of Summer's face, usually stoic, had turned pleading, begging me to believe he hadn't killed Mira. But he had my first name; with it, he could have imagined any number of torments.

My mind sped to the day I'd learned of his proposal. Now that Mab was gone, it seemed everyone was willing to forgo her blessing to secure the alliances they sought. And if we'd married, having my name would no longer matter, because I'd have his too. Had he been seeking a way to mend that damage even after all this time?

I tucked that bitter thought away.

"How's she doing?" I quickly changed the subject, giving myself time to digest this new information.

Foxglove's gaze dipped to the crown of Juniper's curls. "She eats on her own and she hasn't tried to kill anyone since you left. It seems she's been programmed to kill only you, but she hasn't said a word."

His voice was wistful and I was reminded of the male I'd first met two hundred sixty-five years ago. The one who'd loved another low fae, one who was taken from us far too young.

EIGHT

SAV

In my old rooms, I raced to the counter I'd stood at the last time I'd been in Creig's hidden pocket. The last time I'd seen Jack. When we kissed. When he declared he wanted my heart. That same heart thundered at the memory of his claiming, making my palms slick.

New information swirled, leaving me light-headed. If Creig's tale was true, if high fae weren't of Faerie, then we didn't belong there at all. It still didn't account for the missing pockets or the folk who had disappeared. But one thought in my mind shouted to be heard over all else. *Jack.*

Images of him chained, left without food and water; drugged. Stories of Morgan's acts against her own kind had reached me even as a child. My stomach lurched. I knew he needed me. Every breath I spent standing here was another second ISHFA had him, another chance to break him in ways even I couldn't mend.

Jack would die if I didn't move now. I had to free him first. We could regroup later.

I slid a handful of daggers into my belt.

"I won't let you sneak out of here without me." Hazel stepped through the door to my room.

"It's too dangerous. If we go in and can't save him, you'll die, or at the very least have a bounty on your head along with me. Stay here. I'll get Jack and..."

I trailed off. Jack wouldn't be welcome here, and I didn't know where we'd go. The idea circling my mind made my stomach twist, but I couldn't think of anywhere else to go. The worst part was, I knew Kaspar would agree. If I asked, he would say yes. He never denied me anything. But could I take Jack to my new husband's court?

"If you come to Earth with me, you'll have to stay hidden while I rescue Jack. I'm not coming back here. Are you prepared to come with me to Lakes and Streams?"

Hazel squared her shoulders. "I'm coming."

"Us too."

Yolmar and Larek pushed through the door, stopping beside Hazel. She gave them each an appreciative smile.

"Then it's settled." She winked at me.

"No. Your dad will never allow it. And he needs you here."

Yolmar crossed his arms over his chest, Larek mirroring him. "We've been fighting the humans for years. *You* need *us*." Their words bled together.

Yolmar's gaze softened. "Imagine how we would feel if something happened to you, knowing we could have been there, but weren't."

I glanced down at my row of knives. On Earth the bargain forbade me from harming humans, but across from me, three fae were bound by no such rules.

I clasped my hands together, wringing them as I looked between each of my friends. These three were mine. Mine to keep safe. If they fell, I wouldn't recover. I started to shake my head. Better I die trying to free Jack than let any of them risk it.

"I have another reason for going." The twins looked to Hazel expectantly. She reached into the bag she had slung over a shoulder and pulled out a bright emerald stone. Even in the low light it shone brilliantly.

"Why did you bring that here?" I hissed, rushing forward.

"It's pointing to Earth. The signal isn't strong, but there's something there I need to find."

I raised a brow, glancing between Hazel and the scrying crystal. It was pulsing a low green in Hazel's hands—the color of her court. In mine, it had always gone violet. Did that mean Creig was wrong about his theories or could I be of Spring and still be something else?

"What were you looking for when it pointed you to Earth?"

"A solution to the end of Faerie."

-◆-❯-ᴄ-˅-◆-∧-◆-●-●-

Larek and Yolmar raced ahead as Hazel and I moved between the trees. I thought again of Hazel's words. How could the solution to Faerie's shrinking be on Earth? What did it mean?

Just before the portal, amethyst eyes lifted over a fallen log. I slid to a stop. My sister's spy in the missing pocket of Faerie? Impossible. Every time I'd seen the creature, I'd run from it. I was tired of running.

"Who are you?"

The fox twitched its nose. I could almost sense it thinking, deciding, but I was tired of waiting on everyone else to give me the truth. I reached for my innate gift. "Reveal yourself to me."

The fox jerked as if he'd been struck. When I first learned it, I hated how it struck. My skill wasn't subtle or soft, and to ensure I kept my secret I rarely used it. But perhaps the secrets we kept were the reason we were in this mess. If each only knew a part of the whole, how could we ever learn who moved the pieces on the board?

The fox lengthened, bones realigning into Foxglove, tall and very nude. He covered himself with a hand and glowered at Hazel who was ogling him openly.

"But... I thought you were a Libra?"

"*I* didn't know you could compel others." He rubbed his nose. "I guess we're both full of secrets."

His eyes were an exact match for the creature who had followed us on our escape from Sage the day Jack burned his bars, and I wondered how I'd never guessed in all these centuries he was the fox who always seemed to be watching. I supposed it was useful to have a secret gift like that. If no one ever suspected you, they'd never know you were spying on them.

Thankfully, Yolmar and Larek hadn't doubled back to check on us, or Foxglove would have seen them sneaking away too. Better he thought it was just us.

"Princess—"

I held up a hand. "You know there's nothing you can say to stop me."

"I only wanted to offer information."

I blinked, that pressure in my chest returning. Why had I let my pettiness get between our friendship all these years? Why had I so distrusted him when I knew in my heart it was Sage who made us all into her puppets.

"Morgan's gift can be thwarted by fire."

All innate gifts could be countered by one of the elements. If the gift itself was guarded, the thing that rendered it useless was protected at the cost of one's life. I didn't need to ask how Foxglove knew. I suspected he knew a great deal about all of us.

A slow grin spread across my face. What a lucky coincidence that my greatest threat at ISHFA had more to fear from me than I from her. Without her gift, the one she flaunted to the world, she was weak in every way. Perhaps this plan wasn't so foolhardy after all.

NINE

JACK

In my delirium, my mother was my constant companion.

A bucket of ice water startled me out of my latest dream. After several days, Janet had discovered that water masked my pain immunity. I blinked several times, stinging ice lighting up the cuts, fractures, and punctures still healing.

"Wake up! We're going to try something new." Janet's maroon lips were tipped up in the most vile grin I'd ever seen. If a look could kill, hers would slay armies.

Skin soaking wet, I shivered and tracked the movement of her hand as she lifted a rusted-looking nail. Of the objects laid out, it wasn't the most dangerous looking.

"Today, we're going to learn what effects iron has on you."

I nodded dumbly. I shouldn't have. It only angered her more, but my brain had no capacity for logic when it was busy cataloging the myriad of aches and pains spread over my starving body.

Janet rushed forward. The nail punched through flesh to the chair pinning my arm down; black raced up my veins toward my heart.

"So, it does affect you." Her pupils blew wide. "When I learn to harness it, I'll use it to make a drug that will incapacitate your pretty girl-friend. Soon it will be *her* tied to this chair, bleeding for me."

Her words reached into me, rousing emotions I didn't remember I had. But it was Sav she was speaking of; Sav she wanted to cut open and make bleed. Heat stoked to life inside me, lighting me on fire. Steam rose from my torn flesh, causing the wetness to evaporate and with it, the pain. Since learning of my weakness, Janet had spent less time cutting into me

37

and more time, drenching me in ice water, then shocking me until my teeth threatened to crack.

I'd screamed, nothing could have stopped it, and Janet loved nothing more than a good scream.

She'd been too engrossed in her new experiment to notice my dry skin, but my anger ebbed for a moment when the dark veins tracking up my arm began to recede, and she hopped up, dashing to get another bucket of ice. This new heat inside me felt different. It was charged with a protective energy that was fighting the foreign body meant to weaken me. The magic didn't like that.

Flames burst to life along my forearms, racing to my hands and pooling there.

"Baby! I need you!" Her voice shook and some dark part of me enjoyed that.

Janet abandoned her bucket as it filled in the sink, and ran to find Morgan. To command me again. The warmth sizzling under my skin burned hotter. I was tired of being controlled. Poked and prodded. Shocked and frozen, starved and cut open. A raging fire engulfed my handcuffs, and I gasped as the metal dissolved to nothing.

I ripped my arm free of the nail spiking it to the chair, a burst of energy coursing through me when I ripped the nail from my flesh and bone. I'd process the ramifications of all I'd learned today later. Now, it was time to leave.

I burned the ankle bonds and lurched up. Days without food and water had made me weak, and I stumbled into the wall. My ankle, bent at the wrong angle, cracked when I put weight on it and I nearly fell to my knees before I caught myself and continued forward.

Bloody footprints trailed behind me, and I slipped in my own pool of sticky crimson liquid twice. Sliding a hand along the wall, I moved disjointedly down the long glass hall. The flames along my arms were only growing brighter as something deep within me was surging, expanding, pressing against the confines of my skin.

Heat bled through my fingertips; glass webbed and gave. I shoved off before the pane surrendered.

Straightening, I tried again to stand on the broken ankle and steadied myself as I heard the shuffling of feet around the corner. An alarm sounded, ringing in my overly sensitive ears and I brought my hands up to my head to cover the sound. Some distant part of my brain thought I should have burned my ears as I had everything else I touched, but I felt nothing but my own skin against my ears. Was my entire body an inferno?

Someone shouted at the other end of the hall and I threw my hands up to shield myself. Instead of simple protection, a blast of fire shot out, melting paint and plaster. It sizzled and smoked as a line of armed guards rounded the corner, weapons raised. Balls of flame erupted from my still-raised palms causing the guards to dive out of the way.

"I'm sorry." I hadn't meant to harm them, even if they pointed guns at me. But the fire had a mind of its own. "I don't want to hurt you. Let me pass."

The armed men had strange reflective gear covering them, making them faceless strangers. They were used to dealing with the fae. Those whose magic would have overpowered them in moments. "I'm human," I assured them. "I only want to leave this place. What she did to me is inhumane."

I squeezed my hands into fists to stop the sparks shooting off them. Whether I wanted to harm them or not, my body was reacting to the threat. I'd read about the human body's response to trauma in one of my pre-med books. It could manifest all manner of odd and spectacular responses in an effort to protect itself. Sometimes even after unconsciousness. Several medical studies had shown growths or anomalies formed around the heart and lungs inside the body of victims of severe trauma such as car crashes.

Sav had asked if an elemental gift had ever responded to my need to protect myself before. I understood now what she meant. *Fae.* It must mean I was fae. Why did the thought of being like her make my heart swell? I was sure she would have accepted me no matter what I turned out to be, but if we were alike, if we were both fae, then it wasn't illegal for us to be together.

The armed guards had regained their footing and were pointing shiny black muzzles at me. The heat in my veins roared to life, begging to be set free. My sluggish heart pounded against my ribs. Even after days of Janet's torment, I was still afraid to die. I tried to quell the feeling, to slow the flames that would soon seek an outlet, but when safeties clicked off, fire tore out of me.

Metal smoked and pooled at their feet. I squeezed my fists, desperate to drag it back, to make it stop. Men screamed behind their masks and my stomach lurched. I had done that. I had hurt them—burned them alive—because I didn't want to die. No amount of "by accident" could make that right.

I backed away from the carnage I'd caused, hands shaking.

Smog billowed between us, making my eyes water. Overhead, fire extinguishers dropped from the ceiling and burst to life, spraying us all.

Cold hammered down; steam rose. The fire was smothered and pain took its place.

As the room cleared, the scene before me sharpened. Soldiers whimpered and cried, clutching blackened stumps. My insides hollowed out. Power I didn't understand had chewed through guns, armor—and them —as if they were nothing. Bile climbed my throat, a sour mix of acid and guilt.

There was no time. I straightened, dragging my broken leg as I hobbled toward the door. Nothing I said could fix what I'd done to them.

Even as I stumbled along, I could feel my body mending my injuries. The bone that had been cracked in my ankle was knitting itself together. Mindful of the speed with which it healed, I tried not to put weight on it that might set it at a wrong angle.

"Jack, stop."

Morgan's words hit and my knees locked mid-stride. I'd been three steps from the door. Three steps from freedom.

"Return to your chair and sit." My ankle gave as my weight came down, and a scream threatened to tear free. "You will not use magic against anyone here. You will not harm us."

I ground my teeth and moved mechanically, every inch toward the chair a betrayal. I didn't want the fire. Heaven knew I'd had enough of wailing and melting metal, but I wanted that door more. Straining against the command, I reached for the well of power within me, begging it to answer.

Nothing came.

Want sharpened into need as Morgan's words hammered in my head. The urge to return to the chair became my all-consuming desire.

TEN

SAV

At the Central Park Zoo, I donned a glamour. Heavy magic draped over what I'd only just recovered. I wore it anyway. My too bright eyes, now that my magic wasn't bound, would never fool anyone, though.

We left the zoo, stepping through Winter's border, leaving Faerie's wards behind. We were immediately assaulted by the iron, exhaust, and noise. Hazel brought her hands to her head. "Sav, I... can't..."

I rubbed a hand over her back. "Breathe. It gets easier."

I hooked an arm under hers and ushered her across the street, stopping beside a street vendor selling magazines, gum, and other human wares. Looking both ways, I snatched two pairs of sunglasses and handed one to Hazel. "Put these on."

She lifted trembling fingers and pushed them over her nose. Dark lenses hid her tell; in the afternoon glare we passed for human. Our clothes wouldn't. Leather pants were common enough, but our tunics, made of fine silk, weren't common. I knew just where to get scratchy cotton T-shirts to fit in.

"Come on. We need to stop by the bar."

I dragged Hazel behind me. Larek and Yolmar had gone ahead to scout ISHFA. They couldn't hide what they were and preferred to stay out of sight as much as possible. They'd been on dozens of missions around the city and claimed they were comfortable finding their own way to blend in. I had to trust that they knew what they were doing.

We reached Fae'z in Harlem and my mouth fell open.

Where the bar I'd spent more hours in than my small dwelling had

41

stood just weeks ago, a pile of dark cinders remained. They had destroyed it. Completely. Nothing was left. I turned, spinning in a circle. The same graffitied brick buildings stood on either side of Sam's business. None of the other abandoned buildings had been destroyed. True, it was wood while the others were mostly brick and cement, but how had they remained so untouched?

Hazel released my arm and stepped toward the pile of ash. "Was this your home?"

I snorted, but something in my chest spasmed. It wasn't. It was a filthy bar. It had been exhausting and most mornings my head hit the pillow and I slept soundly, only to wake and repeat it all over again. But many of the folk came to Sam's bar too. I'd gotten to know the low fae, to learn a little about them. The Grim came in two nights a week to spin tales of old and while the humans mostly came to gawk, boo, or throw empty pints at him, the folk grew shiny-eyed and sat in silence, a bit of their souls mended by the magic of his words.

We had come together in our shared trauma and comforted one another.

"My home was burned and my things with it." I bit my lip. "But perhaps we will find aid from a fawn I know. Her dwelling wasn't destroyed."

We crossed the street, following the well-worn path I'd traveled many times between Central Park and the bar. My world had been reduced to the fifteen or so blocks I'd stayed within on Earth. It was its own sort of cage. One built of bigotry and hate. The humans had never accepted us, and though we'd lived among them for three years, leaving our designated area was dangerous.

My glamour firmly in place, I didn't have the same fears the others did, but I'd spent as much time protecting the low fae from angry humans as I had working at the bar and it left little free time.

We reached my former housing. Scorch-shadows ringed it, bringing back memories of that night. I swallowed the bile threatening to rise and yanked Hazel's arm, desperate to escape this place.

I stopped, nails digging into Hazel's arm when we reached Clover's home. Or what was left of it. Black earth made my stomach turn. Gone—all of it. The low-fae housing was gone.

Creig's words flashed in my mind. Was I finally with my kind here on Earth when so many of the low fae had been segregated from us in Faerie? Sure Kaspar was there and Creig, but most of those at court were high fae, like me. I hadn't felt the kind of connection to the folk in Faerie that I did these three years on Earth. And now they were gone.

ELEVEN

JACK

My mind floated in that strange place again. It was dark. It was always dark, but here my mother rested my head in her lap. She ran cool fingers over my temple, humming a soft tune. I longed to stay. It was the space between life and death.

My mother's fingers tensed and she looked up.

Her humming cut off; power rose under her skin. I felt it, the sheer magnitude of it. It was like nothing I'd experienced before. Even Prince Fero's magic was a drop compared with what buzzed under the surface of my mother's touch.

"You must go, my prince."

I blinked, sitting up. "I don't want to. I want to stay here with you."

Her eyes were kind when they searched my face, as they had been all her life. "Wake. Wake and break free from your captors. What lies within you cannot be contained by any living thing. You are more. Do not fear the strength within. It will keep you safe."

A shadow moved, creeping along the walls, and my mother's eyes widened as she glanced between me and the approaching danger. "Go, Jacaranda."

I gasped, coming to in the clinical white space that was my prison.

Blood-red eyes found mine and widened. For a moment, Morgan and I stared at one another. Her magic brushed my skin. The dream had been disconcerting, too real, and some irrational sliver of hope that my mother was actually alive somewhere found its way into my heart.

She wasn't. Father had made the arrangements, but her grave sat cold and stony behind the church I'd attended as a child. I had visited it more times than I could count.

"My love, he's awake."

Janet rounded the makeshift cardboard partition they'd erected in the absence of all that glass I'd shattered and appraised me. "What's wrong with his eyes?"

"He's changing."

She closed the space between us, sitting atop Morgan's lap. They were unnaturally close, always touching one another.

"You know what I find funny? You two flaunt your illegal relationship in my face day in and day out." My lip, barely beginning to heal, split open as I spoke, blood dripping onto my tongue. "Yet I'm supposedly being held here for the exact same reason."

Morgan caught Janet's chin; the kiss was hard. When they broke, Janet's mouth was bruised and Morgan's top was rucked.

"That's what happens when you hold the power," Morgan said breathlessly.

One of the many guards stationed around this floor after my escape attempt stepped into the room. "Ma'am."

Janet's eyes narrowed and she spun to face him. "What?"

The guard held a finger to his ear. "Someone's downstairs. Asking for you."

"Who is it?"

"She says she's your daughter."

The hairs at my nape lifted. *Janet has a daughter.* I watched as Janet left the room, shoving the guard's shoulder and knocking him back

Morgan wiped the smudges around her lips and eyed me. "I knew your truth was buried in there. We only want to see what you are. Won't you show us?"

The magic lacing her words dug into my skin. Suddenly, I wanted very badly to reveal all my truths to Morgan. But the same magic inside me, the power that had thwarted these commands before, rose to meet it. Whatever lived in me was stronger, and try as she might, Morgan could not pry this secret from my lips.

It was a pity. I wanted to know, too. I would have gladly shown her if only to see for myself, but whatever my secrets were, they were hidden even from me.

Morgan spoke softly, attempting to wrench information from me, but each question became easier to ignore. Only commands that required no thought were obeyed. I was tired of countering them.

"Slap yourself."

My hand came up, cracking across my face. Fresh blood dripped down my chin. I felt none of it. I was dry once more, but Morgan's hungry gaze tracked the movement, making my skin crawl. I leaned back, a shiver rolling down my spine.

"Baby. Alice has new intel."

Alice? The name snapped me from my revulsion and Morgan gave my blood one last longing look before turning to speak with Janet out of earshot. My mind swam. Alice was Janet's daughter? The spy in my dad's headquarters? They looked nothing alike. Janet's black hair was obviously dyed, but her sharp angles and muscular build made her a menacing presence. Alice's mousy brown hair and soft eyes made her appear fragile. Not a word I'd ever use to describe Janet.

And yet she'd been watching us for years. Watching *me*.

Feet pounded in the hall and Alice slid to a stop outside the door. Her mouth fell open, a tear rolling down her cheek. Janet rushed behind her, wrapping her arms around her daughter. Alice wrestled out of her grip and rushed to my side. She sank to her knees, lifting her shirt to my chin and mouth.

I slid back, away from her touch, old unease prickling under my skin. Alice, who'd always flushed when I walked past her desk, kneeling in my blood like some kind of penitent. I'd imagined a lot of things when I pictured the spy in Dad's office; Alice hadn't been one of them. I flinched when icy skin grazed my cheek, my body bracing for a needle even as my mind scrambled to catch up.

"Jack." Watery eyes met mine. "What have they done to you?"

"Alice, get away from him."

Alice shot to her feet. "You can't do this. Release him." There was more venom in her words than I'd ever heard, all the meek obedience she'd shown Dane gone.

"Honey, Jack isn't human. He's dangerous. Look what he did to the wall."

Alice's gaze darted between me and the cardboard lining the hall. No one was more staunch in the convictions Dane spewed than Alice. She'd swallowed every speech, every slur, like scripture. What would she think of me now, seeing me chained and burned and still not quite human enough for her mother?

"You're lying." Alice crossed her arms over her chest, moving to block my view of Janet. "He's Dane's son. The son of the AFF leader. No fucking way Dane Clyde has a fairy son."

Janet's boots scraped on the tile as she inched toward her daughter. "We think his mom was something else, Honey."

Alice moved, meeting her mother halfway, and shoved her. "And? So what? Your bitch isn't human. Why do you care if Jack has a fairy mother?"

My mouth fell open, even the taste of fresh blood dripping on my tongue not enough of a distraction from the scene unfolding before me. Alice didn't care? Alice, who hung on Dane's every vitriolic word, didn't care that I might be fae? The girl who'd been feeding my father's enemies information for years was shaking with fury on *my* side?

"It shouldn't be possible," Morgan said. "Humans and fae cannot mix. Our DNA is too different."

Alice ignored Morgan, hate-filled eyes still on her mother. "I'll tell Dane what you're doing to him if you don't stop this now."

A flood of gratitude rushed me, sharp and dizzying. Alice would tell my dad and he would come for me. Or at least, that was the story I needed to believe. I didn't know what to do with the girl standing in front of me —a devoted believer who'd followed Dane's every command, yet threatened her own mother for my sake.

I hadn't let the twinge of pain that Sav hadn't come yet sink in. When her people had been taken, she fought tooth and nail to get them back. I had hoped she wouldn't risk herself for me, even as my gaze strayed to the long hall every time I heard boots. But after days in this place, with no sense of time, the hope that anyone would come had dwindled.

But if Alice told Dane of my situation... He would come.

I twisted in my chair to get a better view. Though I could only see out of one eye, it was enough to take in Alice's puffy eyes, the wild look in them. Had her hate for the fae stemmed from this relationship between her mother and a fae? Had it been the reason she'd agreed to join Dane's cult? And what would Dane do to her when he learned the truth?

Janet wrapped her arms tightly around Alice. Her daughter fought like she was possessed, scratching and clawing, but her mother's grip was like iron and inch by inch, she pulled her out of view.

"Jack," Alice yelled from down the hall, her voice becoming more distant with every word. "Jack, I won't let them hurt you!"

Boots squeaked on tile as Janet dragged her away.

Blood rushed to my head from keeping my good eye open in the harsh light so long and I leaned heavily against my chair.

What would happen to Alice? Would her mother keep her safe from Morgan, or would the red-eyed sadist believe Alice was too much of a liability and order her off a roof? My gut twisted. I hoped for both our sakes, she would make it out of ISHFA headquarters alive.

TWELVE

DANE

L eo was still cuffed to the table when I walked in. The room smelled like dust and old wood polish, the kind you found in tacky knock-off furniture stores.

I latched onto that stupid detail, something small and harmless to keep my hands from shaking.

I approached the table. Leo didn't move, didn't acknowledge the power I held over him. "I knew you were former Navy," I said. "Guess I let the cozy little coffee shop fool me."

He watched me.

Jack could be in a room like this. Strapped down. Alone. I shoved the image away before it finished forming and focused on Leo instead. One problem at a time. *Get intel. Then get my kid.*

"ISHFA has Jack." The words came out rough, too tight. I clenched and unclenched my fists at my side, trying to quell the urge to put them through a wall. "I'm getting him out."

He didn't flinch, but his eyes sharpened.

Good. Let him see the part of me that wasn't the smiling AFF spokesman. Let him see the father.

"You want out of those cuffs? Help me. Watch their rotations, text me a clean window, and I'll do the rest."

"And if I don't?" Leo tested the wrist cuff, not because he thought it would give, just to remind me it was there.

My jaw ached from holding it all in, the terror and rage and the bone-deep certainty that every minute I stood here arguing was another minute

47

they had with my son. My training said to plan, wait, be smart. The father in me wanted to kick the door in and drag Jack out myself.

"If you bolt, your 'I'm-just-a-coffee-guy' routine dies. I drop your name in Morgan's lap." I held his stare, forcing my voice to stay level when everything inside me was anything but. "Let her know you're a government spy."

If he made me do it, I would. I'd burn his cover, burn every bridge I had, if it meant one more chance to bring Jack home breathing.

A beat.

"And Jack comes home?"

"Jack comes home."

I left Leo at the side exit to our building, checking the coast was clear before I locked the door behind him. We didn't have any new prisoners to guard, but that didn't mean I wanted eyes inside my building.

I should have seen it. The government had eyes on me. Not the fae. It was a testament to just how corrupt they were.

Grinding my teeth, I strode down the long hall at a clipped pace. It was sorely in need of upkeep. Aconite would have hated how I'd let the building fall into disrepair. How I'd let our son sleep on an old mattress for three years. I twisted the cold metal band around my finger. Still, no matter what the conditions were like at headquarters, they were far better than whatever holding cell they had him in at ISHFA.

I'll find him, I promised. *And bring him home.*

Leo would send word soon—or I'd move without it.

"Dane."

I marched faster.

"Dane!"

I spun around. "Yes, Alice?"

She slid to a stop, wiping her nose with the back of a hand. "I need to speak with you."

I motioned her through the door to my office. She stepped inside and spun around, eyes red-rimmed. "I have an update. On Jack."

My pulse kicked up. She'd texted she had nothing. *Smart girl.* Leo's reminder had me tugging my phone out of my pocket. "Hand me your phone." Alice raised a brow, but pulled it out of her pocket, passing it to me. I set them both outside the door.

"What is it?"

"It's Jack. They're tort…" She tripped over the words and my mouth flattened into a thin line.

"Spit it out, Alice."

Her eyes went round and she shook her head. She glanced frantically around the room, finding a sheet of paper on my desk. "Pen," she gasped.

My temper flared, but I moved around the desk and slid open a drawer, handing her a pencil.

She scribbled on the page, but the lead cracked as she tried to write. I tore the paper from the desk, lifting it to my face. "Torture?" She nodded, face going impossibly pale. That bitch Morgan was behind this, coercing her silence. I eyed Alice again. "How did you get out?"

"They let me go." Her voice shook and she didn't meet my eyes. A lie. Alice was lying...

"Come with me." There was no time to wait for Leo, not when Jack was in pain. I marched for the door, scooping up my phone, and hers. She didn't ask for it back and I didn't offer.

She raced behind me, trying and failing to match my pace. "Please, Dane. You have to help him." Her words were broken, pushed between chattering teeth. Her terror filled the hall. My chest went tight. Alice had always been overly fond of Jack, but I'd seen Janet's handiwork. I had no doubt her fear was justified.

Her phone buzzed and I glanced down. *It's time for you to leave the AFF. It's not safe there anymore.*

The sender's name was Mom.

I stopped, staring down at her phone, mind racing. Alice. Grif had said he was following Alice. Not once. Every time. Every time I'd thought someone was in the hall—listening at the door—it had been... Alice.

I killed him. The realization hit harder than the proof. The hall receded. If I'd listened. If I'd just... But I'd put Grif in the ground for telling me the truth.

A cold sweat broke out on my forehead and needles prickled the back of my neck, nausea swirling in my gut. This entire time, I'd believed I had done what was needed. What had to be done for the cause. Whatever it took to keep us safe from the fae.

My grip tightened on her phone. Alice deserved a slow, painful death for what she had done. For the lies... and for Grif. It took every ounce of restraint I had to keep from clenching my hand around her pale neck. First, I had to save my son.

"Come on. Faster."

We reached the lobby of AFF headquarters, and I pulled the fire alarm. In moments, people spilled out of hallways and doors, flooding the space. Lifting the red lever to silence the alarm, I scanned the room.

"Members of the Anti Fae Faction," I called. "We have a new enemy."

I climbed up onto the desk. "One of ours is being tortured." The word caught in my throat. "We don't abandon our own."

I eyed each person, lingering on those who wore angry expressions. "ISHFA needs you to believe Jack fell for a fae so you won't question what they're doing to him." I let the room settle. "Ask yourselves, does Jack fall for anyone?"

A ripple of laughter.

"He's loved one woman: my wife, Aconite." Faces softened. "She'd have had my head if I left our son in their hands."

A few heads were nodding. Not enough.

"In the hands of Morgan, Autumn Court emissary."

"Let's get Jack back!" Connor shouted. In another world, it would have been Grif following my lead, inciting the mob. It would have been Alice dead at my feet the night I'd discovered a traitor, and I'd be going into battle with the only man I'd ever trusted.

"Jack's one of us!" John chimed in.

Around the room, others shouted, rallying the mob. Soon, everyone was raising fists and yelling their assent.

The sound rose, shaking the panes at our back, and something deep inside me broke loose. For the first time in weeks, hope and fury burned hotter than fear. I stepped down from the desk, their voices pounding in my chest like a second heartbeat.

We were going after Jack, and this time, we wouldn't stop until we brought him home.

THIRTEEN

SAV

I thanked Mab that Yolmar and Larek had gone ahead. New York was scraped clean of magic, the streets quiet by Dane's hand. Dread curled low in my gut. We had gambled everything to break the folk from his cells, and Jack had paid for it. If more prisoners sat below AFF headquarters, there was nothing I could do for them yet. I refused to spiral. I was close, and soon I would free Jack.

We slid into the dark alley behind ISHFA headquarters. A silent clock, ticking down Jack's demise, clanged in time with my heart. I knew in my very being if I didn't act now, soon it would be too late. Phantom lips brushed mine and I touched my fingers to my mouth; a whisper against my ear: *I've wanted to do that for a long time.*

It wouldn't be my last memory of him. I wouldn't let it. *Hang on Jack.*

"Is it a castle?" Hazel murmured, stretching her neck back.

"It's called a skyscraper," I whispered.

"I don't like this place."

The hairs on the back of my neck rose. Hazel had always had a bit of seer magic. Very little, but enough that I trusted her intuitions. "Is there danger?"

"Suffering. And death."

My throat dried. Jack was suffering. I felt it. My skin crawled every time I thought of him locked up with those monsters. Heat pricked the backs of my eyes and this time it wasn't my magic.

A whistle sounded farther down the alley and I peered into the dark. Wicked-looking metal glinted, and a pair of orcs, strapped from waist to shoulder with knives, axes, and other weapons stepped into the light.

"My, aren't they a pair," Hazel sighed.

The twins grinned as we approached them.

I jabbed their arms. "Focus." Hazel batted her lashes and I wondered if I'd have to separate the three of them. "Guys. We're here for Jack. Remember."

"Later," Yolmar said, winking. "After we steal back Sav's boyfriend."

I rolled my eyes, but my heart had slowed a fraction, breath coming easier. We could do this. We could save him and get out without anyone getting hurt.

"The front desk has a panic button," Yolmar said. "The press of a button is all it would take to alert Morgan and Janet."

Larek opened his mouth, but the sounds of shouting and marching feet carried down the street and we all pressed against the alley wall. "Stay here," I mouthed and moved swiftly back toward the street.

Peering around the glass facade of ISHFA's headquarters, my mouth went dry as an angry mob, led by Dane Clyde, marched straight for us. Pressing myself back against the wall once more, I worked to control my racing heart as sparks shot from my fingers in every direction. *Breathe. Then move.*

I pushed off the wall and raced for my companions. "Run!"

Not waiting for more information, the trio darted in the opposite direction, coming out the other side of the alley. I reached the side exit door last and pushed through it, wrapping my fingers around the handle and ignoring the searing pain in my fingers, yanking it wide. "Get inside."

We crowded into a narrow service hall and went still. Shouts and gunfire bled through the building. I eased a shoulder against the exit door. Swiveling my head back to face my friends, I swallowed. "We'll fight through them if we must."

Hazel's eyes were round, but Yolmar and Larek nodded grimly. The look that passed between them said they'd known this was a possibility. They glanced down at the scared female wedged between them, and I knew they'd keep her safe with everything they had. It was who they were. It was why I loved them. I wanted to comfort them, to apologize for bringing them into my mess, but I turned and pushed open the door, ready to meet our enemy.

We were greeted by silence. Where shouts still echoed behind us, the alley was empty. The sudden stillness made my skin crawl. No bodies. No pursuit. Just the wind and the distant crack of gunfire.

I turned in a slow circle, searching for movement, but there was nothing. My pulse thudded in my throat.

Why pull back now? They'd been right behind us, and we had nowhere to go.

My breath caught. They weren't here for us.

Jack. Dane hadn't sent them to kill me, he'd come for Jack.

My stomach lurched. The air was too thin. I turned toward the chaos we'd left behind. "We have to go back."

The scrunched eyebrows marring each of their faces told me none of the others knew. "He's not after us. He's here for Jack." Heat flared in my chest. "We can help them."

Yolmar moved to block the door. "Sav, no. Let them fight each other. We'll take Jack from Dane after."

His words were logical. I knew it. But that tug in my chest, the one that said I had to go in now, wouldn't be ignored. "Stay. I'll be back."

Not waiting for a reply, I pushed past Yolmar, racing down the long hall. When I reached the door to the lobby, I listened. All was quiet on the other side.

Pressing tentatively against metal, I swore when my fingers sizzled. Wedging my shoulder against the door, I shoved it wide and stepped into the massacre.

Bodies were strewn in every direction, some in regular human clothes, others in full tactical gear. The kind I'd only ever seen when ISHFA was called in. I stepped over crumpled forms, following the trail of red to the elevator bank. Eyeing the guns of one of the fallen soldiers, I grimaced. Iron.

I pressed the glass button housing a green arrow pointing up. Stepping inside, I stared at rows and rows of numbers. A red smudge on forty-nine was my best guess. I pressed it and flung my hands out when the world rocked under my feet. I'd seen skyscrapers and tall buildings all over NYC, but I'd never been inside one and the floors I'd traversed had been by way of stairs.

I felt as though I was both falling and flying and I swayed, trying to get my bearings. A ding sounded and I jolted to a stop. The door slid open and the smell of blood and smoke permeated the space.

Peeking my head out, I stepped onto the floor. Pressure built in my ears, making the room spin and my steps wobble. It was the height from the ground. Unnatural and dizzying.

I leaned into the wall, giving myself a moment to acclimate. Shouts and the rapid pop-pop-pop of bullets sounded somewhere down the hall.

I crouched low. The space was nearly all glass, not an ounce of iron to be found. I exhaled a sigh of relief. This far off the ground, the buzz of all that poisonous metal weaving through everything was nearly non-existent. It was clear the building had been updated to suit Morgan's needs, and I was grateful for it.

"Dane!"

My enemy's name was a jolt to the chest and I inched toward the sound.

Screams burst to life as Morgan's low melodic voice spat command after command at her attackers. They were no match for her, even with their guns. "Fire on each other."

A round of shots went off and more yells rang out.

Behind me, the elevator dinged and I spun around. Larek, Yolmar, and Hazel stepped out and I swore. "Get down." They fell to their knees, crawling toward me. "What are you doing here?"

"We weren't going to leave you." Hazel whisper-hissed.

"I need to take out Morgan," I mouthed.

They nodded and I inched behind a conference table. Its solid wood frame was the only barrier between me and the war breaking out on the other side of the room. Sliding to the far side of the desk, I peeked my head out. Dane and Morgan were a few feet away, separated only by a thin sheet of glass.

My gaze snagged on the battered, bloodied form of a man with raven hair and sallow skin, slumped over a chair. My sharp intake of breath did nothing to quell the rising panic in my chest. He was unconscious. I would know if he was dead. I would know...

A raging inferno burst through me and I stepped out from behind the desk.

All around us, bodies were crumpled on the floor. Some moaned or whimpered, others lay still. Morgan had laid waste to them all. Her own soldiers had been little more than fodder to her.

Dane and Morgan's attention shot to me as I flung the table aside and stepped around glass to face them. Dane raised his gun, pointing it at me. "This is your fault," he barked.

My heart jumped erratically as I moved, the pull to end him, the call of the bargain I'd made demanding its due. I would destroy him, but first, flames soared from my palms and I shot them at Morgan. She screamed as they wrapped around her, hovering just over skin. I wasn't ready to burn her just yet. "Morgan."

She jolted, eyes going wide. My magic wasn't soft like hers. "Remove Jack's handcuffs."

She jerked, moving on straight legs to Jack's side and I caught sight of the slow rise and fall of his chest. Dane glanced between us, eyes narrowed. The gun remained on me, but he didn't fire.

My flames parted, giving her better access. "Now the feet."

She undid his leg clasps and I bit back a cry as he slumped over, falling to the floor in a pool of what must have been *his* blood. It was hard to be sure with all the other bodies in the room, but the long strips of skin torn from his abdomen and chest oozed and several other scars told me he had healed from many, many others.

One of the bodies twitched. Janet dragged an arm beneath her, smearing blood across the floor as she forced herself up onto her elbows. Her shirt was soaked, a dark bloom spreading from the bullet holes in her side. Her bloodshot eyes found Morgan first, betrayal twisting her features, then flicked to me. She staggered to her feet with a ragged scream and lurched toward us.

"Kill her."

Morgan fought it. Her jaw clenched, muscles straining against my command, but she wasn't stronger than me, and with her innate gift muzzled, she had no way to break my hold. She charged Janet, slamming into her and driving her back to the floor. In a blur of movement, she pinned Janet down and pressed a gentle kiss to her split, blood-slick lips. "My love," she breathed against her mouth, then sank her teeth into Janet's neck.

A safety clicked off and my gaze swiveled to Dane.

I met his steel-gray eyes and in that moment, I knew I had miscalculated.

Dane had always been so controlled in my presence, even if he was a monster. He'd lived by his own fucked up code. I had thought, wrongly, that it would hold him back now. I should have waited. I should have planned. But the sight of Jack's abused body, sent rational thought from my mind and all I wanted was revenge.

Time slowed as the crack of a gun discharging rang in my ears and the air shifted. Strands of long auburn hair whipped my face and a body crashed into me, knocking me to the floor. I looked up into soft eyes full of humor and life and exhaled a scream as it left them.

"Yolmar. Yolmaaar."

He slumped atop me, full weight pinning me to the ground. His blood was warm against my chest. I gasped for air and pulled in the taste of smoke and metal and something far worse. Rage punched through me, so sharp it made me nauseous.

Larek tugged his twin off me, laying him gently on the floor. He shook him, touching his cheek. "Brother? Yolmar?"

Then Hazel was above me, touching my face, my chest, searching for any sign that Dane's iron bullet had penetrated me.

There was no coming back from this. The thought settled like a stone in my gut. A scream built behind my teeth and had nowhere to go.

I saw nothing but the red haze clouding the room and the evil man who polluted the air I breathed. He lifted his weapon again, a weapon designed to kill my kind, and aimed. At Larek. At Hazel. At any of us.

The rage boiling inside me surged, clawing for an outlet. A thousand tiny moments crashed through me, bright and unbearable. The twins at my side when I read to them as boys. Yolmar splashing me beside the stream as we stared across the border to Summer, planning our next quest. Creig looking in on the three of us before he began nightly rounds outside Spring's palace. Larek's laugh. Yolmar's crooked grin. We would never have new adventures now. Dane had taken that from us, taken Yolmar from his twin, from me.

Something inside me snapped.

Heat coiled in my chest, compact and vicious, pressing against my ribs as if the fire meant to tear straight through my bones. My skin prickled, too tight, my veins burning with it. The air around me thickened, heavy and hot, and every breath seared my lungs.

I screamed, throwing my hands out, and the world answered.

Flame roared from my palms, ripping free of me in a rush that was like being emptied and consumed all at once. The room erupted in fire, swallowing sound, swallowing thought, leaving only blistering, blazing vengeance.

FOURTEEN

JACK

I groaned. The cool tile was tacky, pulling at my damp skin. I opened my eyes, taking in the sideways room. Morgan's ruby gown flowed around her, obscuring most of my view. She lifted her head from a dark shape and smudged the red dripping from her mouth with trembling knuckles. Her gaze jittered around the room, landing on me. She scuttled toward me like some sort of possessed demon.

Sound clawed its way back, her wet lips smacking as she closed in, and dread stitched itself between my shoulder blades. I struggled to move, to sit up, to breathe.

Flames burst to life along my arms and she reared back, hissing. I pushed up to a sitting position, my gaze landing on a strange ring of flames encircling her.

I reached out to touch them, and Morgan leaned back, a strangled scream escaping her. I'd never seen her like this. Terrified, discomposed. My fingers twitched then curled into a fist. She crawled backward, stumbling over the lifeless form she'd been drinking from.

A silver bracelet I knew, Janet's, caught the light. I blinked. How? Why?

Burned fabric and blood, acid on my tongue. Everything hit me at once and my attention shifted past her to the chaos beyond.

"Sav!" The word split my lip and scraped my throat, but I swallowed my next sentence when Sav yanked a blade, dripping with crimson from a form beneath her, blackened nearly to non-recognition.

I pushed to my feet, moving unsteadily, and she rose to catch me. We fell together, crashing to our knees. For a moment, Sav's rain and honey-

57

suckle scent wrapped around me and I blew out a steadying breath. Then, my blurry gaze snagged on the outline of the charred shape behind her.

I inhaled sharply. The nicked wedding band; the scuffed money clip we'd bought together poking out of a pocket, his dark hair, mostly salt and pepper now that Mom was gone. His hand rested on a still chest, ring glinting in my hazy vision. His face and neck were burned so badly I might not have known it was him, but we were built the same, even if I was taller.

I looked up into bright amethyst eyes. It might as well have been my chest she'd buried the knife in. My tongue stuck to the roof of my mouth. "What have you done?" I choked on the question.

Sav's sorrow shuttered; the lines around her mouth smoothing. It was the face she wore for enemies, not for me. "He killed hundreds of my kind."

It's not true. It can't be. The denial came first, sharp, and useless. My mind scrambled to make sense of the scene. His face was too burned to recognize. It was Connor. Or Jim. It had to be. But Connor's hair was blond and Jim didn't have any on top of his head. My dad was safely back at AFF headquarters, not a charred shape bleeding out behind the woman I loved.

Except I'd seen what he'd done. The cages. The experiments. Sav locked in a cell because of him. Two versions of him collided in my chest, the man who'd raised me and the monster who'd tried to carve her apart, and something inside me tore straight down the middle.

I swallowed twice before words came, each one dragging over raw edges. "He was my dad." A thousand-pound weight pressed on my chest, crushing me.

I let go of Sav and sank back on my heels. Distantly, I thought my feet should hurt. Janet had driven a fresh set of nails through them just before I lost consciousness, but my skin was dry again, the numbness back. Numbness to the physical pain, at least.

Heat pulsed under my sternum with nowhere to go, a hole gouged out by the woman I loved. Just as quickly, it cooled, my vision tunneling until all I could see was her blood-slick fingers and the body on the floor behind her.

"He was a murderer." Sav got to her feet, holding out a hand.

I stared at it. At the hand still painted in my father's blood. "So are you." My voice was flat. I didn't recognize it.

Her hands fisted; something raw flashed in her eyes and was gone just as quickly.

"Sav."

Hazel's voice roused me. My gaze slid to one of Creig's sons, Larek maybe, then Hazel, hovering over one of the many bodies strewn across the floor. I tried to count, but my vision blurred at four. Had they come for me? Died trying to save me? As Dane had.

"Sav, we have to leave," Hazel said. There was no coy seduction in her usually sultry voice, only grief.

Sav spun back to face me. "We have to go, Jack. If anyone finds you here, they'll have questions."

I nodded dumbly, getting to my feet. The air reeked of ash and burned flesh. I stepped over the charred body at my feet, half expecting him to shoot up and tell me to stop. To stay with him. To fight with him one last time. He didn't. The silence was a punch to my mangled heart.

Larek hefted his twin into his arms and Hazel scrambled ahead of him to press the elevator button. We stepped into the cramped box: fan rasping, cable humming. Hazel sniffled.

The bell chirped; the doors slid open. Larek stepped through first, followed by Hazel. Sav went next. I stood still.

The doors closed.

They opened again and Sav stepped back inside.

"Jack."

I blinked at my reflection on the walls; at Sav facing me.

"Please talk to me."

My dry tongue scraped the roof of my mouth. The air between us was deafening, but I had no words to fill it.

She pushed a button and the doors opened again.

"Please. We have to go."

The doors closed, both of us still inside. My thumb hovered, then chose—forty-nine.

She faced the doors. Numbers climbed; pressure pinched my ears.

FIFTEEN
FOXGLOVE

Papers and carefully drawn maps flew from the table as Creig slammed a fist down hard enough to rattle it. "You should have told me sooner."

He drew breath to say "soldiers"; I braced. He always went there first.

"Get the soldiers together. I will not have my sons getting themselves killed for another one of Sav's messes."

"That's rather harsh, General. The princess didn't create this mess."

Dark eyes slid to me, his stare pinning me in place. I shuddered and the back of my neck prickled as though a strike were imminent. He exhaled sharply, jaw working. "You're right. Of course. The humans are the ones to blame."

He stopped short. His jaw set the way it did when he was swallowing an order.

"The soldiers are occupied with the injured," I reminded him.

For the fae we'd brought back from Dane's compound, recovery was slow: iron burns puckered along wrists and throats; bandages stuck and bled when changed. On the cots, eyes stared past us, blinking but never truly seeing.

Juniper's condition, the poison they'd forced upon her in that compound, had given me an idea. We'd begun testing them. All had traces of it in their blood. Those at headquarters more than the rest. It could also account for the blank expressions they wore.

At the thought of Juniper, my ribs loosened a notch. It had been centuries since I'd allowed myself to feel anything for another. In truth, if she hadn't been so broken, I might never have let my guard down. I was under no illusions that she would ever have any of those same warm feelings for me. She was fighting the drug's hold and winning a little more each day, but satyrs kept to their own. And rumor had it they took males to their bed only to ensure the continuation of their line.

"Trust that Larek and Yolmar can handle themselves and get back quickly, Creig." He grunted a noncommittal response. "There are no fae living in Manhattan since Dane's last raid. We've rescued all we could. The moment the twins return, it's time to close our portal."

He squared his shoulders. "The guardians live there. The four portals to Faerie are still open. And," he glanced around, "my spies are still there as well. If humans find their way into Faerie, what's left will be destroyed."

I nodded. He wasn't wrong. Our portal, though, had no guardian. Dane had made it his mission to find us and I feared for us far more than for Faerie.

"Perhaps we should allow Sav and her lover to remain here. With most of her magic restored, she would be a great ally should Dane find us."

"Her magic is an inkling of what it should be. She's never manifested what the Lady predicted."

I stuck a hand in my pocket, cold metal biting against skin. The ring I kept with me always. My chest tightened. "She is the Wraith now."

Creig nodded, brows lowering. "I apologize, Foxglove. I didn't mean to bring her up."

I pulled my hand out of my pocket. Thinking of Mira's mother would do us no good at this moment. "It was a long time ago."

His look lingered a beat too long; I looked away first. Like me, his love was stolen, but rather than losing her to a life cut short, Creig's wife had been taken by Mab. Why she'd chosen a pairing between his wife and his brother a century after they were wed, I would never know. But it was a cruelty no one should be forced to endure.

Mab believed her secrets were safe from us. Perhaps that gave her the confidence to carry out such acts. But where her betrayal to Sav had been rooted in her belief that courts should not intermingle, the reason for breaking up Creig's marriage made little sense.

My heart thumped and I looked to the door. Juniper stood, framed by oak and vines. "What is it?"

She said nothing, blinking those golden eyes at me in silent request. Our nightly ritual had brought comfort to my life in a way I hadn't known I longed for. She waited by the table, her comb laid out, the bowl of berries halved just so.

I started for the door, and the one time of day that brought me peace, but froze when Larek pushed through, knocking Juniper aside as though she hadn't been there. That's when I saw what—who—he had in his arms.

"Yolmar?"

Creig's strangled cry hit the room; my hand found Juniper's shoulder before I knew I'd moved.

"Lay him on the table." His voice cracked as he swiped pots of ink and papers to the floor.

Larek stumbled into the room, setting his twin down gently, and I hugged Juniper tighter to me, blinking rapidly. He was so still, skin gone gray; every breath in the room was held. Something split under my breastbone.

Hazel slid through the door, hugging the wall. Her fingers were twisted together, knuckles white.

Creig laid his head on Yolmar. He stayed like that, cheek to his son's chest. No one shifted or breathed.

When he lifted red eyes, peering around the room, I exhaled, a sob catching in my throat. Gone. Yolmar's laugh, the one that cut tension like a blade, was gone with him. Larek's mouth moved but no sound came; his fingers searched for Yolmar's and found only air. I swiped my cheek, inching closer. Yolmar's face was relaxed, and the dark stains on his leathers weren't enough to end him. Or shouldn't have been...

"What happened?" I whispered.

Hazel pushed off the wall, wrapping her fingers in Larek's. She looked from the orc resting peacefully on the table to me. "Dane shot him in the heart. Sav said the bullet must be iron. It was the only way it could have killed him."

"Sav," Creig growled. "Where is she?"

Hazel's eyes widened and she squeezed Larek's fingers. "She's with Jack. They're burying his father."

One of Creig's axes thunked into the far wall. "She's burying my son's killer."

Hazel swallowed. "She killed Dane. She... felt guilty." Her lips trembled and she pressed closer to Larek. Her nearness seemed to rouse him from his stupor and he tightened his hold on hers. She didn't look at Creig when she continued, her knuckles whitening. "It wasn't Sav's fault. She told us not to come. She asked us to stay behind."

Creig narrowed his gaze on his son, a hand still resting on his other. "As did I!"

Larek stiffened.

Hazel tugged him away from the table. His gaze fell to his brother, wetness pooling at the edges of his lashes. "He saved her. The bullet was meant for Sav, but Yolmar saved her."

Creig's fingers found the second axe and trembled once.

I'd stood beside him after the Blood Wood battle and at the great war. He never faltered then.

This was different.

Every line on his face was etched in sorrow even as his eyes promised murder. Blood for blood was the oldest Faerie law; a life was owed. Not Dane. His life was already spent. If Creig laid this at Sav's feet, many would stand between them, myself included. But if he wanted his enemy's blood, only one life would satisfy.

I let out a breath. This was not over, and even the strongest bent under a weight of this magnitude.

Creig was a rock in a storm, but even-tempered he was not. Fear made him harsher. He reached for a second axe, but Larek spoke again.

"I would have done the same. Sav is our friend, our family. We protect family."

SIXTEEN

SAV

Jack walked unsteadily, his bloody footprints leading me on. Counting them was easier than thinking. I didn't regret killing Dane and never would. What I regretted was Jack's slumped shoulders as he carried the body. He had no one now. Because of me. *Murderer.* He'd called me a murderer, and I was. Why then did it hurt so much when he gave me that label?

We reached the Central Park entrance closest to AFF. I pushed my sunglasses in place and scanned the corners.

A figure cut across the street and a knife was in my hand before the thought registered in my mind. One good thing came out of today. The fire at my center, still not fully restored, answered the bargain I'd made with the stars and burned my Earth-bargains to dust. I was free; I could protect myself and my folk. If I could call that fire again, perhaps the rest would burn away—perhaps even Kaspar's.

A man with dark hair and a soft middle rushed to us. "Jack. What happened? Who is that?" *Jack.* They knew each other. The hold on my knives loosened. "You can't be out here," the man added when Jack kept walking. "National Guard is on the way. Minutes. Full gear. If they find you carrying a body, they'll take you in."

Jack stopped. "You called them?"

He nodded. "To pull them off this block. Come inside."

Lightning streaked overhead and the first drops of rain touched us. Jack stiffened; the breath left him in a sharp sound, and his knees went out from under him. He collapsed, still cradling his father.

The man bent, lifting Jack, and his father, up. I took the other arm,

65

careful to avoid the puncture wounds on his forearms. Between us, we got Jack, and Dane, into the coffee shop.

Jack set Dane on the counter and sank into a chair. "Leo," he said, voice rough, "I need bandages and antiseptic."

"I'll help." I followed the man, Leo, to the back.

"Grab Gatorade and granola bars," Leo said over his shoulder.

I looped my shirt over the storeroom handle and pulled it open. I grabbed a six-pack of Gatorade and a handful of bars and hurried out.

Leo put the antiseptic and bandages beside Jack's elbow. "Can you handle your wounds? I need to get outside and redirect them from the shop." His gaze flicked to the counter. "If you can... hide the body." Jack nodded. Leo slipped out the front. "Lock it behind me. I'll come in the back."

I turned the deadbolt with my shirt still around the metal. My fingers shook at the thought of lifting Dane again, but Leo was right. There would be too many questions if anyone looked in.

"What happened to your stomach?"

Jack's voice startled me. I dropped my gaze to the wounds, then looked back up to the near-flame bright of his eyes. I hadn't looked at them in the elevator.

I wasn't ready to share the details of that fight.

At first I couldn't touch Dane with my magic. The bargains made with ISHFA wrapped tightly around my magic and pulled, the same way they had the day I tried to put a sword through a human. He pinned me, stabbing until I was spitting crimson. I pressed both hands to his skin. The fire answered the stars, eviscerating the bargain and bursting from my palms. When his face was no longer recognizable, blood drenching my burning fingers, I pulled his knife free from my side and drove it into his heart.

I unclenched my fists at my sides. "Nothing."

"Come here. I'll dress your wounds," Jack said, an edge in his tone.

I scoffed, moving to his side and surveying the medicine laid out. "You need aid more than I do." The bottle of Gatorade crackled in my hand. "But Leo was right. We need to move him."

Color drained from Jack's already pale face. His eyes shone, and it wasn't because of the bruise at his temple.

"I'll do it," he said. He pushed up, swayed, and limped to the counter.

I gave him room, then stepped in and put my weight against his side. I slid my hands under Dane's head and shoulders. Jack didn't stop me and together, we carried his father toward the back without a word.

A silver door to the walk-in freezer waited in the corner. I reached it first and pulled it open, releasing Dane's head. Metal burned my healing skin, but I held on, gritting my teeth. The pain was a reminder I was alive. And my enemy wasn't. Cold air rolled out, biting the tips of my fingers and nose as I backed up, making room for Jack to enter.

Jack knelt and laid Dane on the metal floor. He bent close and spoke in his ear, too quiet for me to hear. When he stood, he kept his gaze on the ground. A hard knot cinched under my ribs. I held out an arm to steady him; he passed by without taking it. The knot tightened, and I blinked several times to clear my vision. *I'm not sorry. I'm not.*

Fae healing meant the raw edges along my middle pulled less with each step, which gave my thoughts enough room to arrange themselves. Even so, my breaths were short as I followed him down the hall.

Jack dropped into his chair. Wet hair clung to his head and goosebumps erupted along his bare skin. His gaze moved up my body and paused at the strip of bare waist where my blouse had torn. I tugged it down, fingers sticky on the fabric.

He coaxed my hand free and lifted my shirt enough to see the wounds. My breathing hitched when he leaned forward, his mouth brushing one line and following it. Warm breath passed over the hurt. My hand hovered above his head, fingers trembling. I made a fist.

We stayed that way. His lips on my skin; me too terrified to move and shatter the moment.

He drew back as if waking, remembering where he was, who he was touching, his palm still light on my waist, and met my eyes. No hate in them; only grief. He didn't look away, letting me see his pain.

Something in me gave.

Just as quickly, his hand fell, his focus sliding to the back wall.

I drew a breath, held it, let it go. Whether he hated me or he was simply numb from the shock of the past several hours, one of us had to keep steady. I soaked a cotton ball and pressed it to a strip where skin had been scraped raw. Black flecks lifted away—cloth, or what was left of Dane.

Jack flinched.

"I'm sorry." A dry laugh escaped him and his gaze remained unfocused, fixed on nothing. He knew the apology wasn't for his dad. I swallowed a shaky breath. "Drink something."

I held up the Gatorade I'd brought him.

He stared through the bottle for a long moment. "Have you ever been so thirsty the idea of drinking no longer makes sense?"

Spring's dungeon rose in my mind. Two weeks without water for disobeying my sister. A small fox set a cup at the bars. I had taken the fox for her spy, an errand of mercy. No help came from her. I knew that now. "Yes. Drink anyway."

He reached for the lid. His hand shook. Two fingers bent at wrong angles made it impossible for him to twist.

I bit the inside of my cheek to hold in a cry at the sight. Thick scar tissue could only mean repeated breaks. Had they cut his fingers? Had they healed so quickly? Murderous thoughts of Janet and Morgan circled. I set the cotton aside, took the bottle, and opened it for him.

"We need to set those before they heal wrong," I whispered.

He looked down at his hand as if the thought had only just occurred to him. "I need to dry off first."

His bare skin had pebbled, but it must be nothing to the ache in his hands. Surely the shock was making him nonsensical. "We will set them, then worry about drying you," I said gently.

"No." He took a small sip, gaze going distant again. "It will be easier if I'm not in pain."

I frowned. "Explain."

"Water is my weakness," he said. "When I'm dry, I don't feel pain."

It couldn't be. I counted to steady myself. One breath. Two. Three. "Since when?"

"Since Janet started torturing me." The room narrowed to the scrape of his breath and the hum of the cooler. He set his unbroken hand over mine. "Sav."

I looked at his fingers on my skin, the same hand that had lifted my shirt to see the wounds, then at his face. Too kind for what I had done. This was my fault. I had asked him to be bait. No one had paid more for it than he had.

"I'm sorry about your friend," he said.

I pulled my hand free and wiped a tear. "Don't. Don't do that."

He took another drink.

"It was Dane, wasn't it?" he said.

"What?"

"Dane killed him."

My skin pebbled as ice slid down my spine. My throat closed.

"I know you," Jack said. "You would not have killed Dane for yourself. You did it for him."

I crossed my arms over my stomach and took a step back. "You're wrong. I made a bargain with the stars. I swore to end him before I ever met you."

More color left his face, and another crack fractured my heart. Better he knew me as I was. With me, people bled. Died.

He set the bottle down and looked around the empty shop. "Will you find me a towel?"

I straightened. A towel. Right. I had let myself unravel. I needed to get it together.

Outside, rain beat against the window and a siren blared to life somewhere in the city.

I turned, but just a few steps away, spun back and stared at the back of his head, inhaling slowly. He was alive. If he hated me for the rest of his life, at least he was alive. Everything else could be mended with time.

In the back, I tore at cardboard, ripping open boxes in search of a towel. If I could only find one, I could fix things. Dry him, heal his pain, put things right.

"Check behind the counter," Jack called from the front.

I marched back the way I'd come. Had he known where they were all along? Of course he had. Snatching a stack of clean towels from behind the counter, I rushed back to Jack's side.

His body was healing quickly, but flayed skin, puncture wounds, and scars old and new had me seeing red all over again. There was no one to blame but myself for the myriad of bodily injuries he'd suffered because of my plan. And Yolmar. This was all on me.

Working my way south, my fingers hovered at the line of cotton boxers that were wetter than the rest of him. I looked up. "These have to come off." I bit my lip. "Do you want help?"

My cheeks flamed as I tried and failed to ignore the sheerness of the fabric. In a moment there would be nothing between us. It shouldn't matter. Not when every scar marring his skin was on my hands. It didn't. All that mattered now was helping him recover.

He stood and a slew of curses spilled from his lips. I leaned toward him, steadying him as he wobbled.

"Let me do it." I slid wet fabric down his thighs, careful to avoid the flesh still working to close itself up along his right calf.

"Sav."

His boxers sloshed to the floor in a heap and I stood. "Yep?" I kept my eyes on his.

"How does it work? Water nullifying your gift?"

If he was fae. If immunity was his innate gift. The one all fae kept secret if they could help it, only an elemental gift could counter it. An elemental gift like water... He would feel nothing when he was dry. *If...* he was fae.

I laid gentle hands on his shoulders and pressed him into his seat, scrubbing his hair. "Water doesn't negate all gifts. It's different for every-one. But that's a secret you guard with your life."

There were so many things about Jack that weren't fae. His round ears, his dull eyes, his fashion sense, but an elemental gift negating your innate one, that was fae through and through. I struggled to process the informa-tion. To make sense of it. But if he were truly fae, guarding that secret was paramount to survival. We took that information to our grave.

Jack raised a thick raven brow. It had two small white lines running through it now. I longed to run my thumb over it and smooth away all his aches and pains.

"In my case, could I have had a weakness all my life, but not known because my gift was pain immunity?"

I scoffed, tipping his face up to wipe the underside of his jaw. Another new scar. I filed it away. Morgan was gone. So was Janet. But there were others behind this. I would learn their names. "Innate gifts don't manifest before twenty-five."

Jack frowned as I turned his head, wiping the side of his face, counting more tiny white lines. I wished desperately that they were still alive, that I had gotten to them first so I could make them suffer as they had Jack.

"Always?"

His questions brought me out of my murderous thoughts and I blinked. *Always?* What a loaded question. Not always, but was I ready to share all my secrets with him?

Jack's brows lowered, seeming to read my thoughts. "Hand me one." He pointed to the stack of towels.

I did as he asked, and he pressed it to his jaw and throat, careful around a still healing cut running down his cheek all the way to his Adam's apple.

I moved to his right hand and turned it over, inspecting the damage. I wanted to wretch, but Jack was so calm. Of course he was. He'd lived with these injuries for days while I took my time flitting from court to court, choosing clothes for my wedding, rendezvousing with Creig. Another twist in my gut. If I'd avoided going there first, Yolmar...

I swallowed. Jack needed me now. I could do nothing for Creig at the moment. "Are you ready for me to fix these?" I looked him over, inspecting for any wet spots I'd missed. "You're dry enough that it shouldn't hurt."

He didn't flinch as he nodded. "Do it."

Seventeen

Jack

"Breathe in," she said.

I drew air through my nose. A small click came, then a clean pop as the joint slid home. The breath left me in a rush, but the pain didn't come.

"Again." Her thumb found the next joint. "In." A firmer pull answered with a sharper pop. She checked the line of my fingers, tore a narrow strip from the towel, and bound the two together. I watched her, studying the furrow between her brow, the flat line of her lips. The urge to smooth it rose, but emotion was a fickle thing and mine was absent at present.

"Keep them still for a while," she said, tying the knot. Her thumb skimmed my knuckles. "Better?"

Something like desire flared to life at her touch, but the coldness blunting my world forced it down. I flexed carefully. "Better." She had done this before. I didn't ask where she'd learned. The Jack from a few days ago would have demanded an answer.

Her gaze drifted past my shoulder as she ran her towel over my dry skin, checking again for any signs of wetness. A short intake of breath and her fingers traced the intricate design over my back.

"What is this tattoo?"

I hadn't wanted to look, not that I'd wanted to see any other part of my newly scarred body, but if it had been damaged–ruined–my last shred of hope might shatter. I thought I'd been holding it together, but the question punched a hole through my chest. "It is for my mom," I said. "I got it after she died. To remember her."

Sav moved in front of me and lifted my foot to wipe the bottom. The cloth passed over the puncture through the center and a curse broke free before I could stop it. It shouldn't have hurt, but it seemed even a little water was enough to blunt my pain immunity. Or perhaps those wounds hurt that much.

Her brows rose. She lifted my ankle higher and studied the skin. Thin dark tracks still marked the path where black lines had raced up my calves before immunity had rushed in to block it.

"What are these?" Not waiting for my reply, she set my foot down gently and raised the other. "You have iron poisoning." She leaned closer. "Yes. Iron poisoning." Her eyes met mine. "You said iron couldn't hurt you."

I nodded.

She narrowed her gaze, then it widened. "You think your immunity to pain hid the symptoms."

I nodded again.

"Impossible."

"Is it?" My throat was raw. "No one ever got their magic before twenty-five?"

It seemed one emotion could withstand the numbness. Hope was a small thing, but it stood its ground. If iron marked me the way it marked the fae, then maybe I belonged with them. With her. It would not excuse what she had done, but it might make forgiving her a possibility.

She set the soaked towel aside and took a fresh one. "Someone has." She glanced up at me before focusing on my foot again. "Me."

I waited for her to say more. The cooler hummed. Rain threaded the glass. She pressed a towel to a cut on my heel until the warmth ebbed, then worked along each mark with a steady hand. Her mouth tightened at the corners. I watched the tremor she quieted as she focused on her task.

I lifted a hand once more, touching the bloody ribbons of her shirt. She said nothing as I slid the fabric aside. They were healing quickly, but there were still at least a dozen angry red marks around her middle. Heat flared to life, pushing down the cold numbness. She could have died trying to save me. So many others had.

"Dane did that, didn't he?"

She pulled her hand free and wiped a tear with the heel of her palm. "Don't."

I traced a red line. She didn't stop me. Didn't pull away.

"You don't have to tell me. I know those marks are from him."

Her skin pebbled. Her throat worked, but nothing came.

"He would have killed you."

The truth sat between us. Her silence the only confirmation I needed.

They'd fought. One to the death. When I was bleeding only a few feet away, he'd chosen his hatred over his love.

I let my hand fall and looked out the rain-streaked window.

When the quiet stretched, my mind finally accepting all that had come before this moment, I exhaled softly. Sav may have killed my father, but if she hadn't, I was certain he would be the one patching me up now. Offering weak consolations for my loss. I found *she* was the one I couldn't live without.

"There's nothing for me here." I looked up. "Will you take me to Faerie?"

She went very still, then the tension in her shoulders eased a fraction. "Yes."

EIGHTEEN

SAV

"Sav." Jack caught my hand.

The door banged open and Leo appeared looking between us. "I brought you some clothes."

He held up a shirt and pair of shorts that looked much too small, but Jack stood, accepting them, and sliding the shorts up his thighs. Freshly scraped wounds oozed and I pressed a towel to them, staunching the bleeding. Many of his wounds had already closed, but the worst of them, the ones made by iron tools, would take longer.

Shouts rose outside, and I moved to peer out the front window. "The street's still full of soldiers."

Jack joined me and parted the blinds at eye level. Guards clustered at the curb and funneled Dane's people into lines. The smallest group held faces I recognized from the night of the attack on my building or my time inside AFF headquarters. The largest held strangers.

Leo cleared his throat. We turned. "I'll check on Grace," he said. "She will want to know you are alive."

The name meant nothing to me, but I knew little of Jack's life on Earth. He nodded and stared past Leo to the rain. "Tell her not to come until it's safe."

"I can try."

Leo turned to go.

"Leo?" Jack's voice pulled him back. "Check on Alice?"

The name struck my gut. I shouldn't care. Not when Jack may never forgive me. But I did. I'd allowed hope to crowd in when he asked to come to Faerie, but wanting to leave Earth and wanting to go because of me were not synonymous.

Leo disappeared, leaving us alone once more. Jack moved to the door, twisting the deadbolt and leaning against it. For a moment, I thought he would follow his friend, brave the rain and the pain that accompanied it. I wouldn't have blamed him. He had a life here, friends. I had taken the only family he had left, but at least he had them.

"Jack."

He turned and there was more life in his eyes than I'd seen since pulling him out of that awful building. He moved toward me and my heart beat against my ribs. In the moment, I hadn't thought his question through. Faerie wasn't safe for Jack. *I* wasn't safe for him.

I opened my mouth to explain. To tell him, but that would mean bringing up Creig and... Yolmar.

He took another step, a hand stretched toward me, but I backed up. The brightness in his gaze faded. He would sink back into that place again if I didn't give him something.

"Blood for blood is the oldest law in Faerie."

Jack stopped. "What?"

"You can't go to Faerie."

He opened his mouth.

"You can't go anywhere with me."

He closed it, hand falling to his side. I swallowed my next words. The excuses I'd planned to make. The hurt in his eyes was a knife to my chest. After all the pain I'd caused, I couldn't be responsible for more.

I crossed my arms over my chest. "Creig will hate me now. He'll want what's owed. Blood."

Jack's brows pinched, but he said nothing.

I inched backward, needing space in the suddenly claustrophobic room. The ache wasn't in my ribs or skin—it was the pull under my breastbone, a tearing that worsened with each inch I put between us. I hadn't given myself time to think about it before now. What it meant that... Yolmar... was gone.

I tried to say the words, to explain, but my mouth was full of cotton. I swallowed. "He'll blame me."

Jack took a step toward me. "We'll tell him what happened."

I flung a hand out in warning and Jack halted. "You don't know what it means to have Creig as an enemy," I said. "He's loyal... until you cross him." I wrapped my arms around myself. "Then there's nothing he won't do to find you."

"You didn't kill Yolmar." He winced before the name was fully spoken, realizing his mistake.

Too late. It was too late. His name sliced the air between us and everything I'd been holding back broke loose. I gasped out a sob, crashing to my knees. *Yolmar.* The kindest of us. The best of us. Another choked sound worked its way up my chest. Hot tears streaked my cheeks.

Jack fell beside me, wrapping me in the warmth of his embrace.

I heaved, too willing to accept his comfort when I deserved none of it. Not for him or for the friend who'd died on my watch. Just as Creig had feared. I'd failed them both. My shoulders shook as my chest hitched, again and again. I would be dead now if it wasn't for my friend. He had bought me the time I needed to attack.

Jack's grip tightened around my heaving form and slowly, the tears dried.

"You can't come with me," I choked out. "You're safer away from me."

His arms loosened, a hand stroking my hair. It soothed the ragged bits of my soul too broken to give voice to. "It wasn't your fault."

"It was." New wetness gathered along my lashes, threatening to break free. "I went to Creig's hideout. I let them come along."

I looked up, vision blurry. "Don't you see? He'll kill us both if he finds you with me."

The hand stroking my hair stilled and Jack's gaze darkened. "Do you truly think I'd leave you to shoulder this alone?"

The tears did come then, fast and heavy. I wiped my cheeks. Now that I was thinking clearly, a new truth, one more horrible than any other came to me. Creig wouldn't want my blood. He would want the blood of his killer. And with his killer gone...I searched Jack's face. Creig would come for him. Creig would demand what was owed.

"You're right. I can't leave you. It's not *me* he'll come after."

◆→(◡◆❋◆◆

When the rain and the soldiers outside showed no sign of departing, Jack's eyes drooped, his breathing slowed, and I searched the space for something more comfortable to sleep on. I stood, crossing the room to a low corner booth and tugged the cushion off.

Jack's eyes blinked open, a small smile tipping his mouth. "Upstairs," he grunted. "There's a bed."

The stairs were narrow and the room at the top barely held the mattress and a dresser, but it would do for the night. Jack eased down. I sat at the end. The storm drummed the roof. Outside, the city was alive with humans searching for those involved in the massacre that still painted the walls only a few blocks away. While Jack seemed to relax, my heart would

77

not slow. His eyes closed, but it only beat harder. I pressed my palms to my thighs and waited for the shaking to pass.

When my breathing calmed, my heart slowing a fraction, I studied Jack's face. In sleep, he was peaceful. The lines pinching his brow smoothed.

His eyes opened. "Watching me sleep again, Savage?"

His mouth tipped up and I exhaled a chuckle.

"Just making sure you weren't about to die again." The words came out rougher than I intended.

He smiled. "It was close."

Scarred fingers wrapped around my wrist, tugging me toward him.

I gave in, letting him pull me down until I was nestled in the crook of his arm. Quiet gathered. Breath by breath it settled. My shoulders relaxed. My eyelids grew heavy, my breath slowed.

"I learned something," he said at last.

I shifted, pressing into his warmth. "What?"

"I think my mom is alive."

NINETEEN

FOXGLOVE

I was drowning in correspondence, but none of it was critical. Not when there was so much to be done. Mostly, I stayed here to avoid Creig. The lingering anger and grief were so raw it might split me in two just to witness it. I didn't want to see it etched on his face; didn't want to hear it in his voice. It was selfish, but I never claimed to be anything else.

A sound made me look up from my desk. Surely, I was hearing things. It came again. A soft humming. I stood, rounding the desk, and making my way to the chair facing the window. Juniper was staring at the vines swinging in a light breeze. She'd wandered in only moments after I did. She always seemed to find me. We never spoke, but she enjoyed my silent company as much as I did hers.

Her mouth opened and a soft melody poured from her lips. The vines swung faster, stretching for us.

I had heard of wild satyr magic. Of the way it brought life to the land. It was nothing like Sage's oppressive, suffocating magic. Sage's magic forced branches and vines into new furniture, stretching them high overhead until blooms burst on ceilings and along walls. It was beautiful, but not natural.

The tulip fields she cultivated, a not-so-subtle reminder of her power, were not native to Spring. They'd been stolen from Autumn centuries ago and required a great deal of Sage's magic to sustain. Ostentatious shows of magic were Sage's favorite thing. From the enormous cage of pixies in her parlor, to the added walls of blooms all throughout the castle, Sage expended a great deal of energy showing the court just how powerful she was.

But Sage was gone. Taken by the magic eating Faerie, or at least its fae, if Silv was to be believed. Silv, Spring's current satyr clan leader, had claimed both Sage and Alder were taken by the magic the day Sav married Kaspar. But if I knew my brother, he'd use just such an excuse to escape his dying lands and shrinking principality.

I hadn't spent a moment troubling myself over his whereabouts. And if by some miracle he was truly gone, Faerie would be better off without him.

Juniper's song twined around my heart like vines, seeking a stable post to help them thrive. I found I wanted to be that stable force for her. Wanted to be whatever she needed to break free of the poison's hold. Even if breaking free meant returning to her folk.

"Lord Hawthorn."

I glanced to my door, to the orc standing in it, and nodded.

Murz stepped into the room, casting a nervous glance at Juniper. They were all afraid of her. Certain she would grab the nearest blade and slice into them as she had Sav the night we rescued her from the AFF. But apart from the occasional mindless grab for a weapon, she was calm when Sav wasn't nearby.

"We're gathering."

I dipped my chin and knelt down to offer an arm to Juniper. She took it and stood. Silently, she turned with me until we faced the door. We crossed the room, Juniper staring straight ahead and I glanced back once. The vines she'd sung to stretched over the moss-covered ground, straining toward us, but it had stopped a few feet away, new buds lengthening just beyond the shadow of the trees. Pale leaves stretched toward the sky, reaching for the sun.

She had heard their plea and helped them find their way.

-●-➔(⌄♦♠♦●-

Somber faces gathered around freshly dug earth, red eyes cast low. I wrapped my fingers in Juniper's. Hushed whimpers and wordless tears circled the space as we observed in silence. Creig and Murz had laid Yolmar's body to rest, offering him the dignity of a private burial. A moment between his closest family and friends. Now, we gathered as one to witness his return to Gaia.

Creig dropped to one knee, resting a hand atop the soil and a gentle song burst from his lips. In the tongue of his people, he sang to Gaia of his son's strong heart, his bravery in battle, his loyalty, duty, and honor. Over many centuries by Creig his sons' side, I'd learned enough of their language to piece together the story he crafted.

Yolmar's tale would be carried on the wind, whispered in the heart and burned into the minds of all who knew him. His legacy would carry on until everyone in this meadow was gone. When the last creature drew its final breath, Yolmar's memory would pass with it, beyond the veil, to the place all forgotten things dwelled.

Until that time, his spirit would remain, a piece of him in each of us, a memory of who he was and what he stood for. I felt it most in Juniper's hand, her fingers tightening around mine. I looked down, startled, and then up again. Her eyes were clearer than I'd ever seen them, shining, caught by Yolmar's song or maybe by his spirit itself, piercing the haze.

A single tear traced her cheek. My chest tightened, my heart spasming at the sight.

And then she whispered, the words a jagged blade through the moment of quiet: "We have to kill them."

TWENTY

JACK

Half-conscious, I'd thought my mom rested in the place souls went after death, waiting for me to join her, but slowly, my mind was recovering, and with it, the memories. My finger traced the pattern my mom had drawn on my chest over and over again.

Sav's gaze followed the movement, her eyes narrowing. "Let me see your tattoo again."

It wasn't a question, but I didn't feel the urge to obey as I had with Morgan's commands. I rolled onto my side, inhaling shallowly. The worst of my injuries were on my chest and abdomen, but I was afraid to find out how much of my tattoo had been destroyed by Janet's knife.

Warm fingers slid my shirt up, and cool air caressed my back. A calloused finger traced the cursive letters spelling out my mother's name.

"Aconite."

I exhaled. It must not be too damaged if she could make out the letters.

I nodded against the pillow.

"You said this tattoo was for your mother?"

The confusion in her voice made me twist to look; I fell back onto the pillow. "Yes."

She paused, searching my face. "Tell me about her."

I blew out a breath. Where to begin? My mom had been my guiding light my entire childhood. The reason I wanted to help people. To study medicine. I considered her question. Sav didn't want to know why my mom was special to me. She was asking the same question she'd been asking nearly since she met me. Could my mom be fae? I'd refuted it vehemently the first time we talked, but I couldn't shake the strange visions I'd had on the path, or my most recent dreams about her. If they were dreams.

"I think I saw her. Somewhere in Faerie maybe. But she's a prisoner. Someone has her in a cave."

Sav nodded, biting her lip.

Hope swelled in my chest. She wasn't claiming it to be impossible. Did that mean the fae could talk to one another in dreams? Could my mom? But if that was true, why hadn't she ever visited my dreams before? A thought struck me.

"Could one of my innate gifts be visiting people in my dreams? Is that possible?"

Sav's brow furrowed and I leaned forward, smoothing it with the back of my thumb. She stiffened but didn't pull away. We hadn't lost all the progress we'd made before I was kidnapped by ISHFA. I would take it. And I would work to rebuild it. I ran the pad over her wrinkled brow until it smoothed before I let my hand fall, content to bask in those small touches for now.

"I've never heard of it, but that means nothing. Each high fae's gift is unique. What I'm less certain about is the ability to have more than one."

She slid down, resting her head on the pillow. This close, her breath tickled my nose and heated my skin, her scent tugging me toward her, begging me to close the space between us. To touch my lips to hers and claim her as I had in the missing pocket of Spring, what seemed like a lifetime ago.

"So, you only have one innate gift?"

Sav nodded, but frowned. "Maybe."

She searched my face. "You didn't tell them how to get into Faerie."

"No." The relief on her face, the desire to trust me, bloomed in my chest, but I wasn't being honest, and that didn't sit well with me. "They never asked."

She pursed her lips, but after a moment, her features relaxed, smoothing into something resembling a smile. "You wouldn't have."

I traced the line of her jaw. I hadn't meant to touch her again. It had been as natural as breathing and I was loath to release her now that I had her again. She didn't pull away, so I let my thumb slide to her mouth, running over soft lips that parted and the blood in my veins heated.

Sav's pupils dilated, and I didn't think she'd taken a breath since our skin met. She was flushed under my touch and her heart beat wildly in her chest. I blinked. I could *hear* her heartbeat. I let the pad of my thumb trace a line over her full bottom lip, over soft skin and under her chin.

Her pulse increased as my thumb ran over the smooth skin of her neck to her collarbone. The vein in her throat jumped and mine matched its pace. I felt it then. The way our hearts found each other's rhythm, syncing.

"Jack."

My gaze fell to her mouth as my name spilled from her perfect pink lips. "Yeah?"

"I'm worried about Creig."

I swallowed, the image of the orc general, axes at each hip, war paint streaked over his face, flashed in my mind. My hand dropped. There had been no time to consider him before, but he would want revenge for his son. My insides twisted at the thought of Yolmar, dead at Dane's hand.

Could I blame him?

Sav's heart pounded as she considered her next words. I searched her face. There was more she wasn't saying. My heart's rhythm matched hers. "What?"

"I made a bargain."

The hairs on my arms rose. Why did it sound so ominous? "Okay."

"If anything should happen to me, Creig must protect you."

Her eyes were wild and our rhythm stuttered as my heart took off. I cupped her face. "Nothing will happen to you."

She searched my face, her mouth flattening into a thin line. "Jack. You would never survive him if he chose to end you." She sat up. "You don't know what he's capable of."

Was she truly suggesting she would harm herself... for me? After everything? After she'd killed my father in front of me, there had been a moment. An instant where I wasn't sure I could forgive her. Wasn't sure my heart could come to terms with what she'd done. But that moment had passed. If I'd been unsure, her declaration clarified everything.

I wasn't from Faerie. I hadn't seen Creig in battle, but the way she flinched told me enough. She didn't think either of us could stop him.

If she thought that meant I'd ever trade my life for hers, she was wrong.

"I'm serious," I said, brushing her cheekbones. "Nothing is going to happen to you."

"That's not how this works," she breathed. "Creig won't come for me. He'll come for you. You're the blood he's owed."

I went still.

Blood for blood. Dane killed Yolmar. Dane was dead. The payment left was mine.

"He *will* take it," she whispered. "Jack, he will."

My jaw locked. "I'm not giving him anything."

The heat I'd grown so accustomed to in ISHFA headquarters flared to life in my chest. Sparks skittered from my fingertips.

"Listen to me," she snapped. "I won't watch him cut you down to satisfy an old rule." She crossed her arms over her chest. "My bargain with him guarantees he can't harm you. If we're left with no other option, I'm taking it."

I leaned in. "Absolutely not."

The sparks dancing over my fingertips burst into flames and caught at the edges of the blanket. "Damn—" I smothered it. Sav slapped the ember out beside me. We stared at the scorch marks.

I inhaled a slow breath through my nose. I'd just gotten her back. I wasn't losing her again.

Sav looked up, laid a hand over mine, and the heat receded. "Creig isn't in Faerie. We'll go there. It hasn't come to that yet."

I nodded, taking calming breaths. Leo's tiny apartment would go up in an inferno if I couldn't keep my anger in check. All the emotions I'd numbed were coming back. Slowly, they crept in, each finding a new place in my head and my heart.

Sav would stay with me. Together we'd find a way to reason with Creig. I didn't know him well, but the love he had for Sav was plain. She didn't think he could be convinced, but if I could forgive, perhaps he could too.

But first, there was something I had to do. "Before we go, I have to lay him to rest."

Sav searched my face, eyes shining, and she squeezed my hand, nodding. "Then we do it now."

Relief hit so fast it hurt. I stood. "We'll have to be careful." I turned, holding a hand out to her. "And we're not done talking about Creig."

"We will be if you're dead."

I let out a sharp breath and didn't argue.

TWENTY-ONE

SAV

I grabbed his hand and dragged him out of the small bed in Leo's room. We slipped down the narrow stairs, past the quiet of the dark coffee shop, through the back. Jack moved gingerly into the refrigerated space, lifting his father into his arms, and then we were at the rear exit. Beside the back door, I grabbed the rubber handle of a garden trowel, nodding to myself.

When we stepped outside, I pressed a finger to my lips. He frowned at me for the fifth time since I'd told him about my bargain. I'd never seen eyes change the way his did. When I'd been bound, my own had dimmed, as if the very magic in my veins lit them from within. Now that most of it was back, there was no hiding it. I couldn't account for Jack's.

This late, his bright eyes would appear as other to any human paying attention. We didn't have the luxury of explaining that away. It was a fact I could no longer ignore. Iron poisoning in his veins, temper hot enough to spark, eyes that burned brighter when his gift rose to the surface, and most troubling, an innate gift that was nullified by an element.

If it were all true, could it also be true that his mother was *the* Aconite? Not just any fae—in the history of Faerie there had only ever been one Aconite. And more troubling than the thought that he might be the son of Mab's only daughter, was the idea that Dane might not have been what he claimed.

High fae could not mix with other creatures to produce offspring. It was a fact known by all. A truth carried down one generation to the next. We were incompatible. Humans were no exception. So, if Jack existed, that meant one of Mab's rules was a lie. Or Dane hadn't been human.

Leaning against the brick facade, I peered around the corner of the dark alley. Nothing stirred and I scented nothing in the air.

"This way," I mouthed, sprinting across the alley.

I pressed my back to the wall and motioned for him to join me. Bright green eyes met mine, blinking once, and he darted across the space, shoulder bumping mine as he slid up beside me.

When we reached Central Park, crossing the wards and stepping on soft grass, I exhaled a small sigh as all the iron pressing against my skin dissipated. Jack was unaffected, moving on light feet, his father cradled in his arms.

We cut off the path under an elm where the grass grew long. The soil was damp and dark, littered with wet leaves and sparse patches of grass. I dropped to my knees and took the trowel, pinching only the rubber handle between my fingers. The iron gleamed in the low light, close enough to burn if I slipped.

I drove the blade into the ground. It sank an inch or two before roots caught and held it. I worked it back and forth, prying up clumps and scraping them aside. The handle twisted in my grip and my palm slid against the exposed metal. Heat flared across my skin. I hissed and jerked back, the burn settling into a low throb as I tightened my hold and dug on.

Jack's gaze was distant as he clutched his father to his chest, his measured breaths marking the rhythm of my work. The earth yielded quickly under fae strength, but it did not give itself freely; roots tugged back, stones jarred my wrist, and every shovelful landed in a growing mound beside us. By the time the hole was as deep and narrow as I dared make it, a cool, earthy smell rose from the opened ground—leaves and the faint sweetness of rot.

Jack lowered Dane into the grave and sat back on his heels. He smoothed his father's hair. "I remember you sitting by the door when I stayed out late, burning breakfast in the mornings when mom had a headache. You weren't perfect, but you stayed. I love you. I hope you know that wherever you are now."

His whispered words cracked. My hand rose toward him, fingers reaching for his shoulder before I caught myself. I curled my hand into a fist and tucked it under my arm. I had put the blade in Dane's chest. I did not get to comfort his son for it.

The rain had stopped, but the earth was still slick and cold. I glanced between the wet dirt and Jack's face, searching for any sign that the pain in his chest had returned. All I saw was exhaustion, hollow and raw.

Jack leaned down and I looked away, giving him that last moment.

He sniffled, and then the soft patter of dirt on cloth broke the quiet. I shifted closer until our knees touched and reached for the soil. It clung to my fingers and wedged under my nails as we pushed handful after handful back into the hole. Each fall of soil landed with a muted, final thud.

When the mound was smoothed as best we could manage, I set three flat stones at the head and pressed them into place. It was a mark for the living, not the dead.

"May the land keep what it's owed," I said, old Faerie words that were still true.

Jack pressed his palm to the mound and bowed his head. I watched the dark for trouble and stayed close enough to touch. When he swayed, I took his hand and squeezed once.

"We need to go," I breathed.

He nodded. We left the elm and didn't look back.

On our way to Leo's coffee shop, we hugged the wall, keeping to the deepest slice of shadow. Ahead, I heard voices, mechanical over the radios they wore at their chests. Soldiers. Getting closer.

I halted and laid a hand on Jack's chest. A spark of that pull between us flared to life.

There are no true mates, I told my fractured heart. It didn't listen. It insisted his touch was too right, his heartbeat too in sync with mine. But if Mab was still pulling strings somewhere, forcing bonds against our will, I wanted no part of it. She had ruined enough lives with her matchmaking.

I pointed back the way we'd come, gesturing for him to turn, but Jack didn't seem to understand. His anger had banked and his eyes were dim again. Human. I had no hope that mine would do the same. Without my magic bound, my eyes were as good as flashlights in the pitch dark. Coming out now, with soldiers around, had been a bad idea. We just had to get back inside Leo's coffee shop and wait them out.

"Hey!"

Ice slid down my spine as a set of boots jogged down the alley toward us.

He'd spotted us. It was too late. He would realize what we were and arrest us. My heart pounded in my chest as my palms went slick. Soft fingers traced the line of my jaw, and Jack's lips pressed against my ear.

"Will you trust me?"

Boots pounded faster as the soldier closed the distance between us. My vision blurred, the world spinning by.

"Trust me?"

Jack's warmth and his breath, hot against my ear, steadied some of my panic. I nodded, unable to do more.

He ran a thumb over my chin and tipped my face up. His warm mouth found mine, tentative at first, then more insistent. His lips parted, reminding me of the day we'd leaped into the lake and I'd pressed my lips to his, offering him some of my air.

Even then, I think I knew. I'd felt that strange surge in my chest, urging me to claim him as mine. To demand that he do the same. I hadn't believed it. A stranger, thrust into my life through circumstance and bad luck. A creature from another world and the son of my enemy. But somehow, the moment I'd pressed my lips to his, I'd known.

Mates.

His tongue swept in, tasting mine, and I followed his lead. My hands came up, fisting in the too-small shirt that covered most of his new scars. Scars he'd earned in a battle waged between humans and fae. The players in our war were yet unknown, and my gut told me it was far from over.

His hands were in my hair, sliding through tangled strands as he pulled me closer. We were lips and tongues, hands and bodies, minds and hearts and souls. And I wasn't sure who I was without this perfect, broken being who had invaded my life, my heart, and demanded I love him.

"Excuse me."

The words were distant. I was too lost in him. Too found.

"I'll need to see some ID."

Jack's long fingers, the ones that had healed Hazel, traced my scars, loosened in my hair, but he didn't release me. He backed up, shielding me from view.

"I'm sorry. I didn't bring it with me," he said, voice low and rough. "We just wanted a moment alone. Roommates. You know?"

His tone was light, jovial. As though we hadn't just come from burying his father. As though we weren't about to be hauled off to a human jail. My face was buried between his shoulder blades, his heartbeat a steady drum even through his back. He was covering my eyes from the soldier.

"We'll go back in," he said. "We don't want trouble."

There was a long moment of silence, and I wished desperately to see what was happening, but one look at my eyes and we would be in serious trouble. I was sure I could kill the humans now, but Jack would never understand. He would rather us be thrown in prison. My fingers curled in Jack's shirt.

"Get off the streets," the soldier said finally. "Bad things out tonight. It's no place for a young couple."

My grip tightened.

"Of course. We're going." Jack reached for my hand, and I released his shirt, grabbing his fingers in a death grip.

He turned away from the soldier, tugging me behind him. I let my hair fall in my face, lowering my eyes and turning quickly.

"Miss."

I froze. So close. We'd been so close.

"She's a little embarrassed about..." Jack let the insinuation of what we'd been caught doing hang heavy. "I'll take it."

He stretched a hand back toward the soldier without really turning, and I squeezed my eyes shut.

Then we were moving again, Jack pulling me with him, back toward Leo's coffee shop.

He yanked the door open, and we staggered inside. The muddy trowel clanked against the floor as Jack tugged me to him. I crashed into his chest, the door clicking shut behind us.

His arms came around me, hugging me to him, and I sucked in a shallow breath through my nose and another.

His hand found mine, lifting my palm and resting it against his throat.

"In. Out. That's it. Slow, deep breaths."

Jack's chest rose, compressing slowly, and my breathing slowed as I inhaled. His calming words eased the tension in my veins, the magic that had been seeking an outlet. The heat receded. I'd never been able to pull it back once the panic seized me. I'd always needed a discharge. What did it mean? How had he done that?

Soon they beat in sync once more. *Mates.* The word circled my brain, shouting for me to listen. I wanted to shake my head, to argue with myself, but I'd heard legends of mates who were so connected, so in sync, that they could do such things. And our hearts, beating as one, could only mean one thing.

I didn't want to take comfort in that truth, in that terrible, wonderful realization, but even as I resisted, my body melded into his.

"Okay?" he asked quietly.

It was a silly word that didn't mean anything, but I found that I was.

His hold relaxed.

Fae. He *was* fae. I knew it with absolute certainty. My eyes didn't want to believe it, but my senses knew.

TWENTY-TWO

KASPAR

As Eras had reported, Summer's stream was dwindling. Centuries ago, I'd pulled the water back from Summer, draining their supply. When I'd released it, sending it rushing over Summer's border, I'd destroyed my own legion when they were unable to survive on land. The memory of that act lived with me eternally.

All signs had pointed to my uncle. Then, I'd believed he was working with the Prince of Summer. But decades passed, then a century, and Fero had never shown signs of aligning with the Prince of Oceans and Seas. Still, I didn't trust him.

Asking him to ally with me, for the sake of my folk, was no small wave to overcome. But as with all the choices in my life, this was a decision I was forced to make alone.

"Prince Kaspar."

I tilted my head. "Fero." If he noticed my slight, he didn't acknowledge it. I reminded myself that I was here on diplomatic business.

"I am told you wish to speak of a new alliance."

My shoulders relaxed as I fell into the role of indifferent heir. "If the alliance suits us both."

I didn't need to sense emotion to read the desperation on the prince's face. Water was the one resource they lacked. Relocating my lake to his court would be a boon to his principality.

"Very well, state your terms."

I nodded, stepping out of the shallow stream into Summer's court.

⦾⧖⫶⟡⧫⬩⬩

93

Seated on a pile of pillows in shades of white and tan, I accepted the tea handed to me by a ram with rows of piercings down his tufted snout. Memories of a drink given to my sister by the prince of this court sifted to the surface, and I scented the air before setting the cup down.

Fero's thick, dark brow rose, but he didn't comment on my lack of decorum. He leaned forward, sipping from his cup. "Now then, what do you seek in exchange for ready access to your lake?"

I slouched into the cushions. "It is more than access I am offering. It is the relocation of my lake into your court." The corner of my lips tipped up. "Where my lake resides, the land thrives. Within a decade you would have medicinal herbs to equal those of the Spring Court."

The prince's arm tensed as he brought the cup to his lips. "While I long for peace between us, I cannot agree to it at the expense of my folk. Your lake is vast. My folk need the land it would devour."

I let my gaze drift to the expanse of sparkling turquoise just outside Summer's castle. "Your view is breathtaking."

I searched the cresting waves for any sign of my uncle or his spies. Once, the sea had been part of Lakes and Streams. All one domain, ruled by a single king. Though that was lifetimes ago, I still felt the pull of the ocean. The desire to call on its magic, harness it and draw strength from it.

"Too bad it does not sustain life for your folk."

Fero leaned back, mirroring my posture. "Ah, I had wondered when the threats would begin."

I shrugged, hiding a frown. For a court so desperate for our aid, he certainly wasn't willing to play the game. I glanced over my shoulder at the expanse of sandstone pillars caging in an open-air castle. I saw no one but the ram waiting by the wall. I'd known great parts of his court were missing. Taken by whatever blight was destroying Faerie, but with so little of my water flowing through his land, it was hard to say just how much he had been affected.

Was he desperate for more than just water?

"I do not wish to quarrel. My folk have been impacted just as yours have by Faerie's reduced state. What would you propose to suit us both?"

Fero chewed his bottom lip, glancing to the fae standing silently beside us and nodded. The ram disappeared from sight and he leaned forward, resting his elbows on his knees. "You trusted me once. I'm choosing to do the same now."

I sat forward. So much of Summer was a mystery to me. The spy in me yearned for his truths, but the pragmatic part was cautious of the honesty in his next words. What he said could equally be a deception intended to walk me into a carefully laid trap or some great secret he'd been concealing from the world.

"I have a son." He twisted his hands together in his lap. "Spring has him."

Every instinct I had honed as a spy flared at once, a sharp spike of alarm. A son. The Prince of Summer had a son. Heat prickled under my skin, surprise sharpening into something tighter and uglier. I had spies in every court, eyes buried deep in Spring itself, and yet none of them had ever breathed a word of this child. Somehow, Spring had learned of him when I had not—and they had taken him.

"You are aware of the condition of things in Spring?"

Fero dipped his chin. "Much of the land is missing." He set his cup down. "But my son is there. I'm sure of it."

I didn't ask him how he knew. I was certain he would not divulge that information. "You want me to find him." It wasn't a question, and I didn't need to await his response. Why ask me? Why not march in and take him? Perhaps he didn't know the princess was gone. If that were true, I would not be the one to tell him.

"Your son in exchange for a place in your court?"

He nodded.

"With no expiration date on how long we may remain."

Fero's legs widened. "For as long as I am at liberty to offer it."

I tapped my thumb over the pads of each of my fingers. "If I begin the search, you will allow me to relocate my lake now."

"Only if you agree that you will continue your search until my son is found."

I opened my mouth.

"And returned to me," he added.

He was better than I thought, but I would not allow him to trap me so easily. "If your son has been eaten by the missing pockets of Faerie, I will not bind myself to your cause for eternity. I will search for thirteen lunar months or until I find the boy and return him to you, whichever is sooner."

Fero stood, holding out his hand. "A year and a day then."

I mirrored him. "A year and a day, or until I find your son. Whichever comes first."

TWENTY-THREE

SAV

His gaze devoured me, slow and hungry, as if he were memorizing every unfamiliar line. Heat climbed my throat and, under that gaze, the shame loosened. He didn't look away.

"Sav," he whispered, his voice not entirely human. "You're beautiful." Then, softer. More dangerous. "You're mine."

The words slid through me like warmth and gravity. "Yes," I breathed. "I'm yours."

I swallowed. "Now you."

Jack blinked, his brows knitting. "Me? Sav, I'm not wearing a glamour."

That shouldn't have been possible, but it was a problem for later.

He laced his fingers with mine and drew me toward the stairs, and I had no will to resist.

What we were was undeniable; Creig's tale of Mab making mates echoed at the back of my mind. The word *mate* should have tasted like betrayal. Somewhere beneath the waves, a prince still held my vows, a husband in law if not in heart. The bond to Kaspar tugged like a chain beneath my ribs—cold, unyielding—and guilt followed close behind. Not for him.

For the male at my side who did not yet know he was touching another's wife.

Kaspar didn't honor land traditions; mates meant nothing to him. To the sea, I was a contract, not beloved. I would need our history to break my bargain. And I wasn't ready to tell Jack. Not here. Not when saying the words aloud might shatter the only thing in my life that felt like it belonged to me.

My heart drummed as Jack led us to the tiny mattress in the alcove that was Leo's bedroom. He ducked under the door, pulling me down with him, and fell onto the bed. I dropped beside him. Desire burned in his gaze, drying my mouth. I wanted to touch him, to taste every inch, to drown the ache and the guilt both. But there was only so much we could do.

A marriage bargain didn't preclude a spouse from cheating, but when coupled with love, it struck the heart of the betrayer. We could kiss, even perform other acts, but sex, coupled with such emotion, was a death sentence.

A thought needled me. I had killed Dane despite the bargains folk were forced to agree to in the ISHFA integration program. I scarcely dared to believe it, but I couldn't deny something burned away the moment I needed to end him to save myself. Still, protecting myself from certain death wasn't the same as willfully defying a marriage bond, older magic by far, and I wouldn't bet my life on a hunch.

Jack ran a hand across my cheek, fingers sliding into my hair, and tugged me closer. Relief and hunger hit at once. A few hours ago I had thought I would lose him to Morgan's sadistic plans; now his warmth was solid beneath me as I rolled atop him, straddling him, fire blooming as our bodies met in a clumsy imitation of what I wanted.

Our mouths crashed together, desperate. I swallowed his breath like he was air and I had been drowning for centuries. I ground my hips against his growing desire, greedy for the friction, for proof he wanted this as fiercely as I did. He groaned, the sound dragging across my nerves, raw and rough; sparks raced up my veins, my chest, my stomach, turning everything inside me molten.

I wanted to tear his ill-fitting clothes off, to trace the line down his chest to where heat strained against thin fabric. I wanted to know how he felt with nothing between us. But if that barrier vanished, I would have no restraint. A single step and I would tumble straight through my bargain, through my marriage, through every promise that chained me to the sea, to my death.

From what I had seen between kisses, he was healed enough for any acrobatics I threw at him. My fae body knew a hundred ways to take and be taken. I wanted to try them all, to see which of us bent first, which of us begged.

Strong fingers left my hair, slid down my sides, and gripped my hips. He found the band of my pants, fumbling for the buttons. For a heartbeat, my body screamed yes, but I set my fingertips over his and tugged them away.

He deepened the kiss but did not fight me. His hands tightened on my hips instead, anchoring me as if I were the one who might vanish. I let his fingers go and slipped my hands under his shirt, over newly scarred skin, cataloging every inch they had nearly taken from me. He tugged me forward, then pushed back, finding a rhythm that matched our heartbeats as he slid my burning thighs along the hard length of him. Cloth might as well not have existed. It was torment and mercy both.

His grip tightened, guiding me faster. Our tongues tangled, a different kind of battle, until my teeth caught his lower lip and he gasped into my mouth, the sound shivering straight through me.

"Savage," he groaned, and the word curled low in my stomach, a claiming and a prayer.

I drank him in and shuddered as jolts shivered between my thighs. He lifted, kissing the line of my throat, his nose skimming my pulse, increasing the friction until stars danced at the edge of my vision. It would be so easy to let go, to pretend we were allowed to have this.

His swollen lips found mine again, sucking my lower lip, dragging another sound from me I didn't recognize as my own. I was feverish and cold at once, my skin flushed and my bones chilled with the fear that this might be the only time we had together.

When I cried out, my entire body trembling, he pulled me tight against him so our sweaty, sticky bodies were indistinguishable. For a moment I could almost believe we belonged only to each other. I raised a shaking hand and pushed hair from my forehead, trying to catch my breath.

I rolled onto my back; the air kissed my damp skin. "Did we just dry hump like horny teenagers?"

Jack's laugh shook the bed, warm and breathless.

A chill swept over me as all my earlier worries crowded back in. Kaspar would never honor a mate bond; my bargain with him still held fast. Hazel was trapped in the missing pocket of Spring. Creig would use any of it, my bond, my bargains, the folk I loved, to draw blood.

If I didn't break the one truth I'd hidden from Jack soon, it would break us instead.

-●-⟩(◡♦♠♠●●-

I opened my eyes, blinking in the harsh light. I threw up a hand to block the early sun's angry glare. Last night I had thought there were no windows in the tiny space; this morning proved me wrong.

99

Jack's huge foot had knocked aside Leo's blackout curtains, letting the day in to scour the room in our truths. Today, we would face all that had come before.

"Jack. Wake up."

He groaned, a pitiful sound that would once have had me plotting ways to toughen him. If Jack was going to survive in my world, he would need to grow a thicker skin.

I rolled over, slipping free of his arms. "Get up!"

He only burrowed deeper into the pillow.

I growled low in my throat. No mate of mine would be a pathetic layabout. He would need training, and in our cramped quarters, daggers would have to do. I slid a blade from my boot and traced the tip up his shirt, grinning when it reached his neck.

Jack blinked, eyes flicking to the knife. "Savage. Isn't it a little early for knives?"

I pressed the dagger lightly, a line of crimson streaking over his Adam's apple, changing course when he swallowed.

"What did I do this time?"

I curled my lip and tucked the blade away. "You're too easy to kill. I will not have a weak mate."

The word caught behind my teeth, a breath sucked in. Mine or his, I wasn't sure. My heart stuttered once, then beat in time with his, a single rhythm pounding against my ribs. That low, constant pull woke under my sternum again, the aching thread that had been there since I found him. I knew he felt it too.

"Mates?" he echoed, pushing himself upright so fast the sheet slipped down his chest. Sleep vanished from his eyes, replaced by something bright and startled. "You mean actually mates? Like fae mates?"

Heat crawled up my neck. I forced myself to meet his gaze. "Our hearts are synced. And something has lodged itself beneath my ribs and keeps tugging me back to you. You feel it too. I know you do. That is the mate bond."

He stared at me as if I had just handed him the sun. "I *have* felt it," he said slowly. "A pull in my chest. The way it aches when you're far away. I thought I was losing my mind. Or had it bad for you. Or both."

I huffed. "Both are still possible."

A laugh burst out of him. Then he leaned forward, wrapping his arms around my middle and hauling me against him in a crushing hug. The sudden movement knocked a surprised breath from my lungs.

"Good," he said into my hair, his voice rough. "That means you are stuck with me."

I groaned and shoved his shoulder. "That is not how bonds work."

He tightened his hold for a moment before letting me push him back onto the mattress, grinning up at me like an idiot as I stood. "I think that's exactly how they work."

I tried, and failed, to smother my own smile. "You are insufferable."

"Your problem now." He glanced around the wrecked room, the bed, the dresser, the kicked-aside curtains. "Breakfast? I'm in the mood for Crumbl."

My stomach grumbled loudly at his words. "I don't have any human money."

"My treat. Leo stashed my go bag. It has plenty of cash in it." His gaze traced the line of my body, lingering on my lips. "On second thought, it will cost you."

I fought a smile as he reached for my arm, tugging me back onto the bed.

"One kiss for all the Crumbl your heart desires."

I grinned. A terrible bargain for him. He had just agreed to buy me Crumbl for the rest of my life, and all it would cost was one kiss. I let him pull me down, his arms caging me as his lips found mine.

"Food later," he mumbled against my mouth.

"After you learn how to use a knife," I said, but he swallowed my words with another kiss.

TWENTY-FOUR

SAV

Jack looked softer this morning, content in a way I hadn't seen him before, as if some feral thing in him had finally quieted. I leaned against the headboard, my palm resting on his slowly rising and falling chest. A soft smile tipped the corners of my mouth.

The downstairs door banged open. "Jack! Get your ass down here!" a female voice shot up the stairwell, followed by Leo's steadier call: "It's clear. Come down."

Jack's eyes flew open and darted to the pair of blades in my fists. "We won't need those," he said, gently closing his hands over mine. I narrowed my eyes at him, but let him slide them back into my boots.

Untangling himself from the sheet, he stood and held out a hand. "Come on. I want you to meet my friend."

We descended. A woman, no taller than a child, had planted herself at the bottom step, hands on hips; Leo waved us toward the tables.

"Grace," Jack said, relief washing over him.

My back stiff, I followed Jack down the stairs. So this was the woman who was helping him rescue fae before we met? Up close, the air around her prickled against my skin. Small didn't mean harmless, and there was nothing harmless about the woman.

"Nice to finally meet you," she said, not blinking as she took me in.

I nodded, moving past her. I slid into a seat and took the water bottle Leo handed me. I twisted the cap and drank deeply. The taste of chemicals was sour on my tongue, but after three years on Earth my magic knew how to burn it away before it could settle.

The longer I was near Grace, the more certain I was she wasn't human.

Her gaze skated over me, cataloging my torn, stained shirt. I wrapped my arms over my chest. I didn't have the ability to see through glamour. I only knew one fae with that gift.

Sage would have pierced that glamour in a breath. She should've seen through Jack's, too, back in Spring, but she hadn't noticed him until his magic flared in her dungeon. I uncrossed my arms, drumming my fingers on the table. What was I missing?

If Jack was half human, one of our sacred rules was a lie. It was more likely that Dane wasn't what he pretended. There were chameleons in existence, living masks who could wear any face. But I'd never met one.

I shook myself from my thoughts to interrupt Grace's lecture about Jack's obligation to his friends to notify them of his whereabouts. "I need to see Creig. To make things right between us."

Jack's brow furrowed. "Are you sure?"

My gaze lingered on his long fingers drumming the counter, graceful still, but carved with thin white scars that made me see red. I wished Janet were still alive so I could peel back her skin and listen to her choke when I tore the cords from her throat.

Leo set a cup of coffee in front of Jack. Those dexterous, silver-lined fingers wrapped around porcelain. He was mostly healed, but the scars, they would stay. His slight limp said the bones weren't fully mended, but thankfully it was a far cry from yesterday.

Grace moved to the window and nudged the blinds aside, watching the street like she expected trouble.

"No sign of Alice," Leo said as he sat.

"Thank you for checking." Jack set the cup down.

My stomach twisted, but not the way it had yesterday. Knowing he was mine, knowing we belonged to each other, softened the edges.

"They'll be looking for him. Dane," Leo added, darting a wary glance at me. "But with no body, they'll assume he fled. Best case for you."

My gaze slid to Leo. Had Jack told him I was the reason we'd buried Dane last night?

Leo rubbed his face. "Here's what I know. General Thomas knows Morgan's dead, but he hasn't heard from any royals in Faerie. He can't reach out, so he has to wait for first contact. Right now, he's focused on who did this and worried about an attack from the other side."

"General Thomas. Commander of the White House Communications Naval Intelligence Office?" My brows rose. I looked between Jack and Leo. "You work for the government?"

Grace's gaze flicked to me. "He's a spy."

I shot to my feet. A spy. Was Jack—?

"Sav," Jack breathed.

I held up a hand, mind racing. I was hiding in a government spy's shop. He'd seen Dane's body. Was this a trap?

"I'm not working for them," Jack said quickly. "I was helping Leo. *He* works for them."

Informant, not spy. Barely better. "You said you were working on a plan to free the fae prisoners. This was it? You traded information for a rescue?"

"Sort of," Jack said. "They wouldn't move on the compound, but if I could get the fae to a safe house Grace and I set up, they would have extracted them."

"To where?" I threw up my hands. "Back to smoking piles of ash where their homes used to be?" His blank look told me enough. I blew out a breath. "We're leaving. Now. And he"—I flicked a finger at Leo—"isn't coming."

Grace stayed quiet, which only sharpened my suspicion that she wasn't what she seemed.

"She is," I said, standing.

Jack mirrored me. He was steady. Good. I could throttle him later for trusting the human soldier.

Leo rose, too. Before he could speak, Grace's gaze snapped to the window. "Someone's coming."

A hard knock rattled the front. I glanced to Grace. I hadn't heard a thing. How had she known?

"You open?" a voice called.

"I can't ignore it," Leo muttered. "Go. Now."

Jack motioned me toward the back. Grace slipped from her stool and fell in behind us.

At the back door, I caught Jack's sleeve. "We don't have time to make any stops. We need to get out of here."

He searched my face for a heartbeat, then nodded.

The latch clicked; voices bled down the hall and Jack pushed the door wide as we slid into the stinking alley. The bell chimed behind us, another voice, then Leo's reply covered our retreat.

Jack led us east through side streets until iron and brick gave way to trees and concrete paths. The zoo loomed quiet in the morning glow. We stayed in shadow, following the path until we reached a high arch, its letters overgrown in just three short years.

"Here," I said.

They followed me to the low plastic wall, scuffed by a thousand small hands. Beyond, the shimmering light of a small portal sparkled. Not the carefully camouflaged paths carved centuries ago to the Seelie courts, but the quick slice made by amateur hands. Whoever had planned those portals, made them with care, binding so much magic around them that any who did not know the way might forfeit their lives with a simple misstep.

Grace whispered, "You've got to be kidding."

"Welcome to one of the missing pockets of Faerie." I gave a mockery of a salute.

We swung over the plastic wall, boots on damp concrete, and I looked at Jack. His eyes were bright and unafraid. If I was wrong about this, wrong about my long friendship with Creig, I was walking us into another battle. Perhaps death. I had to hope Creig wouldn't claim the blood he was owed. If it came down to it, I would do what I must to keep Jack safe.

"Ready?"

"With you," he said.

I took his hand.

Twenty-Five

Jack

The strange tingling that draped itself over me like a warm blanket each time I stepped through a portal seemed to be growing stronger. The moment my foot touched moss-covered earth, the scent of wild jasmine and pine flooded my senses, something sparked to life in my chest.

I hadn't lost it on Earth, but it was stronger here. As if the realm charged the magic living in my veins. I couldn't think of any other way to describe it.

"Stop."

Sav's panic had me halting abruptly and spinning around in search of a threat. Beyond her, the portal was translucent; there, but only a sliver in the fabric of the world. It sliced through the air, cleaving a shimmering path to my world. Beyond it, I saw nothing. Even the forest, normally alive with animals and a breeze, was unnaturally quiet.

I smelled it then—the tangy, salty scent of blood. Not human. More like Sav's: salty, but sweeter somehow. A realization jolted through me. Not just that Sav wasn't human, but that I'd smelled *this* before. A memory of my childhood, my mom and dad fighting. Dane demanding I go to a doctor to get my flu shot. *Any shot*, he'd shouted, and my mom's voice had dropped. Even now I strained to make out the words. Something about my blood. How the medicine wouldn't work the same on me because I was different. The blood I smelled now reminded me of my blood.

A tortured scream rent the air, and we whirled toward it. Sav raced for it, and I swore, sprinting after her. She moved over dead leaves without a sound. I snapped every twig in my path. Each crack landed too loud in my skull. She stopped at the edge of a ring of trees encircling Creig's camp. I halted beside her, mouth going dry as I took in the scene.

Bloody, torn bodies were strewn about, some so disfigured they were unrecognizable.

"We're too late. The humans found them." Sav hissed.

Something moved at the periphery of my vision, and I ran to it, sliding to my knees. "Poppy? Can you hear me?"

The elf's ear twitched, but a gaping hole in her neck pumped blood in time with her heart's slowing beat. She was bleeding out. I clamped both hands to her neck, trying to hold the life in. She opened her mouth, choking on the stream of crimson that sputtered from between her lips.

"Shh. Don't try to talk."

Sav dropped to her knees beside us. "Can you save her?" she whispered. I glanced up through blurred eyes and shook my head. She nodded, said nothing, and stood, laying a hand on my shoulder. "We need to find Hazel and Creig... and any others."

I pressed down harder on the wound. Poppy gurgled in pain and I bit my lip. "I have to try."

Sav's brows lowered, but she nodded. "I'll be back as soon as I can." She glanced back once before disappearing into the foliage.

"Hang in there, Poppy." I pressed down on the wound with one hand, tearing a strip of fabric from my shirt and wrapping it under her shoulder and around her neck.

"Let me help."

I looked up and nearly stumbled backward. Grace's eyes were too big, gold, and slit-pupiled. White whiskers fanned her cheeks; tufted ears pricked between a snowy white mane, pulled up in a high bun. She'd shrunk inside her clothes; seams hung loose on a smaller frame.

My mouth dropped open. "Grace?"

She blinked, dropping to her knees beside me and lifting two elongated fingers. Her hands, too, had a light dusting of fur coating them, and it seemed to match her frost-white hair. "Hush, child," she crooned at Poppy, sparing no more time for me. "I'm here now."

A red-tinged tear spilled from Poppy's lashes and she stilled, some of her panic receding.

My jaw slackened when glimmering dust sparkled at Grace's fingertips, falling like snowflakes and absorbing into Poppy's skin.

"Don't release your hold just yet, Jacaranda," she said, and ancient magic drew tight beneath my sternum. My name. My true name. She hadn't commanded me, but she could have. If she'd wanted.

I reapplied pressure to Poppy's wound, glancing up several times as my friend worked.

She chanted under her breath, a strange songlike cadence that seemed to call on the plant life around us. Vines wove over grass and moss, curling around Poppy's middle, twining up her arms and over her shoulders. Soon, their leaves tickled my fingers and Grace nodded.

"You may release her."

I sat back, lifting sticky fingers. Vines swept in to take my place, wrapping tightly around the fae's neck and shoulder. When only her face was visible beneath a sea of green, Grace stood, no more than four feet off the ground, and surveyed her work.

"Will she live?" I asked.

"She will. The magic of the forest will restore her."

"I don't understand," I breathed. "Who are you? Why were you on Earth?"

"I was there as a favor to your mother."

"My... mother?"

The creature nodded, patting my shoulder. "Come, Jack, there are no others living in this meadow, but I sense that we are needed elsewhere."

Her thick accent, nothing like the New York one I was used to, was untraceable to my untrained ears, but I climbed to my feet, following numbly behind her. I had never suspected even for a moment that she wasn't human. And my mother had sent her? From where?

A long silver braid hung beneath Grace's bun, trailing the ground behind her as she walked.

Being in Faerie was doing wonders for my strength, and the fractured parts of my mind, damaged by repeated electrical shock, were slowly knitting back together too. But the pain in my chest, the ache of losing a father I thought I hadn't loved, and the brittle, splintering hope that my mother was still alive did not mend the same way. I suspected no magic in any realm could fix that.

We wove through trees that stretched into a murky, cloud-covered sky, and I stored the thought away to be examined later. I hadn't expected it to be the same time of day here as it had been on Earth, but the rapid change in time was no less jarring to my senses.

"Do you know where my mother is?"

Grace glanced over her shoulder, whiskers twitching.

The hope swelling inside me threatened to deflate. She would say my mother was dead, just as I'd known she was and that fragile hope would plummet.

"No."

My gut twisted.

"But she *is* alive."

I stumbled, losing my footing, and crashed to my knees. Overwhelming relief bowled over me and stole my breath. Alive. She was alive!

Twenty-Six

Kaspar

I was drained, physically and mentally. Relocating an entire lake, diverting its folk, and expanding a stream, was no small task. But moving each stone and plant, placing them just as they were, ensuring the air pockets protecting my tombs and scrolls remained intact, setting Sav's room just as it was, those were monumental undertakings. I wondered now if she would notice; if she would appreciate the effort.

It had taken the better part of three days. I raised a shaking hand to shield my eyes, observing the sandy borders of my court. We were now surrounded on all sides but one by Summer. I'd left one escape path for our folk. Into Winter.

Soon, when my magic was restored, I would work to thaw the stream bisecting Summer and Winter and ensure the members of my court could escape should Fero go back on his word. I had preferred to leave Spring at my shores, but with no ruler to protect it and the blight eating up the land at a pace too horrific to catalog, I wanted to give us as much time as possible to escape our fate.

To give myself time to try to stop it.

Sparkling white-topped mountains gleamed in the midday sun at the north border. It was taking a great deal more of my magic to warm the water on the north side of my lake to a temperature my folk could tolerate, and the drain was already beginning to take its toll. On the Winter side of my court, snowy beaches were slowly melting, ice drifting into my lake. I put the least amount of energy there and advised my court to avoid the cold if they were unable to adapt to the cooler temperatures.

The naiads had surprised me when they raced for the area to claim it for their own. I had not seen many of them since. I preferred warmer temperatures, and had situated my castle nearer the Summer side, but the water closest to the desert region was quickly growing too warm. It would take some time for me to find the right balance in our new home.

That done, I left the lake, the bargain's magic tugging me toward Spring. Fero knew his son's general age and gender, but apart from that, he didn't know his name, what he looked like, or who might have him. His mother had died shortly after he was born, never having told Fero he had a son.

It wasn't until he had consulted a seer that he'd learned of his existence. The seer was vague on many of the details, but she was certain of one thing. He was in Spring. Held there under a false name and believing his captor was his mother. I had been surprised by how open Fero was once the bargain was struck, and a part of my cold heart warmed at the emotion in his words.

I followed the stream's path until it reached the border between the two courts and stepped up onto Spring's mossy shore.

TWENTY-SEVEN

SAV

I slid to my knees. "Hazel?" I shook her shoulder. A thin trickle of green blood painted her lips, and she was deathly pale. "Hazel." I shook her again and bent to press my ear to her chest.

My cheek stuck to her hot, damp skin. I held my breath until my lungs burned. Begged the wind rustling the leaves—*shut up, shut up, shut up*—until, finally, a faint flutter against my ear. Weak. There, but barely.

Small cuts marred her knees and fingertips. Wounds that should have sealed in a blink if she'd had anything left to heal with. Nothing else explained why she hovered at the edge of life. I wiped her lip, held my green-tinged finger to my nose, and sniffed. Iron, yes, but something stranger, too, metallic and briny. It nagged at my memory.

Beside her limp body, the ground was wrecked, branches snapped, vines ground into the dirt, a long drag-line scarring the earth away from her. Someone else had been taken; that much was clear. Were they still alive? I didn't have the luxury of finding out. Hazel was here, and she needed me.

She coughed and her eyelids gave a faint, involuntary twitch.

I lay a palm on her burning forehead. If I didn't know better, I'd say—

I inhaled again, and the truth slammed into me. Squid ink poison. It had nearly killed me once, and I'd only survived with Kaspar's blood. I needed him. Whether I was ready to face him or not. Whether I was ready for Jack to learn the truth or not...

I sensed him a breath before I looked up.

Leaves exploded and Jack stumbled into the clearing with a puca at his heels. My gaze flicked from him to the golden-eyed creature. "You found a healer."

Shy. Ancient. More magic than flesh. Pucas didn't come when you called. They didn't come for high fae at all. And yet she stood there, whiskers twitching as she assessed Hazel.

"Hello," I said. Something familiar glinted in those eyes. "Grace?"

"My name is lost to history, but you may call me by that one," she said. The New York lilt was gone. Glamour stripped, her true face was revealed. Not fae... or not high fae, at least. My uncle's puca tales flooded back: wild and near-immortal creatures who slipped into leaf and loam when they wished to disappear from the world.

"What were you doing on Earth?"

"A favor for a friend."

I wrinkled my nose at the non-answer, but she was already on her knees, tufted hand on Hazel's sternum. Grace looked up, eyes going wide. "I cannot heal this one."

Hope cracked down the middle. "We need water magic."

"Not just any water magic," she agreed. "A prince's."

"How much time does she have?"

Grace peered through a break in the canopy as if the stars would answer. "Less than a day."

"Will you come with us?" Jack asked. "Help me find my mother?"

His words made me falter. What did Grace know of his mother? I didn't have time to untangle it now. Not when Hazel was clinging to life.

Grace's whiskers twitched toward Jack. "When your party's whole and woven tight, the thorns will part and grant you sight. Only then will you be ready to find her." She shifted her gaze back to me. "I cannot join you. The forest needs me. Faerie is breaking, and I'm needed to mend what's been torn."

She blinked once, and the space she occupied was empty air.

"Wait!" Jack called, but she was already gone.

I looked at Jack, vision blurring. "I have to go."

He nodded and scooped Hazel into his arms, the tendons in his forearms standing out as though he could save her by will alone. "I'll come with you."

At the tear between realms, Jack shifted Hazel higher and I cupped her burning cheek. If there were any way back that did not cut through Earth, I would have taken it, but only Mab, and once Fero, opened portals between realms. I'd seen no sign of the others or who had attacked. Squid ink poison wasn't a human weapon, though. I wished I could stay in the missing pocket of Faerie to help Creig and Larek and finally mourn Yolmar, but Hazel was dying and Kaspar's blood had saved me once. I was under no illusion that he would save her if I didn't ask him myself.

I stepped through the shimmer into the abandoned zoo and froze. The air stank of rust and old straw.

Jack stumbled out behind me and stepped forward, Hazel cradled tight against his chest.

"Jack—" I tried to warn him, but I wasn't fast enough.

The air shifted, ions buzzing. Kaspar stepped from the shadow of a cracked concrete enclosure, faster than Jack could stop. His free hand shot out, closing around Jack's throat and driving him back into a flaking metal rail. Hazel jolted in his arms.

"Kaspar. Stop."

Aquamarine eyes found mine. He lifted his nose and scented the air, cruelty curling the corner of his mouth as he ensured our bargain had not been broken. He didn't need to say it. He only wanted me to remember that he knew. He couldn't smell the mate bond. Thankfully. I could not let him learn the truth; not yet.

His nails pressed into the side of Jack's throat, easing only a fraction. Crimson beaded where they kissed skin. "He has injured your companion."

"You know very well he has not."

He arched a brow, at last sheathing his claws, and stepped back. "I had wondered when you would return to me."

Jack's sharp inhale was a shard of ice through my ribs. I didn't look at him.

"We need your help." I kept my voice steady. My hands were not.

Kaspar went still, his attention swinging to Hazel, pale and slack in Jack's hold. "What has happened to her?"

"Squid ink." Memories and fear bubbled up. "She needs your blood."

"Come." He turned, and I let out a slow, shaky breath.

We followed and I moved faster to catch up to Jack. The warmth burning off him was enough to make me grimace. "Please," I whispered to Jack, sliding my fingers along his forearm where heat shivered under his skin. "For Hazel."

His magic eased a fraction.

Kaspar dove into a shallow stream, reaching for my hand and lacing his cold fingers in mine. Water rushed over our boots and I tightened my hold on Jack. On land, once Jack had dried, his pain was muted. When immunity failed, every wound could come roaring back. Was he truly healed, or had his innate gift only been holding him together?

We didn't have time to find another way. Hazel's breathing was slowing, and my dread grew with it.

I squeezed Jack's arm tighter and Kaspar's magic shimmered as we slipped through a tear and into his lake. Turquoise scales flared along his back as he hauled us toward the coral gates. They opened like teeth.

Jack's arm went rigid under my hand, his body jerking as Kaspar dragged us deeper. I glanced back at his wide eyes, searching for any sign that the pain had returned. Down here, where Kaspar ruled and water ate away his immunity, he might be in agony and I could do nothing to help him. But the cords standing out in his neck weren't from old wounds. He was running out of air.

I turned, caught his mouth with mine, and poured the last of my breath into him. He wasn't built for Kaspar's depths. He had to survive anyway.

A blink later, Kaspar's magic hurled us into my rooms and we collapsed on the semi-dry floor, heaving.

"Please... Kaspar... There's no time. I need... your blood," I gasped out.

"It seemed you needed a great many things." His voice was cold. Distant. He flicked his hand out. "Bring her to the bed."

Jack set Hazel down. Her mouth fell open and foam slid over her cheek.

"Get her on her side!" I shouted, my throat raw. Jack was faster, bracing her head, tipping her gently. I pressed my ear to her back. Her heartbeat was faint, fading fast.

Kaspar slid onto the mattress, nail slicing the inside of his forearm. "Open her mouth."

Jack turned Hazel's head; I tucked her against my thigh. Indigo welled and fell in slow drops onto her lips.

"We may be too late," he said softly.

"No." I rubbed circles into her spine. "Fight, Hazel."

"Water." Kaspar didn't look up as he gave the order. Indigo drops mixed with the foam at Hazel's lips, staining it a deep violet.

I ran, found an ivory shell by the basin, filled it, and raced back, pouring it over the bubbles foaming on her lips. It slicked over her chin and soaked the blanket.

"It isn't working. She isn't swallowing!"

Kaspar's gaze cut to Jack. "Human. You will make a bargain. You will leave when I have saved her."

"Kaspar. Now isn't—"

"Will you let her companion die?" He didn't so much as look at me as he cut me off, ice-cold eyes fixed on Jack.

Jack's jaw worked. For one suspended breath, I hoped he would refuse, hoped he would not sacrifice anything else because I asked, but Hazel's heart was painfully weak and I was desperate.

Jack's eyes never left Kaspar's as he nodded.

"Bargains require words."

"If you save Hazel," Jack said, voice steady, "I'll leave your castle when she recovers."

Kaspar inclined his head, focus shifting to my friend. "Anastasia Hazel Elm," he commanded, and power crackled through the room, "open your mouth and drink."

My blood ran cold. Why did Kaspar have Hazel's name? How? Hazel's throat worked. Even half dead, she swallowed. He cut deeper and fed her more. Her hands rose, fingers wrapping around his wrist and dragging his arm to her mouth. When he murmured, "enough," the hum in the air shifted and she released him.

"Keep giving her water," he said, standing.

Heat licked up my veins and I moved to follow.

I *would* have answers.

Hazel convulsed, choking up pools of dark blue onto the blanket. I dropped, whispering encouragement into her hair, and counted the strengthening beats under my palm, sliding strands of hair back from her face.

Kaspar turned to the doorway. His gaze flicked to me, cool and sharp, then beyond me as if Jack were a stain. "Sal—"

"Don't you fucking dare," I hissed, standing and stalking after him.

He moved quickly—faster than he ever had when we used to race on land. I refused to think of that version of him. Not with Hazel's full name on his tongue, a thing you did not have unless you were married.

With a single sharp sweep of his hand, the water split before him, a tight pocket of air forming in his wake. I stalked after him, matching his pace.

He reached the end of the hall and turned. I knew the path he was taking. It had been many years since I'd been to his castle and even then, I'd only ever gone to Mira's rooms and his office, but I'd known the moment he showed me my new rooms that they'd been situated near enough to his office that I could swim there even if I didn't have his air magic to clear a path.

"Stop."

He snapped to a halt.

Slowly, he spun, eyes narrowing. "You will never do that again." His voice could have cut glass.

"I think I get to be upset," I said, closing the distance. "You almost used my name to control me. You have Hazel's true name. What else don't I know?"

His shoulders loosened by inches. A practiced smirk curved his mouth. "Well. My lovely wife finally comes home to rule. What does my princess want? A full accounting of my affairs? A better understanding of her court?"

Was that anger in his voice? Emotion? Even storming away, he'd still carved a path so I could breathe. For someone who claimed to have no feelings, he cared a great deal for mine. It should have soothed me. It only stoked my temper.

"I want to know why you have my friend's name."

His smile vanished. "Of course."

He turned. The tunnel of air he'd carved began to collapse; water folded in on itself and rushed for my ankles.

"Don't walk away from me!" My pace quickened. "Kaspar. You owe me an answer."

"I... owe... you?!"

He whipped around as the corridor became a wall of water behind him. I backed up, tripping over my own feet. Malice coated the hall as a wave raced for me. Our eyes met and, for a moment, it was pain I thought I saw in his glowing aqua eyes.

Impossible.

I turned and ran for my rooms, the flood chasing my heels. At the threshold it hit an invisible shield and stopped, thundering against it until the walls hummed.

"Sav? Sav!"

I pushed through the seaweed curtain into the bedchamber. Jack sat at the edge of the mattress, Hazel's head in his lap. Relief washed over his face when he saw me, so sharp it pinched at my chest.

"I'm here," I said, crossing the space in three quick strides. I brushed my fingers over his shoulder as I passed. "You kept her breathing. Good."

Hazel's eyelids fluttered, nearly-black eyes finding mine.

"Hazel." I caught her hand. "How do you feel?"

Her lips twitched in the ghost of a smile. Jack propped her carefully against him. "She's been throwing up Kaspar's blood since you left, but it's working," he said. "Her heartbeat's stronger."

I heard it then. Steady and insistent. Relief buckled my knees. Memories of my own poisoning surfaced. It had taken more than a year to claw back strength, and even then, I was never sure I had ever fully recovered. What would the lasting cost be for Hazel?

"Larek," she croaked.

I bent close. "What?"

"Larek. Taken."

My heart seized. "Who took him?"

Her throat worked. "Juniper."

I swayed. Heart hammering against my ribs. *No. No!* I turned back toward the door. Jack caught my wrist. "Sav, please. We can't leave yet. She'll need more of his blood."

"You don't understand," I whispered, heat spiking under my skin. "Juniper is dangerous. They did something to her. Creig already lost—" The name stuck; I swallowed it. "He can't lose Larek too. I have to go back."

"It's dangerous there. You can't go alone. And Hazel isn't out of the woods," he said, gentling his voice like he could loosen the knot in me. "You have to be here to convince Kaspar to keep treating her. Without you, we don't know what he'll do." He patted the bed. When I didn't move, he held out his hand. "My favorite thing about you is how selfless you are."

I set my palm in his. He turned it and pressed a kiss to the vein that pulsed at my wrist. "Please don't throw your life away when it's so precious to me. We'll go together—when she can come with us."

The words unspooled something in my chest. I nodded. We slid down on either side of Hazel, arms wrapped around the girl who'd kept me alive more times than I deserved.

Sometime later, scales scraped softly against my bare arm, and bright, aquamarine eyes glinted in the dark. Kaspar leaned over the bed, his wrist hovering above Hazel's lips. She drank greedily, color creeping back into her cheeks. His focus pinned me like a claim he had no right to make.

I opened my mouth, but before I could speak, he'd stood and disappeared into the shadows.

By the second treatment, Hazel's breathing had evened. Her lashes fluttered open and I leaned over her, inspecting her pupils.

"You need a mint," she groaned.

A laugh burst out of me. She tried to sit and swayed; I caught her head. "Easy."

We gave her more water. Slept again. When we woke, the worst had passed.

Hazel lived. That should have been enough. But water pressed against the windows, turning the chamber into a glass cage while Juniper held Larek, stars knew where. Once Hazel recovered, we would go back to the missing pocket and make sure Creig didn't bury another son.

TWENTY-EIGHT

JACK

I woke, blinking in the murky darkness. It took me a moment to remember where I was. I'd been trying desperately to reach my mother. As I had each night since ISHFA, I closed my eyes and hoped she'd be waiting in that damp, moldy cave, but since I'd left ISFHA, nothing but darkness greeted me when I fell asleep.

A warm arm was tossed across my chest and the too tight T-shirt I'd been wearing since we left Earth rode higher, exposing patches of discolored skin.

"They cut you open." I jumped and Kaspar's bright eyes blinked in the near dark. He slid closer inspecting my scars. "I've known a sadist or two in my time."

I shuddered, tugging my torn shirt down. My gaze traveled the wide bed. Hazel was wedged between Sav and me, one arm wrapped over each of us, as though she could hold us together no matter what came next. Sav's dark lashes rested against tanned, freckled skin, breathing deeply.

It seemed I was the only one unsettled by the prince's appearance in our room.

He crowded closer to Sav, leaning over us all.

The hairs on the back of my neck rose as he pressed bare, scaled flesh against her back.

He slid a nail over his perfectly unmarred skin and we both watched as blue blood welled along the cut and began to slide over the side of his arm. He lowered his wrist, whispering low by Hazel's ear. She opened her mouth, accepting his gift and another shudder rolled through me.

For Sav, he would save her.

When she'd wrapped her fingers around his wrist, sucking fervently, Kaspar looked up. His gaze trailed the length of Sav, moving over Hazel and back to me. "They belong to me. No matter what silly fantasy you've been harboring."

Fire burst to life in my chest, racing along my veins. Every base instinct in me screamed to put the prince in his place, to show him just how wrong he was. To tell him what Sav and I were to each other, but I wasn't like him. I didn't play games with the woman I loved. That he felt the need to stake a claim only told me how unsure he was of his place in her life.

As quickly as he'd appeared, he was gone, slinking away in the darkness to retreat to whatever watery fortress he dwelt in alone. The shadows moved with him, obscuring him from view before he'd reached the door. What must it be like to spend your life in the cold, dark, away from all you desired and all you wished you could be?

I didn't hate him. I pitied him. It must be a lonely life. One I wouldn't wish on my enemy. And I didn't think Kaspar was my enemy. Not yet.

•◦(◡♦♠♦••

I rolled over, careful to avoid the bodies tangled together beside me. Kaspar's late-night treatment had done wonders for Hazel. Her color was returning, her breathing steadier. Her heart was a drum beating against my ears, and when she woke, her eyes were bright.

Sav sat up, inhaling sharply. "Hazel?"

Hazel smiled a languid, seductive smile. An act for her friend I thought, to hide how terrified she'd been to be so close to her end.

"If I'd known I only had to be near death to get you into bed with me, I would have done it ages ago."

Sav laughed, shoving Hazel's arm gently. She leaned down, wrapping her arms around her friend and Hazel groaned. "Careful. I'm irreplaceable if you break me."

Sav's watery laugh made something in my chest loosen.

Hazel was recovering. That meant a countdown had begun. Soon, Kaspar's bargain would be fulfilled, and I'd have to leave. Would Hazel be well enough to make the swim to shore when it was time? I wasn't sure Sav would leave without her.

"How are you feeling?"

Hazel's emerald gaze swung to me. "I knew we'd end up like this eventually... Didn't I tell you?"

I grinned. "So... better?"

Her lips spread wide, but I wasn't as convinced by her show as Sav was.

I'd seen enough injured people faking for their loved ones—my mom first and foremost—to know when someone was putting on a brave face.

She tried to sit up, but her pupils dilated and she fell back.

Sav's smile fell and she dipped with Hazel, catching her head. "No fast movements."

Hazel waved her off. "I'm just hungry and starved for a companion. Speaking of, did you find my new plaything?"

Sav's face paled. "I will. I'm going today."

I frowned. I'd hoped Sav would forget about the other fae for a little longer. Hazel was in no shape to leave and I wasn't letting Sav go alone.

Hazel's calm demeanor fractured, true pain in her eyes. "You haven't heard from him?"

Sav sat up again, an edge of panic in her jerky movements. She stood, pacing away, wrapping her arms around herself and her gaze shot to me.

I smiled. "I'm sure he's fine." Sav wasn't convinced by my hollow words.

Hazel swallowed. "You can't go alone. You need an army. It was chaos. The fae we pulled out... they weren't right." Her gaze cut to me. "They'd been poisoned but it wasn't meant to end them. It put them under a thrall. I tasted their blood." She turned to Sav. "Blood magic. And more. Iron. And something else I couldn't place. A concoction meant to turn them into mindless killers. You'll die if you go back on your own."

"Squid ink." Sav rubbed her arms. "I nearly died from it once. You would have too. If not for Kaspar." She whispered his name.

My heart clattered against my ribs. Sav had nearly died before I'd ever had the chance to meet her. I would have lived my whole life never knowing there had been someone destined for me. Someone who shaped my every whim and desire. What a tragic life, and I wouldn't have even known what I was missing.

"They don't have Kaspar's blood. They don't know what they're dealing with. I need to go back. To warn them." Sav cut a path through the room, spinning around each time she reached a wall. Finally, she turned back. "Hazel. Why does Kaspar have your true name."

Hazel twisted her hands together, her knuckles going white.

"If I tell you, you must make a bargain." Her gaze fell on me. "Sav, as the ruler of Lakes and Streams, I am not forbidden from sharing this truth with you, but Jack..."

Hazel continued speaking, but it was crackling static in my brain. *Ruler of Lakes and Streams?* But that meant... Fire raced in my veins, igniting every inch of flesh. The room was hazy and distorted as plumes of white burst from my nostrils.

"Jack."

Sav was calling my name. Saying something. Pleading. But I couldn't hear around the screaming in my head. Sav could only be ruler under one condition.

"You married him!" I shot to my feet, backing up as sparks erupted from my fingertips.

Sav threw out her hands. "Jack. I can explain."

Explain... The world was spinning, making me nauseous. *It was true.* She was married to the cold prince. The heat was building in my chest, behind my eyes, demanding an outlet. Hazel slid back on the bed, eyes wide. I took another step back as rage burned up my throat.

Not rage, molten lava. I opened my mouth as white-hot flame burst free, shooting across the room. The wall nearest an air bubble sizzled and sparked, tiny sprays of water shooting into the room and causing it to steam.

"Jack. Calm down. You'll kill us."

Kill. That was an all-consuming thought. I would kill the man who dared lay claim to my mate. My chest was burning, pulsing, and a burst of lava shot up my throat again. It licked along my insides, stoking the anger burning through me. *Kill him.* I would kill him.

Sparks of hissing flame jumped from my hands and puffed from my nostrils into the air. They crackled and sizzled everywhere they landed. I ignored them. Ignored everything as I turned, marching from the room.

"Jack. Stop!"

My limbs jerked to a halt and visions of Morgan's filthy magic flitted through my mind, making my vision red at the edges. I was burning, magic pressing against the confines of my skin as it sought an outlet. I was trapped. Trapped by my mate. The rage increased tenfold. My mate had the same terrible magic as my tormentor.

And she dared to use it against me.

"Let me go, Savage." The name tore out of me, stripped of every soft edge it had ever held. The words were a guttural growl, eaten up by the flames still flaking off my tongue when I tried to speak.

She stepped in front of me, eyes meeting mine. This close, the heat wafting off me should have been enough to burn, but her veins were filled with the same fiery magic mine were. My fire wouldn't harm her. *Good.* There was no controlling this rage.

"You'll drown us all. Please, listen."

I yanked against her command, but it was ironclad, locking my muscles in place. Some of the haze was dissipating. Her nearness soothed the fury inside me. Bright amethyst eyes sparkled even in the dim light and caught me in their grasp. I inhaled a scorching breath.

"I had no choice."

"He forced you?!" A ball of white burst from my palm, sinking into the floor.

Liquid glass pooled at my feet and I glanced down, a flicker of recognition dancing through my mind. My rage would kill us. I couldn't survive underwater and Hazel was too weak to swim. Sav would be forced to choose which of us to help. Heat banked, warmth lapping at the edges of my awareness. It wasn't gone, but I was listening.

"When you were taken, I had to get my magic back."

The haze in my mind was slowly lifting. "Sav."

She held up a hand and tears slid down her cheek. "It was my fault. I sent you on that mission. I put you in danger. You would have died if I hadn't come for you."

She folded her hands under her arms, her lip quivering, but she didn't look away. "I was so scared."

Her hold slipped away, the invisible chains falling from my mind, and I stopped fighting as the tips of my fingers cooled, heat receding.

She swallowed, her throat working around the next words. "When I saw you..." She stifled a sob, eyes glistening. "I thought... I thought..."

I lurched forward, wrapping my arms around her. She sank against me, and I held her, squeezed until her shoulders stopped shaking and her tears dried.

I loosened one arm from its death grip around her, stroking her hair and pressing my cheek to her forehead. "I'm okay. You saved me."

She hiccupped a small sob and wrapped her arms around my waist. She'd married him knowing it was the only way to get her magic back. To save me. The truth didn't stop the ache in my chest, but it took the sharp edge off and turned raw rage into something smaller and sore that still, stupidly, loved her for choosing me.

"I'm still furious," I said quietly, the words rough in my throat. "And I hate that you had to do it this way. But I know you did it to save me."

Sav let out a shaking breath. "Of course I saved you," she whispered. "You matter to me."

Her fingers fisted in the back of my shirt, like she was bracing for me to let go. I didn't.

Hazel cracked a heavy lid, looking us over from where she lay slumped on the bed. "I'm glad you finally admitted it. It was painful to watch you both pretending."

A soft smile slid up the corners of my mouth and Sav laughed as we moved to sit beside her. Hazel sat up, propping her elbow on the bed beside her and leaning across me.

Sav wrapped her fingers in mine and reached for Hazel's with her other. "It's more than that. He's my..." she looked to me as if for reassurance and my heart beat harder. "We're—"

Hazel's eyes widened. "Don't tell me. I can't keep your secret."

Sav squeezed Hazel's hand harder. "Because he can compel you?"

"Because he owns me." She closed her eyes, inhaling a long breath. Nodding to herself, she opened her eyes once more. "I was a gift. A peace offering."

Sav's fingers tightened around mine until my knuckles went white. She glanced at me and my breath caught. My chest still ached at the truth of what she had done, but she hadn't done it because she loved or even desired him. She'd done it to save me. I could strangle her for being so reckless, but I couldn't be angry. I squeezed Sav's hand as Hazel launched into her story.

"Before I was born, more than a hundred years ago, Winter and Water were at war."

Kaspar's jaw flexed.

"Mab never had anything to fear from Oceans and Seas. They are cut off from her queendom. Her court disappears into the distance, shrouded in mystery and fog to the north. To the east, a sharp line of mountains bisects all access to the ocean. To the west Summer reigns, and to the south Spring blocks her border."

"Only Lakes and Streams bisect her land. Where there is land, there is water access, and Prince Kaspar controls it. Mab never liked her tenuous relationship with the court, but she is as weak as the rest of us when it comes to the need for that most precious resource.

"She has a book, a journal. I found it and read it.

"For a time, a millennia ago, she relied heavily on the magic Firethorn, her only son, provided. He melted just enough ice from the peaks of the snowcapped mountains to sustain them, and Mab blocked access from the king. Back then, one king ruled all water. But eventually, Firethorn had melted enough that the king found a way in. This was thousands of years ago. Maybe tens of thousands, long before my time. But it's in the book."

Hazel nodded to herself.

"Firethorn, being far more diplomatic than his mother, went to broker a peace treaty, but when he met with their princess, it was love at first sight. Theirs was a love match for the ages and even though Mab forbade it, he lay with the princess and promised her his heart."

I knew that kind of promise, the kind you made before you understood the consequences.

"The princess gave birth to a great and beautiful seer."

"The Lady of the Lake," Kaspar said, stepping into the room.

Hazel swallowed, eyes darting to the prince, but he dipped his chin and she continued.

"For some time, they were happy, and Firethorn welcomed his new daughter into the world on what Mab described as the happiest day of his life. But Mab's scribblings, often illegible, cataloged strange abilities, and she feared what her grandchild might become. Firethorn cared only that his daughter was healthy and happy and wanted for nothing.

"It should have been the marriage alliance that solidified peace between land and sea, but Firethorn discovered he had a mate. A land fae named Clematis. He forsook his love, taking his mate to his bed that very night. When Princess Lorelei learned of her lover's deception she climbed to the highest cliff along Winter's border and flung herself against its frozen, unforgiving trenches."

"A creature as powerful as Lorelai might have survived such a great fall, but she begged her father, the sea king, to grant her this one kindness and give her death."

The room went colder, the water pressing harder against the air magic holding it back.

"And what of Firethorn," Kaspar asked, but I was certain he already knew.

Hazel ran a hand over her throat. "When Lorelai died, the truth struck his heart, and with hate filled eyes, he turned his accusing gaze on his mother. For it was only in Lorelai's death, that he learned the truth. Mates were true, something wild and gifted of the land itself. So rare, they had no name for it before Mab appeared in their world, but it was old magic. The kind that did not recognize species or rank. It was formed of a desire to mend what folk had broken."

Sav went very still.

"When Lorelia died, Firethorn saw the truth of his mother's deception. She had contrived a mate bond for her son made of false promises and corrupt magic. Mab's gift was that of true name sensor. With it, she could rewrite the world. But one thing was more powerful than her hold over a name. True mates."

Kaspar leaned against the bed, observing our group. "The winter court knows the true history. Those who guard the book at least, as do my folk. Mab holds no power here. When she sought to claim it, I reminded her that she is not of my world, and I will not be cowed."

He glanced at Hazel. "She was my recompense. Reparation for all her folk had done to mine and a plea to keep her secrets."

Hazel's gaze dipped to her hands. As if she bore the shame of her cruel monarch.

"Hazel," Sav whispered.

She ignored her friend, studying her upturned palms.

"Hazel knows what her sacrifice bought her folk. She does not regret it."

Sav's white knuckled fists tensed, and it was the only warning we had before she swung.

TWENTY-NINE
SAV

My fist slammed into cool flesh, and the satisfying crunch of bone made the dark part of my soul rejoice.

"You made my friend your prisoner. She was a baby when Mab gave her to you." The words flew from my mouth, spittle landing on Kaspar's swelling jaw. It was more than that. So much more than that. He knew. It seemed they all did. And none of them ever told me.

He scowled, pushing off the bedpost, wiping his bloody lip. He stared at his fingers, blinking at the smear of indigo as if it might belong to someone else. His hand hovered there a heartbeat longer, then dropped to his side, shoulders rigid as slitted eyes met mine.

Jack got to his feet, crowding behind me, and any regret I was feeling for my actions ebbed away.

Kaspar's gaze darted over my shoulder to the male at my back. "Princess," he said, never taking his eyes off Jack, "do you think it wise to strike your prince when I hold all your lives in my palm?"

I opened my mouth—nothing came out.

Ice shot down my spine, freezing the blood in my veins. I had the sudden urge to take it back, to take it all back and never ask Kaspar for another thing again.

How had I spent nearly three hundred years relying on this male every time I was in danger? Even now, caught between a fake marriage and a mate—possibly true mate, if Hazel's story was to be believed—I had run to him for help. I had placed myself in an impossible situation and had no one but myself to blame when he finally expected something in return for all his favors.

Hadn't I learned that lesson time and again? Yet somehow, I'd never seen how deep the hole I'd dug had been when Kaspar made it so easy to climb in. I was in trouble, and he was there to help me out of it. He was a prince. He didn't follow the land fae laws. He did whatever he wanted, and I had foolishly believed I could do the same.

I backed up. "Kaspar."

"Prince... Kaspar. Better yet. Husband. Or have you forgotten?"

I swallowed.

Jack stepped forward, arms spreading at his sides as the tips of his fingers burned white-hot. My chest caved, stomach flipping. Jack would get himself killed in this underwater tomb and he would take us all with him. Air was suddenly difficult to take in. I sucked hard, trying to gather it into my lungs, but it was just out of reach.

I inhaled a sharp breath, but it wasn't enough. I gasped again, and again, short panting breaths making me dizzy and my head dropped between my knees.

"Sav!"

I heard my name distantly. Images raced through my mind: water rushing in, Jack and Hazel dashed against the wall as waves crashed over them, air torn from their lungs.

I gasped again, vision going dark at the edges.

I tried to call out to Kaspar, to beg him not to hurt them. To plead for Jack to stop, but no words came.

A hand was on my back, rubbing soothing circles. I sucked harder, desperate for air.

Voices blurred together, feet marching away, and I sank to my knees, letting my head touch the cool floor. That calm, reassuring hand was still there, lending strength as my breathing slowed. My heart caught the rhythm of Jack's and calmed.

I lifted my head, looking around the space.

In the silence of the smooth, polished stone room, surrounded on all sides by clear sparkling water, only Jack and I remained.

"Where did he take her?"

"He didn't say."

I grimaced. I hadn't meant to react so violently. I'd never punched Kaspar before, but the pain of his truth was a crushing weight. He knew. All these years, he knew that Mab wasn't a benevolent queen and the truth of mates was more complicated than anything I could have imagined. But most of all, Hazel belonged to him.

All the times she'd appeared in my life were tainted by new thoughts. Had he used her to convince me to marry him?

I shook my head. The first time I'd met her was in Winter and she had never done anything to overtly dissuade me from marrying Bracken. Nothing out of character for her, at least. Suddenly, my uncle's seat made sense. Winter wouldn't want someone sitting on the throne who was controlled by Lakes and Streams. Even temporarily. And Hazel's cavalier attitude towards partners and marriage... It was because she already belonged to someone.

She would never be a wife, have a life of her own, rule her realm, even if Mab never returned. She was trapped.

How could my best friend, my cold... unfeeling... husband... On second thought, I knew exactly how and it changed everything.

I glanced out the window. Bright light filtered through sparkling water and somewhere far overhead was my freedom from this nightmare.

Jack climbed to his feet and held out a hand. "Come on. Let's find food."

I frowned up at him. "We're trapped in here. Unless you want to swim the halls. Are you fully healed? The water–"

"I'm fine. But if we don't eat something soon, I might pass out."

I wrapped my fingers in his, letting him pull me up. The warmth of them bled into my clammy skin, staving off some of the tension from my earlier panic attack. It was so rare I got them anymore. I hated how vulnerable they made me feel, how weak. It seemed in these past two weeks, all the insecurity and fear I'd felt in my youth were determined to pull me down a spiral of doubt.

For years after my poisoning, I'd looked over my shoulder, convinced I was a target, but whoever had killed Mira never took credit for it and although Kaspar had searched, was still searching, he'd never learned the truth.

At least that's what he led me to believe. I wasn't sure what was true anymore. What if Fero *was* her killer, as we'd all suspected years ago? What if that was the true reason Kaspar had offered to marry me when Fero proposed? But no. Kaspar had said it was our bargain. Made when I was at my worst, desperate to be free of my meddling sister and the males of my court.

One he never should have held me to.

We reached the door to the hall, and I held a hand up to the wall of water caging us in. There were only so many places Kaspar could have taken Hazel. She couldn't breathe underwater. But perhaps he'd taken her as punishment for hitting him.

I glanced over my shoulder at Jack, still squeezing my other hand. His thumb traced slow, repetitive circles over my knuckles, but he didn't mention Kaspar or the word husband. I was grateful. I wasn't ready either.

Maybe his silence had nothing to do with Kaspar at all. His gaze had gone distant, and I wondered if he was thinking of Hazel's story, of Firethorn and Lorelai's love, wild magic made to save a realm from a foreign invader by bonding two creatures together. Could the magic want the same from us now?

If Jack's mother was who I believed her to be, and I had the wild magic low fae possessed, was Gaia once again weaving a spell to save our two kinds from mutually assured destruction?

I spun around. "I don't know that we'll find food out there, and I've been meaning to talk to you, but we haven't had any time alone."

Jack squeezed my hand, the corners of his mouth softening. "I'd love some time alone."

Heat crept up my neck. I laced our fingers and drew him back into the room, walking backward until the backs of my knees bumped the mattress. I sank down and Jack followed, shifting farther up the bed and patting the space beside him.

I scooted close until my shoulder brushed his, his warmth seeping into my chilled skin. I bent my knees, kicked the covers loose, and slipped underneath. The mattress dipped as he joined me.

Wrapped in a cocoon of shared heat, I rolled onto my side to face him. He kissed the tip of my nose, and my mouth curved before I could stop it. His hands slid to my waist under the blanket and he tugged me closer, scissoring our legs. Warmth coiled low in my belly and I slid my fingers into his hair, guiding his mouth back to mine.

His heartbeat thudded against my chest, arousal growing firm and insistent against my stomach. My breath came shallow, the rest of the world narrowing to the drag of his lips and the rasp of his calloused fingers as they traced my hips, then hooked behind my thighs, hauling me closer until I was molded to every hard line of his body.

Opening my mouth for him, his hot breath tickled my cheeks as he took his time tracing my nose, my top lip, finally claiming the soft flesh between his teeth before his tongue swept into my mouth, flooding me with the taste of wintergreen and fire. I moaned, wrapping my tongue around his and stroking until his hips moved in response.

His grip on the backs of my thighs tightened, as he pulled me impossibly closer and every nerve in my sensitive body burst to life from the friction building between us. I wanted him, needed him to claim me, to tear the clothes between us aside and sate the hunger eating me from the inside.

But I couldn't have Jack that way.

The realization was a bucket of ice over my inflamed skin.

I slid back, gasping in a breath, pressing my palms against his chest. "Wait. No. I need to talk to you."

Jack's swollen lips split into a wide grin before he nipped my nose. "I'm all ears."

He leaned down, head dipping below the blankets, and slid my hair away from my neck, trailing kisses over heated flesh to my collarbone.

"Jack. I'm serious."

"I'm listening," he mouthed against my fevered skin.

"It's about your mom."

His lips left my chest and the blankets lifted. All mirth vanished from his face. "What about her?"

"I know who she was." I bit my lip. "I think."

"Is."

I quirked a brow. "What?"

"Who she is. She's alive."

The memory of Jack telling me, half-delirious in Leo's tiny apartment, that he'd seen his mother alive in a cave resurfaced. I'd shoved it aside beneath more urgent horrors. ISHFA, Creig, bargains and war. But it lodged now like a thorn.

"Those dreams," I said quietly. "The cave. You believe they *weren't* just dreams?"

"I visited her," he said. "They started when I was at ISHFA. When I was unconscious for periods of time."

"I would wake up in a cave and she would be there, waiting for me. She looked even younger than I remembered her, and her eyes sparkled. She was, *is*, a prisoner, but not chained. They have some sort of magic that keeps her trapped there.

"Once, I'd heard them coming and was sure I'd get a look at them that time, but she told me to go and, as if her command made it happen, I was shoved out of the dream."

Jack's hand wrapped around my fingers, and he brought them to his mouth, kissing each one lightly. "I think I was actually visiting her." He searched my face, as if seeking confirmation, hoping I believed him. "And Grace... She said..."

His brows dipped. "But I haven't been able to return. I've wished each night before I fell asleep that I'd go back there and learn something that would tell me where she was, but I haven't been able to return."

I exhaled a breath. "If your mom is who I think she is, it would explain a lot."

THIRTY

JACK

"I think your mom *is* Aconite." Sav swallowed and tugged her hand from my grip. "At first, I thought she was just using the name, an homage to her court, but your magic. The flames were like the legends of Firethorn. No one has had magic like that in a thousand years."

I shook my head, the ice in my veins freezing over until it was hard to breathe. My mom... Mab's daughter? A princess of Faerie? I remembered then all the times she'd called me her little prince. Could it have been more than just a silly nickname to go with all her fanciful stories?

"Wait."

Something scraped at my mind. A memory. It was hazy. I was young, maybe thirteen. I'd left school early because of a headache. Before I ever opened the door, the sound of Dane's voice carried through the walls.

The words were murky, hard to cling to, but I knew they mattered.

"What?" Sav traced a line over my skin. One of the many scars I'd have for the rest of my life thanks to Janet Glassdon and her lover.

I squeezed my eyes shut, willing the memory to come to me. The moment shifted. The door to our house came into focus, then my dad's voice, but I was older. Already over six feet. I must have been in high school, because I had a set of house keys in my right hand. Mom hadn't let me come home by myself after school until then.

I'd waited until just before final period and ran home thinking no one would be there, but they were. Both of them.

"Damnit Aconite, I told you. You can't ask me to do nothing."

"I'm handling it, Dane."

My mother's soothing tone was lower, but I heard her. It was odd that I could hear them through the walls of our home when they weren't yelling. The sounds around me screamed against my eardrums, drowning them out. It was the reason I'd left early. Everything was too much today. The sounds. The smells. Sometimes, the world was more than I could handle. It beat against my skull until I couldn't think.

I slid the key into the lock as silently as I could and twisted.

"Your mother will destroy everything and everyone if we don't stop her."

Mom was silent when I came through the door and Dane had stopped talking too. She'd heard me—somehow—and silenced my dad.

"Jack! We're in the kitchen," my mom called in an overly bright tone.

I stepped into the room, guilt painted over my mother's face, but Dane... he looked furious.

"What is it?" Sav's soft voice tugged me from the memory, and I blinked, staring into her perfect sparkling eyes. She'd let her glamour fall away the moment we were back in Faerie, and I found I couldn't stop staring at her nose, slightly thinner in her true form, her lips, full and pink and those eyes, rimmed in long, auburn lashes.

My thumb traced the swell of her lower lip and I had to remind myself to speak.

"Mom and dad fought when they thought I couldn't hear them. It was always about the same thing."

"What was it?" Her voice was light and a little breathless, and I knew I wasn't the only one affected by our proximity.

"Her mom." I had never met my grandmother. Her family, anything to do with life before Dane met her, always seemed like a sore subject, so I'd never asked.

Sav bit her lip, and my earlier thought slipped away. I leaned forward, brushing my lips along her jaw, trailing over her smooth skin until I found her mouth and slid my tongue between her teeth.

She gave a teasing bite before letting me in, and soon the only thing in my head was the feel of her wrapped in my arms, her mouth on mine, the taste of her on my tongue.

Her lips left mine. "Jack," she said breathlessly. "Focus."

Her scent wrapped around me, her perfect ass cupped in my palms making it impossible to think of anything else, but I tried again.

"Right. Sorry. So, you think..." I forced the words out. "That Mab is my grandmother. That would mean my mom and dad were fighting about Mab."

Sav sat up, tugging her top down to cover the skin I had exposed. "But that would mean Dane knew about our kind all along. Why would Dane and Mab's daughter be fighting about Mab? And more importantly, who was Dane really?"

I pushed myself upright, leaning back against the bedframe. "Sav." I choked on my next words, but said them anyway. "You... killed him." Bile rose in my throat as Sav's sorrowful face froze, the truth hanging between us. "Surely you knew when he died so easily"—I swallowed—"that he was human."

Sav was silent for a long time.

"He did seem human."

"Is it so impossible that I could have a fae mother and a human father?"

"Yes."

She didn't hesitate, and doubt crept in. But her hand came up, twisting an auburn curl tightly, and after a moment she said, "I don't know."

I waited.

Finally, she let out a long breath. "Mab declared no high fae could ever produce a child with another creature." She looked me over, considering. "What Mab declared was law. Truth."

"But Hazel said—"

"We have always known about Earth and humans," Sav cut me off. "But we were told long ago that they were only playthings for the folk, good for nothing else and certainly not for bearing children. It was one of Mab's many reasons for the rule. What use is there for love with a creature you cannot create life with?"

"But—"

"But," Sav agreed. "If Hazel's story is true, and Creig's, maybe nothing Mab told us was true."

"What about the iron poisoning?"

Sav ran a hand through my hair. When she found my ears, she traced the outline all the way to the lobe. "Could a human and a fae have a half-fae child?"

"There would be iron in my blood," I said.

"Not necessarily."

I frowned.

"If your mother was fae, you'd still be more fae than human," she said softly. "You'd have her blood, even if some of your father's traits slipped in."

The medic in me twitched. "It's a little more complicated than that. We get two copies of every gene, one from each parent. If fae blood works like a dominant trait, then, yeah, one fae parent could be enough to make the child fae. But—"

Sav's brows pulled together. "Iron isn't a blood type, Jack."

I huffed a quiet laugh. Of course she'd pick up the one detail most people missed. "You're right. Blood type is about little markers on the outside of the cells. Iron is just the metal human blood uses inside the protein that carries oxygen—hemoglobin. If fae blood doesn't use iron, there has to be some other molecule doing the job. Something that hates iron enough that it burns you."

I froze as the thought clicked into place. "You were going to tell me about your magic."

Sav rolled her bottom lip between her teeth. "First, tell me why you believed your mom was dead."

My knuckles went white. I laced my fingers together tighter, staring at them so I didn't have to look at Sav.

"She tried to kill herself while I was at school," I said. The words were thick in my mouth. "I was halfway through the semester when Dad called. I don't even remember hanging up. Just... being in the car. Driving home."

Pieces. That's all the memory was. A phone ringing. My dad's broken voice. The road blurring past.

"I got to the hospital and she was..." I swallowed. "Hooked up to a bunch of machines. She kept drifting in and out. Apologizing. Saying she was tired."

Sav didn't interrupt. Her silence made it easier and harder at the same time.

"There was a nurse," I added. My jaw tightened. "Something about her was off. She smiled too much. Kept telling me to leave. Visiting hours are over. She needs rest. Every time I came back, she was right there by the bed, by the IV, watching me like I was in the way."

Heat pricked under my skin. I pushed it down.

"Dad was my rock," I said. "Talking to the doctors. Asking all the right questions. I... sat there." I let out a humorless breath. "Doing nothing."

Sav inched closer until her knee pressed against mine. Her arms came around me, carefully, like she thought I might bolt. I didn't. Instead, my shoulders began to unknot, breathing getting a little easier, her presence alone soothing something in me.

"I remember sitting next to her bed that night," I said. "Holding her hand. The nurse came in again. Told me to get some sleep, that they'd call if anything changed."

In my head, I stood. Kissed my mom's forehead. Walked out into the hallway. There should have been something after that. A sound. A shout. A doctor. Something.

My stomach twisted. I reached for it—and slammed straight into a different memory. Damp ground. A casket. My dad standing beside me. The smell of fresh dirt and flowers.

"We buried her the next morning," I heard myself say.

Sav's arms loosened. She leaned back, and her eyes burned into me. "But what happened?"

I blinked. "We buried her," I said slowly. "The funeral. I just told you."

Her brows drew together. "Jack, How did she die?"

"I—" The word snagged. Hadn't I already said this? I rewound, replaying what I'd told her. College. The call. Hospital. Mom in the bed. The nurse. The hallway—

The hallway dissolved like smoke when I tried to see past it.

"I told you," I insisted, but it sounded wrong even to me. "Didn't I? I was in her room and then... and then..." My chest squeezed. "I just told you."

Sav's gaze didn't waver. "No," she said quietly. "You didn't say anything."

A low roar filled my ears. I shook my head, trying to clear it, but the gap only yawned wider. There should have been monitors, alarms, a doctor saying words I didn't want to hear. Instead, my mind cut from fluorescent lights to a grave.

"I..." My throat went painfully raw, a lump forming that I could barely get words past. "I don't know."

Saying it out loud made it worse. Made it real.

I didn't know how my own mother died.

Sav studied me, something sparking behind her eyes that had nothing to do with me and everything to do with whatever had done this. "That's not just grief," she murmured. "That's a hole. Someone took that from you."

Magic. She didn't have to say it.

She drew a slow breath, jaw tightening. "There are stories in Faerie about mind magic that does this," she said. "It doesn't blur the edges, it cuts them out."

My skin crawled. "You think someone used that on me? At the hospital?"

"I think nothing about this is natural." Her gaze held mine. "If someone wanted to hide what they did to your mother, the first thing they'd steal is the moment you saw it."

The nurse's too-bright smile flashed behind my eyes, the way she'd stood between me and the IV pole, her hand always hovering near the line. My stomach twisted.

Sav's fingers brushed mine, grounding. "Memory magic leaves seams," she said softly. "It has to. If we can find where they stitched you back together, we might be able to pull at the threads."

Hope and dread tangled in my chest. I wasn't sure which one hurt more.

THIRTY-ONE

SAV

The sound of water sloshing in the next room made me jump. Memphe, Kaspar's right hand, hopped into the room. He stretched, letting his long legs carry him in an imitation of a high fae's march, and he moved a table and chairs beside the window, setting down a plate sealed by his frog bubbles to protect its contents. Beside it, he set down a cup, and the bubbles popped, releasing the fragrant scent of seasoned vegetables into the air.

"I've brought food and drink for the princess."

I glanced at the single plate. "What about Jack?"

He squatted low and his long tongue darted out, smacking his round eye. I would have squealed any other time, but Kaspar's insult had chafed hard. "Prince Kaspar... That is... I have no food for your guest, Your Highness."

"And when will the prince be returning?"

Memphe's gaze flicked between me and Jack, half covered by the blankets. I should have moved away or felt even a bit of embarrassment at being caught by a member of my new court with a male in my bed, but Jack was my mate and Kaspar would learn the truth when I saw him again. If he wasn't willing to break our bargain, then he and the rest of his court would be forced to live with it.

"He has left on urgent business."

"With Hazel?"

Memphe backed toward the door. "I'm not at liberty—"

"Did Hazel leave too?"

He ignored me, backing through the seaweed bisecting the space and disappearing into the entryway.

"Memphe." I slid my feet over the side of the bed and marched for the door.

Water sloshed as the frog slipped through the air shield and disappeared into the hall. "Memphe!"

"Sav. Come back," Jack called from the bedroom.

The little creature was gone, swimming as fast as his webbed feet could carry him. I spun around, crossing the claustrophobic space with my arms over my chest.

Jack had already moved to the table.

"Go ahead. Eat."

He looked up, cheeks stained pink. "I'll save half," he said around a mouthful of food.

A laugh burst from my lips. "No. Eat. Your body is still recovering, even if it appears healed on the outside."

Jack pushed the plate across the table and motioned for me to sit. "Sav, you need it as much as I do."

My mouth watered as I stared down at the rainbow carrots, potatoes, and cauliflorets. A dish full of all my favorite things. Underwater, Kaspar kept no land food. He must have sent for the food when I'd arrived. Had it come all the way from Winter?

I sat across from Jack, accepting the fork he held out to me and stabbed a purple potato. It had bright orange seasoning on it, and I wasn't familiar with the flavor as it melted on my tongue. Not Winter or Spring. That only left... Summer.

I looked up. "We can't wait here any longer. Kaspar has been Hazel's keeper for a hundred years. He wouldn't let her die now. We need to find Larek and Creig, and I think I know who might help us."

It was a risk, one I wasn't sure we should take, but who else was left to ask? If what Hazel said was true, Jack and I couldn't take on the poisoned army alone. I wasn't sure who was left to save, but I had to hope that Creig and the others were still alive.

"We need to see Prince Fero."

Once, he'd come to my court to see my sister crowned, and learned my secret, that I had gained my magic early. I hadn't seen him again for nearly two centuries. On my two-hundredth birthday, the zenith of a high fae's power, he had appeared and was gone before I could open my mouth.

Jack's eyes darkened. "The prince who proposed?"

I frowned, sliding the plate back to Jack. "It's not like that between us. The prince of Summer only cares about one thing. Power."

Jack took the fork from my hand, letting his finger trace over mine before stabbing a carrot with it. "You think he'll help?" he asked around another bite.

"I don't know if we have any other choice."

THIRTY-TWO

KASPAR

The lake pressed dark and heavy against the air bubble that kept my office dry. Bands of muted light rippled over the stone walls and the scattered maps on my desk. The low hum of the castle thrummed through the floor, a constant reminder of the water overhead.

Hazel sat in the narrow chair opposite me, spine straight, long white hair falling in a sheet over one shoulder and pooling in her lap. The silence between us wasn't new; it had been trailing us since we left the others, thick with the echoes of what she'd already revealed about Mab.

I turned from the window to face her, and her cheeks darkened under my scrutiny. "I did not expect you to be able to share so much of Mab's truth. Perhaps she really is gone." Hazel looked up, eyes going wide, fingers twisting together in her lap. "Tell me everything they said."

"I'm not your spy."

"I could make you."

Her chin lifted. "You won't. You care too much what Sav would think of you."

I drew a measured breath. Hazel was sharper than a Winter Court fae ought to be. Sheltered, yes—but she'd learned to bare her teeth from years of mistreatment at the hands of courtiers. It was that stubborn, inconvenient virtue that had always reminded me of Mira.

The coat of seduction she wore as armor was every bit as strong as my own armor of indifference. A fact I would have realized sooner if I'd taken greater care to protect her when she was younger. Still, I saw past her guard now, as she often did mine.

"You are right, Hazel." I leaned against the desk.

Silver glinted in the low, refracted light. My gaze caught on the tube poking out at an odd angle, and I stilled. Had someone been here? Touched my things? I stood, strolling to the wall of books and maps, running a finger over their spines. These were the books I'd collected over the centuries, a library of all Sav's favorite stories. Some new, some first editions, and between them, hollow books that hid my most precious treasures. No one knew they were here. Or so I thought.

Hazel stared at the desk, refusing to face me, and I seized the opportunity to push the tube behind a false book, pressing the spine back in place.

"I'm always right. The sooner you accept it, the better off you'll be." She twisted in her chair, raising a brow as I ran a finger over the books once more, ensuring they were in a perfectly aligned row.

I *would* discover who had been in my study and ensure nothing was missing, but first I needed to understand what was happening in the streams of Winter. I'd successfully relocated my folk to Summer, but if it too disappeared, we would be forced to move to Winter next.

Too many things about that court concerned me, though. I wouldn't take them blindly into a part of Faerie that may very well have been where we were being herded all along.

The growing list of demands on my time had a headache starting behind my eyes. Even with all there was to be done, one thought circled like a shark. Sav. She'd rescued the male who smelled less and less like a human each time we met, and now... they smelled like one another.

They hadn't lain together. She would be dead.

Although sea fae never wrote that archaic rule into their contracts, Sav hadn't known that, and my jealousy had gotten the better of me even before I knew how deep her feelings were for the male currently sharing a room with her. My one solace was in the deep satisfaction I derived from knowing they could not truly be together—even if he wrapped his arms around her while they slept.

I shook thoughts of Sav and Jack from my mind. The problem would sort itself soon enough thanks to my bargain, and my folk were what mattered most now. I needed to learn the truth of my restricted access to Winter. Hazel may not have the power to restore it, but she could demand answers from Regent Goodfellow.

I clicked my tongue, choosing to ignore her slight. "If you're recovered enough to travel, I need you in Winter." Hazel opened her mouth—to protest, no doubt. "A quick trip to speak with the regent. I will not leave Sav and her lover alone for long."

Hazel dipped her chin, closing her mouth. Soon enough, Jack would be forced to leave my court, and I wanted Hazel here to comfort my princess when he was gone.

I had left my ward to her own devices most of her life, but now that my princess was in her true home, she would need allies by her side. I'd never dreamed of forcing Hazel to relocate to my court, but the idea of two folk who could command air in an underwater palace appealed to me now. So long as it happened with my consent.

"Anastasia Hazel Elm." Hazel's back stiffened and her eyes met mine, murder in them. "You will not create air passages in my castle unless explicitly instructed to do so by your sovereign." She opened her mouth again, but I continued. "You will not share information about me or my court with anyone other than your ruler unless asked."

Her lip curled back, but she was helpless to disobey.

I closed the space between us, drawing a sharp nail down the inside of my wrist. "You need more of my blood. Drink."

Hazel growled, a feral feline sound that drew a chuckle from my lips, but without further provocation she pressed her lips to the blood welling on my skin and drank.

THIRTY-THREE

JACK

With the last tiny bits on our plate wiped clean, Sav glanced up, preparing to speak, when the light in the room dimmed.

Something huge slid over the window.

I frowned and leaned back in my chair. "Did you—"

Before I could finish, it passed again. The entire wall went dark.

Sav and I both turned toward the bubble of air holding back the lake.

A hulking gray shape drifted into view, larger than anything I'd ever seen in an aquarium. It circled once, slow and deliberate. My stomach dropped as the pointed nose and jagged scars along its snout came into focus.

"That's not good," I breathed.

The shark turned and came straight for us.

I shot to my feet so fast my chair toppled backward, moving toward Sav. The weight of the lake pressed harder against the window as it closed the distance, the entire room shrinking to the size of a dark pit circled by two rows of jagged teeth.

Sav was already on the offensive. She threw up her hands and a ball of flame flared to life in her palm, heat licking my face.

For a beat, I stared. Old instincts screamed that I was the fragile one here, the human in a realm filled with creatures who could kill me without effort. Then fire prickled under my skin, answering some silent call.

I lifted my hands.

Flames burst from my fingertips like they'd been waiting there the whole time, skittering over my skin before roaring up toward the ceiling. The smell of smoke and something sharp and metallic burned my nose.

The shark hit.

The impact rattled the room, a deep *thud* that vibrated through my bones. Its nose punched through the edge of our air pocket, water spraying in cold bursts. Rows of teeth flashed, so close I could've reached out and touched them.

Adrenaline flooded my veins.

I didn't think. I flung my hands forward the same instant Sav did.

Fire erupted from my palms, a jet of white-hot flame that met her blazing arc midair and slammed into the shark's face. The blast lit the room. The stench of burning flesh hit a second later—charred and wrong.

The shark recoiled with a violent twist. Its nose blackened and blistered, skin peeling, blood so dark it could have been black, billowing into the water outside. Bubbles churned around its head as it thrashed to the side, the pressure on the windows easing as it pulled away.

My gut twisted. I staggered, dragging in a breath that tasted like ash.

"Shit," I said, shoulders tensing. "I hurt it." I had no wish to end the creature's life.

The massive shape vanished into the murk, swallowed by the dark water as quickly as it had appeared.

Sav darted to my side, fire still guttering in her palm before winking out. She grabbed my wrist, eyes wide. Not with fear, but something sharper. Brighter. Her gaze tracked the faint embers fading from my knuckles like she wanted to chase them.

"That's some firepower you have," she breathed.

Her pupils were blown, cheeks flushed, magic humming under her skin in answer to mine. She stepped closer instead of away, drawn to the heat.

Fire still thrummed through me, coiled and restless. I flexed my fingers, watching the last embers die.

"Yeah," I said, heart still racing. "I'm starting to notice."

Sav smirked. "It's strong. I've never seen fire melt skin like that. And a shark's skin is especially tough. That's no ordinary fire you wield. It's magma."

I grimaced, glancing down at glowing fingers. On the floor, deep holes had melted into the sea glass where fire had dripped from their tips. I had a sudden memory of the soldiers at ISHFA, of their bloody stumps where hands had been. Even the bones had been destroyed by my flame. I didn't like what my gift could do. Didn't want to become what this gift might make me. A killer.

Sav saw my discomfort. "Whatever happened, you didn't have a choice," she whispered, lifting my hand and pressing a kiss to my knuckles.

I exhaled a sigh, not ready to rehash those moments yet. They were still too fresh, too raw. But I thought the words might not be for me alone. "There's always a choice."

A beat of silence stretched between us as I swallowed down my lingering pain. I had forgiven her; I knew it was unfair to blame her when I was certain my father would have killed her if she hadn't struck first, but it didn't make the truth hurt any less.

Sav released my hand, throat bobbing as she moved away from me. She leaned to peer out the window. Even after the shark's nose had pierced our bubble, whatever magic held the water at bay hadn't been broken.

"I didn't know there were sharks in Faerie." I stood behind her, peering out over her head. Though the sun was still trickling through the water, the shark had unsettled the lakebed, silt and debris obstructing our view of the water beyond.

"It's Kaspar's uncle. He never travels without his envoy."

I waited for Sav to say more. Maybe she'd forgotten how little I knew about her world, or maybe she just didn't have the energy to explain. She crossed her arms over her chest, backing away from the window.

"We can't plan an escape with the sharks swimming around. We're safe here, but if they find us in the water, he can say anything he likes. They're half-wild beasts."

I shuddered, returning to bed. "Come then, finish telling me your theory while we wait."

"I can't." She glanced back. "With Kaspar gone, I'm expected to play host."

⁕⁂⁕

I didn't relish the idea of swimming through Kaspar's underwater castle, but I liked the idea of Sav navigating some new danger alone even less. And although I had yet to spend much time in Faerie, I'd come to realize that every ruler was a threat.

Taking a deep breath, I followed Sav through the wall of water and dove into the hall.

She was fast underwater, even in the turquoise gown she'd pulled from the freestanding closet at the entrance to her rooms and slipped into quickly. I wouldn't have minded if she'd taken a lot longer to get dressed, but she'd been all urgency and no lingering, and now I had to focus on keeping up.

I'd spent most of my summers at the YMCA taking swim lessons, then teaching them for a bit of cash. If I could master holding my breath, I might actually be of some use down here. It had only been a minute, maybe two, and my lungs were already burning. The urge to suck in a breath clawed at my throat. I glanced frantically left, then right, seeing no end in sight.

I should turn back. The next air pocket might be at the far end of this hall, and I wouldn't make it.

Sav spun in the hall, swimming back to me and pressed her hands to either side of my face. Her touch was soothing, calming some of the terror clawing at my chest, and her mouth found mine. She pressed air between my lips, and I accepted it gratefully. She smiled, letting her lips linger against my mouth a moment longer than necessary before she turned around, pointing to a door a few feet ahead.

I followed, and somehow her air seemed to hold longer than mine had. It was an irrational thought; there was no way it could be true, but I made it to the room she'd pointed to and pushed through the air pocket, inhaling more calmly than I might otherwise have.

Sav didn't turn to look at me this time, and I froze as I glanced up and around the massive room. We stood at its entrance. Down the center was a narrow, dry path leading to a single throne. All around it, courtfolk hovered in the water, watching. I had a vague memory of an aquarium I'd visited once with my dad. We walked through a hall of glass and stopped, taking in the wonder of the sea. Sharks and other marine life swam overhead and around us, but we were safe behind glass.

Now, I didn't think we were safe from these creatures, and the too-keen eyes that stared back weren't those of any animals you'd find on Earth.

Sav strode confidently, shoulders back, down the stone path that had obviously been cleared for her. When she reached the throne, she didn't sit, instead standing beside it. She turned, facing the room and spotting me, and motioned for me to stand to her right.

My gut clenched as I took in the angry eyes on her. I wasn't sure if me standing beside her was the message she wanted to send now, but if she needed me, I would not say no.

A dark shape hovered overhead, and I glanced up as I stopped beside her, squeezing her hand. She held mine tightly, nails digging into my skin. A shark with a singed nose pinned me with black, soulless eyes as he prowled the space overhead. If he could, I had no doubt he would tear me open and watch my insides spill across the stone floor.

A second shark appeared, this one less afraid of whatever held the other back. He dove low, mouth stretching wide, and let his jaws skim the air just above my head. He wasn't close enough to truly catch me in his sharp teeth, but the threat was clear.

He darted away, tracing the same figure-eight pattern as his companion, and I looked up as the whole room darkened.

Overhead, a massive black horse with a long silver and black tail where his hindquarters should have been, descended. He stopped just overhead and spun until his seaweed mane dripped from the ceiling and his head slid out of the water. Eyes black as midnight held me in place as they darted to mine and Sav's interlaced hands.

This close, I could see his scales were a deep purple and the streaks of silver that ran along his tail continued up his sides, speckling his flank and neck in sparkling silver scales. He was a creature made of nightmares, and the air sizzled with his magic. He was powerful, no doubt about that, and ancient, but his magic was nothing like Fero's or Sage's.

Before my eyes, the creature's top half transformed and a humanoid head, arms and chest hung suspended in the air. Long strands of plum-colored hair hung overhead, nothing like the perfectly styled waves of turquoise Kaspar wore underwater and on land. I knew he was trapped in the water—unlike his nephew.

THIRTY-FOUR

JACK

"What brings you to the court of Lakes and Streams, Prince Aegon?"

Sav's voice carried clearly down the hall. It had an edge I did not hear often, cool and sharp as the water around us. Beside her, I stood at her right hand, our fingers interlaced, pretending I belonged in a room full of sea folk who would have happily watched me drown.

Overhead, the water churned.

Prince Aegon hung from it, his long body still mostly hidden in the lake suspended above the throne room. Only his head and shoulders broke through the surface. Water sheeted down over a mane of plum hair that hung around his face in dark strands. When he smiled, two rows of black teeth caught the light.

Sharks circled in the water above him, massive shapes sliding through the blue. Every eye in the room seemed fixed on Sav and the throne she refused to sit on.

"I hear congratulations are in order," Aegon said, voice silky. "Taking up the mantle of sovereign by selecting yourself a mistress already?"

A soft hiss rippled through the gathered folk. I looked at Sav. She stood tall beside the throne, chin lifted, shoulders set. For a heartbeat, I saw the hurt in her, the echoes of every time someone had tried to put her in her place. Then something in her gaze hardened.

"State your business," she said, "or I will be forced to rescind your invitation to this court, Prince Aegon."

A sharp crack split the air.

I flinched before I saw the source. Aegon's jaw clenched. He spat a broken tooth that hit the stone path at Sav's bare feet. Several of Kaspar's court made low, pleased sounds. Apparently they approved of whatever she had just done.

Sav smiled. Slow. Satisfied. Not the polite curve she used for strangers. This was something wilder, a flash of teeth in answer to his.

He doesn't scare her, I thought, and my chest swelled.

Aegon's black eyes narrowed. He tilted his head, hair drifting in the water above him. "Where is your husband, Princess?"

Sav glanced around the hall as if only now remembering Kaspar existed. "I do not see him here," she said. "Do you?"

A murmur ran through the room. Someone choked back a laugh. My heart pounded. She was taunting a prince who ruled the oceans while he hung above us with an army of sharks, and she didn't so much as flinch.

"I will not be spoken to with such disrespect," Aegon snapped. "Certainly not by a female who hails from a house of no standing at all."

The smile slid from Sav's face. Her eyes narrowed, violet irises bright against the deep blues of the hall. Every line of her body told me she was done shrinking for him.

He held her stare for a long moment. When she refused to look away, he exhaled loudly through his nose and broke first, dark gaze sweeping the room. "I have come to issue an invitation to my nephew and his new bride." His eyes lingered meaningfully on her hand in mine. "To my nuptials in three days' time."

Nuptials. My stomach twisted. He was getting married in three days and wanted Kaspar present. And Sav. The thought of her anywhere near another royal contract set every instinct in me on edge.

Sav let the silence stretch until it went brittle.

"I will pass your message to the prince," she said at last. Her gaze traveled over him, from the wet strands of his hair to the muscled shoulders emerging from the water above. Her mouth tipped up at the corners. "If that is your only business, I wish you a safe journey home."

Aegon's nostrils flared. "You do not offer me your hospitality. No room to rest. No feast. Are the land fae so disrespectful?"

Her fingers twitched in mine. There was a familiar tension in her that reminded me of our visit to Winter's court, when she'd let her uncle cow her. I saw the moment she chose not to. Her spine lengthened. Her chin rose a fraction higher.

"I suspect you will find out," she said, voice steady. "In three days."

The court stirred. The sharks above cut tighter circles. For a long breath, Aegon simply stared, and I wondered if he would attempt to tear her apart in front of everyone. I stiffened. He could try.

Then he snorted, a harsh, ugly sound, and pushed himself back into the water. His shoulders vanished, his head slipping under as the surface smoothed above us. The sharks followed, shadows sliding through the suspended lake until they disappeared.

Only when he was gone did Sav's hand loosen in mine.

The room buzzed softly as folk shifted, whispering behind their fingers. Some looked impressed. Some looked furious. All of them looked at Sav.

She stood taller.

My chest ached with something fierce and bright. Pride. Awe. Want. All tangled together.

Sav turned toward me and the steel in her gaze softened. "We are done here," she said, loud enough for the nearest rows to hear. Then, in a lower voice meant only for me, "Come on."

•→(~♦∧♦♦♦-

In her room, I stumbled through the door on unsteady legs and barely had time to suck in a breath before Sav threw herself at me.

The sound that tore out of her was half squeal, half battle cry. Her arms wrapped around my neck and her mouth crashed into mine. I caught her by instinct, hands going to her waist. The momentum drove us backward until the backs of my knees hit the bed and we toppled onto it together.

"That was so freeing." She laughed, lips grazing mine.

Her heart hammered against my chest. Mine was trying to match it. I had seen her face off against princes and generals, but there had always been something holding her back. The rules of her court. Her faith in her queen. Down in Kaspar's court, she had cut those tethers one by one.

"You were incredible," I told her. It wasn't enough, but it was all I had. "You told off a prince in front of an entire court and sent him running. It was the hottest thing I have ever seen."

She smiled so wide it hurt to look at, then buried her face in my neck, pressing a line of kisses along my jaw. "I hate that prince," she muttered between them. "I hate all of them."

Her mouth moved down, catching my throat, my shoulder, the place where my pulse jumped under my skin. Her hands pushed at my soaked shirt. I dragged it over my head and tossed it aside.

"I noticed," I breathed into the space between us.

Sav's fingers traced the lines of my chest, lingering on the rough patch of skin near my navel, the square of scar tissue that still looked raw even after it had healed.

"I am sorry," she whispered, mouth brushing the scar. She pressed soft, reverent kisses to each corner of the discolored skin. "For this. For what they did to you."

My throat tightened. I slid a hand into her hair and tilted her face up so I could see her eyes.

"I love you," I said.

The words had lived in my heart for longer than I wanted to admit. Saying them out loud felt less like a confession and more like finally telling the truth.

Tears shone at the corners of her eyes. The rush of battle-high and royal posturing seemed to settle all at once. She let out a slow breath. Too much. Too soon. I had frightened her. I tensed, preparing for her to push me away again.

"Jack," she whispered.

My name held a storm of emotion. Apology. Hunger. Fear. Something that brushed against the words I had just given her, hovering unsaid on the air between us.

Before they could slip out, she surged up and kissed me.

She poured herself into it. Every tremor, every unspoken thing, every shattered rule. Her lips were desperate and sure at the same time, and I felt the answer in the way she held me even if she didn't say it.

I smiled against her mouth when her lungs finally forced her to pull back. "You don't have to say anything," I murmured. "I just needed you to know."

Some of the tension left her shoulders. She swallowed and framed my face with her hands for a moment, memorizing me, then leaned in to kiss me again. Slower this time. Deep and lingering.

When she pulled away, there was a flicker of fear in her eyes that had nothing to do with my declaration.

"There's something I should have told you," she said.

A knot pulled tight under my ribs. "That sounds ominous."

She huffed a breath that might have been a laugh. "It is about the marriage contract. The bargain I signed."

My stomach clenched. "Kaspar."

"Yes." She glanced away for a heartbeat, then forced herself to meet my eyes again. "Part of the contract states that I cannot give my body to anyone else in a way that could produce an heir. If I break it, it will kill me."

The words sank in slowly and then all at once.

"That night," I said. "In Leo's bed. We could have..."

"No." She shook her head. "It has to be sex. Physical intercourse. Something that could create a child. We weren't even close. It's written to protect the royal line. Especially the females. Our bodies are vessels in their eyes, and they don't like the idea of anyone else touching what they believe belongs to them."

The thought of Kaspar and Alder and every other royal male treating her like property made my fingers curl into fists.

"Why didn't you tell me sooner?" My heart sped. "Why would you risk yourself if you knew there was a line you couldn't cross?"

Her throat worked. "Because you're worth the risk," she said quietly.

Her words were a punch to my chest. If that wasn't love, I didn't know what was. The truth was there in the way she looked at me, in the way her hands trembled as she touched me, in the way she leaned in as if distance had suddenly become unbearable.

"It makes things complicated," I said.

"I know." She dropped her gaze, lashes casting shadows on her cheeks. "If you don't want me because of this, I will understand."

"Sav," I said, tugging her closer until there was no space between us. "I told you I love you. There are no conditions."

Her eyes shone again.

"There are other things we can do," I added, letting my mouth curve. I brushed a kiss to her cheek, then the other. "You can't get rid of me that easily."

A startled laugh slipped out of her. Some of the dread eased from her face.

"And we *will* find a way to end that bargain," I said. "Somehow."

She frowned a little at that, as if she knew things about bargains that I didn't, but let it go for now. Her hands slid up my torso again, and I decided I'd spent enough time talking about other males thinking they had a claim on her.

"I meant what I said," I told her, leaning in to kiss the corner of her mouth. "I'm going to take care of you."

Her breath caught. Color bloomed high on her cheeks, but she didn't pull away.

"Jack," she whispered.

I shifted, guiding her farther up the mattress and easing her back, then settled over her without crushing her, bracing my weight on my forearms. She lifted her hips in silent permission while I pushed her dress down, working it until the fabric slid from her body. It pooled on the floor in a heap of damp silk.

Her breath hitched.

"Let me take care of you," I whispered against the flat of her stomach.

She lifted her hips again so I could draw her closer to the edge of the bed. I slid to my knees on the floor between her thighs.

"Tell me if you want me to stop," I said.

"I won't," she breathed.

Something loosened behind my ribs at the trust in those simple words. She had let me see her at her lowest. Let me hear the worst of her past. Now she was letting me have this.

I settled in and took my time.

I learned the sounds she made when my mouth brushed the inside of her knee and the way her thighs trembled when I moved higher. Where she needed more pressure and where she wanted me to linger, how her breath stuttered when I eased back and how she chased me when I gave it back to her.

Releasing her thigh, I ran my thumb over the sensitive spot at the apex of her leg, rubbing gently at first, then harder as she cried out.

Leaning closer, inhaling the sweet scent of her arousal, I kissed tender flesh and let the stubble on my chin trace light pink lines close to her center. This wasn't about proving anything. It was the only language I had for the way I felt about her. Every shiver, every gasp, I took as a prayer I intended to answer.

Her fingers threaded into my hair, tightening, not to push but to hold on. I held on too. To her. To the impossible fact that after everything, she was here, trusting me with her body and her heart.

"Jack," she breathed, and the way she said my name almost undid me.

I buried my nose in soft auburn curls and lost myself in her. My hunger was real, sharp and insistent, but it was tied to the quiet, stunned joy of being allowed to worship her this way.

Her hips began to move, small, helpless rolls that told me how close she was. Her thighs shook around my shoulders. I tightened my grip and stayed with her, tongue working against her, exactly how she needed, until she came apart.

She shattered with a rough, broken cry, her back arching off the bed. I held her through it, easing her down, kissing the soft skin of her thigh as she shook and slowly went limp.

When I lifted my head, she was flushed and glowing, hair a wild halo around her face. She looked wrecked and beautiful and mine, and I loved her so fiercely in that moment I thought my ribs might crack.

Our eyes met. We breathed together for a few long, quiet heartbeats.

Then she tugged me up into bed with her. I went willingly, letting her pull the blankets over both of us. She curled herself around me, head resting on my chest, one leg hooked over mine, one palm spread warm and possessive over my heart.

Outside, water moved and shadows drifted. In here, it was still.

"You're mine," she whispered, so softly I almost didn't catch it.

"Always," I said.

Her breathing evened out above my heart. I pressed a kiss into her hair and let my eyes fall shut.

For the first time in longer than I could remember, I slept without nightmares of what would come when I woke.

⋄→⟨⌣♦⌃♦♦⋄

Pain sliced through me.

I groaned and grabbed my sternum, fingers digging in as if I could claw the hurt out.

"What is it?" Sav sat up so fast the mattress dipped, concern carved into every line of her face.

Water crashed against the walls of the room beyond the bedroom, but it might as well have been miles away. Magic dug into my heart and twisted. I gasped around it, my muscles still loose from sleep, the last warmth of the bed turning cold in an instant. My immunity gift should have blocked any pain, but whatever this was didn't care.

"Sav," I rasped.

Kaspar's voice cracked through the doorway. "Your guest's time is up."

He stood framed by shifting lake light, darkness pooling around him. It took a heartbeat for my mind to catch up. This was the male who had offered us rooms while he healed Hazel. A temporary reprieve. A transaction. I had never mistaken him for kind, but some quiet, foolish part of me had not expected the blade to turn this fast. Or this precisely.

I tried to sit up, to raise a hand and blast him across the room, but my lungs seized. Air came in shallow, useless gulps. My limbs went heavy. I managed only to drag myself toward the end of the bed.

"Kaspar. What are you doing to him?" Sav's voice sharpened. "Let him go."

"Hazel has recovered. He made a bargain."

The words hit harder than the pain. I had agreed. I had thought I understood the cost. Kaspar's magic twisted again and a broken sound tore out of me.

Sav threw the blankets aside. Cool skin pressed to my burning side as her arm came around my waist. She hauled me up, her shoulders shaking with the effort.

My muscles were a raging fire, seizing and trembling. My legs gave out, and I crashed back to my knees.

Magic roared through my veins, the bargain tightening around my heart. If I didn't leave, it would finish the job.

"Sav," I gasped.

"I'm here." Her grip tightened, almost desperate. "Come on. I will get you out."

"I don't think so." Kaspar's tone slid across my skin, cold and controlled. Goosebumps rose along my arms and fire burst to life in my palms. Another spasm ripped through me and the flames sputtered out. A hot metallic tang flooded my mouth. I must have bitten my tongue.

Sav let go of me and surged to her feet, planting herself between us. "We are leaving," she said. "You won't stop us."

Power threaded her words. Compulsion.

"Wisteria Salvia Aestus. You will not use compulsion on me. Ever."

Her full name crashed through the room, every syllable heavy and intimate. For a heartbeat it rang clear in my mind. My brain lunged for it, trying to hold on. The next heartbeat, it slid away, leaving only a hollow ache where the memory should have settled.

Sav screamed.

The pressure in the air snapped. Magic went dead around her. Her hands dropped to her sides, fingers curled uselessly. Color drained from her face.

She stared at Kaspar, horror and betrayal widening her violet eyes, as if the steady, calculating prince had just taken his mask off and shown her what had been underneath all along.

"Come with me, Salvia."

The command wrapped around the room with invisible fingers. Her bare feet scraped the floor as she shuffled forward, body obeying even while her expression begged him to stop. Her fingers twitched, reaching back toward me before her heel dragged her another inch away.

"No," I pleaded.

Her gaze snapped to me, stricken. Pain and panic tangled in my chest. I pressed my palms to the floor and pushed, but my arms shook under my weight. I barely managed to drag myself an inch.

If I left, I might live. If I left, she would be alone with him.

Kaspar was tearing us apart word by word, and all I could do was lie there and watch him lead her away.

The cold prince turned and walked from the room. Sav fell into step behind him, limbs moving stiffly. Flame sparked at her fingertips and she lifted her hands, but Kaspar's low voice cut across the space, a string of commands I couldn't make out, and the fire died.

"I will kill you for this," she said, voice raw, but her hands stayed at her sides as they stepped through the door into the hall. The water peeled back for Kaspar without a gesture, opening a clear path ahead of them and leaving me writhing on the floor behind.

Sav's long auburn hair fell down her back, hiding most of her body from view. I caught one last glimpse of her calves, the flex of her ankles as she tried to dig her heels in.

"Stop," she begged, her voice cracking. "He'll die."

Those were the last words I heard before the water crashed down behind them, swallowing them from view.

Pressure built behind my eyes. My breaths came in short, harsh pants. The bargain was already choosing for me, squeezing my lungs dry. In this state, I would never make it through the water. I couldn't stand, let alone swim thirty or more feet to the surface.

Even in my hazy, oxygen-starved state, I knew this had been his plan all along. He had given us this underwater room. Removed Hazel without telling us when she was well enough for the bargain to wake. It was why he had stayed away when his uncle came. With Sav's true name, he had always known she would be helpless to disobey.

They belong to me, he had said. *No matter what silly fantasy you have been harboring.*

He had been right about one thing. If I lay down and let this kill me, Sav would be his for the rest of her long life.

I couldn't let it end here. I couldn't die on the floor of Sav's prison and leave her to rot with the cold prince. She needed me. On land, with my immunity to pain and fire magic in my veins, I might stand a chance. Long enough to free her, even if Kaspar took me down with him.

My only comfort was knowing he would never harm her. She was everything he wanted. But that didn't mean she would not suffer chained to him forever.

I had to live.

I pressed my palm to the floor and spread my fingers, pushing myself up to my knees. The moment I chose to move, the bargain loosened, just enough to let me breathe. I staggered to my feet and stumbled to the wide window.

It was large enough for me to fit through. My heart thundered at the thought of climbing out.

This was Kaspar's domain. Any number of his folk could be waiting for me in the lakebed. Even if they weren't, I had enough experience with holding my breath to know I would never make it to the surface without help.

Pain dug in again, forcing a gag from my throat. I was dead either way. At least if I tried, I could say I had not gone out without a fight.

I drew in a shallow breath. The pain receded just enough for me to try again. This time I filled my lungs as much as I could and pushed my head through the wall of water, scanning the murk outside.

I saw nothing, which meant very little in a magical lake.

I pulled back into the room, exhaled, cold water dripping down my body, then inhaled again. Another deep breath in and out. Sparks danced along my fingers when I shook my hands out.

This might actually work.

I dragged one of the chairs to the window and reached for the well at my center. The water outside didn't touch it. Only my innate gift hated being submerged, just like Sav had said. My other magic waited, hot and eager.

Flames burst from my fingers when I looked down.

Taking two quick breaths, I held the second and launched myself through the window. I shoved everything I had into my fire magic and angled my hands toward my feet. Heat rushed out of my palms. Even underwater, the force of it shoved me upward, toward the surface. The sky above was darkening, but it was getting closer.

Flashes of silver and blue flickered at the edges of my vision. I reached again for my well of magic. It flared and then sputtered. The push it gave me was barely enough to keep me moving.

In moments, I was hanging in the middle of the lake, suspended between the castle below and the air my lungs were already screaming for. Panic surged through me, clawing at the last thin scraps of breath.

Something navy shot past.

I swallowed my scream as a figure with fins where arms should have been and a scaled tail darted toward me, sharp teeth bared. Her eyes were wide and glassy, lids blinking with a translucent inner membrane, and they locked onto one thing: my throat.

I stretched my arms toward the surface and swam.

My legs kicked frantically. The urge to open my mouth and drag in a lungful of cold water hammered at my skull. The surface looked close, but distance was impossible to judge through the shifting gloom.

Panic took me when bony teeth sank into my ankle.

Every needle point dug in, scraping along bone. The creature began to sink, dragging me with it. I kicked, tried to jerk my foot free, ripping her fangs through skin and muscle. The surface slipped farther away, a fading smear of light.

My chest burned. The need to breathe roared in my ears. I was going to die in Kaspar's lake, dragged to the bottom by one of his creatures. Sav would stay his prisoner forever.

Rage snapped through me, sharp as flint. The fire at my center flared.

Heat burst from my hands. It didn't spark in the water, but my palms burned all the same when I wrapped them around the creature's neck. It shrieked, a thin, terrible sound, and its teeth tore out of my ankle as it wrenched away and vanished into the dark.

I kicked hard, fighting to reclaim the distance I had lost, blood flowing in a thin stream behind me.

My thoughts blurred at the edges. The surface was a distant idea now. The water was soft and cold and my limbs had gone heavy. It would be so easy to stop fighting.

Something grabbed my arm.

Fingers, not fins.

I was yanked upward, dragged through the water so fast the world turned into streaks of blue and black. I lost track of which way was up. My shoulder screamed where my rescuer had hold of me, but I clung to that pain as proof that I was still here.

We broke the surface.

Air hit my face. The dying rays of an orange sun stabbed into my eyes. I coughed and choked, sucking in breaths between bouts of sputtering.

I was dead weight as whoever held me cut through the lake, towing me along. Even my fingers wouldn't cooperate, slipping uselessly through the dark hair that floated around us every time my rescuer dipped beneath the surface and rose again.

Everything hurt. My head. My lungs. My chest. My ankle throbbed where the creature's teeth had torn in. My limbs tingled.

"You are heavy," a rough voice grumbled in my ear.

I craned my neck, trying to get a look at the face attached to the arms hauling me. Not a human face. A fae's. All I could make out was a long, slender nose with a small silver ball through it, glinting in the sinking light.

THIRTY-FIVE

SAV

"Scrub yourself until every inch of his scent is gone."

"I hate you," I shouted as I sank into a tub that matched mine perfectly.

"The feeling is mutual at the moment, I assure you."

I picked up a sea sponge and dragged it over my skin. It was rough and scratchy, and I couldn't soak it in the water. The command wouldn't allow it. Slowly, the tub filled, the water creeping higher with every breath. Kaspar had forced me to march naked through the castle to his rooms. Then he'd scowled, sniffed the air, and grimaced. "Filthy," he'd said, and stinging warmth pricked the backs of my eyes, my arms folding in as if I could hide myself from his gaze. I knew I wasn't dirty, but he'd made me feel that way.

Blood slid down my arms and legs, turning the water pink. Still, I scrubbed, blinking hard, jaw tight. I tipped my chin toward the wall, giving him my back. He didn't get my tears.

"How are you able to use my name to harm me? The bargain—"

"You dare ask me that, when you gave yourself to a male who wasn't your husband? I know you love him. Don't bother denying it. Yet you aren't dead either, so I could ask you the same thing."

"He's my mate."

Kaspar bit down on a reply, eyes flashing. I saw it then—something wild and sharp beneath the calm his kind were supposed to wear. Fury. They weren't meant to feel it. I was learning I knew nothing about my world. Why should it surprise me this had also been a lie?

"Impossible." He stood, glaring down at me as I kept scrubbing,

167

scouring the tender flesh everywhere Jack had branded me with his love. The sponge was crimson now, heavy in my hand.

"How can you be so cruel? You knew I didn't love you. I never lied about my feelings."

Kaspar's went black as water pressure built against his invisible wall. "Well, I have." His jaw ticked. "I have waited three centuries for you to realize what was right in front of you."

His words cut deeper than the sponge. For a heartbeat, my chest squeezed around something that might have been pity—three hundred years of longing, of standing beside me while I looked everywhere but at him. Had I truly never seen it? Should I have? The thought twisted in my stomach... and then curdled.

No. Whatever he felt, it wasn't love. Not truly. He'd taken that time, that devotion, and forged it into a weapon. His "love" held no tenderness, only claim. And now that he knew he would never have what he wanted, he'd decided I wouldn't have it either. If he was drowning, he intended to drag me down with him.

Heat roared through me, hotter than any fire I could summon. My grip on the sponge shook. I didn't pity him. I couldn't. I only wanted him stopped.

"Why don't you put us both out of our misery and kill me?" My voice came out raw. "I don't want to live if you plan to kill Jack."

Something flickered in Kaspar's eyes—shock, maybe even devastation —before it was swallowed by the familiar curl of his lip, the scornful mask he wore so well. I blinked back tears. Not for Kaspar. For Jack.

Could he survive the bargain? I didn't think so. Not without my help.

My whole being had ached to return to Jack, to rush him out the window and swim with him to safety, but with my name in his hands, I was truly Kaspar's prisoner. If he wanted to keep me in this cage forever, inflicting fresh torments on me every day, he could.

"Finish cleaning yourself and get dressed. We have dinner in two hours."

Kaspar swept out of the room, and I bit back a scream. The sponge dragged over my burning thigh and a low sob burst free. Had Kaspar gone to drown Jack? Was he even now drowning him where he lay crumpled on the floor?

If Jack ran, the bargain would be fulfilled, but Kaspar was betting he wouldn't leave me. I closed my eyes as the sponge scraped tender flesh; it dragged over my nipple, making me cry out, and I prayed to Gaia, instead of Mab—who had never answered any of my prayers—that just this once, Jack would leave me behind.

"Sav. Oh Mab. Sav."

I surfaced from a darkness I hadn't meant to fall into and blinked up at Hazel. The room was a smear of stone and water behind her. Hazel dropped to my side, stifling a sob.

"What has he done to you?"

I glanced down at the water spilling over the side of the tub.

"It's not as bad as it looks," I mumbled, but the truth was, I'd passed out before the scrubbing stopped. I wasn't sure if even that would be enough to end my torture. It must have been, though, because I stood, with Hazel's help, on shaky legs and glanced down at my healing body. Angry red streaks still marred my skin, and the worst of it, between my thighs and across my chest, was raw but no longer bleeding.

I leaned on Hazel as I stepped out and nearly slipped in the bloodied water pooling around us. She led me to a chair in the room's corner and helped me sit.

"I'll get a cloth."

She darted around the corner with purpose, and my stomach dipped. She was oddly familiar with where things in Kaspar's room belonged, and I swallowed down my panic.

"Hazel?"

She peeked around the wall into the next room. "One sec!"

Bile swirled in my gut and I choked on the taste.

She produced a cloth and raced to my side.

I looked up, searching my friend's face. "Hazel. Tell me. Please tell me..." I couldn't say the words. They were too vile. "He hasn't made you do things."

Hazel frowned, wrapping the cloth around my shoulders. "Of course not."

The contents of my last meal settled a little. I didn't think she was lying. Hazel was never shy about her partners, but those were by choice. If I ever learned that he'd done the worst possible thing and used her name in that way, I'd kill him, even if it cost me my own life.

"He's not that kind of male, Sav."

I watched her closely. I wasn't sure what kind of male he was anymore.

She helped me rise, walking slowly by my side into his room. I tried not to look at any of it, not to think about the place where he lived while Jack might be dying in his lake. The space pressed in anyway. Too large. A massive bed at the center, as if all of this existed only for his comfort.

Something jagged, made of coral, hung low overhead. I hated it on sight. My gaze snagged on a dressing closet like the one he had made for me, its doors half open to neat rows of clothes from every court. Of course he had planned for every version of this. Even my suffering.

"There is a dress laid out for you," Hazel said, and she crossed the room, picking up a shimmering turquoise gown. On the outside, it looked like shards of refracted glass, sharp enough to cut anyone who got too close, but I knew the inside would be the softest silk. It reminded me painfully of Mira on the last night of her life.

Mira spinning in Foxglove's arms, laughing, the two of them so sure they were proof the world could change. Once, a marriage between high and low fae, especially one from a sea court, would never have been possible. Mab had seen to that with her laws, and Alder had made certain his half-brother did not tarnish the Hawthorn name by reaching beneath his station.

Now Mab was gone, and all the rules she had carved into us were cracking. Kaspar had finally made his move. Fero had tried for his own inter-court match. Even Aegon had secured a union with the princess of Autumn. All of them scrambling for alliances while the courts rotted beneath them.

I couldn't hold all of that in my head and Jack too. Thinking about futures and politics when I didn't know if he was still breathing made my ribs ache. I shoved the memory of Mira back into the dark where it lived. I only had room for one thought.

Jack.

"I'm not going to dinner with him. I can't eat. I can't look at him. Not while Jack could be..."

Hazel's eyes widened. "Jack escaped. I thought you knew?"

My heart spasmed in my chest as my eyes snapped to her.

Escaped. Alive. He would be okay. Just as long as he didn't come back for me.

THIRTY-SIX

FOXGLOVE

I wiped a sweaty palm across my brow and glanced over my shoulder. Larek was still pale, but he was recovering. Creig leaned a shoulder against him, half to steady his son and half to reassure himself Larek was still breathing.

Larek hadn't complained. He hadn't said he was in pain, but whatever was eating at him leached the color from his skin and dug sharp grooves into his forehead with every step.

Juniper moved ahead of us, axe in her hands as if it had always belonged there.

The image overlapped another from hours earlier, when she had taken an ogre's head cleanly from his shoulders. Creig's axe had whistled through the air in her hands and hit with a sickening crunch. It was not a light weapon, but she made it look that way.

The ogre had been one of Dane's executioners, mindless on the drug. When his blood splashed across my face and hit my tongue, it burned instantly, thick and greasy, wrong in a way no living thing's blood should ever feel.

Juniper had rushed to me, cupped my face, and wiped the line of green from my lips with her thumb. "Don't ingest it," she'd hissed, then thrown herself back into the fight. No hesitation, no fear. Only rage. She was a legend covered in other folk's gore, and I ached with sharp pride.

Juniper had dragged Larek back into camp without a word, and from the glazed look in her eyes, I knew I wouldn't get any more information from her. When I'd seen him last, he'd raced into the woods to find Hazel.

He'd been poisoned by the blood tainting the fae army Dane left for us to find, but someone had tried to save him. Sucked the poison from his veins.

Was it Juniper? Did she see Hazel? There had been no time to search for her; the moment Juniper stepped back into camp with Larek, the true attack began.

One moment we were gathered around Yolmar's burial site, and the next Juniper's head snapped up, as if she'd heard a silent command. It was the only warning we had. I didn't know what had triggered it. I only knew they had been programmed to wait until the largest concentration of us stood shoulder to shoulder, unarmed.

They hit the back line first. The healers. The kitchen workers. The ones least prepared to fight. Ogres, dryads, naiads, and all manner of fae we had dragged out of the AFF came crashing into the camp with teeth and claws bared.

One of the kitchen elves went down beside me with a cry, and instead of fleeing, a fawn dropped to her knees and bit into his shoulder, tearing flesh. I didn't have time to react before carnage erupted all around the glade.

Just like Juniper the night we first freed them, they grabbed whatever blades they could reach and swung blindly. When someone dropped, they did not run. They bit. They sank their teeth into our fae and infected them with poisoned blood.

Creig had been the first to answer. Axes out, bellowing, he plowed into the line and four bodies hit the ground in the space of a breath. A troll came at him from behind, slamming him into the dirt and pounding his back with stone fists until Creig rolled and took its head off in a single, brutal arc.

They didn't die the way they should have. That was the worst part. Blows that should have felled them, deep cuts, shattered joints, barely slowed them. Some kept coming after they'd lost limbs. The only thing that ended them was taking off the head.

We had been fighting without rest since the funeral, mere hours ago.

"Now," Juniper mouthed.

I nodded. "Come. It's clear."

Creig slid an arm under Larek's and together we ducked behind the next tree encircling Creig's house. House wasn't the right word for it. It was large enough to be a castle, but from the outside it only took up a fraction of the clearing. Bodies were strewn everywhere. Most of them had died within minutes of the folk we'd rescued from Dane's compound turning on us.

Juniper tore the door to Creig's home from its hinges. It would have alerted any normal enemy, but these weren't normal foes. They weren't hunting sound or scent anymore. They were moving on some buried command, and that command didn't include stealth.

Creig wanted to save them. He always had. He'd built this place to be a refuge. But I'd seen his face when he realized they'd been turned into weapons. Grief had already cracked him open. This was salt in the wound.

Right now, grief didn't matter. Keeping Larek upright did.

"Inside," I said.

Creig and I hauled Larek through the threshold. Murz appeared from a door to the left, and my heart jumped. I hadn't seen him since Yolmar's burial. I'd assumed the worst.

He motioned us forward, and we darted into the strategy room.

Maps and papers were scattered, and green and red blood streaked every surface.

In the corner, Poppy leaped to her feet and my shoulders dropped a fraction. Behind her, at least a dozen folk huddled together. She slid an arm around Larek's waist and helped him sit with the others. Vines crawled down the back wall, pulsing like veins. My gaze snagged on the creature tending Larek's thigh.

Her huge, round eyes flicked up to assess him, and her whiskers twitched in disapproval.

A puca.

I froze in the doorway. A puca, in Creig's house.

Just watching her work was a miracle.

Juniper laced her fingers through mine and tugged me forward. I let her pull me down to sit as the vines along the walls responded to the puca's orders, creeping from the plaster and wrapping around Larek's oozing skin. We'd flushed most of the poison in the stream, but it was stickier than anything plant-based, clinging to him, refusing to let go. The vines tightened. They bloomed. Then withered black as they drew the poison out of him and died.

Larek's face eased. The tight lines at his mouth loosened.

"Are there others?" Creig asked, his voice dropped to a battlefield murmur.

Murz nodded. "At least another dozen in the kitchens." He jerked his chin toward the hallway. "I haven't been able to get to them. There's an ogre blocking the hall just a few feet from the door. He hasn't attacked yet, but things could change in an instant."

Creig nodded and followed Murz's gaze to his son's leg.

Murz elbowed him back to the present. "She'll help him," Murz said quietly. "She can help the ones that aren't too far gone."

The puca dipped her chin to Creig. Her kind didn't defer to ours, not normally. They remembered when the low fae ruled this realm and the high fae were intruders. Orcs and satyrs had once fought side by side to keep sea folk from carving up these forests. If the old stories were true.

Creig stood. Murz went with him.

Larek pushed himself upright, breaking dead vines as he moved.

Creig spun. "Stay here."

"Da. I'm coming."

"You'll stay here. That's an order."

Larek's brow dipped as he shoved off the wall and tore the last of the blackened vines from his shin. "I'm not a child."

Creig's jaw worked. The anger there wasn't for Larek. It was terror. He held out a hand. "I need you here. Protecting them. We'll join you soon."

Larek swallowed hard. He opened his mouth like he meant to argue again, but glanced past Creig.

Juniper sat beside me, breathing hard, glassy-eyed again. Gone from us for the moment.

My stomach twisted. Her lucidity after Yolmar's burial, the way she'd squeezed my hand, eyes clear as they met mine, hadn't lasted. She was slipping in and out. There for moments. Gone for stretches. Still the only one among us who could tear through a mind-broken ogre like it was made of sticks.

Larek saw the same thing I did. He shut his mouth.

"I've got them," he said.

Creig nodded once before he turned and left.

There was more work to do. There always was. And Juniper—the only one immune, the only one who could wade through poisoned blood and not fall—wasn't all the way back yet.

But she was here. And so was I.

THIRTY-SEVEN

JACK

I blinked, my gaze catching on the blurry shape of tanned skin, naked from the tips of her painted toes all the way to the crown of her head. Her outline solidified against the sandstone walls. Overhead, a white triangle of fabric was stretched between two pillars and fastened high on the wall.

It blocked the stars and the sliver of moon in the inky sky.

Behind the woman, whose raven hair reached nearly to the floor, torchlight flickered. Soft firelight illuminated a long, wide stretch of space, broken every several feet by pillars of the same sandstone as those beside me. As fuzzy thoughts filtered in, they snagged on the flames. I had never seen real torches in Faerie, only faelight.

Faerie... I was here and—

I sat up with a groan, and the woman crossed the room, pouring water from a pitcher into a bronze bowl. "Good. You're awake. Drink."

I took the proffered bowl in trembling hands and tried to bring it to my lips. An ache split my head, and I rubbed absently at my chest. A wound was still healing there, where the bargain had nearly killed me before the lake had taken a shot at it too.

I glanced around. "Where am I?"

My voice was scratchy, as though I had been screaming. Flashes of memory trickled in. A man grabbing me from the depths of the lake, swimming us to shore. The hot granules of sand recharging the well of magic at my center after being waterlogged so long.

The desperation that had clawed at me to return to the lakebed. To free Sav from the cold prince who had trapped her down there and tried to kill me with his bargain.

"Sav," I croaked.

"Shh. Rest now."

I set the bowl down on the low table beside me, seemingly made of pressed sand, and pushed myself up. The world spun, and I stumbled against a pillar.

"Calm, Jack. Sit." The woman patted my hand, and the tinkling gold bracelets stacked on her arm clanged together.

"Sav—"

"Sav is safe for now," a deep, rumbling voice said. I spun toward the sound, pressing my hand into the wall. Power crashed into my battered body, rolling and flowing over me like liquid fire.

Prince Fero pressed a steadying hand to my shoulder, and my well of power swelled to bursting. I gasped as heat crawled up my throat, puffing out in small white bursts from my lips. It steadied me, but it also made me dizzy with the overwhelming rush.

"Tha—"

"Don't," the prince growled.

I had nearly thanked him. When would I learn? Still...

"I believe I owe you something for rescuing me." I dragged in another wheezing breath of fiery air. He had released me, but I was burning with the need to expel some of the magic coursing through me. White-hot sparks burst from my fingertips, spitting and hissing when they hit the floor.

The prince smirked, his gaze tracking them as they fizzled out.

"It is I who may owe you something soon enough. Come. Join me for tea."

-•-)(·-•-^-♦-••-

I slid onto a stone bench circling a low table that my long legs didn't fit underneath, forcing me to bend at an odd angle. I glanced around the grand expanse, open as far as I could see. It seemed to be an outdoor palace, but there were no true walls. In places, the pillars held white sheets that cut the space in two, cornering off dark alcoves, but most of the castle was open to the warm night air.

The prince, now clothed unlike the first time we'd met, dropped to the floor, sliding easily under the edge of the table, and I silently cursed, following him. Sitting with my back against what I'd wrongly assumed was a bench, my legs stretched out easily in the open air.

A woman with nothing covering her tanned skin except rows of bracelets on her wrists and ankles came last, standing beside the doorway. Two more women joined her, all in the same state of undress. I glanced up, brows furrowing. Sav had been right, it seemed. The prince might have proposed, but it clearly wasn't her heart he was after.

Prince Fero looked up, giving them a short nod, and the women turned, moving several feet away and giving us their backs.

"Tea?"

I shook my head. "Sav thought you might help her," I said, cutting to the chase. "Was she right?"

The prince's brow rose and he looked me over. Someone had changed me into a long, loose tunic and pants that might have been made of silk. The material was soft as butter on my burning skin, but cool to the touch, and it seemed to wick some of my heat away.

"It was rumored that you may be of my court."

I frowned at the subject change and opened my mouth.

"But apart from your very dark hair, I see nothing in you that speaks of Summer lineage."

"I'm not concerned with your theories at present. I need to save Sav."

Fero barked a laugh, running a hand over his bearded chin. "And how do you propose to rescue the princess from her husband and her court?"

"We're mates."

The prince leaned closer, almost conspiratorial. "Mates are a fallacy."

"Maybe not. Hazel has a book."

Fero's shoulders stiffened. "She told you what's in it? What did it cost you?"

I drummed my fingers against my thigh. The last time I'd seen the prince, his magic had silenced me, forcing me to stand perfectly still while Sav bristled at his declaration. She'd never said a kind word about him. Not that I thought any of the rulers in Faerie were kind. I wasn't sure why she suddenly thought she could trust him. Before I shared any more secrets with him, I needed to make up my own mind.

"Why did Sav think you would help us?"

He leaned back, looking bored. "What do I know of the inner work-ings of a female's mind?"

It was a fair question, and my lips tipped up at the corners. I didn't dislike him when he wasn't using his magic on me. "Does that mean you won't?"

"The prince of Lakes and Streams won't harm his wife. Keep her locked up..." He pressed his lips together, looking me over once more. "Perhaps. But harm her? Never. She is a treasure he has coveted for centuries. Now that he has her, he will not let her go."

Heat flared to life in my veins. I'd had nearly the same thought. There was no better word for it than that: coveted. "But if we're mates, doesn't that mean he would have to?"

Fero snapped his fingers, and a fae appeared, setting down two cups. I ignored mine, drumming my fingers on my thigh more impatiently. He lifted his to his lips, took a slow sip, and made a humming noise. When he set the cup down, he faced the fae, dipping his chin.

"You have my gratitude, Yucca."

The contradiction was sharp enough that my mind ran over the scene again. He'd called three nude women into the room, let me stumble to find my seat, then snapped his fingers at his staff, all to make himself look like a tyrant. But the picture was a little too perfect, the cruelty a little too staged.

His attention flicked to me, and the faint tightening at the corner of his eyes told me he knew he'd been caught.

He dismissed Yucca and turned back to me. "I'll make a bargain with you."

I tipped my chin, hoping I'd done it correctly.

"I'll send you with members of my guard to recover your mate, if you promise to search the lake prince's court for my son. If you find him, you will return him to me."

THIRTY-EIGHT

SAV

The long stone table must have been made especially for hosting guests from the land courts, but the water that had been drained from the room was all for me. I stared around the space, a dull ache leaching into my veins.

I was trapped, crushed under the weight of the lake's unforgiving water. The same thing that kept us alive kept me caged. I'd visited Kaspar's underwater home many times. Then, it had felt like escape from the pressures of the palace—a barrier between me and the obligations my sister forced upon me. A bitter laugh tried to claw its way out.

I hadn't thought about my sister in days. Some part of my cold, vindictive heart believed she deserved whatever fate had been dealt to her. If that was true, what did my fate mean for me? Did I deserve an eternity in this prison?

A chair scraped over the glass floor and I jolted out of my daze. "Ivy?" I stood, rushing to the old Spring healer and throwing my arms around her. "I'm so glad to see you," I mumbled into her fiery curls.

She hugged me stiffly and a chill ran down my spine. Was she another of the prince's prisoners? The chill went frosty when another thought crept in. What if all the members of the Spring Court were here? What if Kaspar had been the one trapping the fae?

I released Ivy, leaning back to get a better look at her. Dark circles rimmed her eyes and her skin was especially pale. She'd been down here longer than I had... but how long? I'd seen her in court before I married Kaspar, before the castle had disappeared, Alder and my sister with it. "Ivy... are they here?"

She gave a small shake of her head, and I let out a barely concealed sob. That brief moment of hope swelling inside me died. She slid into a chair and clasped her hands tightly in her lap. It wasn't fear exactly that I scented. It was regret... unease. I searched her face another moment before small feet skidded to a stop, as though they'd been running.

A boy rounded the corner into the room and straightened his shoulders. His eyes were almost Autumn-red, but not quite—more amber, lit from within.

If it wasn't for the bright glow in them, I'd have wondered if he was some form of mix between high and low fae. Although I'd been told it was impossible, I was beginning to understand that nothing Mab said was true.

"Qaden," Ivy called.

The boy blinked, then scooted around me, standing before Ivy. She straightened his hair, smoothing it down, and looked him over. "Staying out of trouble?"

He nodded enthusiastically, then turned, giving me a once-over. "It's the princess."

Ivy's mouth flattened into a thin line. "Yes."

If I didn't know better, I would have sworn Ivy harbored some anger toward me.

Hazel stepped into the room, smoothing her skirts. Now that the charade was over—or perhaps because Kaspar believed us all to be his puppets—Hazel wore the colors of Kaspar's court. As I did, not by choice. I glanced again at Ivy and the boy she'd called Qaden. They too were dressed in shades of turquoise and navy. It seemed Kaspar was rebuilding his court and decorating it with land fae.

The prince himself stepped through the door and the hairs at the nape of my neck rose. Once, his arrival had been a welcome sight, a sign that all would be well for the evening. No one at court had dared degrade me in front of the Prince of Lakes and Streams. Now, the sight of him made me want to hurl my plate across the room and scream.

He was wearing a shirt, which had me more on edge. We were all dressed for court dinner. Why?

Cool, assessing eyes surveyed us. "We are all assembled, then." He moved through the room, confident on two legs, and bitterness tore through me. Long ago, walking on land had been a challenge for him. It seemed after so many centuries, he was comfortable on two legs.

Kaspar's disapproving scowl jerked between me and the empty chair to his right. I lifted my chin, moving around the long table and sitting as far from him as I could without sitting directly opposite him. If it angered him, he hid it. But then, I was fairly certain my husband had learned to curb those emotions. And I was confident now that he *did* have them.

When the table was set, a feast fit for any noble land court, the five of us lifted our forks. Qaden didn't wait for anyone's approval; he stabbed his into a roll and tore it with his teeth. The gesture reminded me of Jack and made me smirk, only to be chased by a sharp pain in my chest. He was alive. I would continue to remind myself of that fact until the day I stuck a knife in Kaspar's back and freed us both from this prison.

"I thought you would be more comfortable with your old court healer to attend you."

My fork scraped over my plate as I looked up to meet her eyes. "Ivy. I'm so sorry."

She grimaced, her lackluster gaze sliding to Kaspar. "I found myself without a court, Your Highness. You do me an honor."

For a breath, I could only hear the scrape of cutlery and the distant rush of water. Creig's war map flashed in my mind—the neat little Xs carved through Spring. It had been ink and parchment then. Ivy sitting at the table made it real. Spring wasn't just disappearing; it was gone.

My gaze snapped to Kaspar. "I didn't ask for this. For any of this. You can't trap them down here."

Kaspar set his wineglass down. I didn't think I'd ever seen him lift a glass to his lips. Not since...

"I am offering them shelter in the absence of a court."

I ground my teeth. "How many others are you offering shelter to?"

If he heard the edge in my voice, he chose to ignore it. "Only the boy and his mother. With Spring and its border gone, she was not safe from Summer. The boy and I made a bargain."

"Qaden," Ivy hissed.

His amber eyes went round. "I'm sorry, Mother. It's just that you were so afraid of them. I wanted to keep you safe." Tears welled in his eyes, one fat drop rolling down his cheek.

Kaspar lifted a slice of apple to his lips, nibbling it. "Would you have me turn them out and risk their fate?"

My brow wrinkled. A hollow ache opened beneath my ribs. *Spring. Swallowed.* "If Spring is gone, where is your court?"

A glint of something calculating flashed in Kaspar's gaze and he set his fork down. "I have relocated *our* court to safer ground."

I shot to my feet, letting my chair topple behind me. There was only one place he could have gone. Winter would be too cold and Autumn was sealed from us. "We're in Summer."

"We're in Lakes and Streams," Kaspar replied coolly.

"Surrounded by Summer."

He tsked, rising and moving around the table. He dipped his head, gathering my fingers in his and bringing them up. "I have not greeted my lovely wife yet tonight." His mouth touched lightly over my knuckles, his grip loose—the very picture of a prince. "On all sides but one, Princess." He raised a brow, indifferent eyes meeting my violent ones. "I beg you not to attempt a battle of wits with me. I have far more practice at it."

He released my hand, sliding into the seat beside mine, and snapped his fingers. His plate and everything on it blinked out of existence and reappeared in front of him, along with his glass of wine. He slid it toward me and motioned for me to sit. I scowled down at the top of his head and snatched the glass from the table. Knocking it back in one go, I glanced around, spying the bottle. I didn't have Kaspar's neat little appearing trick. As a low fae, he didn't have innate gifts like I did, but he did have a whole slew of other abilities. I ripped the cork out with my teeth and dumped the contents of the bottle into my glass, letting it spill over the rim.

He wanted me to rot in this underwater tomb with him? To become just as miserable as he was? Fine. I would show him just how miserable I could be. I lifted my glass, letting dark henbane wine spill down my arm and stain the semi-sheer sleeve of my dress. Tilting the glass in his direction and sloshing some of the liquid onto his plate, I met each fae's eyes.

"A toast to my husband. The cleverest male in the room."

THIRTY-NINE

FOXGLOVE

Creig took the hit in the side of his face. The ogre's mace slammed into him and drove him back into the stone with a crack that rattled my ribs. He laughed through it, a low, wild sound, and swung again. The axe bit into the ogre's side. It should have dropped him. It did not. He roared and lunged instead, swinging for Creig's head.

Murz slammed into his back. I surged in from the other side and caught his arms. The brute bucked between us, his breath hot and foul in my face as he thrashed. My shoulder screamed, but I tightened my grip and wedged my boot against the wall.

"Hold him," Creig snarled.

The ogre jerked, trying to throw us off. Murz wrapped both arms around his middle and dug in. My grip tightened around his wrist. I pinned it to his ribs and leaned my full weight into it until the joints strained and popped.

"Now," I said.

Creig stepped in close, too close for comfort, teeth bared in a bloody grin. He raised the axe high and brought it down in one clean arc.

The blade met bone with a thick, wet crack. The ogre's body shuddered once and went slack in our arms as his head separated from his shoulders. It hit the floor, rolled, and only stopped when it bumped the vines crawling along the far wall. They curled around it, hiding his glassy stare from view.

I let the body sag out of my grip and stepped back, wiping my hands on my coat. No blood had splattered my face or mouth. Creig had made the swing perfectly; every drop falling where he meant it to. A true warrior's strike.

Creig wiped his mouth with the back of his arm and spat a tooth onto the floor. His jaw was already swelling where the blow had caught him, but his eyes were bright with a savage light I hadn't seen in a long time.

"Come out," he called, voice echoing off the stone. "It's safe."

For a moment, nothing moved.

Then folk began to emerge from their hiding places, blinking in the dim light. A head peered out from behind a toppled table. Two healers unfolded themselves from beneath a bench. They crept into the open, glancing from the ogre's severed head to Creig's feral smile.

I wasn't entirely sure which sight frightened them more.

"Quickly," he barked, and they sped up, letting me know he was the thing that had them running and not the ogre. I might have laughed at the scene, but Creig was a creature born for battle and war made his soul sing. Only children had softened him. Now that one was gone, I feared what would become of him.

We gathered the forty or so folk, some limping and bloody, and ushered them toward the portal to Earth. Creig spun around, facing Murz. "Close it the moment we come through. I don't want to risk even one of the infected getting out."

Murz nodded, and I tugged Juniper behind me, ushering the last of them forward. Some had narrowly escaped Earth; others had only passed through on their way to the missing pocket. Most, though, were Creig's soldiers. They had plenty of experience on Earth.

Juniper's blank eyes had me most worried for her mental state. She was shutting down because we were returning to the place she'd been captured. Made to do terrible things.

Crowded into the empty seal pool, we stood around Murz as he worked. I didn't think any of them had ever seen a portal created or destroyed. There were only two that I knew of who could do it. I had suspicions about others, but only time would tell if I was right.

Murz raised both hands overhead and clapped, dragging his tightly pressed palms down the center of the line. As quickly as he'd made it, it slid closed. A silver line traced the empty space until only shimmering dust hovered in the air.

In moments, it had dissipated to nothing, and only the wall of the seal pool was visible all around us. I squeezed Juniper's fingers tightly, saying goodbye to my favorite part of Faerie for the last time. Her hand squeezed back, and I glanced down. Her face was blank, but I thought she knew, felt it too. A piece of Faerie being severed from our lives.

"Let's go," Creig whispered.

Luck alone had brought us to Earth in the late hours of the night. No matter how we'd tracked it, we'd never found any way to measure time between realms. We could go in at midday and come out at the exact same time, or in the middle of the night, like now. The only thing we could rely on was that it was always the same day.

Some things about fae magic I would never understand.

We huddled close together, and the urge to shift and run ahead so I could scout for us was strong, but Juniper's hand, warm in mine, kept me rooted in fae form.

We stopped beside an abandoned building, covered in graffiti and old AFF slogans. Without Dane here to hold them together, I hoped no new threat would rise to continue his mission. I would never know what made him hate the folk the way he did, or how he knew about us before we revealed ourselves. Creig believed his wife was fae. That Jack was half human like Murz. If it were true, there was a good chance whoever she was, he had killed her when he learned the truth.

Jack's appearance was so human, though. If I hadn't seen the magic for myself, I never would have believed it. Of all the fae who were half human, and there weren't many that I knew of, they always manifested their fae form. Their truth was a closely guarded secret. For if Mab had known about them, it would have been immediate death.

It was the reason Creig had left Faerie all those years ago, seeking refuge for his captain's son. It shouldn't have been possible, and had Murz's father not disclosed the truth, none of us might know today. The city air was too thin in my lungs as I thought of Xeg. He had been of the Winter Court long before he came to Spring. Mab sent parties to Earth to spy and report back, and in some cases their stay was long.

When Xeg's lover risked her life to come through the portal, Xeg had learned of another of Mab's lies. She'd died delivering Murz and left him with the truth. Humans and fae could produce children, just as high and low fae could. A secret Mab had killed to keep.

My own great love, Mira, had been such a secret. The product of Mab's only son and a low fae princess. Indirectly, of course. That union was many centuries before my birth or Mira's. But the Lady of the Lake, Mira's mother, was a creature of both land and sea, like her daughter. Impossible, the folk would say. But I had held Mira's warm body in my arms, breathed her seafoam and grass scent, and loved her all the more for it.

Creig lifted a hand, pointing all four fingers ahead, and we moved in a quick, single-file line into the Seelie side of Central Park. I strained to listen for any sign of Connor or his patrol, but when there was no sign of them even after two rounds of patrols should have come, I nodded.

Spring Court's pocket entrance was dangerously close to AFF head-quarters, but, with Dane dead, I wasn't sure there were any active members left. Larek and Yolmar had never gone to Faerie to ensure some of Spring still remained. I could only hope enough remained to get us through.

Larek went first, followed by the puca, then Murz. A group of folk raced behind them. When the first group had made it, Creig motioned for me to go. I shook my head, pointing to the next group.

He made a slashing gesture pointing two fingers. I growled low. He was wasting time we didn't have. Juniper's grip tightened in mine, and I glanced down. Her eyes were clear, and they were shining with tears. "Please," she whispered. "I can't stay here."

My heart seized in my chest. Creig had seen something I hadn't. I had been so lost in my thoughts, as I often was; I hadn't noticed Juniper waking up. I might have missed our window. And she was in so much pain.

We dashed forward, stopping as a small knot formed around the dryad twins who guarded Spring's pocket. "Why are you not going through?" I asked the fae standing nearest the tree. She was sobbing and didn't answer.

I tugged Juniper forward, pushing through the group to the tree with the great shimmering light at its center. "Sisters, let us pass. We must return home."

Sap rolled down Melia's cheek and she wiped it with a branch. "You cannot return."

"Spring is no more," Trillia finished. The twins wrapped their twining branches together, cutting off access to the portal.

The last of the folk crowded in around us, Creig bringing up the rear. "What is it?"

I spun to face Creig, cold flooding my veins. "Spring is gone."

FORTY

JACK

"I will. I swear it. What does he look like?"

Fero's raven brows drew together over his long nose. It was slender for his face, but somehow made him look more dangerous. I wondered if he'd cast a glamour to make himself seem more imposing. To craft the persona of a vicious prince, where Kaspar might just have done the opposite.

"I do not know. But you'll know him when you are in his presence."

I frowned, sliding a hand over the smooth fabric covering my leg. "How can you be sure?"

"Magic sensor."

"What?"

"You are like me in that way. Your innate gift is that of a magic sensor. You can tell how strong their ability is, if not exactly *what* magic they have. In that, we are different."

I pursed my lips, trying to puzzle out his words. "My innate gift is immunity to pain."

The prince's lips tugged up at the corners. "That is *a* gift. But not *yours.*"

I blew out a long breath. His riddles were maddening. "I'm sure it's my ability. I've used it many times."

His full lips spread wide in a true smile. It was a little terrifying. "That is your mother's gift, but she gave it to you. Or loaned it. She may yet take it back."

My mother's gift. His words were true. I couldn't say how I knew, only that I did. If it was still hers to lend, she wasn't gone. My chest went tight.

She had been lending it to me for years, maybe since I was a kid. A memory surfaced of the candy store, lights and sound pressing in until my stomach rolled and the room tilted... and then, in an instant, it was gone. Mom had smiled and told me I was fine as she winced, rubbing at her temple.

It had happened other times too. On days when the world was too much for me, when I woke up buzzing or sick for no reason, the feeling would vanish as if someone had flipped a switch. Her bad days always followed. She took the weight instead.

Had she been using her gift to shield me every time I needed it?

Sav was convinced my mother was Mab's daughter. If that was true, maybe gifts could be passed down like that.

"So we can give our gifts away?"

Fero laughed, a deep chuckle that vibrated through me. "When you are the daughter of Mab, you can do many things."

I pushed out from under the table, climbing to my feet. Was he also a mind reader? How could he know I was thinking of that?

"Calm yourself, Prince of Winter. I am not reading your mind."

I held his gaze.

"Magic has a signature. I need only feel it once to know who it belongs to. I met your mother many centuries ago. She kept my secret and for that, I will be forever grateful."

I sank back down, absorbing his words. So it was true. My mother was a princess. Not just one of the court members bickering over titles, the daughter of Mab. Queen of Faerie. And both were missing. "Do you know where she is? Or... if she's alive?"

Fero's grin fell. "No. But your mother has more than one gift. She can open and close portals to realms. I must admit, when pieces of Faerie began to disappear, I had wondered if it was not your mother, punishing us for whatever has happened to Mab."

I braced a hand behind me. "So... she created the portals to Earth?" Too many thoughts swam through my mind—small, inaccurate memories from my youth. One rushed to the forefront, screaming for my attention.

Fero was speaking, but I didn't hear him. My mind was fixed on that single thread. I closed my eyes, letting the memory solidify.

I was a teen again, standing outside my parents' bedroom with my hand on the door. I should have been at guitar lessons, but halfway there I'd stumbled to my knees, clutching my head. When I could breathe again, I got up and raced home to find my mom. But her voice, low and sharp, stopped me.

"If you ever see her, Dane, run," she said. "Take Jack and run. She would never come to Earth unless she was sure she could win. She's afraid of humans."

"She's fae. What could she possibly have to fear from humans?" Dad scoffed.

"She's not like me and Jack. She isn't strong. She hides behind her gift. And human blood only makes our kind stronger."

"Ac—"

"Listen to me, Dane." Her voice shook. "Mab doesn't tolerate threats to her power. If she comes to Earth, there will only be one reason. She'll erase the threat before it can touch her."

Dad had believed her. He'd built an army on Earth expecting an invasion.

When I opened my eyes, the prince was silent. The women were gone. At some point, he'd sent them away.

The hallway memory snapped into place.

My stomach clenched.

"Mab was going to wipe Earth out."

FORTY-ONE

SAV

Kaspar grabbed my wrist and I tore it from his grip. "Don't touch me!"

"You've had enough tonight, Princess. Go lie down."

"Monster." I spat the word in his face and he wiped my deep plum spittle from his cheek. After polishing off a second bottle of henbane wine, the room tilted. "Jailer. Captor."

"Enough," he barked, closing the space between us. "Go take a bath and compose yourself."

"I don't want to. I want to dance. Clear out the ballroom. Make it ready for your princess."

I staggered in a clumsy circle, crashing against the wall in the hall. Kaspar's eyes rolled to the ceiling, and he marched away from me, all his cool composure and charm spent for the evening.

When I'd begun to sing at the top of my lungs at the banquet table, Ivy had grabbed Qaden's hand and dragged him away. Hazel stood, eyes darting between me and Kaspar. It was clear she feared him and who wouldn't fear the male who held their name in his grasp. I needed only to think back to earlier that night when he'd forced me to scrape my skin until it bled to be reminded of how cruel he could be.

"Sav, can I get you some water?"

Hazel's voice was cloying in my ear, and I spun away from her. I wasn't upset with her, but my intoxicated brain didn't know that.

"I don't need your assistance, Hazel. My *husband* is taking me dancing." I stretched out the word to ensure he didn't miss the bite. Sarcasm worked better sober. Drunk, it only came out sharp.

191

"That will be all. You may go, Hazel."

I stopped spinning, glaring at Kaspar. "You can't force her to leave. She's my friend. *Friend.* I know you don't know what that means, but it means if I want her to stay she will."

Hazel's wide eyes darted between us and my stomach sank. Some part of my brain knew it was wrong to put her in the impossible position of leaving me alone with Kaspar or disobeying him.

I sank against the wall, pressing my temple to the cool, wet stone. When I closed my eyes, indigo swept past behind my lids, disturbingly fast, and the corridor canted. I tipped—until cool arms wrapped around my waist.

"To bed, Princess."

I said no. I think. But when I opened my eyes, I was staring at a cold, gray ceiling and I didn't remember how I'd gotten there.

Leaning over the side of the bed, dark liquid spewed from my mouth, spilling across the glass floor. It reeked of sour wine and bile, and I winced. My head wasn't throbbing and that could only mean I was still a little drunk. The bad part would come later.

I tried to piece together the evening. The last coherent thing I remembered was my fifth toast. When I'd demanded another bottle be brought out even though I was the only one drinking. Each toast included one new nickname for my *husband* until by my fifth one, his name took longer to say than whatever new insult I'd come up with.

I smiled to myself, remembering the water shooting from Qaden's nostrils when I'd added horseface to the list. That *had* been a good one. Today was a new day though. A new day in this wretched place, without... Jack. I didn't know where he was or how he was faring in a world he wasn't prepared to survive. Worse, Larek and Creig were fighting for their lives, if they were even still alive, and I could do nothing to help any of them.

But perhaps that wasn't true.

Annoying Kaspar hadn't worked. Perhaps embarrassing him was the push he needed to give me my freedom.

-●-➔(⌣◆▲◆●●-

I smoothed my skirts, sitting straight-backed in the lone throne-room chair. "Attention, Court. I will hear your cases now. Please bring them forward." News traveled fast in Lakes and Streams, but I wasn't sure if the folk had come to truly meet their new princess and have their cases heard, or to gawk. Whatever the reason, it seemed no one had bothered to inform Kaspar yet. That meant I still had time.

I straightened the delicate silver crown woven in the shape of thorns with three small seashells melded into the metal that Kaspar had left at my vanity table. It was the perfect size for my thick curls, nestling atop my head when my hair ran down my back. That's why I had heaped my hair on top of my head and perched the crown precariously.

He should have known better than to give me a crown. He knew how I felt about them. Adornments of any kind.

A pair of eels slithered forward, hovering to my right. Bubbles shot from their mouths as they spoke in a strange murmuring tongue I couldn't decipher. Their voices came muffled through the water, mercifully dull against my skull.

"Memphe, translate."

Kaspar's first in command twisted sticky fingers together. I'd gone to his room first. Perhaps that was why no one had warned Kaspar. I didn't think anyone kept the prince so well informed as his faithful spy.

"The pair wishes to relocate to the cooler depths near Winter's border. It is becoming too warm here."

I nodded, giving their request serious consideration. "Why not? You have my approval."

The pair of eels murmured again and I glanced to Memphe. "They say the naiads there have grown quite ferocious. If they go without protection, they will be eaten."

"I see." I glanced around at all the folk gathered in the hall. No sharks that I could see and the few kelpies still residing in Lakes and Streams had not found it worth their time to attend this farce. "We can't have that. Our subjects deserve protection."

Several voices chirped or mumbled from behind the water on either side of the throne. I couldn't tell if they were in approval or anger. Their expressionless faces were impossible to read. "Memphe. You'll go with them."

Gasps that could be nothing but outrage followed and I swallowed my smile.

"Your Majesty," Memphe gulped loudly, large round eyes darting around again. I have duties to attend to here. I cannot—"

"Nonsense. I can think of nothing more important than the safety of our subjects. You'll go as soon as they're ready."

A wall of water crashed down the formerly dry center of the great hall, racing for me and I fought with everything in me to compose myself as it crashed to a halt against some invisible shield inches from my face. I could see how having air magic would be useful in this court. Too bad I didn't.

Aquamarine eyes locked with mine as Kaspar halted less than a foot from me in his mer form. Rage sparked, then iced over. His eyes swept the room, assessing, and the mask of indifference slid back into place. "I see the princess is playing court."

His words scraped against my nerves, setting my veins on fire. He'd forbidden me from using my innate gift on him. Three years ago, that might have sent me into a rage, but I'd spent all that time learning to live without my gifts. Learning I was stronger than my magic, and no matter how powerful he was, he had a part to play in front of his court.

"Just taking a few things off your plate, Dear. I know how busy you are." I smiled at him. All teeth.

His shoulders relaxed and although he was floating on a calm current, his eyes, only for me, told me he thought he'd win this battle. I was about to show him how wrong he was.

"You must be tired after the night you had." His lips tipped up in a lazy grin.

"You mean the private dinner you held for the closest members of your court?" I batted my lashes as the hisses around the room told me they had landed their mark. "It was invigorating. Meeting your new spymaster." A ripple of snarls. "And your new right hand."

Memphe's tongue shot out, sliding over his eye. "Sire?"

Kaspar's soft smirk became a grin. He spun in a slow circle facing the room. "My wife is confused. Those were *her* new court appointees. Land creatures relegated to the air pockets of my court. I would never force my faithful folk to walk or crawl when they can swim at my behest." He finished spinning, triumph flashing in his eyes as he faced me.

The creatures in the room turned their cold glares on me. He had made it clear that I attempted to misguide them, and in the court of Lakes and Streams, honesty was the key to their loyalty.

Fine. *First point to you, Kaspar.*

FORTY-TWO

JACK

"Jack!"

I sat up as Fero shot to his feet and sprinted out of the palace.

I lurched up and chased him down the stone steps, my boots sinking into the sand as I tried—and failed—to keep up with the way he glided over it. My gaze slid past the prince to the figure racing toward us.

Larek dropped to his knees, hands up, just as Fero reached him and pressed a blade to his throat.

I stumbled to a halt, chest heaving. "Wait. He's my friend."

Fero's blade lifted a fraction. "Whom have you invited into my court without my permission?"

Larek's fingers came up, two of them bracing lightly under the blade. Maybe my earlier assessment had been wrong. The viciousness was not all an act. So why had he welcomed me so easily?

"There are less than fifty of us left," Larek said, voice rough. "We escaped to Earth, but the portal to Spring is closed. Our only way in was Summer. The Bitter Wraith has lost her senses."

Fero looked from Larek to me and back again, then blew out a slow breath. "Who is among your party?"

Larek swallowed. "My Da, Foxglove, Murz, some we've rescued, plus a few who came with us from Spring when we left."

"Bring them. I will speak with your father privately." He lifted his blade, turning to me. "Your mission will wait until we speak with the refugees."

When the remaining fae who had escaped the missing pocket of Spring were situated in open-air rooms in the summer palace or in the forest bordering the court, according to their preference, Creig, Foxglove, Murz, and Larek met us at the low table.

The naked women who had hovered nearby were gone, as were all the other members of Fero's court who had appeared to help those who needed medical attention, food, and water. Now it was only the prince of Summer, what was left of Creig's free army—and me.

Creig's black stare found mine across the table, a menacing glare skewering me where I sat. His eyes promised death. I shuddered, looking away. He hated me for my father's part in his son's death. I knew it in the marrow of my bones. Sav's words came back to me. A blood debt. Would he attempt to collect that debt now? In front of everyone? I was reminded then that I owed him a favor, and another tremor rattled through me.

"I am sorry to hear of your losses, General." Fero dipped his chin in a sign of respect, and I pursed my lips. If I didn't know better, I'd think the prince and the general weren't enemies at all. But that didn't make sense considering Summer and Spring had been on the verge of war when we were there last. Creig hadn't been Spring Court General in over a decade, though. My gaze slid from General Creig to Prince Fero, his words coming back to me. Magic sensor.

I wasn't sure how I had done it the other times. It had just happened. It came in uneven flashes, driven more by instinct than control, but it was there. I reached for that extra sense again, the one that let me brush against people's gifts. It was there, unfamiliar but steady, as real as sound or scent. Not something I could touch, but a way of feeling what I could not see.

I stretched the ability toward Larek. Something tickled my senses. If I could have given it a color, it would have been dark gray. It was wild and firm, but not very strong; solid like stone.

Creig nodded at Fero. "Your sympathy is appreciated."

I turned my attention to Foxglove, pressing my awareness over him. He had air magic. It was stronger than Hazel's, but something else was stronger. *Shifter.* He could change forms, also the same as Hazel's magic. I pushed harder. If I tried, could I find his innate gift?

His gaze flicked to me. *Don't go poking around in people's private affairs, Princeling.*

I gasped, sliding backward, bumping the back of the bench. All eyes shot to me and I schooled my gaze into something I hoped looked like indifference. Foxglove's attention had never left Prince Fero.

Princeling? What gave him that idea? Had I been in his head or had he been in mine? I'd only just learned of the possible truth from Fero... *Mind reader.* What a horrible, powerful gift. What secrets could one glean from everyone around them with a gift like that, and what would they do with the knowledge they found?

My gaze darted to him again as I pushed my magic-sensing gift toward him, and he flashed me an angry glare. *A gift like yours could get you killed.* Something akin to two strong arms shoving against my consciousness knocked me backward. My eyes rolled in my head and I had to catch myself from falling.

The entire battle had taken place in my mind.

Everyone must have wondered what was wrong with me. Everyone except Foxglove—the mind reader.

"Yours may stay in my court until we find a solution," Fero said, pulling his attention away from my odd display and back to Creig. "But I must say, pooling our knowledge seems like the better plan, given all you know and the resources at my disposal."

Whatever Creig had said, I'd missed it. I hadn't missed the fact that he'd be staying in Summer. That didn't bode well for me, but I had no plans to remain in Summer. Once I freed Sav we would go... Where?

"I have a theory, but I won't put anyone else at risk until I've followed it to its end. I only ask that Juniper be allowed to remain in your court." From Foxglove's composed tone, one might never have known he'd just battled mind to mind and won.

Fero nodded. "Of course, Prince Hawthorn. I do hope you find your missing folk."

Foxglove dipped his chin and stood, marching away from us without a backward glance. Murz slid into Foxglove's empty place. "We need to talk."

I glanced at him, trying—and failing—to keep up with the conversation between the general and the prince. They were discussing the parts of Faerie and the folk that had disappeared.

"I can help you with your gift."

My attention shot to Murz. Was he a magic sensor too? Someone willing to help me was a welcome change.

He dipped his chin, standing and motioned for me to follow. I glanced between the orcs and the prince. Their conversation was in no danger of slowing, so I stood, following Murz to the beach. "I knew it the moment I met you," he said as he spun to face me. "You must have sensed it in me too."

I hadn't attempted to read Murz, but I did now. Like Larek, there was something wild about his magic, but apart from the elemental gift—something to do with water, possibly—there was a bright hue refracting from his center. I hadn't seen any of the others' gifts; I'd merely felt them. With

Murz, when I searched for it, it was not only something I could feel, but something I could see. "Is that how you see it? A bright light?"

Murz wrinkled his brow. "A light? When you open a portal, you mean?"

I frowned. "When I what?"

His face lit and he slapped me on the back. "Come. It's easier if I show you. You've done it before. It'll be easier a second time."

On the beach, Murz raised his hands and brought them together with a sharp crack, and a light erupted in the air. I stepped back as he spread his palms apart and, between two silvery lines of light, a new scene appeared. I blinked, staring at white snowcapped mountains as a frigid gust of wind blasted through the tear in reality.

I retreated another step. "What... did you do?"

A bead of sweat ran down Murz's brow and he gritted his teeth as if it had taken something out of him to create it. "It's a portal. All of us half-humans can make them." He clapped his hands once more, sliding tight palms down the seam, and it closed. "Your turn."

I considered telling him he had the wrong guy. I'd never opened any portals. But something warmed my chest. Burned bright. Hope. If I could open them, I could open one into Sav's room. I wouldn't need Fero's army. I could appear right now, grab her, and bring her back safely.

"Just clap?"

Murz held his hands up again. "Open your hands wide and picture where you want to go. It doesn't have to be somewhere you've been, as long as you have a connection to someone in the place. Then push with the magic at your core." He clapped his hands together, wincing as the strain etched itself into the lines of his face. "Or you've seen it on a map or in a book."

When he spread his hands this time, it was Earth peeking through, but the smell was all wrong.

"I've been here."

A lopsided grin tipped the orc's lips. "This is where I found you the first time we met."

I peered through the shimmering tear in reality. It looked like New York, and had I not been so dazed from traveling the Seelie path, I might have noticed. That other New York, wherever it was, wasn't mine. It was close, but there were differences. The billboards were larger, placed slightly differently. Come to think of it, there wasn't a Ralph Lauren store in Times Square. Not in my Times Square. Did that mean there were other Earths? In other universes?

And the man who had helped me, the one who bought my suit, was from a different universe too. My shirt was from a different universe. My mind was spinning. The possibilities were endless.

Murz clapped his hands together, closing the portal, and bent at the waist, inhaling as if he'd run a mile. "Now you try."

I watched him warily. "Are you okay?"

He shook his head, catching his breath slowly, and when his breathing had steadied, he straightened. "Portal magic isn't like the regular stuff. It takes a lot out of you. I shouldn't have done two so close together."

"But you'll recover?"

He grinned. "I can't open another for at least a few days. I was showing off a bit, but I'll be all right."

I frowned, caught between wanting desperately to learn this new skill and not wanting to waste it when I needed to get back to Sav. The color he'd lost in his cheeks was returning and he was recovering quickly. If I portaled into the Court of Lakes and Streams, I'd be relying on pain immunity, the gift my mother let me borrow, to ensure I didn't need time to recover.

Fero's words had stung and I still hadn't fully processed them. My mother. Princess of Winter. Daughter to Mab. But I was more certain now than ever that she was still alive. What if Fero was right? What if something had happened to Mab and she left to find her?

My mother was kind and loving. Not the sort of vengeful fae who would destroy a realm. Memories of the visions I'd floated in during my delirium swam to the surface. In them, she was trapped, held captive in a dark, dank cave. Had someone forced her to use her portal gift? I had to save Sav, but my mother needed me too. A war raged in my heart.

I would be stronger with Sav by my side. She knew Faerie. And if I was being honest with myself, a selfish part of my heart wanted—needed—to save my mate first.

Two portals should be more than enough for what I needed to do.

Making up my mind, I nodded. I didn't have to think to know where I wanted to go. I brought my hands together. When I spread my palms, pushing the magic in my chest into it, sparks shot from my fingertips and the air distorted.

"Focus, Jack."

I closed my eyes, bringing an image of the dark, tomblike room—streaks of blue light shimmering against smooth stone walls—to mind. It was a prison, dark and foreboding, and the walls had felt as though they would close in on us at any moment. Another emotion crowded in. Guilt. I'd left her, choosing to save myself.

I blinked, and an image of a dark, musty cave filtered in between my palms. The air crackled like bad radio waves and I gasped when I locked eyes with bright, emerald-green orbs that were twins to mine. My throat closed around everything I wanted to say, *I'm coming, I'm sorry, hold on,* but only one word made it out.

"Mom?"

Thick air poured in, drowning the image.

"Jack?"

I strained to hold the fabric of this place and time apart, but it slipped through my fingers, reality closing in around the tear I had made.

"Mom!"

Swirling light, sparking white at the edges, burst to life, clogging the air with thick gray smoke.

"Jack!" Murz shouted. "Close it. You'll burn yourself up!"

My fingers lit with strange white flame, but I was immune to the pain, and I clawed at the opening even as the smoke choked my lungs. Straining to pull the rip in reality apart, the flames raced up my arms and I coughed, choking and gagging. The edges of my tear began dissolving, slipping through my fingers like sand, and still I struggled to hold it apart.

"Mom," I cried as the air grew thicker.

Murz's cold hands pressed against mine, forcing my palms together. I fought, but the smoke was making my head spin and, in moments, he shoved my palms down, sealing the portal closed. The air was heavy with fiery ash and smoke and my eyes burned, my lungs poisoned, but none of it mattered. I had seen her. I had seen my mom. She truly was alive.

I sank to my knees. She had been there. So close. And still unreachable. And the reality of what I had seen was nothing like my dream.

I dropped my head into my hands and let out a sob.

FORTY-THREE

SAV

Kaspar thrust his hands out to either side, parting the wall of water in his throne room. I stood, chin high, and made my way down the long, cavernous walkway to the exit. The eyes of the court burned my back, but I didn't falter or trip under the weight of their stares. When I reached the hall, the water continued to part. He would show me this kindness after his victory.

I wondered bitterly if he would do the same when I won.

At the end of the hall, I turned toward my room, but paused. I wasn't the only land creature here. My friend was somewhere in this watery tomb, and Ivy was here too, her son with her. I wanted to make things right between us, needed her to know I had never meant for him to trap her.

Tossing the silver crown to the floor, I reached up, yanking my hair out of its high bun. It spilled down my back, loosening some of the tension in my skull. The pounding that had rattled my brain all morning softened slightly, and I sucked in my first full breath of the day. I hadn't let them see how much it hurt, would not give them the satisfaction of seeing me at my worst, of thinking me weak.

Diving into the water-filled corridor, going the opposite direction from the throne room, I followed a long hall I hadn't been down before.

I reached the end, none of the doors opening into an airy space, and turned around. I searched a second long hall, but had to turn back when my lungs began to burn. I swam faster. The headache from too much wine was overtaken by icy fingers wrapped around my neck, squeezing. My arms pumped wildly, and by the time I reached my room, I collapsed to the floor, heaving.

Sucking in lungfuls of air, my heart slowed, the headache from too much drink returning, and I twisted onto my back, arms outstretched on either side as I stared up at the ceiling in my stony room.

Wherever Hazel and Ivy were, Kaspar had spaced us out enough that we could not reach one another without his permission.

The confines of this underwater palace chafed. It was time to step things up. If I wanted him to let me go, I would have to push harder. The memory of the night he had found me in bed with Jack reared up, phantom pain ghosting over my thighs, and I grimaced.

Exhaling softly, I shook my head. No matter how I pushed him, he wouldn't do that again. Though I had seen no remorse in his eyes as he watched, his gaze had not met mine at dinner later that night. A part of me still believed he was not as cruel as he was pretending to be. At least... I hoped.

-◆→(↲◆▲◆●●-

I had nothing but hours on my hands as I waited to be summoned by the prince. I used that time to brush out my hair, twisting the strands around my face into intricate braids that looped behind my head, resting atop the thick hair cascading down my back. I searched the newly stocked closet for a dress that suited my mood. Like my sister, Kaspar fancied fine things.

To him, they were an extension of the face you showed the world. Unlike them, I had never put much worth in the things I wore. I favored free-flowing clothes that fell over my skin, rather than those that made a statement at the expense of my comfort. But I had spent more than two centuries in my sister's court. *Wear this dress, Sav. This brooch, these ear cuffs. Dust your cheeks with fairy dust. Your eyelids. Make yourself a dream and everyone will forget what you truly are.* Her words clung to me as I slid the navy dress from the hanger. Did Kaspar know I had worn one very nearly like it the first time Jack and I had attended a ball together?

Did he know Jack and I had shared our first kiss that night? The next morning, I had gone to Kaspar to save Jack when Heath accused us of being more. Even then, it had been obvious to the world. To everyone but Kaspar. And me.

Thin straps dug into my shoulders, a little too tight. I had gained weight somehow, and the measurements were not quite right. Something Kaspar had missed. His ever-intrusive gaze, always watching, always calculating, had missed a detail. An important one. I had been happy. Even if I had not known it, I had been happy, and I had gained weight.

Now Kaspar was threatening to take that happiness from me and I would not let him.

I heard a sound, one I had come to recognize well down here, as water parted and an air bubble burst into the receiving room. I stood, brushing back my hair to reveal my freckled shoulders, when Hazel stepped through the pondweed in my room and looked up. Her eyes were dull, cheeks pale.

"Hazel. What is it?" I rushed forward, grabbing her hands.

I tugged her to the bed and we sat. She squeezed my hands, meeting my face for the first time. "I'm worried."

I searched her face, waiting for her to say more.

After a long pause she continued. "You'll think it's silly. But I'm afraid for Larek." I tightened my hold, opening my mouth to speak, but Hazel barreled on. "I know what you'll say. I barely know him. I'm not the sort of female to get emotional over a male." Her eyes misted. "But he's broken without his twin." She bit her lip. "I'm not in the same situation, I know. My... position doesn't give me the freedom to dream of happily ever afters with anyone, but I feel..." She looked away, searching for the words.

"Kindred?" I offered.

She looked up. "We're both damaged."

I nodded, and I couldn't help comparing her words to my relationship with Jack. We had lived very different lives, mine already much longer than his, but the world had been cruel to us and there was a comfort in being broken together.

"We'll find him. I promise."

Hazel's eyes narrowed. "Not if you keep going on the way you have."

The words hit like a slap. I flinched, sliding backward on the bed as if I could dodge them. "What do you mean?"

"You've given up. You've accepted your fate."

I shook my head hard and pushed to my feet. "I haven't."

She wasn't entirely wrong and that was the worst part. I had spent days pushing back in small ways that wouldn't truly rouse his ire. Watching. Waiting. Telling myself I needed more information before I moved. Tonight I had finally decided it wasn't enough. Tonight I had promised myself I would stop letting Kaspar's name around my neck decide everything for me.

Hazel's gaze didn't soften. "No? What are you doing to escape?"

The question burned. It sounded too much like the accusation I had just thrown at myself. My mouth opened, but the answer I gave only burned my tongue. "Hazel. He has my name. And yours. What can I do?"

She stood too, mirroring me, one hand planted on her hip. "The Sav Briar I know wouldn't let something so simple cow her."

The words stung. My fingers curled into fists at my sides, nails biting my palms. I had been plotting. I had. It just felt so small against the weight of Kaspar's power that I could not bring myself to say it aloud.

"I'm not," I said through my teeth.

"No?"

"No." This time it came from lower in my chest. "I'm not."

Hazel studied me for a long heartbeat, as if she were measuring whether she believed me or not.

"Good. Let's go to dinner." She spun, parting the water as she stepped into the hall. She glanced back over her shoulder. "Coming?"

-•→(◡◆▲◆••-

We reached the banquet hall and I stepped inside. How had it not occurred to me that Hazel had air magic? This prison was not as constraining for her. Why had she not come to me sooner? My gaze met hers across the table. She had that look on her face. The one that said *hurry up and figure it out, bitch.*

"You can't help me unless I ask."

Her eyes lit with amusement, but she said nothing.

"And you can't tell me anything that would help..." I bit my lip. We were still alone, but I didn't know for how much longer. "Can you answer my questions?"

She gave me a stare that said everything she was thinking. Right. No answers. I needed to know what the contract would let her do. "If I command you, as the princess of this court, will you obey?"

"Your wish is my command, Your Highness."

Okay. So I had to ask her to come to me.

"Hazel."

"Yes, Princess?"

"Clear all the halls of water so any land creatures and shifters can use them."

She raised a brow but dipped her chin. Her face said, Not bad, but you can do better.

I chewed my lip. I was certain she couldn't tell me any of Kaspar's secrets. My gut twisted at the memory of my wedding day. She had been surprised, even delighted. She had acted like she had never seen my rooms before. Had it all been a lie? If so, her words were cleverly coded to give me a message.

She couldn't tell me his secrets, so she had used that moment to tell me something important instead. She had commented on the bathroom, the way everything was as I would want it to be. She had wanted me to know he loved me. "He loves me."

Her brows flattened. Okay. Not that. I retraced the conversation. *Lock me up with hot prince, because I would live here forever.*

I looked up. "You know where your contract is." Her eyes were glowing with excitement. "You know where both our contracts are!"

FORTY-FOUR

JACK

The pain scorching my lungs evaporated far too quickly, leaving only the dull ache that accompanied my mother's gaunt face and her torn, battered body. She shouldn't be alive. That was the thought that cycled through my mind. No one could survive that. But she had. Wide emerald eyes that glowed too brightly had found mine, and, impossibly, she had called my name. It had been a feeble whisper, spoken over pale, cracked lips. Her back arched at a strange angle and the tree blooming from her chest had spiky crimson leaves. It couldn't have been a dream. Even I couldn't have envisioned a nightmare like that.

"Come on, Jack. Stand up."

Murz tugged my arm, pulling uselessly. I could no sooner stand than I could ever picture my mother any other way again. I looked up, watery eyes overflowing with tears, and he stumbled back.

"Jack," he tried again.

He took several more stumbling steps backward, and I tracked the movement, seeing only my mother's emaciated form, impaled on that blood-red tree.

My mouth fell open, a silent cry bursting to life. But it wasn't a sound that erupted from my center. Liquid fire exploded from my mouth, pelting the beach in flaming ash and sparks of white-hot fire.

Murz turned, running as fast as his legs would carry him, kicking sand up in his wake. He grunted as several sparks landed on his back and thighs, but did not stop as he bolted for the safety of the summer palace.

Red and orange flames caught on the swaying palm trees nearest the beach, and soon thick smoke drifted into the sky, blotting out the soft afternoon sunlight. My vision blurred as the torrent of heat and flames continued to pour out of me, a lifetime of pent-up anguish and rage expelling from the center of my being.

I pressed my palms into the sand as the energy drained from me, but didn't stop. Couldn't stop. The granules between my fingers melted, pooling around my hands in molten glass as my palms sank deeper, melting the sand.

I swayed, a chill starting in my stomach and leaching the fire from my veins. It wasn't enough. White smoke billowed from my nose and mouth as sparks shot out in every direction.

Distantly, I heard pounding feet. Shouts and commands to stop, but they were drowned by the utter despair that had taken hold of my soul. My mother was alive, but I wouldn't wish that sort of torture on the worst beings in any realm... except perhaps whoever had done that to her.

An icy wave washed over me, knocking me onto my back. Steam rose off me, but a deeper ache speared my lungs and chest. It was an ache unlike anything I'd ever known. Water continued to pummel me, and I choked and gasped but made no move to sit up. Perhaps they would end me. They would bring the wave down atop me and erase the visions pounding against my skull.

Water dissipated, leaving me trembling and sore. I closed my eyes and prayed I wouldn't open them again.

●→)(╰◆∩◆●●

I blinked against the harsh light and groaned, rolling onto my side and squeezing my lids tightly. Brightness filtered through a thin bit of fabric, scorching the backs of my eyes. When I opened them again, they had adjusted, but only slightly, and I squinted around the sandstone room. It was empty apart from the white sheet stretched taut above me and the bed I was lying on.

Pressing my hand to the silken sheets, I pushed myself up and bit back a moan of agony. It felt as though someone had run a knife through my insides a dozen times and left me to bleed out. A pounding headache split my head in two, and my throat tasted like ash.

"He's awake."

Lifting a hand to my head, I looked up at the blurry outline of the tanned male, his arms crossed over his bare chest. I would have been glad for my double vision, but two princely penises in my face was more than any man deserved after feeling like I had been run over by a truck.

I closed my eyes, looking away. "Water?" I croaked.

"Nita, please bring our guest water."

One of the women I had seen earlier stepped into the room, carrying a bronze bowl, and held it up to my mouth. The cool liquid slid over my lips and down my throat, and I swallowed gratefully, ducking my head when she lifted it. My mind was hazy, and sandpaper coated my tongue, but when I opened my mouth to offer Nita my gratitude, the name tasted wrong.

Prince Fero uncrossed his arms. "You were playing with magic you don't understand. That was dangerous for you and for us all."

His words were a shout against my ears, and I held my hands up to block it out. He moved into the room, sitting in the single chair in its corner. He waited as the room swam in and out of focus and I tried to regain my bearings. When the ringing in my ears stopped, I met his bright orange gaze.

"I'm sorry if I hurt anyone."

A smirk crept onto Fero's lips. "Murz will not be able to sit for a while, but no one was badly injured."

The hollow ache in my chest expanded. I looked up, and his gaze softened.

"He told me what you saw."

I said nothing. If I lived a thousand years, I'd never have the words.

He nodded, climbing to his feet. "Rest. Recover, and when you are well, we will find her."

I shook my head. Tried to tell him there was no time, that every moment we wasted, she suffered. That I wasn't sure how she was still alive, but he crossed the room, slipped through the arched door, and, before I found my voice, he was gone.

Nita, or not Nita, I thought, mind still too fuzzy to make sense of my own thoughts, refilled the bowl from a pitcher by the archway and sat beside me on the bed. She held it up and I reached for it with shaking fingers.

"Please." I swallowed around my cracked throat. "Don't wait on me."

She nodded, rose, and stepped out of the room.

Alone, with only the memory of my mother in that awful place and a hole in my chest where a well of magic had once been, I collapsed back onto the bed and closed my eyes. Images flashed across my vision, searing my retinas, and I opened them again, blinking back tears. How could I sit here, languishing in comfort when my mom was...

I sat up, pushing to my feet. Every inch of my body ached, and although I hadn't known I had a drop of magic a month ago, I was already beginning to understand the difference between physical pain and the pain of magic depletion. I was dry, my body either already healed or masking the symptoms of whatever physical limitations I had. Now, only the lack of magic chilled my veins.

The absence of pain was a gift... from my mother. She had given it to me. What did that mean for her? Did she feel her pain so I didn't have to? I swiped at my face, moving unsteadily out of the room.

In the open air palace, several arched walls and pillars crisscrossed the space, and as I passed, I saw folk sitting on beds, standing, changing, going about their normal lives, all out in the open. It was a strange contrast to the other castles I had been to in Faerie. Where Winter had been all grand rooms and long ice halls, Spring had been a maze of vines and blooming flowers. Here, it was vast and wide open, sunlight and salt-laced air spilling through every arch. No assassins or lovers in dark corners. Just the everyday life of the people who lived here.

Under different circumstances, I might have enjoyed my stay in Summer, but today, my only thought was for the two women I loved.

"Human."

My ears pricked at the recognition in that voice, and I spun around. "Grace?"

My round-eyed friend blinked up at me, her whiskers twitching. Her eyes were soft, and I wiped my cheeks again.

"Grace." The word cracked over my dry lips and she reached me faster than she should have.

I sank to my knees, the weight of everything suddenly too much. Grace's long fingers came around my shoulders, squeezing tightly.

"It's okay, Jack."

"Mom. She's..."

Grace's palm skimmed my hair, light as air. "You're almost ready to find her."

"I have to go now. She's..."

"When your party's whole and woven tight, the thorns will part and grant you sight."

I lurched to my feet, tearing from her grip. "What does that mean? Why do you keep saying it? Do you know where she is? What happened to her?"

Grace tipped her face up, gold eyes searching. "Your mother kept you safe."

The words split me open. "I don't..."

Grace held up a hand. "You cannot save her until your party is complete. Your true mate, the shifter, and the boy prince at your side. Without them, you will fail."

I opened my mouth, but Prince Fero appeared as if from nowhere and laid a hand on Grace's shoulder.

"Lady, the folk are in need of your aid."

Grace swiveled her gaze up to the prince and dipped her chin. "I am no lady, Prince."

He smiled. "To me, you will always be a lady."

She huffed, twisting out of his hold and backing up. "Fae titles that mean nothing." She twitched her whiskers, and her gaze found me again. "Gather them, Jack. Then, you will be ready to face those who have imprisoned your mother."

She blinked. Her whiskers twitched once more, and she was gone.

I inhaled a steadying breath, realizing the pain in my middle was gone. Grace, or whatever her true name was, had wrapped her arms around me, pulled me close, and restored my magic.

FORTY-FIVE

SAV

I glanced up from the stack of papers on Kaspar's desk.

I'd thought I heard something. Again. Time was ticking at a rapid pace, my heart pounding a rhythm in my chest, and with each moment we didn't find our contracts, a noose tightened around my neck. I wished I'd known how I burned away the bargain the day I killed Dane. If only it were as simple as igniting a fire in my veins and ridding myself of all the restrictive demands placed upon me, but even if I could figure out how to do it again, he had my name... and Hazel's.

With them, there was no escaping him.

"Sav." Hazel waved a silver tube in her hand. "I found something."

I moved, snatching the cylinder from her hand. I loved Hazel, but I wouldn't trust anyone with my true name for the rest of my life. I pressed my thumb against the tube and pushed. Nothing happened.

"How do you open them?"

Hazel shrugged. "The others opened for me."

I handed it back to her warily. She pushed. Nothing happened. She tried again. Still nothing.

"Let's keep looking. We can take it with us and figure it out later."

I nodded, looking at the tube. It was a match to the one my sister produced the day I signed my name, and my freedom, away, but there were several scrolls on Kaspar's shelf, hidden behind false book spines, that looked similar to one another. What if Kaspar had the true names of several fae? What if each of these was a contract with some poor soul's fate forever sealed? I slid a hand over the tops of each. Nothing. All the tubes on this shelf were sealed.

"We're taking them all."

Hazel's brow shot up, but she said nothing as I slid more than a dozen scrolls into the waterproof bag Kaspar made for me, meant to transport clothes when I traveled between Lakes and Streams and Spring. Since the night he forced me to scrub Jack's touch from my skin, I hadn't been allowed to leave.

Had he explicitly forbidden me? If he hadn't, he could at any time. I needed my contract or I'd be trapped here forever. Hazel had warned me, but I hadn't heard her. I'd chalked it up to Hazel being Hazel.

Now I could hear the plea under her words, the way she'd begged me to see past the facade she showed the world and recognize the truth. And I'd failed her.

When I'd stuffed every last tube into my bag, I looked up. Hazel's eyes were brimming with tears.

"What is it?"

She shook her head.

"Hazel?"

She stood between me and the door, and the hairs on the back of my neck rose.

I lurched for the door. She lunged, claws extending.

"I'm sorry," she breathed as sharp nails pierced my skin, pinning me to the floor. "I can't..."

Her broken words trailed off as she changed, shifting into snow leopard form and pressing all her weight into me.

I gasped around the pressure in my chest, wriggling in her hold. She bared her teeth, hot breath misting my cheeks. A tear dripped over fur, slid between white whiskers, and splattered against my neck.

I should've known Kaspar would never allow anyone to leave this room with his precious contracts. The room was unprotected, unguarded; it didn't need guards when no one who came to his court could take them.

I sucked in a shallow breath, the pressure easing slightly, and wheezed an exhale.

"Hazel." Another breath in. "If I put them back, will you release me?"

Her massive head shook. No. It was too late. I'd tried to leave, and now I'd be pinned here until Kaspar found me, trapped beneath his pet.

Pet. Hazel had called Jack her pet once. Was it another clue? Another desperate plea for anyone to save her? I'd never know now.

What would he do when he found me? Once, I'd been sure he'd release me, give me my freedom back. Now I feared I'd never known the male at all.

One thing was clear. He was a master strategist. There was no scenario where I outmaneuvered him. I'd been a fool to think I could. A prince forged in the turbulent waters of his sea court at the age of eleven, left to rule cold-hearted creatures, must've felt so alone. A piece of my heart cracked for the dear friend who so regularly sought my company on land.

What must it have been like for him, trapped by duty and obligation? Did he long for escape? Had he trapped me here with him so he no longer had to be alone? A single tear slid down my cheek.

I didn't want to empathize. Didn't want to accept there could ever be a good reason for making someone their prisoner, but he hadn't trapped me. That was the part that stung the most. He'd given me a choice, in his own way, and I'd willingly swum into his world. What must he have felt, knowing he'd finally have someone to share this prison with, only to learn I had no plans of remaining here with him?

"Rise, Hazel, and release your princess."

Kaspar's cold voice cut like ice through the room, and I inhaled my first full breath when Hazel sat back.

I scrambled to my feet, wincing at the tug in my shoulder that was only beginning to knit together. I lifted the satchel's strap up, avoiding the gashes Hazel's claws left behind, and backed up, bumping into the desk behind me.

Kaspar stalked into the room in fae form. "I knew I would find you in here eventually."

My hand tightened on the strap, my gaze never leaving his as he stopped less than a foot away. His gaze trailed the length of me, taking in the navy gown I'd dressed in for dinner. My heart beat frantically against my ribs. His eyes lingered on the blood streaking down my exposed shoulder. The wounds had healed, leaving only three red lines of drying blood. His jaw tightened and he glanced to his left.

"Hazel, you will not use force to restrain the princess in her castle. In future, any blood of hers you spill will be taken in kind."

Hazel's large emerald eyes dropped to the floor and heat flared to life in my veins. I narrowed my eyes as Kaspar's head swiveled back to me. Our eyes met and his widened just a fraction, as though he'd forgotten I was there, or perhaps he thought I blamed her for what happened. But the villain was standing before me.

His brow smoothed and he held out a hand. "Hand them over."

My grip tightened on the strap. "No."

His lips tipped up. Did he think this was a game?

The warmth in my veins exploded into fiery anger. "You can't take people's names and force them to be your puppets. That's what a monster would do." My voice softened. "I know you aren't a monster, Kaspar."

His eyes darkened, a shadow of something I couldn't name passing

215

over his features. "I am the cold, unfeeling prince. What do I care if you think me a monster?"

Some of the heat inside me cooled. His words were clipped, but his eyes were pleading, begging me not to believe them. For a moment, a fraction of a breath, I thought a sliver of my old friend might shine through, but it was gone, replaced by the glacial mask he wore when he was preparing to make the hard choices he thought no one else would.

"Hand me the bag."

My chin lifted. "You'll have to take it from me."

I lifted a hand, letting the fire in my veins ignite once more, and sparks danced to life on my fingertips.

"Will you burn me, Princess?"

He stepped closer, and the faintest exhale brushed my cheek. The space around him carried the scent of sea air and ozone.

My hand lifted, prepared to do just that, to will the stars to grant me the magic I needed to burn away our bargain, when a sound crackled in the hall. Kaspar cleared his throat, backing up a step.

He flicked his gaze to Hazel. "Go check it out."

She bounded away without a backward glance.

I held my sparking fingers out.

When he turned back to me, his gaze dropped, his expression going hollow.

"Would you truly do it?" His words were soft, nearly a whisper, and a spasm tore through my chest. I never thought I'd find myself on the opposite side of a battle from my oldest friend. *Would* I do it? My fingers trembled, some of the sparks winking out. I hated what he'd done to me, even if some twisted part of him believed he was justified in his actions, but I could never hate him.

"Please. Let me go."

A crash sounded and my gaze snapped up as a raven-haired female burst into the room, wielding a spear. I had no time to process what was happening before the weapon was flying through the air. It lodged itself in Kaspar's shoulder, knocking him back several feet, and shock ripped through me.

"Kaspar!"

I lunged toward him, fire dying as I grabbed the spear and tore it free. Indigo blood oozed from the wound, leaking down his arm, and his eyes were unfocused. Poison. It was the only thing that could've stunned him so easily.

"Sav!"

I spun around, my heart in my throat as Jack barreled into me, strong arms closing around me and pulling me against him. His fingers tangled in my hair, hugging me close, and I inhaled his wintergreen scent, something in my chest knitting together. Alive. Well. And he had come back for me.

"You came back." I'd meant to sound chiding, to scold him for risking his life to return here, but there was only gratitude in my heart.

"I'll always come for you."

I backed up, eyes wild. "He'll kill you."

Even as I said it, the moisture in the air hummed and I didn't have to turn to know Kaspar was recovering from whatever poison had struck him.

"Come on. We have to go now." Jack's fingers laced with mine and he dragged me from the room. My heart was in my throat as we ran, but a part of me wanted to turn back and check on Kaspar. Would he die? I'd wanted to escape this place, but not at the cost of his life.

Two women, bare from head to toe, their long, shining manes of hair tied back, had Hazel pinned against the wall with wicked-looking blades.

"Don't hurt her!" I screamed, releasing Jack's hand and rushing to Hazel, wrapping my arms around her fluffy neck.

"She attacked us," the female said, not lowering her dagger.

Jack wrapped an arm around my waist, but I planted my feet, putting myself between Hazel and the women's poisoned weapons.

"She had no choice. If we get her out of here, she won't be forced to follow his orders." I bared my teeth at them. The look in their eyes was menacing, but they hadn't lunged. Hazel was bunched against the wall, unwilling or unable to attack with me in the way.

"She is Sav's friend. Don't hurt her."

My mouth fell open when they dropped their knives at Jack's words.

There was no time to worry about it now, though. At any moment, Kaspar could be recovered enough to follow. If he gave Hazel the order, she'd be forced to attack. It would mean the women's deaths, and possibly Jack's along with them.

"Hazel, can you fight his control? Escape with us?"

She huffed against my ear.

No, I thought. A tear slid down my cheek. I couldn't leave her... but if her contract was among those I was carrying, I'd find a way to destroy them and free her. To free them all. I couldn't do that trapped down here.

"I'm sorry," I whispered against her soft ear.

She lowered her fluffy head, pushing me away from her, but I squeezed her tightly one more time.

"I *will* free you."

The massive snow leopard dipped her chin and turned, loping away from us.

I swiped my cheeks several times, turning back to Jack. "Let's go."

The words had barely left my lips when pressure built and the hairs on my arms rose. It was our only warning before a wall of water erupted at the end of the hall, barreling for us.

"Run!" I screamed.

Not fast enough. We turned, racing away from the wave, but it caught us, crashing over us, and in seconds, the weight of all that power pummeled me to the floor, knocking the air from my lungs. The world went black and I was swept up in a whirlwind of churning water, spinning in all directions before slamming into the stone lining the hall.

When the world settled, my lungs burning from lack of oxygen, I peered around in the flooded hall. Jack was several feet away, his eyes gaunt as though some great pain racked his body. He must still be injured, the pain immunity gone underwater. Images of his torn, ravaged body rushed me, battering me anew, but I swallowed them, attempting to quell the panic threatening to consume me.

I swam to Jack, glancing around. The only safe place would be my room. Even in Kaspar's poisoned state, he wouldn't flood my room. It wasn't close, but it was our only chance. Jack's eyes were wide, veins along his neck bulging. I had no air to spare, but he had less. Tugging him close, I pressed his lips to mine and forced what little oxygen I had left into his mouth.

He swallowed it down, some of the panic in his eyes receding, and together we swam for my room.

The hall stretched out before us and my vision darkened at the edges, my head light. My arms were sluggish and dragged through the water, some invisible force weighing me down, making it harder with each passing second to continue.

Jack glanced back, his eyes going round, and he reached for my hand, dragging me behind him as he kicked furiously for the room at the end of the hall. My lungs no longer burned, but a dull ache had started behind my eyes, and I could think of nothing I'd rather do than rest here in the tranquil water and let it lull me into a much-needed sleep.

Sleep. Sleep was what I needed. My eyes drifted closed.

We broke through the air seal, tumbling to the floor of my room, and I inhaled a sharp breath, my head exploding with pain. My lungs were filled with shards of glass. More than once, the room went in and out of focus.

A warm hand rubbed soothing circles on my back and liquid burned its way up my throat, dribbling from my lips.

"Just breathe."

Jack's steady voice stilled the raging torrent of fear coursing through me, and slowly my heart found a normal rhythm, my breathing growing less ragged.

When I could sit up without swaying, I peered around the room. We were alone. The two warriors Jack had brought with him were gone. My chest spasmed. Were they dead? Drowned in this underwater prison? I expected Kaspar would do nothing less to the fae who attacked him in his own home, and guilt buried itself in my gut. They'd come to rescue me, and it had cost them their lives.

"We have to go."

Jack stood, holding out a hand.

I took it, climbing unsteadily to my feet.

Behind me, someone stepped through the air shield and I spun around.

"Larek!"

I stumbled toward him, throwing my arms around his neck. My chest squeezed, the air struggling to come as if I was still submerged, as I gasped around the sorrow and guilt.

"I'm so sorry."

He wrapped me in a death grip, hot tears dripping onto my shoulder. "Me too."

We held each other, all the unsaid words between us circling but not yet ready to be spoken. Without him, without Yolmar, our hug was incomplete, but if we didn't leave now, Creig might have twice as much reason to hate me.

The sharp, quick bursts of air piercing my lungs solidified into full breaths and my head was clearing, bringing with it the urgency of our situation. Kaspar might not fight to keep me, but the satchel heavy on my shoulder was a prize he'd kill for, and I didn't think Jack could survive him a second time.

FORTY-SIX
FOXGLOVE

Among the group of folk settling in Summer's forest, Juniper was doing better. Her eyes were clear more often than not, and she'd climbed high into the trees, disappearing into the foliage some time ago and still hadn't returned.

Satyrs relied heavily on the wild magic of Faerie to replenish their well. Coming here might have been the best thing for her.

A cool brush of thought slid against my own, softer than the breeze stirring the leaves. *You're counting again, Foxglove.* Her mental voice was soothing. *You will not find anyone you've lost. Not tonight.*

I let the truth of that settle. *I know.* The admission was quiet, meant for myself, but with her it was hard to tell where my thoughts ended and hers began.

You can stop watching me too, she added, the faintest thread of warmth twining through the words. *I'm not going to vanish.*

I like knowing where you are, I thought back, before forcing myself to ease my focus away from her. She lingered at the edge of my awareness anyway, a steady, living presence. I could stop counting the ones I'd lost, but someone had to make sure we hadn't left anyone behind.

My gaze trailed the group as I skimmed their thoughts one by one. I believed we had retrieved everyone who survived Creig's pocket, but I checked anyway. My innate gift was powerful, and I'd rather Jack not look too closely. His gift, like Prince Fero's, was dangerous for the high fae.

Unlike Fero, though, Jack had a clear picture of our elemental gifts and could sense the exact nature of our innate gift as well. Where I could hear thoughts, Fero saw magic like colour. He could spot power and lineage at a glance, but the finer edges stayed blurred.

Jack's gift was something else altogether. It had my skin prickling and my veins icing. Not only could he tell what our innate gift was, if he looked for it, he'd find the elemental gift that rendered it useless. It wasn't Mab's gift of true name sensor, but it was close enough that he could bring us all to heel should he choose.

A stray mind hooked me and I looked for the body it belonged to. Not one of ours, too jagged and too frantic. I couldn't hear gender in thoughts, only words, and too often they wore my voice. I'd learned to live with that. What I'd never grown used to was the other kind. Minds that did something unforgivable and then repeated the same excuse until it sounded like truth. My brother's was the easiest to recognize, and the hardest to shut out.

I avoided him, and those like him, when possible. Minds like Sav's, always reminding themselves to do right, were a welcome balm to the constant chatter of self-serving rationalizations in the more vapid members of the court's minds.

I dropped to four legs and ran. The change burned like it always did, bone melding into my fox form, blood singing in my veins. When the change was complete, my connection to the land humming between me and the dirt under my paws, I stretched my legs. That magic wasn't Mab's. It was older than her courts, older than her laws, older than her crown. Gaia claimed us. Luna blessed us. And Mab had nothing to do with it.

Darting into the bushes, I followed the out-of-place mind's musings to a stream. Peering between thick foliage, I spied something I'd never expected to find in Faerie. A human.

I crouched low when her gaze swung toward me. Had she heard? I was silent. Few ever knew I was there unless I wanted them to see. Sav excluded. Her gift of sensing emotion made it impossible to hide from her, no matter what form I took.

Her eyes met mine and my blood ran cold. Impossible.

Beside her, the stream shuddered and deep navy claws pierced the surface. The woman yanked a dagger from her belt, swiping wildly, but the naiad's claws were faster, and her thumb was severed cleanly from her hand. The blade sank into grassy soil and the naiad reached for the woman with mousy brown hair and round blue eyes again, digging her claws into her shoulders and dragging her under. Her scream became a choked sputter as she disappeared below the depths.

Her thoughts were loud in her head for a few moments as, even under the water, she fought her attacker. Then, silence.

I'd never know what brought Janet Glassdon's daughter into Faerie with us. I could only assume she'd snuck in when we passed through Summer's portal, but that problem had just resolved itself.

Outside the summer palace, I trotted up the back steps. Unlike any other castle in Faerie, Summer was open, no doors to speak of and no true way to sneak in and out. Although in fox form I was far stealthier, the black of my feet and ears contrasted dramatically with the sandstone floors and walls.

At the top step, I darted into the nearest room, the mental chatter of two folk nearing. They passed quickly, neither saying a word, but their thoughts were loud. With everyone occupied with the arrival of the last remaining Spring Court refugees and Jack, the pair planned to escape to the sea for a tryst. Even in their excitement, though, one was frightened of the ocean. Of late, the prince of Oceans and Seas had let his more aggressive folk off their leashes.

More than one creature in Summer had returned with missing limbs and some hadn't returned at all. I mulled over the information, stepping out into the hall once more, and nearly collided with Nita. She had been utterly silent. In her haste to escape wherever she was rushing from, she hadn't noticed me yet and I ducked behind a woven basket.

In my nearly five hundred years, I'd never encountered a completely silent mind. Even Juniper, drugged and trapped within her own head, had thoughts. This female's shoes made more noise than her mind. Odd was an understatement.

She spun around, searching the darkness. Spying no one, she continued on light feet toward the exit. I followed.

At the sandy edges of Summer Court, she glanced over a shoulder once more and I crouched low, pressing my ears flat. I couldn't risk lifting my head over a dune to see if she'd spied me, and her silent mind left me feeling vulnerable in a way I never had before.

After several heartbeats, I dared a glance. She was gone. I scrambled over sand, pressing my nose low to the ground. She'd gone deeper into this empty stretch of forest at the edge of our camp. Following her trail, I climbed over tangles of briars that grew thicker the farther we moved into Summer's woods. Unlike the other courts, they'd never named their forest, choosing instead to leave the wild places to themselves.

Nita's scent intensified and I froze, ducking behind a fallen log. I waited, breath shallow.

Prince Fero believed the stories. Unlike most high fae, he thought of us as intruders on foreign soil. Although my brother knew the truth, a secret that had cost our line for centuries, Fero, like Sav, only had the legends told to him by the low fae who lived in and around his borders. It made him dangerous in a different way.

His magic was great and perhaps that was why he believed himself above Mab's laws, but in truth, a magic like hers, the ability to sense a creature's true name, was undeniable. If she learned he'd once colluded with the ocean prince to remove her from power, a fruitless endeavor that had ended the day he learned of Aegon's plan to use him as bait for Prince Kaspar, his life would be forfeit.

But I was no longer confident Mab lived. She had been missing for six years and in that time, no one had heard from her. She could be off world. It wouldn't be the first time she'd traveled to other realms, but she'd never left Faerie without one of her children to guard it. Not since the day she arrived and sank her claws into the land some ten thousand years ago.

Besides, who could end an immortal?

We were near the Autumn border and my nose twitched at the thick magic hanging in the air. A branch cracked and my gaze darted left. There, between two winding vines, her dark hair swung forward.

I crept across the mossy floor on my belly, ears pinned low.

She lifted a hand and tugged the vines apart, slipping through the invisible wall between Summer and Autumn and, in a blink, was gone. I hopped up, racing toward her, and slid through the tiny space between vines before they wrapped themselves tightly together once more.

It was reckless. Dangerous. But no one except members of their court had been in Autumn in years, and I wouldn't pass up the opportunity to find out what was happening inside their border.

FORTY-SEVEN

KASPAR

Pulsing heat seared my arm, radiating to my chest and slowing my heart. It was burning me from the inside, but my magic rose to quell it. The ice in my veins met the foul Summer poison and froze it before it could reach my heart, even if a part of me welcomed the release it would bring.

Sav had raised those flaming fingers, searching my face for any trace of the friend she once cared for, finding none. I had seen it in her eyes, the conviction that lived in her soul. The reason I had fallen for her all those centuries ago. In me, she had seen a monster and she would do whatever it took to rid this realm of its villains. She could not truly hurt me. I had ensured that, but if I had not used her name, compelled her not to harm me, I was no longer sure she would not have.

I had been wrong to believe she was mine. Could ever be mine. No amount of time by my side would change that. She had been angry with me. Furious. When my temper slipped, I took my frustration out on her in the bath. I had watched her scrub until her skin split and bled. The memory slammed into me now; the pink water, the raw lines along her thighs, the way her shoulders shook while I stood by. My stomach rolled. I pressed my fingers to my temple, as if I could scrub the image from my mind.

I had blamed Jack for it. For touching what I wanted, for smelling like her even when he stood across the room. I had let that fury turn me mindless. There had been a time when I believed she might forgive me for it. That thin hope died when she learned the truth. I *was* the monster. The cold prince who stalked this world, protecting my folk at all costs.

225

Each scroll she now carried held a name. A fae who had bargained with me and lost. Though I rarely called in favors, I owned them and they never forgot it. Inside her, the magic was buried, the ability to burn those contracts, but thanks to my misguided attempt to protect her from the Spring Court more than two centuries ago, she would never wield it. When Ajisai Antor, leader of the Spring Satyr clan, tricked me into giving Sav a tea meant to protect her until her twenty-fifth birthday, she had hidden the truth.

I had thought myself so clever then. A fae barely over twenty-five myself, desperate to protect the one I loved from the machinations of Spring Court royals. Ajisai had seen through my facade, my mask, and used it to stop the threat she thought Sav posed. When I understood what she had done, I demanded she undo it.

Oh, I had shown her I could not be used, but she had been stoic to the end, taking her secret with her to the grave. Now, the satyrs and I were at odds.

As the ice did its work, I called the current of my lake to me, flooding my veins and washing the vile poison away. Sav was gone. She had taken my contracts and fled with her mate. The word was like ash on my tongue. I rolled my shoulder experimentally. Pain lanced through me, but I moved. How had Jack infiltrated my court without my knowledge? How had he breached my coral walls?

Hazel had been busy clearing passageways, making routes for Sav and the others to traverse. She had ignored her duty to me to aid her friend.

I squeezed my fists.

No more.

Raising both hands overhead, I sent a wave crashing through the hall outside my office and let it flood the castle. Not Sav's room, or the other land faes'. But they would not use my halls to meet in secret, to plot and plan against me. I had ensured they were on opposite ends of the palace for a reason and Hazel would not thwart my plans again.

Shifting into kelpie form, my hooves clacked over stone as I raced down the passage. Hazel was gone, and so were Jack and Sav. Only two bloated, disfigured Summer fae floated at the end of the long hall, sightless eyes staring blankly as their long hair tangled around their bodies. I would deal with them later.

I raced for Hazel's room, stepping through the air shield and sniffing the air. Her shifter magic lingered, but she had not come here. Backing up, I continued down the hall to Ivy and Qaden's room. I had made a bargain with the prince of Summer to search thirteen lunar months or until I found his son and returned him, whichever came first. The devil was in the details. Thirteen months was a long time to keep a useful piece on my board. If I had known the shifter cat who asked me to keep his mother safe was Fero's son when I met him, I would have claimed him then.

But he did not look like Fero, and I had thought his strangely colored eyes closer to Autumn's than Summer. Fero had secrets I still could not puzzle out, but I would learn them. In time.

Pressing through the air shield into their room, I huffed great plumes of frigid air when I found only emptiness.

The thought returned. How had Jack come to Lakes and Streams? And who had he brought with him?

I did not expect her to be there, but there was only one place left to check. Galloping at speed, I reached Sav's room in minutes and stepped through. Gasps and panicked whispers came from the other side of the pondweed, and I stomped into the room, eyeing the gathered horde.

Sav stood in front of a small group of fae, hands raised, and beside her, Jack lifted flaming fingers. They looked like a unit, two halves of the same inferno, and something tightened low in my chest. Once, I had told myself that fire and water made a perfect balance. Looking at them now, I saw the truth. Only another blaze could truly meet Sav's fire. Where her magic burned wild in reds and oranges, Jack's was molten lava, so hot it whitened at the tips. I had only heard legends of Firethorn's magic, of its explosive raging power, but I imagined it might look something like this. My eyes narrowed on Hazel, transformed into fae form, clinging to an orc at the back of the room.

She was deathly pale and I scented the lingering effects of poison in the air. She had been struck by Summer's weapons too. I saw no visible injuries, but their poison was more deadly even than the squid ink Sav had nearly succumbed to all those decades ago. It did the most damage after the superficial wound closed, working its way to the heart. She did not know it, but her time remaining on this earth was fleeting.

I dismissed her, my gaze lingering on the boy shifter. He had stepped around Sav and Jack to guard the others and a flicker of amusement flared to life in me. I had him in shifted form. A cat. A tiny little thing whose claws would not hurt a toad, but his bravery was commendable. One day, I had no doubt he would be a force. And if his father truly was the prince of Summer, his magic might mirror his courage.

I shifted into land fae form, leaning back against the door frame.

"What now, Princess?"

FORTY-EIGHT

JACK

Murz had found us in Sav's room, bringing the boy with him, and Hazel had bounded through the door shortly after. Qaden was whole, wide-eyed, breathing hard, but in one piece. Ivy wasn't with him. There wasn't time to ask why. With the child here, I could leave now that I'd fulfilled the bargain with Prince Fero. But we'd delayed for Hazel. Larek refused to leave her and Sav refused to leave him. No amount of pleading from either of them had convinced him.

Sav had asked me to take the scrolls, to burn them and free her and Hazel.

It was a dirty bit of magic that had me fuming, but my anger could wait. First, I had to convince Sav to go without them. Because I wasn't leaving her a second time.

When the surge of water crashed over us as we raced for Sav's room, every ache I hadn't known I was carrying sprang to life, weighing me down. I'd leaned into Sav, needing her nearness to lend me strength. Then the air shifted, Sav's gaze snapped up, and she moved to block us all from the door. Somehow, she knew when he was near. A crawling sensation slid over my skin. I didn't like their connection. Hated how easily they sensed each other. Fire begged for release under my skin, demanded I vent the rage building every time I thought of their bargain. Their marriage.

When Kaspar stepped through the door, all that heat crackled. White-hot flames licked at my palms, jumping and sizzling in the puddles we'd left on the floor.

"Give me the bag, Princess."

Kaspar's words dripped with venom. Whatever was in that bag was

229

more important to him than anything else, even Sav. I glanced to my mate. She had both hands raised, flames lashing in a circle in her palms. A fiery wind curled around her, sending her hair flying around her face, and her amethyst eyes glowed inhumanly bright. She was wild and beautiful.

"Let us go, Kaspar."

His aquamarine gaze slid over my shoulder. I didn't have to look to know it was Hazel he was staring at. "We both know neither of you can leave without my permission." He pushed away from the door, and I lifted my hands. "I'll give Hazel her freedom if you give me my scrolls."

Sav went very still.

The flames around her stuttered, the wind she'd called faltering. Her jaw tightened. Her mouth flattened. Her eyes flicked to Hazel, then to the strap across her chest. I knew that look. I'd seen it when she was prepared to sacrifice herself for everyone else. When she'd stepped forward instead of back.

A cold weight dropped through my ribs.

She was about to choose for all of us again. About to hand herself over.

Sav's flames flickered, the air around her dying. She glanced at me, eyes widening.

"No. Sav. No."

Her fire winked out. One hand slid to the strap over her shoulder and I knew she would do it. She would trade her freedom for Hazel's.

Fuck that.

A ball of flame shot from my palm, scorching the wall beside Kaspar. "That was your one warning." I raised my arms, heat gathering in them. "Release them or the next one finds its mark."

Kaspar's icy glare landed on me. "You dare threaten me in my own castle. I could drown you all where you stand."

The ions in the air buzzed to life and a chill swept through the room. Water pressed against the walls, bowing the windows until wetness began to spray through cracks in the stone and run down the walls. I shot another ball of flame at him, calling his bluff. This time it crackled as it flew, singeing the tips of his hair floating on that invisible current.

His eyes narrowed and he stalked forward, but he didn't charge me. Instead he reached for Sav, and I fired again, scorching him. He still got hold of her, and I seized his biceps with flaming fingers. "Get your hands off her."

A guttural sound erupted from his mouth as his temper snapped and the dam burst. Water exploded through the windows, blasting me. My flames sputtered under the spray, but I poured magic into my hands, fueling the fire as I gripped him tighter, wrenching his grip from Sav.

Beside me, Qaden had shifted into a small cat, and he was scratching furiously at Kaspar's leg. He kicked the creature, who yowled in agony as he hit the wall and slumped to the floor. Hazel let out a strangled cry and rushed to him, Larek dropping beside her to inspect the small creature.

I wrapped a second hand around Kaspar's other arm and his scaled skin bubbled under my hold. Still, he didn't release Sav. She glared at him but didn't fight or try to stop him as he dragged her away, instead she tried to shrug off my hold.

I funneled more magic into my palms, feeling the heat begin to penetrate his scales and finally he released Sav, attention dragging to me. The room was submerged up to our knees, and I struggled in the rising liquid as he turned on me, shifting in a blink. In moments, my hands gripped nothing but air and I rushed him.

A massive turquoise head slammed into me, knocking me back, and I sent flame after flame at his hide, but it seemed in this form he was even more impervious to my fire. Or maybe that wasn't entirely true, because black marks charred his scales and his eyes squeezed shut as he opened his mouth, exposing two rows of sharp teeth, and snapped at me.

I narrowly dodged the bite, backing up and stumbling into Larek, who was cradling the cat in his arms.

"Jack, I can't help you. Kaspar has forbidden me from harming him." Sav was backing away from Kaspar and I was sure the only reason we weren't all already drowned was because she was with us.

I swallowed, understanding her meaning. I didn't think Sav was asking me to kill him, would ever ask that, but she wasn't opposed to hurting him to give us the chance we needed to escape. A memory flashed, my mom's hands on my shoulders in our cramped kitchen, her voice low as she told me strength was for shielding, not breaking. She'd always nudged me toward kindness instead of harm, taught me to see what I could do as something meant to protect, not destroy. She'd known the truth long before I did, knew the power I carried and what it could become if I let it.

Even if I wanted to kill him, I wouldn't. Not with Sav and Hazel trapped in his castle. In my own way I was just as trapped as they were. But just because I wouldn't kill him didn't mean I couldn't give them a chance.

Backing up, I raised my hands overhead and clapped them together, thinking of the Summer Court. I spread my hands wide and the fissure in reality slid apart, those same strange sparks sizzling at the edges. It held, as it had the last time I made one, when I'd entered Sav's room but hadn't found her.

"Larek," I said, gaze darting to him. "Take Qaden and go."

His gaze shot to Hazel and back to me. "I..."

"Go. Qaden needs medical attention."

He looked down at the creature whose chest was rising and falling slowly, then back up, searching Hazel's face. She nodded, eyes brimming with tears. "Go," she breathed.

Kaspar, in massive kelpie form, charged forward and Larek turned to run, looking back at Hazel once before he darted through the opening.

Kaspar slid to a halt, huffing cold air and narrowing his eyes on me.

"Jack, take the satchel and go through with them," Sav said. "Destroy them all and you'll free us."

I eased my hands apart, keeping my focus locked on the shimmering tear. The magic tugged at me, hungry to snap shut.

"Don't fight it, guide it," Murz said behind me. "This is advanced working. Most fae take years to hold a tear like this. Keep your mind on Summer and let the magic hold the seam."

My arms shook, but the portal stayed. The tear in space hung there between us, the view of the Summer Court clear on the other side.

"I'm not leaving you."

Sav closed the distance. "Jack, I'm calling in one of my barg–"

"No!" I cut her off before she could say the words, before she forced me to leave her behind. "I'd rather die here than leave you again."

She closed her mouth, lips pressing tightly together, and my heart soared. If she'd forced me, if she'd said the words aloud, I would have had no choice but to step through that portal or wait for the bargain to claim me. Suddenly, all her warnings made sense. Even those you loved most could use a bargain to harm you in ways you'd never imagined.

Sav dipped her chin, and I exhaled a shallow breath. She wouldn't do it.

I bristled when she stepped around me, but said nothing as she lifted a hand and held it out toward the kelpie. Kaspar backed up a step, the hate in his eyes softening. She stretched forward, fingers hovering inches from his bared teeth. "Please, Kaspar. You aren't a monster. Let us go." He huffed again, but pressed his nose into her palm, closing his eyes.

My teeth ground together, muscles in my jaw flexing, but I remained still. Hazel couldn't leave without his permission and Sav wouldn't leave without her friend. Much as that grated, I wasn't prepared to take his life if he refused her request. We needed him to agree.

Hazel stared longingly through the portal at Summer's rolling sand dunes. Her eyes glazed and I sensed it then, her innate gift. Hazel was a seer. She was searching the future, not for her own outcome but for Larek's. She wanted to be sure he would survive whatever came next, already resigning herself to a fate underwater with the prince. She trusted that Kaspar wouldn't harm her. But I didn't.

Thunder boomed through the halls and the walls shook. Sav stumbled, falling backward, and I caught her before she could hit the ground. Kaspar's eyes flew open and he jolted as another boom erupted down the hall, followed by screams. In a blink, he shifted to fae form, gaze wild.

"What is it?" Sav gasped.

"An attack." Kaspar turned away from us, but Sav called out to him again.

"Kaspar!"

He spun, facing us and a beat of silence hung. Another loud boom and the walls shook again. The water was up to our waists, but at the last crack, it began spraying from several tiny fissures in the walls, rising faster.

Kaspar searched Sav's face for a long moment. Something passed between them, something that made the fire in my veins ignite, but he nodded once. "Hazel, I release you from this place. Go."

Hazel whimpered, but I wasted no time waiting to see if the prince would change his mind. I grabbed their hands, yanking them with me through the portal as another thunderous boom sounded and water began flooding the room in earnest.

FORTY-NINE

SAV

Murz lurched through the portal behind us, tumbling to the ground in a roll.

I glanced back as we burst into Summer, and caught Kaspar's eyes. Behind him, a wall of stone crumbled in the water, spraying the room, but Kaspar didn't turn, didn't watch as his castle began to collapse. His eyes were on me, and there was so much sorrow in them that something in my chest fractured.

Jack released our hands, raised his palms over his head and pressed them together. He dragged them down the line of the portal, fighting the rush of liquid pouring through. Silvery light trailed his fingers as the tear in the world stitched itself closed. In the space of a breath, the shimmering wall was gone and we were left on sunbaked sand, dripping and cold.

A thunderclap cracked across the lake.

It hit my chest as much as my ears, a deep boom that rattled my bones. For a heartbeat I froze. Then the surface of the water erupted. Bubbles boiled up from the depths, swelling and bursting in sharp pops that sprayed the shore.

The next sound was a roar.

A wave rose, racing straight for us.

"Run," I gasped.

We spun and bolted for higher ground. My feet slipped on wet stone, sand skittering out from under me. Hazel stumbled and I grabbed her arm, fingers digging in as I hauled her up the nearest dune. On her other side, Murz caught her elbow and kept her moving, helping her push forward. Jack's hand brushed my back, steadying and shoving, all at once.

The roar grew louder, chasing us. Wind tore at my hair. Fine spray kissed the backs of my legs a moment before the water hit.

Lake water crashed over the low dunes, slamming into the spot where we'd stood moments ago. It surged around our calves before sucking back, dragging sand and pebbles with it and leaving the beach a soaked, streaked mess.

I turned, chest heaving, and stared at the churning lake. My heart clenched. I squinted into the murk, searching for any sign of who or what was attacking Kaspar's castle, the court I'd left behind, but all I saw were clouds of sediment and drifting debris.

For a long moment, nothing moved.

Then silver bodies rolled up from the depths, breaking the surface and floating on their sides. A small school of them, fewer than a dozen, gleamed in the weak light.

My breath caught.

I scanned the water for any other shapes. Any flash of movement. Any hint of Ivy. She couldn't survive a castle with no air.

When no more bodies surfaced and the lake stilled, I exhaled a slow breath through my nose. I hadn't known any of Kaspar's silverfish by name, having had little interaction with the non-shifter folk in Lakes and Streams, but I felt each of their losses just the same. Was this what it meant to be responsible for the lives of others? To carry them in your soul even when you didn't know their names?

I sent a prayer to Gaia that Kaspar would defeat his enemy. I knew in my heart that we were no match for him. If he'd wanted us dead, any of us, we would be. He wouldn't have killed me, but Jack... I had no doubt he'd left him alive for me. Another piece of my heart cracked and fell to the bottomless depths of my soul.

Whoever had attacked, he'd end them. He didn't need me for that. What he needed was his tether to mercy, and without me, I feared it would break.

Jack laced his fingers through mine, tugging me toward Summer's castle. Hazel stumbled a few paces ahead of us, saying nothing, her face pale and her lips trembling. Murz stayed close to her, matching her pace as we climbed the rise.

Ice leeched into my veins the moment we crested the hill and Summer's castle came into view. I'd escaped one tyrant who held my name, one I once thought I could trust, only to be thrust into the court of another I trusted far less. Prince Fero might not hold every syllable of my true name, but he still had my first name, and it was enough to make my skin crawl. Centuries ago, before I knew what my innate gift was, before I knew Fero could borrow others' gifts, he'd used mine against me and dragged my true name from my lips.

He'd never spoken it aloud, but I'd avoided him at all costs. On the few occasions he came to Spring after my sister's betrothal and wedding, I'd made myself scarce.

Ahead of us, Hazel and Murz continued toward the castle while Jack and I slowed behind them.

I stopped moving, forcing Jack to halt with me. He spun around, searching my face. "What is it?"

I looked down, grateful that through it all, I'd managed to hang on to the satchel. "My contract. I have to burn it." I swallowed. "Let's go to Winter."

Jack's hand tightened in mine. "Sav." My grip loosened on his fingers as I stepped back. "Fero's been helping us. I'm not saying we can trust him, but everyone's there. And..." He tugged me forward gently. "My mom."

I inhaled sharply. "You found her?"

He nodded. "I'll tell you everything, but we have to hurry."

My hands were clammy and I released his, wiping my palm on the wet fabric of my gown. Up here, under the harsh sun, I felt oddly overdressed. It had seemed like it was nearing dark below, but the sun still hung in the sky, scorching us the way it did on Earth. Perhaps Faerie and Earth were more alike than I thought. Was it my imagination, or was the air more humid here than it had been the last time I'd visited?

The scent of rain hung in the air and I could swear it would begin at any moment. But rain... in Summer?

It didn't matter now. Jack's mom was alive and he'd found her. We had to get her back. My marriage contract could wait, for now. First, we'd find Aconite. Would she know where Mab was? And did I still want to find her, if everything I'd learned was true?

-◆→(◡◆∩◆●●-

I ran my fingers through damp locks, my heart stuttering every time feet marched past my door. In Summer, it was wide open and only a thin sheet offered any sense of privacy. Jack hadn't wanted to leave my side, but I needed a moment. To collect myself. To breathe, to process all the emotions beating against my chest.

I wouldn't forgive Kaspar for what he'd done. Ever. But I was afraid for him, for the folk I'd sworn to protect when I took those vows, and up here, free of his prison, I could admit he had a right to be furious with me for the way I'd used him. Still, I never could've imagined how many secrets he'd kept from me. Hazel. All the other contracts he hoarded in his underwater castle. The emotions he hid from the world... from me.

Might things have been different between us all those centuries ago if he'd told me the truth? But it was too late now, and there was no space left in my heart for the creature he'd become. I only hoped we could forgive each other one day.

"Princess?"

I stiffened, my fingers stilling in my wet hair. As with the time we'd crossed paths in the woods a few weeks ago, a lifetime ago, his magic pressed against me, suffocating in its strength. "Yes?"

"May I speak with you?"

I chewed my bottom lip. I'd promised myself I would listen to him. Even gone so far as to seek his aid. But that was before. My raw, scraped skin had healed quickly, but it left a different wound, one that wouldn't heal with fae magic. Now that I was here, forced to face another male in possession of my true name, ice chilled my veins.

But I needed to speak with him. To exchange information. He'd sworn he wasn't Mira's killer. He'd lied for me and protected me when the Autumn prince tried to kill me all those centuries ago, but his motives were as unclear to me today as they'd been in the months leading up to my twenty-fifth birthday. And I wasn't sure who I could trust anymore.

"I need a moment."

I could climb out the stone window hovering just a few feet above me. Escape to the forest. But Spring was gone. Where would I go? And I wouldn't leave Jack and Hazel behind.

Running my fingers through the final strands of my damp hair, I straightened the loose tunic an ewe had brought me. After towel-drying my body and hair, I'd slipped it on and exhaled a soft sigh. It was gorgeous fabric, devoid of the adornments found in Spring and Winter. Simple, yet elegant.

My thoughts strayed to Fero's revelation at Summer's border a few weeks ago. How different might life now be if I'd known about his proposal? If I'd accepted? My magic wouldn't have been bound. I'd never have gone to Earth, met Jack. A stone settled in my stomach, hollowness threatening to rise up and swallow me. I hardly knew Jack and already I couldn't imagine life without him. Even now, his absence left me cold and empty.

Sliding the thin sheet aside, I stepped out into the wide-open corridor and looked up, meeting bright orange eyes. They danced with amusement and a small smile touched his mouth. "Summer attire suits you."

My lips flattened into a thin line. "What did you need to speak with me about?"

He mirrored my expression, indifference painting his face. "I'd thought you would show some gratitude for my rescue efforts."

"Jack rescued me." I crossed my arms over my chest.

"Ah. But who saved Jack?"

My mouth hung open, but I recovered quickly, uncrossing my arms and stepping around the prince as I attempted to collect my thoughts. I hadn't asked Jack how he escaped Kaspar's castle. Hadn't realized someone had helped him. But of course they had. Jack couldn't have made the swim to the surface on his own, and Kaspar would've had his naiads patrolling. Any one of them would've attacked Jack the moment he fled the castle.

But the portal, the portal I still needed answers for... hadn't he simply made one of those when he left?

I spun around. "Jack rescued himself."

"Sav." I glanced past Fero, spying Jack's large form striding toward us. He stopped beside me, gaze tracing my outline, checking for any lingering injuries. I did the same, finding him intact. "He's telling the truth."

"Prince Fero," the prince grumbled.

I blinked, glancing between the two males. Were they... friends?

My attention returned to the prince. "Truly? You saved him?" I arched a brow. "Why?"

"Sav." Jack laced his fingers through mine, tugging me closer to him. "He pulled me out of Lakes and Streams. He's the one who gave Creig and the others a place to stay."

My gaze shot to Fero. "Have you? Done all that?" My mind snagged on the rest of Jack's words and I swiveled to face him. "They're here? Juniper?" I swallowed. "Creig?" An ache burst to life in my chest. Yolmar's grinning face blossomed to life in my mind, his infectious laugh, and the heaviness in my chest sank deeper. Creig was here and I needed to see him. To hug him. To mourn with him. To beg him not to take his revenge on Jack.

I released Jack's hand, backing up, but Fero's words stopped me.

"General Creig has left. He returned to Earth to gather what remained of his free army."

A tear slipped from my lashes and I wiped it away. I owed him so much more than our last parting, but I wasn't sure when we'd get that chance. "And Juniper?"

Fero nodded. "Come. I'll take you to see them."

We reached the edge of Summer Court, a border of pines rising into the distant sky, rimming the sandy dunes, and a small, broken sound slipped out of me when a mane of golden curls swiveled, matching eyes meeting mine.

She stood.

For a heartbeat we stared at each other across the space. Her skin was sun-warmed instead of sallow. Color sat high on her cheeks. Her eyes were bright, alive, not the flat, glassy stare I'd grown used to since we'd rescued her from Dane.

She rushed toward me and my feet moved too, but we both stopped a few strides apart, catching each other's expressions, wary on instinct.

"Will you try to kill me?" I asked.

She grinned, and it was all teeth and mischief, the way it used to be. "The urge to stab you is strong, but I think I have it under control."

A laugh bubbled up my throat, half sob, half relief. I closed the last of the distance and threw my arms around her. She squeezed me so hard my ribs protested and I let out a shaky sigh against her shoulder. She was solid. Warm. Herself.

I pulled back, hands on her arms, drinking her in. The spark in her gaze. The curve of her mouth. No vacant fog. No faint tremor from the magic that had hollowed her out.

"You're better," I breathed. "Foxglove helped you?"

Her cheeks darkened and she smiled, softer now. "He did. But..." She glanced over her shoulder, as if she could see all the way back to the Summer palace. "Grace has been unwinding some of the blood magic's hold."

"Blood magic?"

Juniper released me, tucking a stray curl behind her ear. "Grace," she laughed. "I've never met a puca with a name before. She can sense magic in the blood. It's what makes pucas so great at healing."

I swallowed. There was only one court that practiced blood magic. Autumn. But how could their magic have gotten into the hands of a human who hated the fae?

"We mostly have it under control now, but promise me if my eyes go glassy, don't ask questions, just run."

I nodded, glancing at the puca who'd come up beside us. Slowly, others from the missing pocket gathered around us. It was a small crowd. Far smaller than the number we'd left behind. I searched their faces. Qaden's eyes were red and puffy and I knelt before him. "I'm sorry for what happened to you in Lakes and Streams."

His lip quivered. "He'll pay for what happened to Mother."

I glanced up and Juniper nodded. My heart constricted. He wasn't certain. He couldn't be. But what other fate could've met my old healer? I squeezed his hand. "It wasn't Kaspar's fault. He lost many in his court to whoever attacked."

The boy lifted his chin. "He shouldn't have brought us down there."

I longed to wrap him in my arms and comfort him. He was so young to have lost a mother. I knew the feeling, but even I hadn't been as young as he was now. Perhaps only Kaspar could truly understand.

Jack cleared his throat behind me. "I don't want to rush you."

I swallowed. Jack had been so patient, knowing his mother was somewhere out there. "Of course." I stood, grabbing his hand, but Juniper touched my arm. I turned back to her. "What is it?"

She looked down, meeting Grace's large, round eyes—then lifted her gaze back to me. "Before you go, there's something I must tell you. Something you'll need."

FIFTY

JACK

My chest ached for my mother, even as relief surged at Sav's return. As much as I wanted to give her this time with her friend, this reunion, they hadn't seen my mother.

"We don't have time."

Sav glanced back at me and nodded. "It will have to wait, Juniper. I'll be back."

Grace snatched Sav's arm, holding her fast. Sav yelped, staggering, but Grace held firm. My friend's strange, familiar eyes met mine. "She must do this, Jack."

I tried to still my hands. They didn't listen. My mother's body on that tree kept flashing behind my eyes—gasping, blinking slow, fading right in front of me.

But the urgency in Grace's voice raised the hairs on my neck. If she knew something we didn't, I couldn't afford to ignore it.

Sav looked to me. Waiting. If I'd learned anything in Faerie, it was that I knew nothing about this place or its rules. We'd need all the help we could get if we hoped to rescue my mother.

I nodded, squeezing Sav's hand. She held my gaze a beat longer, then turned back and dipped her chin.

Juniper led us to a massive oak deep in Summer's forest. Its roots were gnarled and moss-covered, spreading over the earth like tendrils of smoke seeking air. Juniper backed up, bent furry knees, and leaped. In moments, she was high in the branches.

I tipped my head back to track her. Overhead, she grabbed a thick vine, one that shimmered more than the others. It twisted around a single branch, its leaves catching the light in metallic flashes of green. She reached into a pocket and produced a small knife. The last embers of evening sun sparked off the blade, casting it in orange light, making it look like the vine itself was burning.

Sav's fingers tightened around mine. I inhaled her scent, honeysuckle and rain, grateful she was by my side again, her warmth and nearness soothing some of the raw ache of the past several days.

Juniper dropped from her perch, landing hard on twin hooves. In her hand, she held a length of the vine, severed cleanly on both ends. She stalked toward us and, this close, I saw the thick, sharp thorns protruding from it. Each one gleamed pale at the base, darkening to brown at the tip.

"My mother," Juniper said as she sliced one of the thorny tips off, "gave you a tea when you were about to turn twenty-five."

Sav opened her mouth. She blinked. "Kaspar gave me a tea."

Juniper nodded, eyes narrowing. "Indeed. And my mother gave it to him. He killed her for it when he learned what it truly did." Sav's throat bobbed. "It was meant to block your magic."

Sav gripped my hand harder, leaning into me, eyes wide, but she didn't say anything.

"Our clan feared what your magic could do." Juniper's gaze slid to Grace. "All low fae who felt it coming did." Grace dipped her chin in acknowledgment. Juniper held out her hand, and Sav stared at it, shoulders squaring. "But I've grown to know you."

"So you were spying on me."

Juniper smiled. "I was sent to watch you, yes." She dropped her hand when Sav didn't reach for it. "Even with the tea in your blood, Ajisai feared you'd one day harness a magic too powerful for one of your kind to wield. Before she died, she tasked me with making sure you never had access to it."

Sav's brows shot up. "But I only met you on Earth. Ajisai Antor died two centuries ago."

Juniper's eyes darkened, her grip tightening on the vine. "A satyr never forgets."

The words carried enough menace that the magic in my veins flared in response. I took a step forward, but Sav laid her free hand on my chest. "She isn't upset with me. It's Kaspar she's cursed."

Juniper dipped her chin. "True. I've made my bargain with the stars."

Magic swirled in the air and I tasted, or maybe sensed, Juniper's. She had earth magic. It was similar to Larek's but tinged green, calling to roots and leaves instead of rocks and stone. I understood what Fero meant about recognizing a signature. I'd know it if I felt it again.

"High fae weren't meant to have wild magic. Wild magic belongs to the folk who are native to Faerie." Juniper bit out the words. "But Grace has seen the future, and if we're going to survive it, you have to have access." She lifted her hand again. "Give me your hand, Princess."

Sav lifted her fingers and I tensed beside her. Juniper's words were sharp as blades, and I was half sure she meant to use them. Grace knew my mother though. She'd promised my mother she'd look after me, and somehow, this felt like part of that promise.

Sav's outstretched hand reached toward Juniper, and Juniper raised one of the sharp points to meet it. "Prick your finger."

"Do it to me first." I stepped in front of Sav, putting myself between them. No matter what Grace said, the satyr had malice in her heart. Toward Kaspar, Sav said, but that wasn't all. She hated me too, and maybe my mate, for leaving her in Dane's compound. I wasn't ready to trust that she wouldn't turn that anger on Sav.

Juniper's amber eyes narrowed, her gaze swiveling to me. "You don't need it."

"I don't trust you."

Her lip curled and the magic in my veins rose to meet the challenge. I straightened, let go of Sav's hand, and held up my finger. The absence of her touch, even for that brief moment after being separated so long, left a chill on my skin, but I ignored it and met the satyr's slit-pupiled stare.

Soft fingers wrapped around my wrist and my blood heated at the contact. "Jack. She won't hurt me."

My gaze dropped to Sav's hand, warm on my arm, then lifted to her face. She smiled softly. I'd half expected her to chastise me for doing the wrong thing again, but she looked genuinely touched that I'd offered to be the guinea pig. My heart kicked, beating against my ribs as it swelled in response to that smile. For me.

Crinkles formed at the corners of her bright amethyst eyes and, for a moment, I was lost in them.

"I'll be okay." She turned toward Juniper and held up a trembling hand. I felt her magic rise, ready to shield her from any threat.

Before I could argue or try to pull her back, she pressed her fingertip down onto the thorn. Blood welled at once, bright against her skin, and she lifted her hand again.

Juniper's gaze snapped to the bead of red. She rotated the vine, angling the cut thorn so the thick, honey-colored sap dripping from it fell onto Sav's wounded finger. It fell once, twice, three times.

"That's enough, Juniphera." Grace, who'd been silent until now, reached for Sav's hand and tugged it toward her. She pressed her lips to Sav's bloody fingertip, now smeared with resin. Light flared from Grace's mouth and glitter rained down, dusting the mossy roots at our feet.

I watched, throat tight, as a glowing streak of warm light flared at Sav's fingertip, then shot up her palm, over her wrist, and along her arm. It raced for her heart and I wrapped an arm around her waist as she stumbled, catching her as she collapsed into me.

"What did you do?" I sank to my knees, cradling her head in my lap as her eyes slid closed. "What did you do to her?"

I skimmed a hand down Sav's burning cheek, brushing strands of auburn hair from her face. Her eyelids fluttered violently and her breathing went shallow. "Sav? Can you hear me?"

I pressed two fingers to her throat, counting her racing pulse. Unlike the fae who'd been injured in Faerie and slipped into some slow, drifting coma, Sav's heart hammered, and mine matched its frantic pace.

I looked up, eyes narrowing on Juniper. "Fix it," I growled. Juniper's angry glare had gone slack, her face softening into something like fear, and my heart jerked in my chest. I turned to my friend. "Grace. Please help her."

The puca knelt beside me and rested a hand on Sav's forehead. Sav shuddered and my blood ran cold.

Grace looked up, letting her hand fall. "Sav isn't like any other. She was chosen by Gaia to be a vessel, a bridge between our two kinds. She carries high fae blood, but her magic belongs to the land." She spread her fingers, taking in the forest and everyone in it. "No single being could hope to contain so much magic."

The words hit like bullets to the chest, each one punching through something vital. I looked down, fingers pressed over Sav's pounding heart. I'd been right not to trust the satyr, but Grace... Grace had been my friend for years. She'd said my mother sent her. I looked up, vision blurring. "We have to help her. I can't. I can't."

"She won't die, child. She'll mend what's been broken."

"What do we do in the meantime?" My voice didn't sound like mine.

"She needs rest," Grace said, nodding toward the distant glow of Summer's castle through the trees. "Let her sleep. When the magic settles, she'll wake."

I slid my arms under Sav and lifted her. She burned against my chest, limp and heavy, her head lolling against my shoulder. Hazel fell into step beside me without a word as we started toward the palace. Juniper and Grace stayed in the clearing, their shapes swallowed by shadow and firefly light.

When we reached the guest room, I laid Sav down as gently as I could. Hazel took the chair, her fingers closing around Sav's like she could tether her here by will alone.

"You should sleep for a bit," I said. "I'll stay with her."

Hazel's jaw worked. "If you let anything happen to her, I'll gut you."

"Fair," I rasped.

She squeezed Sav's fingers one more time, then pushed to her feet and slipped from the room. I settled beside Sav on the bed, laced my fingers through hers, and let out a breath I felt like I hadn't taken in days. She was here. Warm. Breathing. Close enough that some tight, frayed part of me finally loosened. I counted her heartbeats, letting the steady rhythm pull me back from the edge, and for the first time since we were torn apart, I let myself rest beside her.

FIFTY-ONE

CREIG

Earth reeked of smoke and wet iron. I'd forgotten that. Or maybe I'd just tried to bury the place where Yolmar died from my memory.

Icy wind whipped off the frozen lake, cutting through flesh and bone. I stood at the shore and let it take what it wanted. Breath steamed in the dark. Somewhere far behind me, a road hummed with human engines, the steady thrum of a world that covered its tortures with sickly sweet perfume and rotting trash.

Yolmar should've been beside me. He would've laughed at my plan; told me I was growing too old for such schemes. He would have shared a private joke with Larek, and Larek would've shoved my shoulder and convinced me not to go through with it. I let the memory sit in my chest until it hurt.

Even as babes, Yolmar and Larek wailed if parted, curling together under the thistle blanket Shel wove for them. Years later, they'd lie the same way, pressed close, listening to Sav tell tales that always ended in victory for Spring's army, no matter the foe.

I raised them to stand for those who weren't strong enough to stand for themselves. To fight when the fight found them. Could I fault them for doing just that? Yolmar followed my rules into the dark and didn't come back. That was on me. Not Sav. Not the boy she brought with her. *Me*.

Still, when I saw Jack, Dane's face cut into a different jaw, that same penchant for darkness in him, I wanted what was owed. Blood for blood. That was the law of Faerie.

But Sav loved him. And I—Gaia help me—loved her. Even furious,

249

even hollow from a grief I knew would never leave me, I couldn't raise a hand against her. She was like a daughter to me. But Jack... Wasn't.

"Your fault," I told the black glass of the lake. The wind stole the words.

I'd left Summer without a farewell before I did something I couldn't take back. Now, all that was left for me was the mission. Humans were still here; cruel as ever. There were fae who still needed my help. Folk in hiding, ready to carry out my command. And I wouldn't leave them to be captured. Tortured. Humans had caged us once. They'd try again.

I walked the shoreline until my feet were numb, with only the cold and my memories for company. The ice groaned where it met the rocky shore. Stars hung low, a faint reminder of the faelight that twinkled in Faerie.

Sound stilled around me and the hairs on my arms rose. Shadows pooled, gathering in anticipation of her arrival, just as they sometimes did for the Prince of Lakes and Streams. The air froze, burning my lungs, and I knew I'd found her.

The outline of a creature white as a ghost, yet made of nightmares, solidified in the black mist swirling above her frozen lake. Onyx eyes, set beneath snowy lashes, met mine. Ice coated my brows as the air became impossibly colder.

"Another mortal come to offer false bargains?" Her voice was low, but the magic lacing it was enough to send several winged creatures scattering into the night sky.

I stepped into the moon's silver light. "I'm no human." I flexed my fingers at my sides, prepared to reach for my axes. Not that I believed it would do much good against a creature who was more magic than flesh.

"Lies taste the same no matter the mouth, General." She drifted closer and the ice prickling the air leeched into my skin. Or perhaps it was that she remembered me after all this time. "He promised me a name. He died with it in his throat. I am owed a name."

"Who?" I whispered.

Snowflakes began their lazy descent, obscuring my view as she stilled before me. "The human. *Dane.*" She bit his name out as though it tasted vile on her tongue.

I flinched. Dane had tricked The Wraith? He had been more dangerous than I could have fathomed. "It seems we share a common enemy." I let the wind carry away the heat from the words. "He—" I choked on the next words. "Took my son from me."

Her mouth stretched wide in a silent scream of agony and I braced myself for her banshee's cry. It didn't come. Instead, she lifted her chin after a few seconds. "There is nothing worse than losing a child."

My heart cracked, the memory of Yolmar's broken body, laid out on my table, scratching the backs of my eyelids. I blinked rapidly, clearing it away. I would not remember him like that. I tried and failed to replace the image with those of him laughing, singing, dancing, but try as I might they didn't come.

"I want blood." I seethed, bitterness coating my tongue.

The Wraith frowned. "You cannot have it, bound as most folk are from harming humans." She made a slicing motion through the air.

My mouth bent into something resembling a smile. Not truly. For that would never come again. "I'm not bound and neither are you."

She was quiet long enough for the wind to change direction, sending thick flakes of snow out over the vast, black lake. In that silence Yolmar's laugh tried to find me and failed. I held still and let that hurt, too.

"You wish to make a bargain?" Her words were laced with enough menace that I wasn't entirely sure she would agree.

"I won't demand anything of you." My temper flared hot. I let it burn. Let her see my rage. "If you choose to fight with me, you do it because you want to see them pay as much as I do."

A flicker of emotion was there and gone in her pitch-black eyes.

"I can't give you Dane," I said, and the truth of that scalded. "And if I could, I'd take that life myself. But we can stop the others. Put an end to their violence."

"Vengeance," she said.

"Retribution," I corrected, and didn't bother to soften it when she tilted her head like she'd caught me in a lie. "Call it what you want. You and I both know the difference is just where you're standing when the blood hits the snow."

For the first time, the biting chill abated.

"You would use me," she growled.

"I would stand beside you." The words came out rough. "And when the day comes where I decide to lay a blade at Dane's son's neck, I'll be the one to bear it. Not you." Sav's face flickered in my mind—the way she looked at my boys as though they were family. The thought cracked something in my chest, but I pushed it down.

She glided closer until the edge of her shadow kissed my boots.

"Let us take what is owed then." The Wraith gathered her shadows like a cloak, blackened feet lifting as she stepped off the ice of her lake for the first time in more than two hundred years. Gnarled toenails dug into the snow, sending fissures racing over the ice. It was a glamour, one she wore to hide who she once was. She chose to show the world the version of herself she believed she was now that her only child was gone.

I had never understood that pain until now. If I could don a glamour, show the world the monster I had become, I would be the most terrifying creature the humans had ever known. But glamours were reserved for the high fae and those few creatures whose magic was so great it could take many forms.

I closed my eyes and saw Yolmar's smile. When I opened them, only ice and shadow remained.

FIFTY-TWO
HAZEL

Rough sandstone scraped the bottoms of my feet as I padded down the long corridor of Summer's palace. We'd only been here a handful of hours, and the quiet still felt wrong after drowning walls and the memory of a collapsing castle.

I had attempted to sleep, as Jack suggested, but oblivion wouldn't come; every time I closed my eyes I saw breaking stone and silver bodies floating in dark water. Assassins swimming the halls of Lakes and Streams bent on ending me. I needed something to take my mind off the terrors behind my lids.

Beneath the cold rock and torch smoke, his scent cut through everything. Midnight and sorrow, with a hint of fall leaves crushed underfoot. The sorrow was new. It hadn't been there the first time we met in his hidden pocket of Faerie.

What might it have been like to have a hidden pocket of my own for nearly a decade? To escape my duty and the bargain I was forced into at birth. I would never know. No one had ever offered me refuge. Or shown me a way out.

Sliding the curtain aside, I slipped into the room. Larek jerked up, a dagger in each hand, eyes wild. His black gaze crashed into mine and silence hung between us for a moment before he slid the blades back into their sheaths at his waist.

His skin was pale, a sickly-sweet scent mingling with his sweat. The poison was mostly gone, but enough lingered that I knew he would be weakened for some time from its effects. I'd only ingested a fraction of the tainted blood, and it had nearly killed me. Without Kaspar, my jailer—my savior—I would be dead.

My hand came up, running absently over my chest, the memory of the dream that had woken me resurfacing. But was it a dream? The Summer assassin's poison-tipped blade had only grazed flesh through all that fur. I'd been so sure none of the poison had found its way into my bloodstream. But the dream suggested otherwise.

Just a dream, I told myself again.

"Are you alright?"

I blinked. Larek's voice was scratchy, and dark lines still marred his throat where he'd been strangled by the ogre in their struggle. He should have healed by now. It had to be a side effect of the poison.

"I had a dream."

Larek lifted his thin sheet, and I padded to the bed, sliding in beside him. He drew me in until my back fit flush to his chest, and my shoulders relaxed.

"Do you want to tell me about it?"

I swallowed, pressing myself against his warmth. As a shifter from the Winter Court, my blood ran hot, but he was a furnace. Winter was bitingly cold, and fires burned at all hours, but Summer was a different sort of cold in the deep hours of the night. Its chill leeched into my bones, draining me and making me shiver. The mattress dipped as he shifted closer.

"I have dreams too. About—"

I twisted in his hold, lifting, and my lips found his, swallowing his words. My tongue slid between his teeth, curving to meet his, drawing a groan from his throat. I smiled into the kiss. He would have spoken about his brother, his other half. He would have given voice to the nightmares that plagued his soul. No good came of words.

I pulled him in, deepening the kiss. He rolled us smoothly until I was straddling him, and my tail slid around, parting my dress and tugging the fabric out of my way so our skin was touching.

I broke our kiss, dropping my lips to his chest, trailing lower as my fingers found the buckles crisscrossing his midsection and waist and began to undo them.

"Hazel."

I ignored his inquiring tone, working faster. In my experience, the hesitation never lasted. It was always just a pause—long enough to pretend restraint before taking what I offered. I let the leather bands strapped with knives slide over Larek's scarred chest and focused all my effort on the belt at his waist.

He caught my hands and stilled them. I lifted my mouth from his muscled abdomen, glancing up. His dark eyes were serious, devoid of the lust normally staring back at me. Ice slid down my spine. Why was he looking at me that way? As if he didn't want... me.

I sat up, sliding back and wrapping my arms around myself.

He didn't want me.

But he'd made his interest clear the moment we met. I blinked furiously.

"Hey. I'm sorry. I just..." He reached for me, but I jerked back.

"It's fine." I slid off his lap, twisting as I dropped my feet over the side of the bed.

Strong arms came around my waist, and I stiffened. Hot breath puffed beside my ear and his warmth pressed against my back. "Hazel. Don't go."

A tear slid down my cheek as confusion rattled my thoughts into a jumbled mess. Only one male had ever rejected my advances, and I'd known he would before I ever teased him. This male was sending so many mixed signals my head spun. What else could he want from me? I was no good for anything else. No one's companion.

Larek's lips brushed the shell of my ear, and a shiver ran down my spine. "Just... lie with me."

I spun around to face him and searched his face. In his gaze I saw only sincerity... and sadness. My chest swelled, a painful ache blooming to life. Perhaps he wasn't aware of my situation. It was possible he didn't know I couldn't give him anything other than my body. I bit my lip.

"I can't give you what you want."

Carefully, he smoothed my hair behind my ear, his touch feather-light. The pad of his finger grazed my cheek. "I don't want anything but your company." His eyes met mine and he smiled. It was weak, and it must have cost him a great deal. "Let me be the one to offer you comfort. Would that be okay?"

Hot tears slid down my cheek, and I wiped them away. No one had ever made such a declaration. No one had ever cared enough. I nodded, and he leaned back, tugging me with him. He held me close, steady as a wall, and I laid my head on his slowly rising and falling chest.

"We don't have to talk. Sleep. I'll keep watch."

My eyes fluttered closed, his slow, steady heartbeat thrumming against my ear and warmth stretching through my softening limbs as the world went dark. Somewhere above us, Summer's palace settled into silence, the night pressing close around us, granting a few stolen hours of peace.

FIFTY-THREE

SAV

Dark, twisted memories dragged me under, all of them circling my sister. She'd been missing for more than two weeks. A crown of thorns. Wedding silk soaked in blood. Sage's hand slipping from mine as shadows swallowed her whole. We'd only had a few hours to rest, and even then, sleep offered no mercy.

I jerked awake with a gasp. Rough sheets rasped against my skin. Pale stone arched overhead, unfamiliar and too bright, and every muscle ached like I'd been torn apart and sewn back together wrong. The last thing I remembered was forest loam under my knees and golden sap burning through my veins.

"Hey. Easy."

Jack's voice anchored me. His fingers were wrapped tightly around my hand, knuckles white. I twisted toward his warmth, finding his burning gaze fixed on my face, and my heart gave an involuntary tug.

"You passed out," he said softly. "Grace said you would wake when the land finished healing you." He brushed a stray curl back from my face. "You've been out for a while."

Heat flared in my chest, some of it magic, some of it him. Was this how life would be now? Someone always there when I stumbled. Someone looking at me with so much adoration it hurt. It was everything I'd never let myself want, and so much more.

"You're awake."

Hazel stood in the doorway, hair mussed, eyes wide and shining. She crossed the room in three strides and caught my free hand in both of hers. "Don't you ever do that again."

I choked on a laugh, half sob, half relief. "I'll add it to my list of bad habits."

Behind her, Nita, one of Fero's house attendants, stumbled to a halt in the doorway, the tray in her hands giving a soft, startled clatter. Her eyes blew wide as they flicked from me to the other two, then back again.

As Nita's gaze bounced from me to Jack to Hazel, Hazel's eyes went glassy and distant.

My heart picked up speed. I'd seen her like this once before—eyes distant, breath caught in her throat.

"Hazel?" I pushed up on my elbows. The room tilted, but I forced myself upright. "Are you okay?"

She blinked hard, focus snapping back to me. "I'm fine. I just..." Her jaw clenched. "I need some air."

She squeezed my fingers, then let go. "I'll be back," she said, more to herself than to us, and slipped past Nita into the hall.

Nita ducked her head, shuffled in to set the tray on a low table, then backed out again, letting the curtain fall closed behind her.

I bit my lip, caught between wanting to go after Hazel and letting her breathe. Kaspar's castle had left its marks. I sank back against the pillows. She'd come to me when she was ready.

Jack didn't try to stop Hazel. Didn't ask questions I couldn't answer. He only stayed, his hand still in mine, like he could keep me tethered by touch alone.

Two fae still held my true name.

Kaspar. And Fero.

The thought tightened around my throat, sharp and ugly; different prison, same fear. In Kaspar's castle, I'd learned there were far worse things than death. Stripped of my ability to fight back, to defend myself, to use my gift, I'd finally understood what it meant when someone held that much power over you.

Sage had lived with that kind of leash for two hundred and sixty-five years.

And I'd been so busy surviving that I'd let myself forget what it must feel like to breathe with someone else's hand around your throat.

A soft rap sounded at the doorway, knuckles against stone, and I looked up.

Prince Fero leaned in, assessing me with bright orange eyes.

"May I enter?"

My gaze shot to Jack. Surely, with him here, Fero wouldn't attempt anything. But try as I might to banish memories of Kaspar's cruelty, now that I was free, they seemed determined to drag me back down with him.

Fero stayed where he was, filling the frame, waiting for my answer.

What answer could I give him? I couldn't strip my name from his memory the way I could with Kaspar. Our contract's magic would erase Kaspar's hold when the scroll burned. Fero had no such leash. He'd used my own gift against me, pried my name from my lips. There was no undoing that.

"Yes. Enter."

He stepped into the room and Jack's shoulders stiffened.

"I wish to speak with you—"

"Would you consider a bargain?" I cut him off before he could say more. Before he could shape my name on his tongue. We hadn't had a chance to finish our last conversation, but I knew what I needed from him now. I could compel him, use my gift, but he could do the same to me. Better to set the terms myself. "If you truly want to mend things between us."

"I did try."

I swallowed. As I'd suspected. He would have married me to give us equal footing. I didn't want to think him chivalrous. Not when I still wasn't sure if he was Mira's killer. Who else could have torn her heart out and left her strewn across his beach like so much trash? But Kaspar believed him. And Kaspar did not trust easily.

"Unfortunately, another male has claimed that avenue."

Jack leaned back, eyeing Fero, teeth grinding together. He was getting better at remaining silent when he wasn't privy to all the facts. Watching him hold his tongue, for me, warmed something tight in my chest. He could be taught.

My gaze slid back to Fero. "Agree to never use my name against me. For any purpose, good or ill."

"And in exchange?"

I lifted a brow. "I thought you wanted to make amends?"

He crossed his arms over his broad chest. "A bargain requires two sides. One that is open-ended does not suit."

The corners of my lips tipped up. Of course it didn't. "Very well. Name your terms."

"Sav," Jack hissed, and I glanced back at him. "Is this smart?"

In that moment, I wished I could slip into his mind, or find some other way to show him how important this was without Fero hearing. Instead, I smiled and leaned in, soaking up his familiar warmth. When our lips were nearly touching, I cast my voice so only he could hear. "Life and death."

My lips brushed his, and he leaned into the kiss, his hand sliding into my hair to deepen it.

Since the bond between us had made itself known, it only seemed to grow every time we were near one another. If we weren't touching, I wanted his hands on me. If we weren't kissing, I thought of his mouth. But we weren't given the luxury of time to let our bond grow. Instead, we were thrust into this vicious version of Faerie where everyone and everything wanted us dead.

Jack's hand tightened in my hair and I moaned softly.

Fero cleared his throat, and I jerked, remembering he was still there. I pulled back, face and neck flushing hot.

Fero was grinning, something feral in his eyes. "I suppose it is my turn to be a voyeur."

Heat burned higher in my cheeks, dragging me back to our very first meeting. I cleared my throat. "And your bargain?"

Fero pushed off the wall and came closer. Jack stood, but I reached for his hand.

"Jack." He glanced between us, saying nothing, but his fingers twined with mine.

"It is just as well you are both here," Fero said. "My ask is for you both."

"Jack owes you nothing."

"I'll take her half of the bargain," Jack said.

Fire burst to life in my veins. Of course. Two males deciding my future like I was a piece on their board. Kaspar. Fero. Now Jack. Different intentions, but the same damned pattern.

Fero's grin widened, all teeth, and I wanted to take back every complimentary thought I'd had about him.

"Even better."

"No."

"I have not named it yet, Princess."

I narrowed my eyes at the pair of them and curled my fingers into the sheets to keep from setting the room on fire, just to remind them I was here.

"I ask only that if a need should ever arise for someone to look after my son, that you offer him refuge in Winter."

I bit the inside of my cheek. Was he so confident of Jack's heritage? If Jack couldn't meet the terms of the bargain due to lack of claim, he wouldn't be held to it. But would Fero give up his hold on me—the princess of Lakes and Streams—on the chance that Jack's mother actually was princess of Winter? I didn't think so.

If it were true, the ask was no great thing. In Summer, royals were not chosen by bloodline. Unless the child was more powerful than his father, or any other fae in his principality, he would not become their prince.

Offering aid when Fero had already offered his was nothing, and if Jack wasn't who Fero thought, the bargain was moot.

"I accept."

"Jack." I huffed in exasperation.

I'd barely had a moment to consider before he blurted the words, and thoughts of stabbing something through his eye were vivid in my mind. The male would drive me to madness. And we *would* discuss bargains later.

"Then it is done."

Fero spun, turning on his heel, and left.

Fabric fell across the doorframe, and silence rushed in to fill the space he left behind. Jack's shoulders were still tense, jaw tight, like he was braced for another blow. He'd just tied himself to a favor from a dangerous prince without blinking.

For me.

"You didn't have to do that," I said quietly.

He huffed out a breath. "Yeah, I did." His gaze dipped to mine, hot and steady. "I'd do worse for you."

Something in my chest twisted.

I had spent centuries promising myself I wouldn't hand anyone that kind of power again. No more names. No more pieces of my heart.

Too late.

Not because he'd taken anything.

Because this time, I was the one reaching.

I leaned closer, hooked two fingers in the front of his tunic, and pulled him down until our foreheads touched. "Jack."

"Sav?"

I swallowed thickly. "I love you."

His breath caught, and for a moment, the whole world held still with him. Before he could say anything, I kissed him, swallowing whatever answer he might give and letting the warmth of his mouth drown out everything else.

FIFTY-FOUR

JACK

I love you. Three little words, and suddenly breathing was hard. Sav's hand cupped my cheek, warm and sure, and the rest of the world dropped away.

I set my knee on the bed, leaned in, and tangled my fingers in her hair.

I'd thought she would die; our future unraveling with every step as I carried her back to the castle and laid her in this bed. Now her warm breath ghosted over my mouth, and the soft press of her lips on mine would be enough to send me happily to my grave. I caught her bottom lip between my teeth. She melted into the kiss, her hand skating over my chest. Warm fingers pressed into my shoulders and she pushed.

Pushed.

"Jack."

I blinked, dragged out of the haze of need by the sound of my name. "Yeah?" The smell of honeysuckle and rain filled my lungs, and my body wanted to follow it down again.

"Jack," she said more forcefully.

My eyes opened fully. I searched her face. "What's wrong?"

She scooted back, putting distance between us. "That bargain."

The word sobered me faster than a blade. Fero's grin flashed in my mind. His voice.

"Sav."

"Bargains have lasting effects," she said, voice tight. "Some extend beyond your life. You accepted his terms without thinking through what that means."

I dropped beside her on the bed and motioned for her to lift her head.

263

She did, and I slid my arm under it, tucking her into my side. I kept my touch careful.

Grace had been firm. Waking didn't mean healed. The land would keep stitching her together for hours after her eyes opened, and if she pushed too soon, she could come apart again.

"His intentions were pure," I said anyway.

Sav craned her neck to look at me. "How would you know that?"

I swallowed. The sensation still clung to my tongue. "I tasted it."

She sat up, facing me fully. "Your innate gift? Sensing intention? I thought it was pain immunity."

My throat tightened. "Fero says that one isn't mine. Pain immunity." The words came out rough. "He says my mother loaned it to me. That my gift is sensing magic."

Sav's brows drew together. "Loaned?"

She didn't laugh. Didn't dismiss it.

Hope, stupid and desperate, caved in my chest.

"So you believe him," I asked, and hated how small it sounded.

She nodded once. "If anyone would know, it's him."

Her gaze lingered on my face, softening. I hated it. I didn't need it. I needed to save my mom.

"Then my gift is sensing magic," I said quickly, shutting the door before she could pry it open wider. "But I can sense more than that. I can tell when someone means harm or not."

Sav's mouth parted, then closed again. Her eyes went dark with thought. "That isn't common."

It didn't reassure me. It only gave my fear a sharper edge.

My thoughts snapped to my mom—so much pain, for me. But I swallowed it down. Sav had already burned herself raw for us. I couldn't let her see my panic when I knew she'd risk everything and go right now if she saw it.

She settled back against my chest, her body warm and reassuring. Alive.

"That thing you did to me," I said quietly. "In Kaspar's castle. When you told me to stop... was that your gift?"

Sav shuddered.

"It's called coercion," she said. "A form of mind control."

Something in me went tight. The word cracked open memories I'd buried deep. Morgan's commands clawing through my skull. Sav's *Stop* locking my limbs in Kaspar's hall. My stomach lurched.

Sav lifted her head, searching my face. "You're angry." Tears gathered at the edges of her lashes. Her eyes darted between mine. "With me..." She swallowed. "I'm sorry, Jack. I'm so sorry."

The apology landed like a blow and a balm all at once.

I was angry. I was grieving. I was a mess of jagged edges I didn't know how to smooth. But I wrapped my arms around her anyway and pulled her close until her heartbeat pressed against mine.

I'd wanted those words more than I'd wanted air. Even when it wasn't fair to ask them of her. When I'd needed them and she couldn't give them, something in me had split open and stayed that way.

Now she meant it.

I kissed the top of her head and let myself breathe for the first time in days. Fero, Morgan, my mother, everything could wait a few hours. Right now there was only Sav, alive and warm in my arms, and the fragile space between us finally mending.

I loosened my hold, and she crawled up my chest. Her lips found mine again, but this time the kiss wasn't hunger. It was a promise. Her hands traced my jaw, slid into my hair, and tugged the leather tie free. My hair fell loose around my shoulders.

Sav swung a leg over me and settled on my lap, knees braced on either side of my hips. Her weight grounded me. My hands still shook.

Her touch gentled. "Hey," she whispered.

"Yeah." My voice came out rough.

"You're mine," she said quietly. "Stay with me."

I would've agreed to anything in that moment.

She kissed me slow, careful, as if she wanted to memorize me the way I did her. My hands slid to her waist on instinct, but I didn't pull her down. I let her set the pace. Her fingers threaded into my hair and tugged just enough to draw a sound from my throat.

Her smile curved against my mouth. "That sound," she breathed. "Do it again."

She rolled her hips, pressing down, and heat coiled low and sharp. The air punched out of me.

"Sav," I rasped.

"I know," she murmured, moving again, steady and sure, until my grip tightened on her hips and I had to force myself not to take control. I didn't. I held her as if she might shatter, because she'd burned herself to ash for us and I could still feel how close to the edge she'd been.

Her breath broke. Mine followed.

"Beautiful," I whispered, and her answering shiver nearly undid me.

"Stay with me," she said again, voice cracking.

"Always."

When it was over, she sagged against me, boneless and warm. We lay there breathing hard, her cheek pressed to my shoulder. I smoothed a hand down her back in slow, steady strokes until her lungs stopped fighting for air.

"I'm here," she mumbled, already drifting. "I'm not going anywhere."

I kissed her temple. "Good," I whispered, wrapping my arms around her and pulling the blankets over us both. "I need you right here."

Her eyes fluttered closed. I kissed her lashes, her cheek, the steady pulse at her throat. Even in sleep, her body curved into mine, and I curled around her, holding her in warmth and quiet.

Tonight we'd rest, just for a while. Sav needed the land's healing to finish its work, to settle deep where none of us could see it. Then, when the window closed and she was strong again, we'd leave this bed in the dead of night and go after my mother. ·

FIFTY-FIVE

SAV

Sav. Wake up.

I blinked into the dark, disoriented for half a breath. Jack was curled against my side, breathing deep and heavy, his arm warm around my waist. The room was still. Quiet. The kind of quiet that made me second-guess my own senses.

Had I dreamed that?

We'd only given ourselves a few hours before we left to retrieve his mother. Jack needed the rest more than I did. Portal magic was draining. He'd used it too many times in less than twenty-four hours.

Sav. Now.

The voice came again, not through the air but straight through my skull, sharp enough to raise the hairs on my arms.

I sat up too fast and the room tipped. Nausea rolled through me and I braced a hand on the mattress, breathing through it until the dizziness thinned. When it cleared, my thoughts did too, snapping into place with a steadiness I hadn't felt in... I couldn't remember.

Juniper's sap had done something to me. I could feel it in the strange absence beneath my skin, as if something cinched tight at my center had finally let go. When I reached for my magic, it answered without pain. No strain. No burn. Just there.

Come outside. Now.

"Foxglove?" I whispered into the dark.

Jack stirred, his arm tightening instinctively around my waist. I froze, breath caught, waiting for him to wake. He only shifted, exhaled, and went still again.

267

Was I losing my wits?

I slid carefully out from under his arm and eased the blankets aside.

Now.

I padded to the doorway and tugged the privacy sheet back, peering into the corridor lit only by Luna's glow. Empty. No shadows moving. No servants. No sound but my own pulse.

Sav. Outside.

Either I was going mad... or Foxglove had finally shown his hand.

Something he'd kept buried for centuries.

I let the sheet fall and moved fast, bare feet silent over cold stone. Drawn curtains lined the hallway as I slipped past them. The castle slept on, oblivious.

Outside, the night air hit my lungs sharp and clean. I took the steps two at a time, sand cool beneath my feet as I reached the beach. The ocean glittered under Luna's light, waves whispering against shore.

Something moved near the tree line.

I spun.

A small shape burst from the shadows, racing straight for me. Violet eyes flashed as the fox bounded across the sand.

Even before he reached me, I felt him. Panic, raw and feral, battering at the edges of my mind.

I dropped to one knee and held out my hands. He leapt into my arms hard enough to sting, claws scraping my forearm as he clung to me.

His heart hammered against my chest.

"Foxglove," I breathed, tightening my hold. "What happened?"

Nita isn't Nita. A chameleon. Tried to catch me. Cage me.

The thoughts hit in jagged bursts, not spoken aloud, not even shaped into sound. Just meaning shoved into me with all the subtlety of a blade.

My stomach turned.

I scanned the woods again, expecting movement, expecting pursuit. There was nothing. Only the hush of waves and the frantic rise and fall of his breath.

Why are you still in fox form? I tried to send back, clumsy and uncertain.

Need to calm. Can't shift like this.

I ran a hand over his wiry head, slow strokes meant to steady us both. He panted, leaning into my palm as if he could anchor himself there.

"It's okay," I murmured, though my own pulse had started to race. "You're safe. I've got you."

His breathing stuttered, then eased by a fraction.

No. Hazel. Trapped.

My hand went still.

"What?" The word came out too sharp. I forced myself to breathe. "Hazel's trapped? Where? By who?"

Foxglove shuddered, and the air around him prickled.

He jerked out of my arms. I stumbled back as his body wrenched and unfolded, fur receding, limbs lengthening, snout retracting. Red-brown curls spilled loose around elegant pointed ears as he swayed on bare feet, blinking like he'd been dragged out of a nightmare.

I stared up at him, throat tight. "What happened to Hazel?"

"We need to get the others," he said, voice rough. "Now."

He turned and strode for the steps like the answer was already chasing him. I followed, not thinking, just moving.

Inside, the corridors were wrong. Too many places to hide. Too many curtains drawn. Too much quiet.

Minutes later, other footsteps joined ours.

I shook Jack until his eyes snapped open. Foxglove roused Fero. Murz and Larek came next, half-dressed and armed out of habit. We gathered in an open chamber meant for receiving guests, every face tightening.

Juniper stayed with the rescued fae, watching over them while we figured out what to do next.

"It's Prince Aegon," Foxglove said. "He's in Autumn. So are the missing fae." His gaze met mine, then slid to Larek's. "I thought I heard Prim calling my name. I went to her." His jaw flexed. "It was a trap."

Larek's voice went flat. Dangerous. "Hazel."

Foxglove nodded once. "He has her. They do. Prim and Aegon."

"But... Prim is my friend." The words sounded foolish even as I said them. I hadn't seen her in decades. Not once since I returned to Faerie. I'd told myself it meant nothing. Prim was always traveling. Always working.

Foxglove's expression didn't soften. "She tried to catch me," he said. "Tried to cage me."

Jack's hand wrapped around mine and squeezed.

"Where are they holding her?" Larek demanded.

"In Autumn's castle," Foxglove said. "There are wards around it. Stronger than the ones blocking their border."

I opened my mouth, questions stacking up, but a small weight bumped my hand. Grace. She appeared beside me as if she'd stepped out of thin air, eyes bright in the dim room.

"It is time, Fire Fae."

Every gaze swung to me.

I swallowed. "Time for what?"

Grace's voice didn't waver. "Time for you to break the wards."

FIFTY-SIX

JACK

Sav's pulse thrummed beneath my thumb, blood pounding where our fingers laced. She tightened her grip as we moved to the edge of the forest. Grace had asked us to wake Fero's son, Qaden, and to bring Juniper. Foxglove swore under his breath when we knocked on Juniper's door, where she'd been keeping watch. When she joined us, clear-eyed, a reluctant smile tugged at her lips at the sight of him, and some of his nervous energy stilled.

They met at the edge of the trees, and he cupped her face, checking her over.

"I'm better. I promise." She laughed, and he pressed a kiss to her forehead.

They were an odd pair. Juniper laughed, and something in his eyes softened. Love did that. I felt it in my bones—the same way I'd felt Sav's love long before she'd been willing to admit it, even to herself. Through the bond, her feelings had bled into mine until I couldn't tell where one ended and the other began. The connection had rooted itself so deep I couldn't have carved it from my cold, dead heart if I'd tried.

I'd love Sav through death and whatever came after. She was the quiet force that kept me tethered when everything else shook loose.

When everyone and everything else was breakable, she wasn't.

She glanced up, eyes meeting mine, and a soft smile touched her lips. Her pulse steadied beneath my hand. If anyone could do this, it was her. And if I wasn't there at the end, I knew she'd find a way to carry on.

"Jack."

Grace signaled me forward. I released Sav's hand and stepped into the center of our circle.

"We go to Autumn's border. Have you traveled there before? Can you picture it?"

"Why not tear straight into Autumn?" Murz asked, stepping closer.

Grace frowned up at him. "The wards won't allow it."

A memory flashed: a smoking, flickering portal, the one I'd created when I'd tried to reach Sav and found my mother instead.

"We must take down the ward," Grace continued. "Once we're through, we'll be free to portal within Autumn."

"I'll make the first portal," Murz said, lifting both hands.

Grace rapped her knuckles against his thigh.

"Ow," he hissed, dropping his arms and grabbing his leg.

"Jack will open it first," Grace said. "Go stand with the others."

I smirked. It was good to know Grace was sharp with everyone. I'd thought her tone was reserved for me.

Her large golden eyes fixed on mine. "You aren't close enough with anyone in Autumn to use them as an anchor. I'll give you a vision. Picture it when you open the portal."

I nodded, lifting my hands. I'd given up trying to pin down what Grace could do. Her emotions were as hazy as her abilities. It seemed I still had much to learn.

An image bloomed in my mind: a fog-drenched forest, moss heavy on ancient trunks, the air damp and cold. It shimmered, then blinked out.

"Do you have it?"

"Yes." I inhaled slowly, my gaze darting to Sav. She gave me an encouraging nod, and I spread my arms apart.

Silvery light streaked the air and split. Reality tore open in a jagged seam, and our group gathered around it. Within the tear, a murky forest loomed. Crisp wind whipped my hair, cooling my heated veins, and I exhaled softly. Summer's heat had been suffocating. The cold felt right.

I looked to Grace. She nodded.

One by one, we stepped through.

Fero went first, holding Qaden's hand. Larek followed, then Murz. Grace held out her arms and Juniper lifted her, glancing back as Foxglove stepped through behind them.

Sav stepped up last and held out her hand. I grinned, lacing my fingers with hers, and together we passed through the fabric of reality and into the forest at Autumn's edge.

Behind us, the portal crackled. Summer's golden sand glimmered through the narrowing band of light.

I turned, lifted my hands, and drew my fingers together. The silvery tear shuddered, pulled inward, and thinned to a single shining line before it snapped out with a soft crack, leaving only damp air and shadow behind us.

The portal was gone, but magic still pressed against my skin, nearly suffocating in its strength.

This wasn't my magic anymore.

I saw nothing between us and the forest, but when I stared directly at it, the trees seemed to stretch away into an impossible distance. The moment I blinked, the branches were close again—low and grasping.

"Summer, step forward," Grace called.

Fero released Qaden's hand and stepped to her side.

I forced myself to look away as dizziness washed over me. The forest tunneled endlessly when I stared too long.

"Lakes and Streams."

For a heartbeat, I expected Kaspar to emerge from the shadows, aquamarine eyes sharp and unforgiving. Instead, Grace's gaze landed on Sav.

Ice speared my chest.

She was Lakes and Streams now. Not Spring. Not any land court at all. I had no idea what rules she was breaking simply by standing here. Whatever the cost, I'd make sure she didn't pay it alone.

Sav glanced at Fero, steady now. I wanted to go to her, to shield her from the weight pressing down on her shoulders, but it wasn't him that set her on edge anymore. It was the mission ahead.

She stood tall, shoulders back, unbreakable.

"Clasp hands," Grace commanded.

"How do you know what to do?" I asked.

Sav shot me a narrow-eyed scowl. I knew how it sounded. I still needed the answer.

Grace chuckled, the sound like bark scraping stone in a storm. "The land keeps no secrets from me, Winter."

I jolted.

She'd always called me Jack, even after she'd shown her true face. *Winter.* Sav and Fero had both circled it without saying it outright. Grace had just named it.

I believed in threes.

We were headed into enemy territory to save my mother, and I was more certain than ever that we were also saving the princess of Winter.

FIFTY-SEVEN

SAV

My fingers wrapped around Fero's, and fire burst to life in my veins.

Siphon.

Except it did not feel like being drained. It felt like a dam breaking.

I'd hoped for a chance to test it, to practice. The first time my magic had poured through me, I'd been unable to control it. It was lucky I hadn't injured anyone. Now I would have access to its full potential.

Grace's voice threaded through the roar. "Do not fear it, child. The magic is fed from the land, through you. It feels the blight laid upon it and riots. The land wishes to be free of its shackles."

I swallowed and opened myself to the magic swirling around me. A wash of multicolored light burst behind my eyes, sending dazzling shards of crystalline energy skittering across every surface. I could see it, everything around me, as if the elements swirled in perfect harmony. But though they were all present, only one bent toward me. Heat. Energy in motion. Turbulent and wild. The giver of life and bringer of death.

The almighty flame.

I called it, and it answered. Every tendril of crackling warmth raced toward me, burrowed beneath my skin, invaded my veins until I was alive with it. Until I *was* fire. Fero's grip loosened, his touch sliding up my arm, never fully leaving.

"Place your hands on it," a voice said from a distant corner of my mind.

I struggled to master myself, to regain control. Fire was chaos and light. It demanded an outlet, and I would give it one.

As I thrust my hands out before me, my palms met a sticky, invisible wall.

The forest warped behind it, distance folding wrong—branches close, then impossibly far. The magic caught anything that pushed through. Once you stepped into it, there was no end but death

I leaned into it. The ward grabbed me, syrup-thick, locking my arms mid-thrust. Inside the magic. That was where I'd burn it to the ground. I pushed. And the magic pushed back, swallowing my hands to the wrist, then the elbow. Fero's hand tightened on my shoulder as he was drawn in with me. I couldn't look at him. I couldn't spare him an ounce of energy. My focus was on the magic holding me in stasis, trapping us in its web.

But even here, fiery energy sparked and sizzled.

I called, and it answered.

My veins were flaming, raging, ready to ignite the world. I tipped my head back, opened my mouth, and screamed—screamed for the injustice so many had been dealt, for the lies I'd been fed all my life, for the queen who had been just another jailer.

It wasn't sound that burst from my lips.

It was flame.

Wild, untamable fire whipped through the air, smoking and crackling as it found each ribbon of sticky magic woven together, bent on catching all who flew too near. Strands popped and smoked, and my back bowed under the strain of all that energy funneling through me.

It wasn't like the magic I usually called. There was no bottom to this well. It came in endless waves and exploded from my mouth, my hands, my chest, devouring the taint poisoning the land. Even if burnout wasn't possible, my body strained against so much power. Sweat slicked my forehead, stinging my eyes, and the skin on my palms and chest began to blister and peel.

My lips cracked, salty liquid seeping into my mouth. But there was no off switch. No reins. Once it started, it wanted everything.

The land craved vengeance. Not just for the poison Autumn inflicted, but for the centuries of wild Faerie magic controlled, redirected, and forced to bend to Mab's will. It shouted in my veins, in my very being, demanding to be freed. She had shaped the seasons, commanded the elements to obey, but they would no longer submit.

Lightning streaked overhead, thunder rolling close behind. Howling winds rose, tearing at my hair and clothes. Still, the magic poured through me, escaping into the black clouds forming above, joining the lightning crackling in the sky.

The pressure of Fero's hand eased on my shoulder, and something inside me narrowed, a valve turning, a great faucet kinked in the line.

Flames sputtered and spat, tiny orange and red embers landing on my cheeks.

My hands dropped. As the last flames died, I sank to my knees in the moss.

Strong arms hooked under mine and hauled me back the instant the last flame winked out. Warmth enveloped me, wrapping me in its embrace. I smiled up at two pools of sparkling emerald.

Safe.

I was safe in Jack's arms.

FIFTY-EIGHT

KASPAR

Aegon's sharks had destroyed my coral walls, leaving my court defenseless against future attacks. Had Sav's display in my absence riled him so much that he took it as an affront to his court? Perhaps it was that we hadn't attended his wedding. I'd known the invitation was coming and intentionally left court so he couldn't deliver his summons.

I hadn't expected Sav to play hostess in my absence.

Whatever his reason, my uncle was done playing nice. His sharks, the lot of them rather than his usual two, had reduced my castle to boulders on the lakebed. All my folk were accounted for—alive or dead—apart from two. My soft heart thudded painfully as Kila and Twila made another pass over the rubble. They'd been circling the ruins for hours, with nothing to show for it but more broken stone.

If Memphe was gone, I would not be merciful when I came for my uncle.

The time for courtly politics was over. My uncle's attack had cost me a great deal. Not only my heart's desire, but all my leverage over the land fae. Apart from one. I touched the waterproof satchel at my hip containing my maps of Faerie, the history of my folk, and one silver tube. The one I'd kept locked away rather than with the others.

The one that meant more to me than any castle or court.

At last, Twila appeared before me and bowed low. I waved a hand and she rose, shaking her head. My chest tightened. Memphe was more to me than my right hand. More than my spymaster. He was as close as one might come to companionship beneath the deep.

I dismissed Twila, my gaze roving the wreckage of my home. Centuries of portraits, baubles, and intel lay buried beneath the stones my ancestors had built. Moving my court was far simpler than rebuilding. Could I disband it? Go it alone? Drift until even the land forgot my name? My power would be diminished if I didn't claim my realm, and who would bend the streams, bring water to the land creatures who needed it to survive? What would become of my folk?

I pressed water through my gills and sighed. No. I couldn't abandon them now, not when Aegon might wipe them and all land creatures from the map. The thought burned in my chest as a new board assembled in my mind.

I'd assumed my uncle wanted to crush me under his thumb, to rule over all water, but what if he wanted something worse? Without freshwater in Faerie, the land would die. He could, in one fell swoop, destroy them all. The only thing standing in his way was me.

A memory floated to the surface. A long-buried dream of the time I'd been captured by Autumn. After so many centuries with no movement from him or them, I'd chalked it up to a nightmare, even if the faint, ghost-like bites from Dahlia, Autumn's seer, still stung my neck when I closed my eyes.

My uncle had lured me to Autumn's court. Then he'd pretended he, too, was a guest, invited to witness the coronation of a new princess after the death of Prince Helenium. But my uncle had been working with them, and their aim had been me. He'd wanted the magic of the sea, something he believed I had, stolen by my father. But the magic had been gone centuries before my father was born. Long before Aegon's reign.

My mind drifted to the night Dahlia performed blood magic, tasting mine and revealing a truth I'd never fully grasped. Her words came back to me.

"He has the gift of portal magic," she'd hissed to my uncle, spitting my blood onto the floor of the dark, cavernous space. "With a gift like that, the magic could be anywhere."

My uncle had screamed, spittle landing on my face, but I was powerless to move. He struck me, commanded Dahlia to bite me again and again, draining me until I was weak and crumpled on the floor. "Where have you hidden it, boy?"

The veins in his neck had strained as he hovered half out of water, half in the stream beneath Autumn's mountain fortress, but he was trapped, unable to set one foot on land. That thought roused something in me. Like me, my father had been a shifter, able to transform and move about on land. His gift hadn't been as strong as mine. His treks were restricted to short distances from the lake, but if he'd wanted to hide something from my uncle, what better place than land?

I wasn't sure how I knew, but I did. My uncle had figured it out. He was looking for his missing magic. The magic of the sea. With it, he would be stronger. He could raze Faerie and send all the creatures of the land to their watery deaths.

I had to find it first, and I had to do it without Memphe.

He was dead.

Many had thought him small, weak, but he was all I'd had when Mira and the rest of my army died two centuries ago. There was comfort in knowing someone shared your secrets, someone bound by so many bargains his tiny heart would have ceased beating the moment he betrayed me. But he never would.

Now he was dead. And my wife was beyond my reach.

I squeezed the marriage contract in my fist, silver warping under my grip. The time for games was at an end.

I swam to the bottom of my lakebed. The very center of my court, what was left of it, held a massive seashell. The last remnant of my ancestors' legacy. Ten thousand years ago, before Mab landed on our planet, my ancestors had ruled this realm. Not by might alone, though we had that in spades.

I ran my tongue over the smooth grooves of its surface, then backed up, setting my satchel and Sav's contract down beside it. If Memphe were here, I'd have commanded him to guard my most prized possessions, but he was gone, and there was no one left I trusted.

A long pink tongue unfurled from the depths of the shell, and I swam inside. Soft flesh retracted, coiling around me until I was wrapped in darkness. I closed my eyes, feeling the magic wash over me as the shell stripped away my bargains.

This was where our true power lay. No land fae could escape a bargain. It followed them to their death, and sometimes beyond.

When my recent bargains were stripped away and the shell's magic restored me, I inhaled clear water and let out a long, slow exhale. The pain carving its mark on my heart eased the moment the shell closed around me. The relief was sweet, and some part of me still wished for the reminder of what I'd done.

I'd used my wife's name to punish her, and the bargain had taken its revenge. It wasn't a true betrayal, not enough to take my life, but magic didn't see in black and white. It judged in shades of gray.

My punishment was fair.

When the shell cracked and light filtered in, my gaze snapped to the contract. The one that no longer held my fate. Now only Sav was bound by it. A vicious sliver of my heart still craved vengeance for her disloyalty after all my years of silent suffering and hoped she would break our vows and succumb.

Another, quieter instinct wanted to free her from the shackles I'd sworn she would never wear.

I couldn't worry about her now. My folk needed me. I suspected the entire undersea realm was in need of my rescue, and that meant finding the magic that should have resided at the heart of the sea. A nagging thought wondered if Faerie would have suffered as it had if that magic had remained in its rightful place.

But my uncle couldn't be trusted. So much magic in his hands would mean ruin for all.

I was certain now it lived on land, but where?

Like Mab's daughter, I could carve portals between realms. Did my father share my gift? Had he gone so far as to move it off-planet? Had the portals, the bargains, all of it, come from my uncle's suspicion that it was on Earth?

FIFTY-NINE

JACK

"Sav. Can you hear me?"

I whipped my head toward Grace. "What have you done? This is the second time I trusted you." The words fractured, turning into a sob.

Sav was ice-cold in my arms, limbs heavy and unresponsive. I feared she'd pushed the fire past the point of return.

When I'd torn Fero's hand from her arm, he'd looked as dazed as she did, stumbling a few paces back before collapsing to his knees. Juniper dropped beside him, one hand braced on his shoulder like she could keep him upright by touch alone. The rest of our group hovered in a loose ring at the border, silent and watchful, the woods hemming us in.

Sick terror twisted my gut. The strongest fae in Faerie looked on the verge of death, and sparks still snapped off Sav's fingertips.

"Sav." I hauled her against my chest, flame igniting inside me, and pressed that heat into her, fighting to warm her.

Grace knelt beside us. I slid back on my heels. She held out a hand, but I tightened my arms around Sav. "Don't touch her."

I spat it, but Grace didn't flinch. She reached out and laid her palm on Sav's forehead.

Her brow pinched.

My chest cracked in two. Grace had never shown an ounce of concern before. Would Sav survive this? Could she? I'd trade places, beg Mab or Gaia or whoever ruled this place, if it meant she lived.

"Let me help her, Jack."

I curled around Sav like a wild animal backed into a corner, fire licking to life along my forearms.

"I can heal her."

Heal her. That was my job. I was supposed to be a healer. But I didn't know the first thing about fae magic. How did you mend something you couldn't even name?

Grace lifted her hands and the land answered on both sides of the border. In front of us, the Autumn forest no longer stretched away out of reach. Vines spilled from its trees and from the shrubs at Summer's edge, curling through the air and skimming over moss and grass as they raced toward her outstretched palms.

"Let me ask the land to give back what it has taken."

My hold loosened as I stared at the border—at Autumn, the same forest that had tried to devour her. Vines crept up my thighs and wound around my arms.

"No," I pleaded.

The flora ignored me. It tore Sav from my arms, wrapping her tight until only her face and the tips of her fingers were visible. I stared down, trying to make sense of it. How could she be better off without me? How could the forest give her what I couldn't?

Grace's hand settled on my shoulder. I jerked like I'd been struck.

"She'll be safe here," Grace said. "We must find your mother."

I wrenched free. "I'm not leaving her."

My voice cracked. "She needs me."

Grace's eyes softened. "Jack. She'll be safer here. Away from battle." She tipped her chin toward the dark stretch of Autumn beyond the line. "Your mother's time is running out. Aegon draws closer to what he wants with every breath she takes. If he accomplishes his goal before we find her, all of Faerie will pay the price."

My gaze snapped back to Sav. Her lashes rested against her cheeks, soot smeared along one temple. None of this mattered if she didn't wake.

Murz dropped beside me, careful not to touch the vines. "I'll stay with her. The moment she wakes, we'll get her to you."

My vision swam as I looked between my mate, cocooned in living green, and Murz's steady face. I couldn't leave her. Couldn't walk away without knowing she'd open her eyes again.

I shook my head. "No."

"There are things you don't know," Grace said quietly. "About your mother."

I choked on a sharp retort. Those were the truest words Grace had ever spoken. I was certain there were a great many things I didn't know about my mother.

"Portal magic isn't unique to those who are half human," Grace went on. "Your mother, Aconite, has the strongest portal magic left in Faerie. Her power is woven through every gateway that still holds. If Aegon gains full control of her, if her magic succumbs to him, the portals will collapse in on themselves. Faerie will crumble with them."

I stared at her. The ring of bodies around us was suddenly too far away, like I'd stepped into a narrower world and couldn't climb back out. "What are you talking about?"

"I believe your group already knows Mab had two children: Firethorn and Aconite. Though Aconite was the younger sibling, she was no less powerful. When she was only a girl of fifty, she accidentally created her first portal between realms. She found Earth."

"Unlike Mab's ability to travel throughout our realm, Aconite's gift let her search for hospitable planets *across* realms. Mab, no longer satisfied with ruling one realm, wanted to expand her reach. But the creatures inhabiting Earth weren't as docile as those she'd encountered here, and they had one thing our realm did not."

Grace's gaze flicked once to the listening circle. Then her eyes locked back on mine. "Iron."

"Iron was poison to Mab's kind. But Aconite had many gifts the others did not."

"Pain immunity," I breathed.

Grace nodded. "Because of that gift, she could travel to Earth without the agony Mab and the others endured even near iron. She was the bridge your queen needed."

Images of my mother flickered in my mind. The way she rubbed her temples after a long day. How she refused every pill a doctor tried to offer. I'd thought Earth itself was killing her. Maybe it had been the weight of holding that bridge.

"Why not just close it?" I asked hoarsely. "Why spend time on Earth if no one could really live there but her?"

"Because," Grace said, and her fingers tightened on my shoulder, "the humans were more compatible with her kind than those native to Faerie. When a fae and a human procreated, their child's gifts were amplified. Mab was obsessed with creating a stronger, better race. One that could rule across the multiverse."

My stomach dipped. Stronger. Like me.

"But those children were also harder to control," Grace continued. "Mab's true name magic could compel them, but it couldn't hold them the way it held full fae. She saw what they might become. A race that could challenge her."

"So she made the rule," I said. "Never fall in love with a human."

"Yes. At first, the rule was for humans and fae. Then, when she saw how unpredictable other pairings could be, she grew wary of any bond that might create power beyond hers. Even unions between high and low fae began to worry her. Mab feared anyone who might one day be stronger than her, so she wrapped the world in rules and bargains and called it order."

I thought of all the times my mother kept us tucked out of sight. The way she watched the horizon for a threat that never came. I'd known she was hiding something. I just hadn't understood who she was really afraid of.

Larek stepped forward. "I have to go." His gaze cut across the circle, then pinned me. "Hazel."

I nodded. I understood. And though the need to find my mother beat in my skull like a second pulse, I still couldn't bear the thought of Sav waking to find me gone.

Grace studied my face for an uncomfortably long moment.

"She'll understand, Jack."

I reached for Sav, brushing my knuckles over her exposed cheek. "I know she would. But I'd never forgive myself."

Grace mirrored the motion, her small fingers tracing a scatter of freckles on Sav's cheek. "When she wakes, she'll want to come with you."

I dipped my chin.

"But she won't yet be strong enough to fight." Grace's voice sharpened. "Would you have me save her now only to risk her in the coming battle?"

My throat went dry as my heart sped up. I understood her warning too well. What lay ahead could mean death. The only way to ensure Sav lived was to leave her behind.

My gaze fell on her again. Color was creeping back into her cheeks. Her breathing had steadied.

She'd recover.

But if she woke and we were still here, she'd demand to go with us. And she needed time to heal.

I lifted my eyes to the faces around us. The mission waiting. The war to come. Sav, the girl who'd burned herself out to save all of us, bound in living vines at my feet. My mother running out of time.

"Let's go," I said.

Murz opened his mouth, but Grace lifted a hand. "You're needed in the battle, Orc. Qaden and I will stay with her. We'll guard this place until she wakes."

Murz dipped his chin and climbed to his feet.

I leaned down and pressed my lips to Sav's forehead. Her skin was already warmer.

Grace was right. Sav wouldn't stay behind when she woke. She'd demand to help save Hazel, to help save my mother. But with no one to take her, she'd be forced to stay. I hated myself for it.

I straightened and looked back once more. Qaden stood beside Grace with his arms folded, those strange amber eyes fixed on my face as if he were memorizing it.

I swallowed and turned away before I could change my mind.

SIXTY

FOXGLOVE

On light feet, I led our expedition over rocky terrain to the cliff overlooking the ocean. Once, this cliff had gazed upon an endless stretch of forest. Now, turbulent waves crashed against a jagged shore, stony spires jutting from the surf.

Aegon had found his way into Autumn.

How they'd managed to cut off whole portions of Faerie was a mystery that Creig, Murz, and I had been working to solve for several years. We knew it had to do with portal magic—usually the kind only half human, half fae could create. Aconite was the exception. But of the few who existed, none possessed the power to carve such massive rifts that entire sections of Faerie could be removed.

Only Aconite had power like that. And perhaps her son.

Aconite didn't just go to Earth. She vanished from it. That narrowed the list of who could've reached her, taken her, and kept her to a very small group.

I stepped to the cliff edge and leaned over. Below was a several-hundred-foot drop to craggy, jutting rocks and a frothing sea. Death for most.

Just beneath our feet, several sea-facing caves had been carved from the rock. The caves' prisoners had nowhere to go. Even a shifter like Hazel couldn't hope to survive the leap. Her thoughts were near, just underfoot —a slew of curses and fiery retorts she'd offer my cousin if she ever saw her again.

Primrose.

My cousin.

The wind shifted, salty and sharp, and I forced my attention back to the cliff. One misstep up here and we'd join the bones at the base. Still, that single word kept echoing in my head.

How had Primrose masked her thoughts and plans from me so long? We'd grown up together. Centuries at court, surviving my brother and the lords and ladies who plotted our demise. But of course, she was one of four creatures who'd known my innate gift. Three, now that Mira was gone.

Even so, hiding one's thoughts was a skill that required great mastery. Hadn't I wondered at Nita's ability to mask her thoughts? Hadn't I followed her to Autumn? But that would mean my cousin had two such gifts. Chameleon fae weren't the rarest, but I'd only heard of one who could change not just their face, but their scent. Puck. A legend. Not real.

Unless...

Could the famous creature have been Prim all along? She was older than me. More than a century older. None of us knew what life had been like for her before.

But there was no denying that stray thought—the one I didn't think she'd meant me to hear when her fake cries for help had brought me to the castle.

My brother was a horrible ruler. A terrible fae. Selfish, stubborn, completely unaware of how his actions affected those around him. But his cruelty had centered around his wife. Primrose had been spared much of his attention. Prim's hate, the vicious thoughts she'd carried toward him, said otherwise. How had she kept them from me all those years?

I shook my head as a gust of wind shoved at my shoulders. Glancing back, I met Murz's eyes. He lifted the rope—secured to a tree several feet down the ridge—then nodded once.

Larek tightened the knot at his waist at my signal and stepped to the brink. I took my position at the edge, close enough to keep the line lifted clear of the jagged rock.

Larek didn't hesitate. He turned, ran two steps, and launched himself over.

The rope snapped taut. The shock of his weight ripped through my arms and dragged me forward. I dug my heels into the dirt and lifted the line higher, fighting to keep it from grinding against the cliff's sharp lip. Loose stones skittered under my boots and clattered down the face below.

My white-knuckled hold slipped when something cracked—one of my fingers. Pain shot up my arm, hot and blinding, but I clenched harder and held the rope up anyway.

Behind me, Murz hauled back, taking the load and yanking me away from the brink. My knees buckled, then caught, and I heaved for balance as the line sang between us.

"Got her!" Larek shouted from below.

Now came the hard part.

SIXTY-ONE

JACK

The Blood Wood wasn't what I expected.

It reminded me of a trip I'd taken with my mom to Tennessee one October, back when her headaches had started getting worse and she'd insisted nature would do us good. My mom didn't fly. Ever. After eleven hours in a rental car, I'd stumbled out, stiff and half-delirious, and the sight had stopped me cold.

Back home in New Jersey, trees fought for space among brick and asphalt. Here, the forest swallowed the sky in every direction, a canopy of reds and golds so vivid it tightened something in my chest.

It was much the same in the Blood Wood. The shades were deeper, most of them veering toward red and ember-orange, but green and gold still threaded through the branches. A gust of wind shook loose a slow cascade of leaves that drifted down around us, brushing my shoulders as they fell.

The ground wasn't Spring's moss and root-tangled carpet. It was layers of fallen leaves, damp and decomposing, pressed into a thick, rust-colored bed. From a distance it looked like the forest floor had been flooded with crimson and left to rot, turning the woods into a bog of red-brown decay.

Under other circumstances I might have appreciated the beauty of the scene.

Juniper moved ahead, nearly silent, her golden hair the only bright thing against the dark trunks. Fero kept close behind me, close enough that the heat of him brushed my back when he shifted. We weren't alone out here, even if the forest tried to swallow sound.

Juniper glanced back and lifted a finger to her lips.

293

I froze, listening.

Nothing. No footfalls. No voices. Only the faint hum of night creatures and the brittle crunch of leaves when I breathed too hard.

She motioned us forward.

We'd barely gone a dozen paces when she stopped so abruptly the hairs on the back of my neck rose. No sound warned me, but my other sense flared to life. Magic—weak at first, a distant pulse. The moment I caught it, it latched on and refused to let go.

Now I understood how Fero had found us in the woods that day. He'd said he only needed to sense a fae's magic once to know its owner.

I reached for that pulse, letting it thread through me, searching for what always rode beneath it. Not words. Not thoughts. Something truer. A sharp edge of fear. A desperate urgency that scraped down my spine.

There.

It was—

I broke into a run.

"Jack," Juniper hissed behind me, but I couldn't stop. Fero's footsteps pounded after mine. I didn't care. I knew that magic. I'd borrowed it so many times, believing it was mine.

Mom.

Branches clawed at my arms as I tore through the trees. Roots snagged at my boots, the ground sloping down toward the mountain. Ahead, the trees thinned and a black gash split the rock face. Cold air spilled from the cave mouth, sharp with stone and something metallic.

I pushed harder, lungs burning as I charged for it. I didn't look back. I didn't need to. Nothing was going to stop me from getting to her.

A troll slumped just inside the entrance, eyes half-lidded, a spear hanging from one meaty fist. His chest rose in slow, heavy breaths. Then his nostrils flared.

His eyes snapped open.

I didn't hesitate. I flung both hands out, white-hot fire tearing across the space toward his chest.

He jerked upright with a roar and thrust the spear between us. My flames hit the wood and it caught fast, fire racing up the shaft. The troll bellowed, trying to hold on, but the spear blackened, split, and sagged in his grip. He cursed and flung it aside as embers scattered across the cave floor.

He lifted both hands over his head.

The cave answered.

Stone groaned above the entrance. Dust sifted down in thin gray streams. Pebbles began to rain from the ceiling, skittering across the floor as the mouth of the cave shuddered.

He wasn't trying to trap me inside.

He was trying to shut me out.

"No!" I shouted, diving forward.

I threw myself across the threshold as rock shifted behind me, the air thickening with grit. I hit stone hard and slid, skin scraping over jagged edges until I crashed against a sharp outcrop.

There should've been pain.

Nothing came.

My mom's immunity wrapped around my nerves and swallowed it whole.

I sucked in a breath, scrambled to my feet, and spun back toward the entrance.

The opening was gone.

Boulders filled it, wedged tight, dust still drifting from the cracks. No moonlight. No forest. No Juniper. No Fero. Just rough stone and the fading echo of falling rock.

The silence that followed pressed in on my ears as the darkness swallowed me whole.

Sixty-Two

Sav

I blinked awake, cocooned in the warm embrace of Jack's arms.

I must have fallen asleep.

But when my eyes opened, it wasn't the open sky above Summer Court's castle, or even the linen sheets we'd hung for privacy. A canopy of thick foliage arched overhead, so dense it swallowed what little light there was.

I tried to move.

The arms I'd thought I was wrapped in were vines, coiled tight around me from head to toe. I wriggled my fingers, reaching for the knife strapped to my waist, but my hands were pinned in place. Panic hit hard and sharp, and I squirmed in earnest, fighting the living bindings.

"Calm, Child."

My gaze snapped left to the puca who had been masquerading as Jack's friend. "Grace? What's going on?"

She moved without sound, standing over me, her silhouette a dark cutout against the leaves. "I'm afraid I can't let you leave."

My heart hammered as I tried to remember how I'd gotten here. Was she working against me? Had she trapped me? Trapped all of us?

"Where's Jack?"

Grace smiled, showing rows of needle-sharp teeth. Not a vegetarian. "He is completing a mission."

Memories flickered in, jagged and bright. Flames. Wicked magic licking at the edges of my vision. The Autumn border. Our group planning to rescue Hazel and Jack's mom.

Had they left me behind? Had something happened?

297

"I have to go to them."

Grace's expression didn't shift. "No."

I blinked, twisting against the vines until they bit into my skin. What did she mean, no?

"Sav."

A smaller shape appeared beside Grace.

"Qaden."

Fero's son grinned at me, carefree. "I'm glad you lived."

"Um. I appreciate that."

"You're welcome."

"To what?" The question slipped out before I could stop it, my mouth moving on instinct while my brain screamed at me to shut it. The fae didn't make bargains with children. Not like this. Not ever.

Qaden glanced at Grace, suddenly wary.

Grace dipped her chin.

"To..." Qaden looked around, eyes tracking over the space. "That stick." He pointed at a sharp-looking branch on the forest floor.

I pressed my lips together, fighting the urge to laugh and cry at the same time. Of course. Of course that was what he wanted.

I wriggled my fingers, testing the slack Grace had left me. "Bring it here."

Qaden darted away, swiping the branch up and brandishing it as a sword before he knelt beside me and shoved it into my hands.

Grace had been wise to leave my fingers free.

My body felt wrecked, heavy with exhaustion, as though I'd been scraped hollow. The memory of what I'd done returned in flashes, enough to know I'd been close to death. But this vined cocoon felt less like healing and more like a cage.

With what little I had left in me, only embers would come if I tried to call my fire.

But embers were enough.

"If you go now," Grace said, "you will likely die."

The words sent ice racing down my spine.

"You don't know that."

"You are not ready, Fire Fae."

My heart pounded harder now, each beat a blunt weapon. Heat gathered in my palm. The dead wood in my hands caught, flame licking up the grain, bright as fury.

Grace watched without moving to stop me.

"If I might die," I said, voice rough, "they surely will. I have to help them."

"Some may have already lost their mortal life."

Terror sliced clean through me.

Only one in our group had a mortal life.

Jack.

I slashed at the vines, feeding more magic into the flames. The fire surged, the bindings hissing and blackening. An ache sparked in my chest, the well inside me dangerously empty, but I didn't care. I couldn't let Jack die.

I tore the last of the vines from my legs and stumbled to my feet, the world tilting.

"Where is he?"

"You won't reach him in time."

Her words landed as a punch to the gut. The terror became fuel, hot and frantic.

"Help me," I begged. "You did it before."

Grace exhaled a long, slow sigh.

Time was racing by, and every second was one closer to Jack's death. I didn't understand her. She wanted to help. She didn't. She was smiling one moment and barring my path the next.

"Please."

Qaden had backed up, eyes round.

"I don't have portal magic," Grace said. "Neither do you."

"I'll run." My knees hit the ground before I meant them to. "Please, Grace. If it's a bargain you want, name it."

She studied me. The desperation rolling off me in waves was its own kind of magic. I would have offered my firstborn in that moment if she'd asked for it.

After a beat, she nodded.

"One day," she said, each word drawn out, "when your line is called to end a great tyrant, no blood of yours may spill the Lady's blood."

I chewed on the words, trying to make sense of them through the panic. A generational bargain. Not meant for me, but for some distant future. The Lady could mean a dozen different monsters and myths, but my mind snagged on one.

"The Bitter Wraith?" I asked, and hated how unsure it sounded.

Grace blinked at me, wide-eyed. "She is and always will be the Lady of the Lake."

There wasn't time to make sense of it.

But the name hit like a bell in my bones, ancient and cold. The Lady of the Lake. The one whispered about in Spring Court as a warning. A creature said to be immortal once. A deity, almost, until grief reshaped her into something else.

Mira's mother.

Exiled. Guarding the Winter portal on Earth. Choosing solitude over a realm that held too many ghosts.

And I had just agreed to something that would reach forward through generations and wrap around my bloodline as a noose.

I swallowed hard.

"Yes," I said. "It's a bargain."

The magic struck, sharp and immediate, snapping into place so violently it stole my breath. This was no easy out. No harmless pact.

Grace stepped closer and wrapped her arms around me.

Her power surged through my body in a hot, living wave, filling the hollow places, stitching me back together from the inside out. Breath snapped into my lungs, strength into my limbs. My vision cleared, sudden and sharp.

More of my memories returned all at once. Grace showing me how to channel Faerie's magic instead of burning through my own—how my strength had been sapped from my body, not my power. How, once my body recovered, all of Faerie's fire would be within reach.

My knees steadied. My lungs pulled in a full breath.

I ripped myself out of her grasp and took off.

SIXTY-THREE

JACK

I lifted a hand, a small tongue of flame curling over my fingertips. My stomach churned as the black, slick walls flickered in and out of focus. On the wall, a sconce held an ancient-looking torch. I grabbed it and touched fire to it.

Taking it with me, I moved deeper into the cave and my mom's magic grew stronger, tugging me toward her, urging me on. I knew these walls. Recognized the damp, mossy scent and the underlying decay. This was where my mind had gone whenever I'd needed somewhere else to be, somewhere the pain couldn't reach. Here, in my mother's arms, I'd thought they were dreams.

"Mom," I whispered.

Farther ahead, I heard a steady drip. It splashed against rock. Behind me, shouts and the sound of a fight breaking out. Juniper and Fero had arrived. But they were trapped behind the collapsed entrance. First, I'd find my mom. Then we'd find a way out. One problem at a time.

A thin stream of light appeared, a pinprick in the distance, and I followed it.

As I drew closer, it widened into a shaft of light, piercing the darkness and stretching into a chamber beyond.

I set the torch in an empty wall sconce and stepped into a room that rose hundreds of feet, narrowing to a small opening at the center of its roof.

"Mom."

The word came out raw, catching in my throat as I rushed forward, stepping into the patch of moonlight and halting beside the massive red-leaved tree reaching toward its single, pale beam. It was exactly as I'd seen when I tried to open a portal. She was motionless, caught in the tree's trunk and branches.

For six years, she'd been dead.

Six years of talking to her headstone. Six years of waking from dreams with her voice in my ears, forcing myself to remember they were only dreams. Only a few days ago, Grace's words and those dreams had cracked that certainty. I'd barely let myself hope.

Now that fragile hope collided with the sight in front of me and splintered into something sharp.

A different memory rose up—hospital lights too bright, the steady beep of machines, the thinness of her voice when she tried to sound fine for my sake. Nurses speaking softly in the hall, thinking I couldn't hear. I hadn't understood everything, but the fear had hollowed me out.

Back then, I'd folded in on myself, drowning in my own panic instead of seeing hers.

Then, I'd been too late.

My chest cinched as the same cold thought tried to anchor itself now.

I swallowed hard against the sob clawing its way up and forced my feet to move. I came to her side and lifted a hand, then stopped with my fingers suspended inches from her skin.

Pain was etched into the fine lines of her otherwise smooth face. A shock of silvery-white hair, stained red and brown, tangled in the branches cradling her in place. When I'd seen her last, she'd been nearly forty, black hair threaded with gray at her temples, faint lines at the edges of her eyes from smiling at me across the table.

This woman looked untouched by time, too perfect in her stillness, as if the years had slid off her and left only something polished and waxen behind.

I searched her face for some trace of the mom who burned pancakes and hummed the most beautiful other-worldly melody while she did the dishes, something familiar I could hold on to.

A drop of water slid off my chin and landed on her collarbone, disappearing against her skin.

I was crying.

My fingers trembled as I finally closed the distance, brushing a silver curl back from her hollow cheek. Her skin was cool, not frozen. Not dead. Heat pricked behind my eyes. Was there real warmth there, or was I just desperate enough to invent it?

Either way, I wasn't ready to hope.

"How did you do it?" I whispered, voice cracking. "How did you lend me your gift when you were already gone?"

My chest swelled, but I forced the emotion down.

Noises at the end of the hall grew louder. Rough scraping sounds. Grunts. The cave itself felt like it was holding its breath.

I ignored it all and flattened my palm carefully over her chest, avoiding the branches piercing through her. No human would've survived this for even a day, but fae were more resilient. Had she lived? Suffered? Hung here all this time while I went about my life in New York?

Under my hand, something fluttered.

Brilliant viridian eyes snapped open and locked on mine.

I stumbled backward, tripping over a stone and crashing to my knees before scrambling up again. "Mom!"

She blinked, eyes softening when she saw me. That one look reduced me to a child. Twenty-five years of life—of hardship and pain—the last six without her, and one look from her reduced me to a boy. I was fragile and small, wanting nothing more than for her to open her arms and protect me from the world. But she couldn't protect me from this.

"Jack."

"Don't try to talk." I scanned the length of her, searching for the best way to remove her from the monstrosity pinning her in place.

"Jack," she whispered again. "I've missed you, my little prince." Her throat worked, trying to swallow around thick barbs piercing her collarbone.

Fresh tears streamed down my cheeks, but I slid my hand under her head, lifting so her weight didn't press into the bark. Blood welled where the branch speared her chest, but I continued lifting. If I could free her from the tree, she could heal. She was fae. She could recover.

Her fingers twitched, catching my attention, and I glanced at the arm run through with another thick branch. I pulled and she let out a blood-curdling scream. I froze, my limbs trembling with rage and anguish. "Please. Mom. Take your immunity back. Please..."

Our eyes met, hers glimmering with a bone-deep agony carved from years of pain.

Dry lips forced a smile. "I knew... you... would come."

"I'll get you out of here."

"I never left you." Her soft, tender voice, even ravaged as it was, was a balm to my soul. The comforting voice in the dark. The soothing sound of the hero who chased away my nightmares with a kiss.

"I never thought you did." My words were punctured by sobs. I tried and failed to get them under control. I had to be strong for her. Had to keep a level head and get her out.

I wiped my wet lashes with the back of my free hand, bending toward her to try again, when her eyes went wide. "Ja—"

Her croak was cut off in the same moment something sticky touched the side of my neck. I tried to turn. Tried to call the flames inside me to fight off an attack, but I was stuck. Frozen in place. Only my eyes could move, straining to the left to see the owner of those strange, spongy fingers.

They didn't feel like skin. They pressed and held with a damp suction, clinging to my throat as if she could drink my breath through my skin.

Violet eyes met mine.

I tried again to jerk out of her touch, but my limbs were leaden, my feet stuck to the floor. My gaze swiveled to my mom, still wide-eyed, but the woman who held me frozen in place rested her other hand on my mom's shoulder.

I wanted to shout at her, to scream, but I could do nothing but stare.

"Our prisoner has been quite the honeypot. She's lured many into this trap." The woman smiled, glancing between me and my mother. I tried to convey my rage and hatred with a look, but her grin only widened. "It isn't her you should be worried for, Jack." She knew my name. A chill crept down my spine. "Mommy has immortality. A gift she's kept quite close."

My gaze returned to my mom, taking her in again. Immortality. Did it mean she couldn't be killed? No matter what? It was all at once the best news of my life and the worst. If I couldn't save her, she would be trapped like this—impaled on this tree—for eternity. Long after this sick woman and her co-conspirators were gone, my mom would be here.

I had to do something. I couldn't let it end this way.

As if she'd heard my thoughts, the woman said, "I'm sorry, Jack, but I need you out of the way." Her grip tightened on my neck and the magic holding me in place intensified. My breathing grew labored, my heart slowed. "You're a wild card, your gifts still untested. While the idea of using you to learn more about mixed blood appeals to me, I don't know enough about your gifts to take that chance."

My vision blurred as I struggled to suck in another breath, even my panic sedated by the vile magic coursing through me. My attacker went on as if nothing was wrong. "I don't know why you all care so much about her." The woman's hot breath fanned my face. "I'd think as a half human you'd hate her for helping Mab try to end your kind." Her magic pressed into me as darkness danced at the edges of my vision. "You knew she was a spy, didn't you? That she made Xcess to enthrall the humans so Mab could enslave them? Just as she did with us."

Her words were sharp, a little crazed, but I could only focus on one thing. My mom. Her immortality would save her and doom her to this eternity.

"But Mommy might finally be willing to give up that immortality if it means saving you." Her gaze burned the side of my face. I tried to shout. To tell my mom not to listen to the vile woman's words, but my tongue was stuck to my teeth. "Shall we find out?"

Her finger lifted from my mom's shoulder and a wicked dagger glinted in the moonlight. I tried to mouth the words to my mom, blocking out the purple-eyed woman's voice. I had failed her. I had failed her and she would watch me die.

"Jack," she cried, free of the other woman's magic. "Close your eyes, my prince."

I didn't, even as the knife slid painlessly into my neck.

Blood pumped from the wound as the knife clattered to the floor. It was a slow rhythmic pulse. Hot liquid gushed down my neck, through the woman's sticky fingers, soaking my tunic.

"What do you say, Aconite? Will you give up your immortality for your only son?"

My heart kicked, blood pumping faster. My vision tunneled, the world going out of focus. Only the same green eyes that had haunted me for six years held my attention, even as my lids grew heavy.

A face flickered at the edge of that blur, freckles and violet eyes and a crooked almost-smile, the one she wore when she finally told me she loved me. Sav. I wanted one more breath with her. One more second.

Distantly, I heard my mother's voice, begging for me.

The blood soaking into my shirt was hot against my rapidly cooling skin and I swayed, registering too late that the woman had released me. I stumbled to my knees, palms drenched in the pool of blood at my feet. My blood. I stared down, but it was gray, not red. Color was slipping away.

Thud. Thud... Thud.

The beats faded, sliding farther and farther out of reach. Then nothing.

SIXTY-FOUR

SAV

I knew where Jack would go.

The Blood Wood.

The memory of that conversation while I lay in stasis shouldn't have been mine, but I wouldn't look a gift kelpie in the mouth.

The Blood Wood was forbidden to Spring Court. Which, of course, meant I'd been there half a dozen times.

From the border, it would take half a day. I didn't have half a day.

I called Faerie's magic into my limbs—not from the well inside me, but from the world itself—and ran until the forest blurred, colors smearing into streaks as trunks flashed past and the ground vanished beneath my feet.

As I moved, Grace's bargain gnawed at me.

Too careful. Too precise.

Had she kept me wrapped in vines to protect me from something she believed would happen, or had she only needed me helpless long enough to extract what she wanted?

What did she care about Mira's mother's fate?

I knew so little of the wilds of Faerie, of the truly old creatures who remained hidden from our kind. If we were nightmares and legends to the humans, then the puca, the Lady of the Lake, the Winter Hag, and Barbegazi were the legends whispered among ours.

But if the Lady was the daughter of Firethorn, Mab's only son, and Lorelai, a princess of the sea, how could she be immortal?

The question chased me as the air grew colder, the trees darker.

I slowed at the edge of the Blood Wood.

It was nearly dawn. A sliver of burning orange crested the horizon, peeking between the black trunks and gilding the forest floor in flaming crimson. It looked like a lake of fire poured beneath the trees.

I stepped lightly into it, scanning the ground for signs of their party.

A trail of broken branches greeted me.

Thank Gaia. Jack would never be adept at traveling undetected.

SIXTY-FIVE

JACK

I blinked. The world snapped into violent clarity, then immediately blurred at the edges.

"He's awake."

The words drifted down from somewhere above me. I squinted up. Two shapes leaned over me, swimming in and out of focus. A glittering silver nose ring, a pair of bright orange eyes, a familiar sharp jaw. Fero. Beside him, Juniper's wild hair framed a face pinched tight with worry.

Fero's arm moved and suddenly his hand was in front of my face. I stared at it for a heartbeat before my brain caught up. My own fingers were tacky with drying blood as I reached for him, and he hauled me upright. The room pitched sideways. My knees buckled.

"Whoa." His grip tightened around my arm, steadying me. "You've lost... most of your blood. Can you walk?"

His words wavered in and out, like they were coming through water. Shapes around us hardened at the edges. Then I saw her.

Mom.

The tree's black trunk loomed behind her, branches spearing through her arms and shoulders. My chest cinched tight. I lurched toward her, legs wobbling.

"Mom." The word tasted like chalk. I pressed my hand to the trunk, leaning my weight into it so I wouldn't fall. "We need to get you out."

I grabbed the nearest branch. The bark bit into my palm, rough and painted in ruby where her blood had dried on it. My knuckles went white as I wrenched. The branch snapped with a sharp crack that echoed up into the hollow space.

Before, I'd been afraid to touch any of it, sure the tree was the only thing keeping her from bleeding out. But if she truly couldn't die, then freeing her had to be the first step to letting her heal.

I wrapped my fingers around the splinter skewering her arm and pulled.

She screamed.

The sound ripped through the chamber, raw and piercing. My stomach heaved. I stumbled back into the trunk, dragging air into my lungs in sharp, ragged pulls. "Take back... immunity," I choked, my tongue thick and clumsy. "Please. Take it back." I couldn't watch her suffer one more heartbeat.

A hand landed on my shoulder and I flinched.

"She can't," Juniper whispered.

"She has to." My voice came out in a broken rasp.

Juniper's nails dug in, sharp crescents through fabric. The pressure barely registered, but it anchored me. I dragged my gaze back to my mother.

Her face had gone corpse-pale, lips ghastly blue. A tremor ran through her, as if the tree itself was shivering around her. Something in the room had shifted. Wrong.

"She'll die when you remove her from the tree, Jack," Juniper said softly.

"No. She's immortal." The words felt like a lie.

The satyr shook her head, but I stepped around her, reaching for my mother's freed arm. I caught her hand, careful to avoid the wounds. She smiled. Skin flaked and cracked at the corners of her mouth.

"My little Jacaranda."

My senses crept back, stitching together the torn edges of memory. I'd been dead, should've been. "What did you do?"

Her weak smile warmed. "Saved my child." She coughed; red slicked her lips. I slid a hand beneath her head so she wouldn't choke. "As any mother would."

The words hit, and something inside me shifted. "Take it back. I don't want it." A tear slipped hot down my cheek. "I want you."

Her grip tightened, strong, even with torn biceps. "I have lived a full life." Another cough. "I have loved." Her eyes misted. "And I have known the joy of motherhood, a gift I never expected."

I pressed my forehead to her cheek. "I can't lose you. Not when I just got you back."

She closed her eyes. "Promise me you won't blame your father." A ragged breath. "He only did what I asked."

The words cut new and deep. My father was barely in the ground, and she was asking me to forgive him.

But if she wouldn't take back her immortality, she would die. I wouldn't let her last moments be a different kind of pain. I wouldn't tell her what happened to him.

I'd kept my anger like a weapon for years. If I let it go now, I didn't know what I'd have left.

I had believed she was already dead. Now I'd lose her all over again. "Please, Mom. Take back your immortality."

"Your life is just beginning." Her fingers squeezed mine. "You can do so much good. Let me join my people beyond the veil." She coughed. "Free me from this tree."

Juniper came to my side; Fero braced me from the other. She was asking me to do what I couldn't six years ago: let her go. But I was selfish. I wanted to keep her.

"I won't. I can't..."

"My prince." Her voice was gentle. "Faerie needs you. And even with Mother gone, Earth does too. My time has passed."

Heat flooded my eyes. "Take your pain-immunity back," I whispered. "I won't free you while you're in pain."

She nodded and closed her eyes.

White-hot fire exploded behind my brow. My arm screamed—broken, I realized only now. Smaller aches flared. My lungs burned. My heart hammered, desperate to restore the blood I'd lost.

Nothing compared to what she'd borne daily. Lines in her brow softened; the fine crinkles at her eyes eased. She was ethereally beautiful, skin smooth, luminous silver hair sparkling. But the hollows beneath her eyes and the pallor stayed. Numbness couldn't cure what would still kill her.

"Together?" Juniper murmured.

I drew a shaky breath. Fero reached up and cracked the remaining branches pinning my mother's arm in place.

Mom smiled, opened her eyes, and met each of ours in turn. "Thank you."

An open-ended bargain brushed my skin. I wanted to scream. Where was her justice? What kind of world let a perfect soul endure so much while monsters roamed free? I scanned the shadows. My attacker was gone. I'd find her later.

I cradled my mother's head and squeezed her hand. Juniper set her palms to the thickest bark through Mom's middle. Fero wrapped both hands around the lengths spearing her legs.

Mom met my gaze and nodded, the gentlest smile. It shattered me.

I had never taken a life.

CASSANDRA ASTON

Now I would end my mother's.

We lifted together. I never looked away from her. No flicker of pain, only relief swelling in her emerald eyes. My thumb found her wrist out of habit, searching for a pulse I already knew was slipping. I fell to my knees, her head in my lap. Juniper and Fero turned away to give us a final moment.

"I'm so sorry," I sobbed.

"Promise me," she whispered. "Promise you'll forgive your father."

"Mom..."

"I asked him to protect the humans from my mother."

The ice that had been living inside my ribs, years of cold, hate-soaked grief, cracked. I had never reconciled the man who raised me with the one who tortured and killed fae. He'd done it for her. Then why had he said she betrayed us? Now, I would never be able to ask.

Her gaze traced the outline of my face, memorizing it. "Listen to me. They used me to create rifts in Faerie." She coughed, a wet rattling sound. "The missing pockets should have been destroyed..." She coughed again. "But I fought it. Fought the taint so that they were only hidden. When I go, Faerie will be restored."

She swallowed and a tear slid down my cheek. "Shhh. Mom. Don't talk."

Trembling fingers lifted to my face. "They must not learn you have that gift too."

My vision blurred. "They won't. I promise." It was a hollow promise. We both knew fae like Foxglove existed, those who could pry any secret from your mind. But none of that was my mom's burden.

The pad of her finger skimmed the path my tears made, wiping them away. "You've grown into a man." Her smile pierced the ruins of my heart. "I would have given it to you sooner."

"What?" I rasped.

Her hands cupped my face, tugging me close. I leaned in, breathing in her scent and memories of nights under blankets, a flashlight's glow, her voice reading while lightning split the sky outside.

I fought the sobs. I'd be strong. For her.

She drew a pattern over my heart, the one she'd traced a hundred times, but backward this time.

"The immortality my mother gave me just before she died. But you're —" Her breath hitched; her eyes flew wide.

"Mom? Mom!"

Her body trembled; small spasms shook through her. I folded her thin frame into my arms, stilling the shudders. "Shhh," I breathed into her hair. "I'm here. Your little Jacaranda is here."

312

Wet seeped into my collar, soaking my chest. I rocked us, whether to comfort her or myself I couldn't say. "I'm here," I whispered. "I'm here, Mom."

The tremors ebbed. I loosened my hold and tipped her face.

Her eyes were open, staring at nothing.

"Mom," I gasped. "Mom?"

Something tore inside me, something vital. I traced the line of her cheek with shaking fingers, the way I used to when I was small and she'd sit on the edge of my bed with a book and a flashlight, making the whole world shrink down to her voice.

I wanted that voice again. Just one sentence. One more breath.

My throat locked. I pulled her closer and pressed my forehead to hers.

"I love you," I whispered.

Wherever she was, I prayed she heard me. I prayed she'd found my father, and that for the first time in six years she wouldn't be alone.

Sixty-Six

Sav

The ground surged under my feet, and my heart climbed into my throat. Crackling energy swelled in the air. Something had happened. Something big.

I reached the mouth of a cave and slowed. A massive troll lay on his side, a vicious-looking knife buried to the hilt in his throat, another in his ear. I would know those blades anywhere. Juniper.

I climbed over the rockfall choking the entrance and listened. Beyond the wall, darkness stretched forever while earth and rot pressed thick in the air.

On the balls of my feet, I reached for the dagger at my hip. Soft voices grazed my ear. I eased forward and winced when my boot nudged a stone. Silence snapped taut ahead. A trap? Would I find Jack already bleeding? Worse?

Cold silver touched my neck. Hot breath lifted the hairs at my nape.

"Sav," Juniper whispered. The blade slid away and sheathed. "Come. He'll want to see you."

My breath hitched. "Is he... okay?"

She touched my arm. I flinched. "You'll see."

I abandoned stealth and ran, skidding to a halt in a cavernous room washed by the first light of morning.

I froze. A male who might have been Jack looked up. Brilliant emerald eyes met mine.

"Jack?"

Tear tracks streaked cheeks now carved into sharper angles. Hair like poured silver curled around ears that tapered to rounded points. Lips, deep blue like Hazel's, were pinched with grief. His tunic, once creamy with bronze accents, was stained in crimson. I searched every inch of his exposed skin, finding no wounds to account for it. Not his blood. I exhaled softly.

My gaze dropped to the still form in his arms and my breath caught.

I knelt and rested a hand on his shoulder. Indigo-tinged fingertips brushed his mother's waxen cheek, tracing the hollow along her jaw.

"She's gone," he whispered.

My heart cracked. Grace's warning slid into place. Jack had lost his humanity. The last vestiges of my terror drained away as I wrapped my arms around him and squeezed. "I'm so sorry."

Unusual magic stirred in the chamber, and I couldn't tell if it belonged to Jack, his mother's passing, or something else entirely.

Magic jolted through Faerie again and the floor tilted; I fell into Jack. When I looked up, steadying myself, the cave seemed to stretch into an infinite distance. Jack's shoulders went rigid. Light flared from the body in his arms, a soft shimmer that burst outward, momentarily blinding me. When the dim returned, the air still glimmered, but his arms were empty.

"Mom!" He lurched to his feet. I stumbled back. He *was* taller now, bigger. His clenched fists glowed in the dark.

"She's gone," Juniper whispered at my shoulder. "Gaia has accepted her."

Jack's eyes, glowing and bloodshot, swung to us. "Where? Where did she go?"

"She is part of Faerie now."

He raked the room with a frantic gaze as if she might be hiding in the stone. I had never seen the rite. High fae were buried or burned. Low fae had their funerals, and when Gaia accepted them, the land carried their memory and magic forever. The goddess had granted Jack's mother a rare honor.

I reached for his fist. He flinched, as if remembering me. Heat fizzled under my palm and died so quickly I might have imagined it. Our magics should be compatible, his fire should've slid off me harmlessly, but his felt hotter, more dangerous somehow. For the first time, I wondered if it could hurt me.

He turned to me, tears glinting in his green eyes. He closed them and leaned into my shoulder. Energy rolled off him in waves. His glamour had fallen away, revealing what he was. Hadn't I always known he couldn't look that human without help? He must have worn it his whole life.

It was a powerful shield meant to hide his form *and* his magic. To keep him invisible in the human realm. To keep him hidden from Mab.

The realization hit hard. Aconite had feared what her mother would do if she learned of the half-human child. My thoughts snagged on Mira, Kaspar's half-sister, another child with two parents from different worlds. The Lady of the Lake remained one of Faerie's great mysteries to me. What did that make Jack?

His shoulders shook. I held him tighter and grimaced as raw magic pressed against my skin. I would need to teach him control now that the leash was gone. Later. We would talk about everything later.

"We must leave this place," Juniper said, cutting off my thoughts.

Jack scrubbed a hand over his face and straightened. His fingers found mine and laced tight. I had to crane my neck to meet his eyes. He had grown into the tallest male I knew, taller even than Creig.

He searched my face. His grip tightened and he pulled me closer. I stumbled, and his eyes went wide. "I'm sorry."

I eased my hand free and shook it out. "You're stronger now, too."

Terror flickered across his features. He looked from his blue-tipped fingers to the corded muscle in his forearms, then to my much smaller hand. "I'm sorry," he whispered again.

"Sav."

I glanced at Juniper. Her jaw said she was done waiting. I nodded. "Where are they?"

Fero stepped into a shaft of pre-dawn light. "Autumn's castle."

I frowned.

"I'll bring us to them." Jack lifted his hands. Without looking back at the place that had caged Winter's princess, he cut the air. Space split open, a pocket forming into a vast stone chamber lit by flickering red candles.

Anguish rolled through the opening, hot and steady. It hit my skin and my instincts screamed.

Before I could say a word, Fero charged through.

Juniper tore her daggers free and leaped after him.

Jack stepped forward.

"Wait," I called. "Something's wrong."

He paused and turned. "What?"

I opened my mouth to warn him, but the world slowed as a spear shot out of the portal and punched into his shoulder.

Jack's eyes went wide. He staggered, momentum carrying him forward, and he fell through the opening.

"Jack!"

There was no time to think. I launched after him.

Fire surged in my palms as I crossed the threshold, candlelight and shouting swallowing me whole.

SIXTY-SEVEN

JACK

I hit the stone hard and rolled, tearing the spear free from my shoulder. Blood followed it out, hot and fast, before the wound cinched and began to knit. I barely had time to suck in a breath before hands were on me.

They came from everywhere. Nails raked my arms. Weight piled on, dragging me down. Their eyes were empty and glassy, mouths working as they lunged.

Fire burst through the portal.

Sav.

Flames tore across the chamber in a single violent sweep, driving them back long enough for her to reach me. The heat flared bright, blinding, and then it guttered out.

Gone. Something in my chest went cold. She'd burned herself out again.

Sav stumbled as she landed. Her breath hitched. For a heartbeat she looked stunned, like she hadn't expected the fire to fail her.

Then she pulled her blades.

She was on them anyway. Steel flashed. A dagger sank into a spine. Another into a throat. She fought with what she had left, fast and ruthless, carving space around me as the blank-eyed fae surged again.

"Sav," I choked, pushing up on my elbows.

She didn't look at me. "Stay down."

A creature scrambled over my shoulder, teeth bared. Sav drove a blade into its back and wrenched it free.

"Stop," I said, catching her wrist.

She ripped free, breath sawing, eyes blown wide. "They'll kill you."

"They're drugged," I forced out. "They're not choosing this."

Another fae lunged.

Sav lifted her blade again.

Her knees buckled.

She dropped hard, the fight spilling out of her all at once. I caught her before she hit the stone, hauling her against me as her weight sagged boneless in my arms. "Sav!" I tightened my hold, refusing to let her go.

Her whole body trembled. Tears slid down her cheeks, her lashes fluttering as her gaze lost focus.

Too soon. Grace had warned us she would need time to recover. Her head tipped back and her eyes rolled shut.

Pain exploded across my back as another blade struck. I hissed and turned, bracing Sav against my chest as I put myself between her and the attackers. I felt the wound already closing as I shifted my stance, shielding her with battered limbs and muscle.

Fero went down under a crush of bodies with a curse. Juniper swung her axe in a brutal arc, dropping three attackers at once.

I scanned the chamber, breath ragged.

Foxglove and the others were nowhere in sight.

It was a trap.

The air thickened, damp and oppressive. The fine hairs along my arms lifted.

Water surged up from the darkness ahead, rising into a towering wall. A massive black kelpie broke through the surface and shifted in a blink, spreading his arms wide.

Cold slammed into me. Spray wrapped around Sav and me hardened in an instant, turning clear and unyielding—glass. It locked us in place, molded to our bodies. I couldn't move without risking her.

Behind us, Juniper screamed as glass closed around her. Fero froze in place from the neck down.

A low hum vibrated through the chamber. The sound came from a weapon shaped somewhere between a trident and a tuning fork. Recognition hit like a fist. I'd seen him in Lakes and Streams when he came for Sav.

Aegon. Prince of Oceans and Seas.

"Welcome," he said, smiling with two rows of black teeth. "To my kingdom."

◆ ➔ (⌣ ◆ ⌒ ◆ ◆ ◆

Glassy-eyed orcs hauled us down stone corridors and dropped us into metal-barred enclosures surrounding a vast cave. Magic buzzed thick enough to make my stomach hollow.

Sav stirred in my arms, breath uneven, her skin slick with sweat.

Something pressed down on my senses, smothering my gifts. I reached for my fire. Nothing answered.

Candlelight caught on the bars in dull, lifeless lines. Shapes shifted behind them.

"Juniper?" a voice called.

"Foxglove?" Juniper answered.

"Yes. I'm here. Are you injured?"

"They tried."

"Murz?"

"Yeah."

"Can you see them?" Foxglove asked.

"No. Only Larek."

Sav shifted again, eyes fluttering open. Relief hit me so hard it stole my breath. She swallowed. "Jack?"

"I'm okay," I said immediately.

Her shoulders eased a fraction. Then her brow furrowed. "Hazel," she rasped. "Where are you? Are you hurt?"

"I'm here," Hazel called from another enclosure. "I'm okay. I just can't shift."

Sav sagged back against me with a shaky breath.

"I can't move inside this glass," Juniper muttered.

"It should melt within an hour," Foxglove said.

"Are your gifts suppressed?" Fero asked.

"Mine are," Larek answered.

"I can't sense emotions," Sav said quietly. She swallowed. "And I can't compel anyone."

"My fire wasn't working before," I whispered against the shell of her ear. "I can't test it now."

"When the glass melts, we break the bars and run," Sav said, restlessness threading through her exhaustion. "Can you do that?"

I shook my head. "The moment I stepped through the portal, my magic dulled. Down here, it's worse."

Her brow creased. I wanted to promise her safety.

I couldn't.

Anyone who could cage us, command an army, and smother our gifts was powerful beyond anything we'd faced. Grace had said we'd need to be together. Maybe this was what she meant. But we weren't complete. The boy and Grace hadn't come with us.

Voices murmured through the chamber. Foxglove spoke quietly with

Juniper. Hazel and Larek whispered. No one mentioned what I had become.

I was grateful.

As the rush of battle drained away, grief filled the hollow it left behind. Sav murmured something I couldn't catch, and I focused on her breathing, steadying myself with it.

Then silence fell.

A fae with tufted ears and speckled, deer-like legs stepped into the chamber. Her eyes were vacant. She didn't react when Sav called her name.

She drew a thin black blade across her forearm. Blood welled. She smeared it along the bars of our enclosure, crouched to trace the line across the floor, then rose and dragged the mark up the far side, sealing the rectangle.

"Can you hear me?" Sav pleaded. "You don't have to do this."

The fae moved on, cutting herself again. Foxglove pressed to his bars, voice low and coaxing, but nothing reached her. When she reached Fero's enclosure, the room went still. We watched as she grew paler, feeding whatever binding magic held us. When she had finished her work, she slipped quietly into the shadows.

Time dragged.

At last, the glass softened and ran away, leaving us cold and damp. I slid down the bars and Sav followed, crawling into my lap. I wrapped my arms around her, holding her close. Without the glass, the chill sank deep. I reached for heat. Nothing answered.

Metal clanged. Trays scraped beneath the bars.

"Don't eat," Fero warned. "It's drugged."

I leaned my head back against the bars. Sav slept on, breath warm against my throat. I closed my eyes, praying she'd recover quickly.

Praying she'd be strong for whatever came next.

SIXTY-EIGHT

SAV

I blinked, taking in my surroundings. It was dark; crimson candles flickered against stone walls, our only light. There were no windows or cracks to let in the sun. No way to tell if it was midday or midnight. Jack's arms held me tightly even in sleep. My clothes were stiff, finally dry after an immeasurable stretch in our cell. The smell of roasted vegetables tugged my gaze. Two trays sat against our bars, but even Autumn's seasonings couldn't hide the poison underneath.

They meant to drug us. To make us compliant the way Juniper had once been.

They underestimated us.

I rolled my shoulders, working out battle kinks and the ache of sitting too long. Jack mumbled and hugged me closer, lashes still pressed to his cheeks. White lashes that had been black before. I studied his sleeping face, free to catalogue the differences. A scar cut his right cheek, crossing the spot where his dimple showed when he smiled. His jaw was sharp, white stubble roughening it after days without shaving. Snowy curls fell over his brow, hiding the darker shadows under his eyes.

My gaze traced the exposed skin through the tears in his shredded Summer Court tunic. Smooth, whole, as if the drugged folk had never slashed skin at all.

I tucked a loose curl behind one tapered ear. They weren't as long as mine, and the soft, rounded tips made them oddly similar to human ears even as they stood proudly. I ran a fingertip along the lobe, following its line.

A thought surfaced. Mab looked more like humans than the rest of us.

She too had ears that were less pointed than ours. Her features softer. I could have blamed Jack's strange ears on his human father, but something in me said that was wrong. These were the alien ears of those who came from a distant world and crashed into Faerie ten thousand years ago.

Either way, there was no denying his lineage. Mab's line bore a single striking feature. In ten thousand years, no Winter royal had hair of any other color. It made sense that Aconite glamoured their hair. If Mab's spies had ever searched Earth, they would never have guessed the human boy with black hair was her direct descendant.

"Watching me sleep, Savage?"

I grinned and kissed his nose. "Is it a crime?"

White lashes lifted. Emerald eyes met mine, impossibly bright. The invisible tether between us pulled taut, dragging me closer. I pressed my mouth to his and he answered, fingers flexing at my waist.

"Did you sleep?"

"A little." I rested my brow to his. "You should too. You need it."

He lifted his head and scanned the room behind me. "We have to get out of here."

I nodded. "Autumn's blood magic isn't like anything else in Faerie. We'll need a way to neutralize it."

A deep voice rumbled through the stone. "I tried my blood. It didn't work."

"Fero?" I turned toward the wall.

"Yes, Princess. And don't think this cage dissolves our bargain. You two must live so my son has a place to call home when this is over."

I laughed, brittle and dry. I'd used my magic too soon and I was still recovering from its effects. "If your blood wasn't strong enough, I don't know what hope we have."

"You have Mab's grandson in there, do you not? I can think of no better blood."

I straightened. He was right. If any blood could unlace wards, it would be Jack's. "Jack."

He nodded before I could say more and eased out from under me, rising to the bars. He slid an unused dagger from his belt and set it to his wrist. I guided the blade higher on his forearm. The edge kissed his skin and crimson welled along a thin line. He looked to me.

"Do as the fawn did," I said. "Trace it along the bars."

He did, reopening the cut three times to finish the line. The wound closed almost as quickly as he drew it. Even for a fae, he healed fast.

Jack gripped the bars with both hands and pushed, putting his weight into the metal.

Nothing.

"Try the seam," I said, frowning. "Drip your blood between the bars wherever the magic seals it."

He tried again, digging in his heels and heaving. Still nothing. He might as well have been human. I took his place, teeth gritted as I shoved. The door held.

"I'll try," Larek called. We held our breath through a series of grunts, then his sigh. "No."

One by one, each of them tried and failed.

"I can try." I lifted a dagger to my arm.

"Sav." Jack's voice flattened. I glanced back to find his mouth a hard line.

"I have to."

He folded his arms, watching.

I understood his urge to protect. I felt the same. But we would face worse before this ended. I was sure of it.

I drew a long, thin cut and let my blood fall, smearing a line across the floor, up the bars, then rose onto my tiptoes to reach the top rail. Fingers wrapped around my waist, lifting me and I closed the loop. Jack set me down and I leaned into his warmth, eyeing my work.

Satisfied, I braced my hands on the bars. And... fell straight through.

Cold stone scraped my palms and I pushed up, staring through the gaping bars in disbelief.

I'd done it. *My* blood had freed us.

SIXTY-NINE

JACK

Sav spun to me, shock still written across her face. I moved cautiously, unwilling to rush into another trap. When no army of drugged fae leaped from the shadows, I dropped to a knee, scooped her up, and spun her.

"You did it!"

"I did."

"Sav. Hurry." Fero's clipped tone carried tension. I set Sav down and scowled at the prince. Sav pulled a dagger from her belt loop and traced the same blood line over his cell door. It swung open. She flashed me a grin, then crossed to Foxglove's cage and began again.

My chest tightened as I looked down the long row. There were at least a dozen cells. Only ours had held two.

Hazel's door swung open. She wrapped Sav in a tight hug. "I'm so sorry," she breathed. The hurt in her eyes told me what she thought. That she was to blame.

Sav hugged her back. "It's not your fault."

"She's a chameleon," Hazel said, cutting her off.

Sav studied her a moment, then moved on and freed Larek. "Who?" she called over her shoulder as she continued working to free the others.

Larek lifted Hazel off her feet. Her cheeks flamed as she glanced around, but when he set her down, she kept his hand.

Sav moved to the next cell, staring blankly at it, then looked back at the group. "Where's Murz?"

"The drugged fae took him away while you were sleeping. That was hours ago, and we haven't seen him since." Sav opened her mouth, but

Foxglove spoke again. "Come on," he said, wrapping his hand around Juniper's and bolting toward a dark corridor. "We'll look for him on our way out."

I closed the distance to Sav and lifted her arm, inspecting her wound. It was healing quickly, but not quickly enough.

"Pr—" Hazel began.

Her words were swallowed by a booming laugh that rolled through the chamber.

Only then did I notice the stream running through the cavern had been rising. Frothing water spilled over the stone and soaked the floor around our boots. Instinct said to jump back. But the pain-immunity was gone, and down here my gifts were dead. I didn't even know what could neutralize what I really was.

"Going somewhere?"

My heart slammed against my ribs as the kelpie prince loomed over us, blocking the tunnel that led to our exit. Aegon had been waiting, testing whether we could break his bindings. None of us had, except Sav.

I tightened my grip on her fingers and drew her in at my side. Pieces of Aegon's plan clicked into place. Murz's absence was not a coincidence. He had portal magic like my mother. Her dying words resurfaced, clearer now. With her gone, they would need someone with portal magic to continue their plan. Could he survive it? He wasn't a powerful fae royal with immortality. He could make small tears in reality, only two before he needed to recover. If they pushed him past that limit...

Aegon rose on a tide of water. I reached for my power. Nothing. I was as helpless as I'd been most of my human life. A quick glance told me Fero's hands were empty of flame. Foxglove's clenched jaw and flickering gaze said his gifts were deadened too.

Larek moved first, a knife spinning from his fingers. A wall of water surged up and hardened to glass. The blade bounced off and skittered across the floor.

Aegon chuckled, flung his arms wide, and sent spears of water across the room. They solidified on impact, pinning Larek to the wall. More spears shot out in a wide arc. Several punched into Juniper's thighs and ribs, sending her crashing to the floor. Foxglove grunted as he dropped to his knees and crawled toward where she lay, a thin line of crimson trailing behind him.

"Give me the princess, Mab's heir."

Mab's heir. *Me.* I ground my teeth and yanked the last shard from my shoulder. My wounds were closing, but not fast enough.

Sav tore free of my weakening grip, darted in front of me, and spread her arms.

Aegon's grin slipped. Flame bloomed in Sav's palms. She screamed and hurled bright red blasts of flames at him.

"Sav! Don't!" My heart hammered in my chest as I pushed up. Too soon. Not again. How much could her body take?

He threw up another water wall and smothered the blast, but she ran for him, firing shot after shot.

I followed, begging my gift to answer. If I couldn't strike, I could still shield. As Aegon gathered another volley, I tackled Sav and covered her with my body.

Pain should have lanced through me. Instead, a solid weight crashed down. Water hardened to glass around us.

We were trapped again. I braced my back and shoulders and pushed. It didn't give an inch. Sav still had her fire here, and Aegon knew it now. I suspected it was why he had caged us together.

Sav was the most selfless creature I knew. She would not burn me even if it meant freeing herself to attack him.

Air thinned inside the glass. *I* wouldn't die for lack of breath. But she would. Her struggling slowed, then stopped as the realization hit her. She didn't have an hour.

"Sav," I said, keeping my voice low. "There isn't enough air."

"Yeah." Her breath stuttered. She went still for half a second, then dragged in another shallow pull that ended in a rough cough.

"I'm going to buy you time," I said.

She tried to twist, and the effort knocked a grunt out of me. "No."

I shifted my weight just enough to reach my belt and felt for the last blade. My hand moved at my hip. Her whole body went rigid beneath me. "Jack," she said, breath breaking. "Don't."

"I can't die," I said. "I'm immortal."

For a heartbeat, she didn't breathe at all. Then a thin, strangled sound tore out of her. "What?"

"I can't die," I said again. "But you can."

Her shoulders started to shake, whether from fury or panic I couldn't tell. "You're lying. Don't you dare pull some chivalrous act on me."

"I'm not."

"Jack. Stop." Her voice cracked, sharp and furious.

"There isn't time," I said.

Her breath hitched hard. She squirmed beneath me, uselessly, glass holding us fast. "No," she said, the word tearing out of her. "I don't agree. I don't accept it."

"I know," I said.

Another breath scraped out of her, thinner than the last.

"I won't let you," she said. "I swear to Gaia, Jack—"

"I've got you," I said, and slid the blade down.

I drove it into my thigh.

Pain detonated under my palm. Hot blood spilled, slick and fast. Sav made a sound that wasn't a word, her body bucking once beneath me before the glass stopped her.

"Stop," she gasped. "Stop it."

"I can't," I said, reopening the wound as it tried to close. Each gasp she took sounded smaller. "I'm stealing your air."

Her breathing broke into shallow, desperate pulls, each one shorter than the last. She shook beneath me. "I hate you," she choked. "If you do this—"

"You can hate me after you live," I said, cutting again.

I sliced along the same line, pressed harder, hit bone, and saw white. Blood pumped faster, but the wound knitted even faster. If there were room to reach my throat, I'd make it quicker, but Sav was fighting under my weight, trying to force space between us.

I stabbed again and sawed at skin that fought to hold my lifeblood in.

Dark crept in at the edges. Sav's words blurred under the heaviness in my chest. My grip slipped on the slick hilt.

It was working.

Just a few more. Just...

SEVENTY
FOXGLOVE

I crashed to my knees beside Juniper, digging jagged slivers from her torn, bleeding skin. Sav had accessed her magic, drawing all Aegon's focus, and he had trapped her and Jack, but I couldn't spare more than an instant for them.

Juniper tried to stand. Green blood pooled under her, slicking my hands. There was too much, and she wasn't healing fast enough. She had only just shaken the last of Dane's blood magic, only just started laughing without that hollow, brittle edge in her eyes. The sight of her sagging under her own weight sent ice down my spine. The idea of her slipping away again made my stomach lurch.

"Juniper. Don't move."

She ground her teeth and fought me. Her muscles bunched beneath my fingers, but blood loss made her weak. My grip tightened anyway, as if I could hold her together by sheer will.

Her gaze flicked to Aegon, to the bodies scattering the chamber, and I saw the moment she reached the same conclusion I had. Our group was no match for the Prince of Oceans and Seas with our two strongest fighters out.

Larek tore free of the shards pinning him to the wall and sprinted to Hazel, who looked dazed and unfocused. My innate gift was dead in this cave, but even without it I could see she was drowning in visions, her complexion dulled, eyes far away. Why was her gift working when mine wasn't?

Seer magic was strongest in Autumn. Had they left that line unblocked on purpose? Or, as with Sav, was some other magic at work here? The questions crowded in, but Aegon fired another volley of glass and I shoved the thoughts aside. I wrapped my arms around Juniper and grunted as two spears punched into my forearms. She grabbed the last dagger at my hip and hurled it. It went wide, clattering uselessly against the far wall, and my chest tightened.

Our last weapon. Missed.

I dragged Juniper backward toward the nearest cell and pulled her inside, pressing her to the wall. Glas shattered at our feet, just out of range.

"Release me," Juniper demanded.

"We have no weapons and you'll bleed out," I said, searching her face. "We need to regroup, then strike."

Her brows slashed low. For an instant, stubbornness flared in her eyes, then she nodded. I let my arms fall.

"You're bleeding too," she muttered. She stepped in close, the scent of rain-soaked moss and wild mint wrapping around me, and leaned over my shoulder. Her fingers brushed my skin as she gripped the shard. I braced and she tore slivers from my arms and back. Pain flared, but my pulse stumbled for an entirely different reason. Her.

I hissed as bloody shards clattered to the floor.

I edged to the door frame and peered out. I didn't risk a wider look.

Larek dragged Hazel across the stone floor, a smear of green trailing them as they disappeared from view in the cage beside us.

A guttural roar erupted. Prince Fero. Another wall of water crashed over the stone. Fero dropped to his knees near Aegon and water whipped around him, pinning him in place.

We were losing. Badly.

My gaze snapped to the glass mound shaped like two bodies across the room. I ached for my gifts. Either of them. Shifting, or even mind-to-mind speech, would change this fight.

The bars of our cage swung shut.

I lunged for the door and shoved. *Sealed. Damn.*

Larek shouted in the cell beside us. Trapped as well.

Aegon's laugh echoed. Juniper forced herself upright, wounds knitting just enough to slow the bleeding. She limped to my side and glared up at the kelpie prince.

"Your group has been a thorn in my side for some time," Aegon said, meeting each of our eyes and lingering on Fero, still outside the cells. "I had hoped to lure the princess out alone, but she never travels by herself, does she?"

His mouth curled. "And my nephew kept her guarded night and day for years."

My brows shot up. I knew Kaspar's true feelings for Sav. He'd shown his hand the day she was unbound, not by her sister but by a satyr of Juniper's clan. But that he'd guarded her all this time, even on Earth, was a secret he'd kept from every land fae.

If anyone had known, I should have.

"I planned to keep you all alive," Aegon went on. "Leverage for her compliance." Black eyes drilled into Fero's as the prince fought the water restraining him. "But you're more trouble than you're worth." He lifted a brow. "And I only need one to make her obey."

Twin streams shot from the water and speared Fero through the chest. He grunted and sagged forward. Hazel cried out in the cell beside us. Fero's head lolled to one side, a thin line of crimson trailing down his arm. My heart seized.

If Aegon meant to keep only one of us alive, I knew who it would be.

I found Juniper's hand and laced our fingers. She squeezed and looked up at me.

I was no use to anyone, disposable, but Juniper mattered. Perhaps I could convince Aegon of that. She was Sav's closest friend on Earth, and even after Sav learned why Juniper followed her there, she still cared.

A fawn stumbled into the room, eyes black as onyx, moving woozily. She was starving. Aegon hadn't treated his army well. I wasn't sure how long they had. How long any of us had.

She cut her palm and smeared blood down the cage beside us. The door swung wide. Larek shoved past her, twisted her neck, and dropped her. I winced. She hadn't chosen to be our jailer, but mercy wasn't his aim. Larek was bred for battle. He wouldn't go down without a fight.

He leaped.

Aegon raised both hands and a dozen water spears flew.

It hardened and glass peppered the air. Larek dodged most, slowed only when one struck his thigh. He snatched a knife from the floor, the same one Juniper had thrown. Summer's poison laced that blade. If his aim held, he had a chance.

Larek's arm rose.

A spray of glass punched his middle.

He crashed and slid, the poisoned knife skittering away.

From here I couldn't see his chest move. Without my gift, I couldn't reach his mind.

Hazel screamed and bolted from her cell.

"Hazel! No!"

My shout was drowned beneath her snarl. She slid across the wet stone and grabbed Larek's fallen blade.

Aegon watched, amused. He didn't consider her a threat, even with that poisoned blade. But perhaps he didn't know how deadly it was. One nick was all it should take. A slow, silent killer that would work its way to his heart with time. Summer's poison wasn't quick, but it was lethal.

He raised a hand, but she ducked before the spears formed, anticipating his move.

My breath hitched. Her sight was sharper here, surrounded by Autumn's seer magic. Could she outmaneuver him?

Another strike dodged. Instead of leaping at him, she dove into the stream beneath his feet.

Juniper let out a sharp cheer.

The air pressure shifted; ions buzzed over our heads. Hazel moved under the surface. Could Aegon shape spears underwater?

The wall of liquid he rode collapsed and crashed around us.

He dove.

My stomach flipped.

Even without magic, water was his domain. Hazel couldn't beat him below.

A crack split the din. I jerked toward the translucent coffin trapping Sav and Jack. Crimson glowed under the shell. Another crack. Then the cage shattered.

Sav screamed and burst free, hurling blast after blast of flame. Aegon was fully submerged, and her fire died against the flood. She didn't hesitate. She dove, vanishing beneath the surface and taking the fight out of view.

A groan dragged me back.

Jack forced himself to his knees, deathly pale and swaying. Most of his clothes were burned away. White lines and discolored patches webbed his skin, old scars now exposed. He should have been torn apart. He should have been bleeding. He wasn't.

I lunged for the bars again and shoved until my shoulders burned. They didn't give.

Juniper's hand tightened around mine.

Out there, Sav and Hazel fought in Aegon's water. In here, I had nothing. No gift. No blade. No way to reach them.

Only the sound of the stream, swallowing the fight while I shoved at bars that would not move.

SEVENTY-ONE

SAV

I sucked in a breath and dove for Aegon. He was sinking fast, his weight dragging him toward Hazel. Her eyes were wide, shock carved into her features. I hadn't seen the fight trapped under Jack's hulking form, but I'd heard every sound.

Jack had bought me a few extra breaths, and I wanted to shake him for it. Later. Right now, Hazel needed me.

Aegon reached Hazel and closed sharp talons around her throat. She slashed with her small knife and buried it in his shoulder. He grabbed for the hilt with his free hand but couldn't reach it. I surged closer, tore the blade free, and drove it into his neck. He twisted, tightening his hold on Hazel. Bubbles streamed from my mouth with the scream I couldn't stop.

I struck again. He caught my wrist, and pain detonated as bone cracked. The knife slipped from my hand.

I kicked to break free, but it was useless. He was stronger in water. He shot upward, hauling us both, one hand clamped around my arm, the other still locked on Hazel's throat. Hazel and I broke the surface together, gulping air. In the same frantic sweep, I found Fero sprawled across the stone, chest rising. Alive. For now.

Her breaths hitched and cut off under his grip; her face went blue. I roared, summoned flame, and seized his forearm, igniting his skin, the way I had centuries ago when another male had wrapped his fingers around another friend, attempting to choke the life from her.

He bellowed and wrenched my arm aside. White-hot pain flared; the joint bent wrong.

Aegon flung Hazel to the stone. She coughed and gagged, bile spilling as she crawled toward Larek.

I called another fireball and hurled it at Aegon's head.

"Enough, brat, or your friends die," he hissed, shaking me.

A wall of water shaped into six spears, all aimed at Hazel and Larek.

My stomach dropped. The flame in my palm winked out. I stilled. "Let them go and I'll do whatever you want."

He dropped me on the stone. I swallowed my scream of pain and nodded to Hazel, praying she would take Larek back into a cell.

Fero, still unconscious across the room, was temporarily forgotten by this monster. I would keep it that way as long as I could.

Jack was awake, alive, but still struggling to stand.

Heat climbed my throat so fast my vision pulsed. What had he been thinking, draining himself like that? Immortal or not, it would take time to recover from... death. I pushed up, teeth clenched against the throb in my arm.

"Let them go. I'll make a bargain."

"No!" Jack staggered toward us.

"Stay there, Jack!"

Hazel dragged Larek into a cell beside Juniper and Foxglove. Juniper ground her teeth and spat through the gap in Aegon's direction. Foxglove's gaze narrowed, focus shifting to the far wall.

Jack hadn't stopped moving. Soon, he would put himself in Aegon's line of fire. I started toward him.

"Stop," Aegon commanded.

I kept moving, boots skidding on blood-wet stone.

"Stop, or I kill them all."

I froze. My muscles locked before my brain could argue. I turned. "What do you want from me?"

A cell door to my left slammed. Good. Hazel and Larek were behind bars again, out of Aegon's immediate line of fire.

"Tell your lover to get in his cell and we will talk."

I frowned. Jack was stubborn on a good day; immortality wouldn't help. I looked back. He had made it two steps and dropped to his knees. Maybe not so hard.

I reached him in four strides and slid my good arm under his. He grunted, eyes catching on my mangled limb. "I'll kill him," he seethed.

A smile tugged at my lips before I could stop it. A few weeks ago, Jack wouldn't have stood a chance against a prince of water. Now, magic no longer trapped, Mab's blood in his veins and death no longer permanent, he just might.

If he survived his own idiocy.

"Come on. Listen to me for once."

A wide grin broke across his face. His blood was still too thin; not enough air had reached his brain. I braced and tried to haul him up. He had at least a hundred pounds on me.

"Please, Jack. I can't watch you bleed out again." I swallowed the lump in my throat. Somewhere behind us, Fero lay where Aegon's spears had dropped him, silent and still. He'd been unconscious for too long; I didn't dare look to see if his chest was still moving. Fero and I had our differences, and I feared him, but I didn't want his story to end here. He'd pushed us into a bargain. Had he known? Had he guessed this was his end? I might never know now.

Jack leaned hard on me and pushed to his feet. One step. Another.

"That's it. Almost there," I coaxed.

He smiled again, eyes glazed and a little too bright, and even as I cursed him, warmth curled through my chest. At least Jack would live.

Even if the rest of us did not.

We made it to the nearest open cell. My legs shook. My arm hung heavy and wrong at my side, each breath jarring it and sending pain blazing up into my shoulder.

"Inside," I whispered.

"Sav, no," he rasped. "I'm not leaving you with him."

"You're not leaving me," I said. "You're resting. There's a difference."

His fingers brushed my cheek, clumsy and too cold. "You promise you won't bargain yourself into something stupid?"

"Never," I lied.

He snorted weakly and let me guide him through the bars. The moment he cleared them, an orc with dull, glazed eyes stepped out from behind the nearest column. He sliced his palm and smeared blood over the metal. The ward shivered and sealed, leaving Jack on one side and me on the other.

I stepped back, swallowing the instinct to grab the bars and shake them until they broke.

Aegon rose higher on his rolling wave of water, the stream frothing around his hips. "Good," he said. "Now you will do something for me, Princess Aestus."

He wrapped the title in contempt, like he still didn't believe it was mine. I turned to face him, jaw tight. "What do you want?"

He flicked a webbed hand toward the line of cells. "The seer. Bring her."

Hazel stiffened. Larek pushed in front of her, hand braced on the bars. "Take me instead."

Aegon only smiled.

The same orc shuffled from Jack's door to theirs, lifting his bleeding palm. He smeared blood in a neat rectangle over the bars. Metal shivered. A gap opened.

"Don't go," Larek whispered. "We'll find another way."

Her fingers tightened around his wrists. "We both know this is the only way any of us survive," she said, voice so soft I almost missed it. She rose on her toes and kissed him, quick and fierce. When she drew back, her hand slid up, cupping his cheek. "I'm glad I found you," she breathed.

He held on for a heartbeat longer, knuckles white, then his grip loosened. Hazel slipped from his hands and stepped through the opening.

"Sav," Hazel called.

Her gaze snapped past me to the cavern floor. "He has it," she whispered, horror tightening her voice. "The crystal."

I crossed the chamber, every step sending a fresh pulse of pain up my ruined arm. The crystal sat near the center of the floor, a rough knot of faceted green stone, tide-pearl sized—wide enough that I had to cup it with both hands. It pulsed faintly, a Winter green that matched Hazel's eyes.

She stopped beside it, close enough that the glow painted her skin gray. Up close, she looked worse than she had in the cage. Sweat beaded along her hairline, her pupils blown wide.

"Will it hurt?" I asked.

Her throat bobbed. "No," she said. "It only amplifies what's already there."

"Enough," Aegon snapped. "Hands on the crystal."

Hazel set her palms to the stone.

"Picture a vast and violent ocean," Aegon ordered.

Her brows darted up, but she closed her eyes and did as he asked. The crystal brightened under her palms.

"Now you, Princess. Feed it your fire."

I lifted my good arm and winced.

"Sav," Jack called from his cell.

The flame starting to gather in my hand faltered. I glanced back. He gripped the bars, face pale, eyes dark with a worry I didn't have time for.

"Please," I mouthed. "Let me do this."

He shut his mouth, jaw clenched.

I turned back and called my fire properly this time. Heat crawled up my good arm, gathering in my palm until orange sparks danced across my fingers. My broken arm throbbed harder with every heartbeat, but I ignored it and pressed my hand to the stone.

Fire leaped from my skin, skittering over the crystal. It flared green, sending fractured light across Aegon's stream and the cavern walls, sharpening into trees and shadows.

Hazel's face pinched. Sweat beaded on her brow.

"Now narrow your focus to its center," Aegon said, voice low and intent.

The picture sharpened. Manicured paths cut through snow-laden boughs. Dark shapes speared the sky beyond the trees, blocking out a heavy gray light. A bridge arched over a rise of white-dusted green.

The frozen lake at its heart gleamed, a sheet of white. I knew this place.

I crushed the thought. If Aegon saw recognition on my face, if he guessed this world meant anything to me, he'd force me to talk and Hazel would be useless to him. I kept my features smooth, locked my jaw, and fed another surge of fire into the crystal.

"More," he demanded.

Hazel whimpered but didn't let go. The green glow brightened until it was almost white, the image zooming in, closing on the tree leaning lazily over the frozen lake. My stomach twisted. I refused to let my gaze linger.

"That is it," Aegon breathed. "Nearly there."

Hazel's knees buckled. She stayed upright only because she braced herself on the stone. Her teeth flashed red when she sucked in a breath.

"Stop," I said. "You're going to kill her."

Hazel shook her head without opening her eyes. "I'm already dead," she whispered, lips cracking on the words. "Let me save the rest of you."

The flames in my palm died as I gasped. My throat burned. I wanted to drag her away from the crystal, throw her over my shoulder, and run.

The image shattered, breaking into shards of green light. Hazel collapsed against the crystal, then slid down on her side. I dropped my hand and went with her, catching her before her head hit stone.

"Hazel. Hazel?" I looked up. "She needs a break!"

The orc moved again at Aegon's gesture, blood-slick fingers reaching for the bars of an empty cell beside Jack's. Another rectangle of smeared red. Another door shivered open.

"Fifteen minutes," Aegon said. "Then we resume."

Carefully, I helped Hazel stand and we moved slowly into the empty cell. She collapsed against the wall and I slid down beside her, careful of my still-healing arm.

"You can't go on," I whispered, cradling Hazel's burned, shaking hands in my good one. Her palms were blackened now, skin cracked and angry.

She smiled, but her eyes were tired. "I can," she said. "For you. For them."

Larek rattled his bars so hard they screeched. "Please, Sav," he croaked. "Please. Don't let her go back out there. It will kill her."

My chest ached. If it were Jack in Hazel's place, I knew exactly how I'd answer. Hazel's hands shook, but when her gaze met mine it didn't waver. No panic. No pleading. Just that quiet, unmovable resolve that made my stomach turn. She'd seen something in that crystal. Something that told her there was only one way out of this.

Aegon turned toward his stream, ready to sink beneath the water and wait.

The air changed.

Pressure built so fast it made my ears ring. Ions buzzed along my skin, prickling every hair on my arms.

Every head in the cavern shifted. Even the mindless fae twitched uneasily.

Aegon spun, eyes wide, and threw up a shield.

Lightning cracked the air. The stream frothed and twisted into a whirlpool, tearing itself out of its usual smooth current. Something old and familiar surged through the shifting water, a magic that lived in the space between waves.

My heart stumbled.

The whirlpool tore open, and a figure stepped out onto stone, turquoise hair floating on an invisible current as if he were still underwater.

"Kaspar," I breathed.

SEVENTY-TWO

KASPAR

The air shimmered. Power rolled off the portal in crashing waves, and every head in the cavern turned.

I stepped through.

Aegon's shield caught my first gust of wind and squealed under the pressure. He smiled, showing off two rows of teeth. "Nephew."

"Uncle." I didn't bother to look at the cages. I could feel Sav's eyes on me. I didn't need to turn to know there would be hope in them. She thought I'd come for her. She was wrong.

He waded to the edge of the stream, current licking at his hips. "You brought yourself to me. Brave."

"I brought your death."

The wind in the chamber whipped angrily, eager to do my bidding. I held it back.

He tilted his head toward the cages. "You think you're stronger than me, boy? Even your pretty wife chose a human over you. Though I suppose he isn't really human, is he?" His gaze flicked toward Sav, then past her to her lover. "Females flock to a strong male. That's why you'll be alone all your life." His smile widened.

His words hit. My magic faltered. I could sense the suffocating blood magic prodding for weakness, but my uncle, in his arrogance, hadn't shielded the castle against sea fae. His arrogance would be his downfall.

"Careful, Aegon," I said. "You're bleeding."

He blinked. A stain of blue-black at his neck, where a poison-tipped blade had sliced through scaled skin, had crept over his collarbone. Another stain at his shoulder told me he'd been struck twice. Summer's

341

poison traveled differently in waterfolk. Slower. He could flush it from his system, but he would be weaker for some time.

"So you challenge me now when I'm not at peak strength?" His grin turned malicious. "You're just like your father. Weak."

The chamber narrowed. For a moment, my vision tunneled. "Don't speak about my father."

"What about your mother? Would your pride be offended if I spoke of her?"

Sav said my name. Soft. The sound slid under my armor and pressed on a bruise.

I dropped my hand. The stream at Aegon's waist circled him, a whirlpool tightening around him. He flung his arms wide, sending glass spearing for me, but I flicked a wrist and a gust of wind knocked his weapons harmlessly aside.

"Is that all you've got?" he asked, gritting his teeth.

I stalked across the stone floor. Darkness peeled off the walls and spilled from the corners, gathering at my feet.

Aegon's eyes flicked to it, finally wary. "Since when do you—"

"You aren't the only one who can keep a secret, Uncle." Dark ribbons dove into the whirlpool, riding the current as they closed in on Aegon, wrapping around his wrists and neck. He choked out a command and mindless folk gathered along the walls jerked forward. With half a thought, I raised my arm again, sending a fresh wave of water at them. They were dragged across the floor to their silent deaths at the bottom of the stream.

Aegon sputtered in rage as he fought my shadows' tightening hold.

My attention snapped to Sav, pale and shaking in her cage. Purple bruises marred her arm, but she was otherwise unharmed. I looked away, scowling. *I'm not here for her,* I reminded myself.

I closed the distance between me and my uncle, loosening the shadows around his throat a fraction. "You did all this for the magic?" His plan, this court, the shrinking of our world, it was extreme, even for him.

His mottled skin flushed. "I did it for all of us. Mab was a tyrant who took without remorse. Your grandfather knew that. I am the one who ended her reign so the rest of you could finally breathe." He spat at my feet, and I glanced down. "Your worthless father took the only thing that would have made me strong enough to defeat her on my own."

My focus cut to the room's corners. He had accomplices. I'd known Janet and Morgan were his puppets, but I didn't know the other players yet.

"I wouldn't have had to kill him if he'd just told me what he did with it."

My cold blood iced. I narrowed my gaze on him. "You... killed my father?"

Aegon's gaze leveled on me. "I'd have let him live had he told me where it was."

I ground my teeth. "And my mother?"

He scoffed. "She was never good enough for our line."

Inky tendrils of shadow at his throat cinched once more as my vision went black at the edges, all the darkness within me consuming me from the inside.

"Kaspar—" He tried to say more, but his eyes bulged, the tendons in his neck tightening. I lifted him from the water and wrung every drop from him.

I went very still.

"You killed my sister."

Something in me slipped for the briefest moment.

His pupils blew wide. "I—"

"No." I tightened my grip until a snap sounded and he screamed. "You don't get to speak."

My hands curled into fists and the energy around me crackled. I had suspected him for years, but held onto the hope that he wouldn't harm family. That hope died today.

Indigo ran down his cheeks. He fought with what little he had left, but he was a fish out of water, and I relished his slow end. Memories of my silver fish army, begging for water when none could be found, filtered through my mind. Alaco's final gasping breaths. Mira's lifeless form, torn and bloody. Memphe, buried beneath the rubble.

His body stilled, eyes staring past me at nothing.

Silence rippled outward. Stillness followed, heavy and absolute. Only the stream slapping against stone could be heard.

My shadows released him and he hit the floor with a crack, navy blood soaking the stone around him.

I turned. The crystal lay against a wall, and I called it to me with a wave of water. It flared aquamarine in my palm for my court, then rippled brown, as if silt rolled through it. Then blue again, muddied at the core. I frowned, but filed that bit of information away for another day.

I looked at Sav's cage. She held my stare, chin high. Not a trace of remorse from my wife.

I crossed the room and stopped in front of her. My heart clenched and I almost reached for the bars. "You," I said instead, "are unfit for Lakes and Streams."

Her lips parted, hurt slashing across her face, but she closed her mouth and nodded.

I let the crystal rest in one hand and reached into my bag with the other. The marriage contract was a weight I had carried too long. I pulled a long, slender tube out and threw it at her feet. "I have committed your name to memory. I have overridden our bargain. Remember that before you consider crossing me."

She flinched, then set her jaw. "Kaspar—"

"You are no princess of my court. Our bargain is dissolved." My voice was level, though something in my chest cracked. The pain in her eyes cut deeper than I would admit, so I held onto the only thing that did not waver: my anger. I turned.

"Save her," Sav said, voice raw.

I froze. Not wanting to turn around. Not able to face her again.

"Hazel's dying."

I glanced over my shoulder. I'd known. Hazel had survived longer than expected. My gut twisted. She was mine. I had agreed to care for her the day she was gifted to me, but the memory of her betrayal sat heavy in my mind. She didn't deserve my help.

"She's not my responsibility any longer," I said, striding for the door.

"Kaspar," Sav begged. "Please."

I'd saved them all from the male who had imprisoned them. Even that wasn't enough. I owed her nothing. I owed none of them. I kept walking.

"I know where the magic you're looking for is." Jack's voice was dark. I'd carefully avoided him since setting foot in the room. But even without looking, I heard the change in his voice. Something had altered him. There would be no more pretending he was human. My lip curled and I took another step away.

"I saw the images on the wall," he said. "I recognized them. You aren't from Earth. You won't know where to look. But I do."

I stopped. The crystal had worked then. I could waste months searching for a seer, tracking the magic's pull, or I could make a bargain. With Jack. "What would you ask of me?"

"Hazel lives." He put a hand to the bars. "Heal her."

I spun around, eyes catching Sav's mournful stare first, then Hazel, pale and huddled in the corner of their cell. Finally, I met Jack's burning green glare. He was much transformed. Something in my chest flared to life: bitter jealousy. He was the embodiment of everything I hated. A direct descendant of Mab. And he had the thing I needed most.

"It's Qaden's blood you need. Not mine." Fero lay somewhere to my right, already nearly bled dry by Aegon's spears. He was Summer's heir too, but if they took any more from him, they might finish what my uncle had started.

"Qaden?" Sav gasped. "But—"

"I won't tell you more without the information." I leveled the words at Jack.

Jack nodded, silver hair shaking with the movement. He'd been insufferably tall before. Now he was a giant. "The frozen pond in Central Park. Where Winter's access portal lies. That's where it led."

I swallowed the sharp twist in my chest and dipped my chin infinitesimally. "Any blood of the current royal line in Summer counters its poison. That's their secret. You should hurry. I'd wager she has minutes."

-●-●·)·(-●·●·◆·●●-

Sirens wailed, too many to count, and the iron in the air would split my skull if I was forced to remain too long on Earth. Creig had made his mark in the days he'd been back in this wretched realm. The city was crawling with armed patrols on the hunt for the creature responsible for bombing several of their buildings.

Centuries ago, when I enjoyed sneaking past his patrols in Spring and he still turned a blind eye to my spying, he'd told me an eye for an eye was the only way to live. If I caught him in my court, he expected equal treatment to that which I received on the occasions when he caught me in his.

On Earth, it was clear he was taking his own advice.

I moved silently between blackened remnants of trees and debris in Central Park.

When I reached the frozen lake guarded by the Bitter Wraith, I stopped. "Lady. Will you grant me audience?"

The lake shuddered. A figure rose, swathed in white, and raced toward me, a scream tearing across ice. When she reached me, her mouth snapped shut, black eyes going round.

"What are you doing here, Prince?" Her voice was hollow.

I prepared to offer her a bargain, to plead if I must, for her to return the thing which had been missing for so long, when, in my satchel, the crystal pulsed. I glanced down at it, then back up, raising a brow.

I had believed I was searching for an object. An artifact that belonged in the sea. But what if the magic at the center of the ocean, its heart, was not an artifact at all?

My father and the Lady had produced a child. My sister. The rest was only legend. Some claimed my father seduced her from the ocean, pulled her from her depths and made her leave. But the Lady was not only of the sea. A creature born of land and water, she could reside wherever she chose. Leaving was not the same as being taken.

Could it be?

I studied her face. Far older than any living creature. Rumored immortal. Was *she* the magic?

But the Lady would never return to her birthplace without payment. Blood for blood was the oldest law in Faerie.

I took a tentative step forward. "I bring news."

The nightmare facade slipped, just a little, showing her true beauty beneath. "Of my daughter?"

I dipped my chin.

Black tears slid down her cheeks and she sank atop her frozen lake. I moved to catch her, shuddering as I stepped onto its surface. A cold so biting it burned traveled up my calves. I ignored it, cupping her hands in mine. Ice leeched into my bones, but I held fast. "It was my uncle."

She looked up, eyes flashing. "Blood demands vengeance."

I nodded. "I have taken it for us both." I bared my throat. "But if you require more, my life is yours."

Her glamour flickered, and bright, white light scalded my retinas before her muted form returned.

Silence sat between us, and I tensed. If I'd miscalculated, if her grief was too strong...

"No." She climbed to her feet, releasing me, and I exhaled a puff of frozen air, flexing my fingers. "Enough blood has been spilled."

I stepped back, feet crunching in frozen grass. "Will you return with me? Help me restore what has been broken?"

"I made a bargain with the general," she said, watching me. "I promised to drown the human world. But when I searched their future, I saw a fate far more deserving than the one I would bring." Her mouth trembled. "And I grow weary of a life without Mira in it."

My cold heart clenched. I would never know the love of a parent. There was only one fae I was selfless enough to consider such a path with. And she would never be mine.

The Lady stepped off her lake, seeming to hover on air. She nodded. "Take me home, Prince."

SEVENTY-THREE

SAV

Kaspar's words echoed after he'd gone.

No princess of my court. I have committed your name to memory. Remember that before you consider crossing me.

I clenched the silver tube that held our contract, the bargain I'd made to get my magic back, to save Jack. My shoulders loosened when it hit me that I was free, but my throat tightened anyway, a hard ache catching behind my ribs. I forced it down. He deserved none of my compassion. He would have let her die.

"Hold on, Hazel," I whispered.

Her breathing rasped, wet and uneven.

I bit the pad of my thumb. Blood welled. I drew the line along the floor, up the right bar, across the top, down the left, and pushed.

"Sav?" Juniper's voice dropped low.

"I'm getting Qaden," I said, already moving.

I stepped into the cold stone room and kept my eyes off the bodies still strewn across the floor, but I didn't manage it for long. My attention snagged on one form. "Fero," I breathed. Why had Kaspar suggested Qaden when Fero was only feet away?

I crossed the room, fast enough my lungs burned, and stopped short, the sound that tried to tear out of me caught behind my teeth.

He was still. Worse, blood no longer streamed from his wounds.

I grabbed the first spear and hauled it free. It clattered to the floor. A slow trickle followed, and I let out a breath I hadn't realized I was holding. "Hang on."

I yanked the second with more force. The third spear, lodged deep in

347

his shoulder, fought me, but it came loose with a final jerk. The last two were shorter, driven in at cruel angles, and my hands shook as I wrenched them out one after the other.

When all five lay on the stone, I dragged him back to our cell and propped him against it.

He didn't move. I couldn't see his chest rise. But he was the strongest fae of our generation. I had to believe he was alive. That he'd wake.

"Hazel, can you move?"

A hand slid out of the dark and closed on my wrist.

I twisted, instinct screaming, but my body didn't follow. Spongy fingers locked me in place, pinning me.

"Sav," Hazel croaked.

"Careful," a familiar voice purred, warm and soft. "I've waited a very long time to do this properly."

Prim.

The name burned my tongue, but it wouldn't come. My mind scattered, thoughts skittering in every direction, and one beat louder than the rest cut through the noise.

Run.

Prim turned me, and my body obeyed the command. Inside, I fought. Outside, I complied.

She guided me onto a slab.

"Let her go," Jack barked.

"Prim. Don't do this," Foxglove shouted.

Her palm pressed my shoulder. I laid back, staring up at the dark ceiling far overhead, breathing shallowly through my nose.

Foxglove's voice hammered through my skull, and a memory broke loose in jagged pieces. A trap. He'd been lured to Autumn. He'd been warning me about Prim.

A tear slipped toward my ear before I could stop it. I tried to hold on to the version of her I'd known. It couldn't be Prim. She'd been my ally. My closest friend in Spring when I'd had none.

Pain bit my arm.

A sting ran up my forearm, sharp at first, then heavy. I couldn't turn my head to see what she'd done, but I felt the wrongness of her blood mixing with mine. Heat flushed through me, dulling everything it touched.

"Just give it another moment or two to sink in." Prim's words near my ear blurred at the edges. For a second I didn't realize my senses were sliding away, one by one.

Her touch left me, but I couldn't move. I couldn't even lift my chin.

The magic holding me down didn't feel like iron chains or bindings. It was personal; inside my skin.

Voices rose around me, overlapping as they shouted for her to stop. The sound should've steadied me. It didn't.

Prim tsked.

With an effort that made my eyes sting, I dragged my focus toward her. My head turned just enough to see her face.

Her lips twitched as her eyes met mine. "Do you see the double standard I'm forced to work with? Where were their shouts and protests when Aegon was your attacker?" She sighed. "But I'm just a female, right? Why would they fear me?"

She slid around the slab and ran a finger down my side.

Numbness bloomed wherever she touched. My stomach lurched, my pulse jumping against the drug's heaviness, and I tried to curl away. My muscles didn't answer.

"Just because I don't have an appendage swinging between my thighs, the world thinks I'm less of a threat."

My tongue felt thick. I tried to shape her name again. Nothing came.

Her eyes met mine, bright violet, too bright. "But you know all about that, don't you, Sav?"

I fought to keep my gaze sharp, to stay present, but fog pressed in, muffling the room and softening the edges of everything.

"Don't bother fighting it," she went on, almost bored. "I've given you my blood. The effects will last hours. What do you think the secret ingredient in the drugs Dane used was?"

Prim cackled.

Cold spread through my veins, fast and wrong, and my stomach rolled hard enough I thought I might choke. It couldn't be. Prim couldn't be behind the mindless fae army Dane had drugged and experimented on.

"I'll kill you!" Juniper shouted.

Prim's attention flicked away from me. "One drop of my blood, and you'll be back in line," she said dismissively. "I don't know how you overcame it, but it will be fun to study you."

"Pppprr," I tried.

Prim's violet eyes lit with amusement. Something in my sluggish mind snagged on it. Her eyes had been dull for as long as I'd known her. Something had changed.

I tried again to speak, to reason with her, but she cut me off. "I wish I could catch you up on everything, Sav. I really do. Not that you've ever been a very good listener." She leaned closer. "But I'm not here for you. I need something from your boyfriend."

The thought of Prim turning toward Jack jolted something awake in me. Heat flared deep in my chest, fierce and panicked, then stalled, trapped under her blood in my veins.

"The Winter line is tricky. I'll give them that." Prim paced, voice calm. "Mab was more selfless than I thought, choosing to save her daughter rather than herself."

She left my slab.

For a moment, hope sparked. She wasn't going to Jack.

Prim stopped at Hazel's cell instead.

Hazel shrank back, shoulders curling, breath hitching. Prim ignored her and studied Fero's limp form. Then she glanced over her shoulder at me.

"Smart," she said, almost approving. "But Kaspar already told you his blood wouldn't work to save your friend."

I swallowed. The muscles in my throat thawed just a fraction against her magic. It was small, but it was something.

Prim snapped her fingers.

Several mindless folk marched into the room. Without a word, they crossed to Fero, lifted him into their arms, and dragged him toward an exit in the far wall.

My eyes tracked them, refusing to miss it. There hadn't been an exit there before. It had to be cloaked.

The mindless fae vanished through the opening and the wall looked solid again.

"Still," Prim murmured as she moved away from Hazel's cell, stopping at Jack's.

I called for my magic, begged it to answer. Heat gathered in my chest, then sputtered. Nothing reached my hands.

"Can't be too careful," she went on. "Your little seer could be a complication. Better to let her die."

Hazel whimpered.

Larek rattled his bars, voice raw as he hurled curses at Prim.

The fae who'd taken Fero returned and formed two neat lines behind her. The room tightened around me, closing in with every silent body.

Prim stared through Jack's bars. "Interesting."

"What's that?" Jack spat.

I pulled again, harder, reaching for the fire under my skin. It had worked before. It had to work now.

"You don't look immortal." The guards shifted, closing in around her, blocking her and Jack from my view. "But neither did your mother when Mab transferred the gift to her."

I yanked harder, forcing the heat to climb, willing it to burn through the fog.

Tiny orange sparks flickered at my fingertips.

A spike of adrenaline punched through me.

"I'll give you whatever you want," Jack said. "Just let Sav go."

Shut up, Jack.

I tried to shout it. My tongue wouldn't cooperate. Maybe it was better. Better not to remind Prim I was fighting.

I focused on the heavy blanket of her magic draped over my skin and pictured it catching, curling, blackening, breaking apart.

My concentration wavered at the sound of metal creaking on its hinges.

Jack.

No.

The metal clicked.

The door swung open.

SEVENTY-FOUR

JACK

I rushed through the doors. "Sav!"

Blank-eyed soldiers pinned my arms. I fought, but even if my new magic had worked here, I wouldn't have hurt them. I couldn't.

Prim—the female who murdered my mother—smirked. Recognition was a slap. Rage unfurled inside me. I had never truly wanted to kill before. Aegon had been bad. This creature was evil.

She lifted her sticky hand. "Come along then, Jack."

I fought to cage the hate eating me alive. Sav was more important than my pain. I had to save her first. Then I'd...

"I don't know how to give it," I said. "But I'll try."

Her mouth curved. "You'll figure it out or she dies."

Sav lay still, eyes tracking us. The tether between us pulled tight.

Prim reached for me and I braced myself for the familiar feeling of her magic.

Sav moved first.

Orange flame burst in her palm as she caught Prim's wrist.

Prim screamed as two of her guards lurched forward, tearing Sav's hand away. They pinned her down even as they burned. The flame, mirrored in her eyes, grew. The smell of burned flesh and clothes filled the air, but they held firm.

"Sav," I breathed, Dane's charred skin flashing in my mind.

She didn't hear me, intent on the fury that lit her soul on fire.

"Enough," Prim snapped, setting a hand on Sav's neck. Flames winked out and the soldiers straightened, their skin smoking and black.

I wrenched free of their grip. Prim was so close, but the guards' arms were iron, and I still wouldn't break them. I reached for the fire anyway, for the new wild magic coiled inside me, and slammed into a wall of suffocating power. Pain burst behind my eyes. Nothing answered.

Prim glanced back at me and panted through the pain. A feral smile crept over her face. "I'm a female of my word, Jack. Give it to me or watch her die."

She snatched a blade from the floor, one coated in black residue, and I didn't have to ask to know it was the same poison on Hazel's blade.

Panic flared to life inside me as I tried desperately to find a way to give her what she wanted. "Don't. I—"

The blade flashed, and my words were swallowed by a shout as Sav's eyes met mine, round with terror. Prim stepped back, a satisfied smile painting her lips.

"Sav! Sav!"

A shrill giggle burst from Prim. "It's in her heart. Only immortality can save her now. Go ahead, Jack."

The part of me that was human cracked. I shoved against the guards again, screaming her name, desperate to reach her. She was dying and I couldn't reach her. I grabbed for my magic a second time and hit the smothering barrier again, agony ripping through my skull. The tether between us shrieked, a soundless scream in my chest.

Something tore loose.

White-hot rage erupted through me, dissolving the heavy magic that had held it at bay. The room exploded in fiery embers, molten lava shooting from my palms. Creatures burst into flames and dissolved, melting to nothing. Fire flooded my veins, bursting from my mouth, my eyes; the world went black and red as my magic devoured everything.

Prim tried to run, but nothing could escape my fury. She fell, writhing on the floor as flames swallowed her, dying screams reverberating off the walls, then cut off all at once.

The fire guttered. I crashed to my knees, lungs burning, the taste of ash thick on my tongue. Every inch of me shook. My skin was scoured raw.

I crawled the last distance and slid a hand under Sav's head.

"Please," I said, hauling her up, cradling her head. "Don't leave me."

I willed the immortality to go. Begged whatever gods were listening to save her. But I was lost. I had no idea how the magic worked. I ran a thumb over her lips, wiping the smear of crimson away.

"You killed her," she breathed, managing half a smile.

"Don't talk."

Her smile broke; she coughed, flecks of blood striking my cheek. "Have to... get it out."

I pressed my forehead to hers. I couldn't tell her the blade, even poisoned, was the only thing keeping her alive. That the moment I tore it free, she would bleed out. A tear slid down my cheek. I silently pleaded again for anyone to help us.

A boot scraped stone and I looked up, meeting large yellow eyes.

Grace stood less than a foot away, Fero's son close at her side. She took everything in; her knowing gaze landed on the blade buried in Sav's chest. My vision blurred.

"Can you help her?"

"No, child."

A crack fissured through my center.

"Only you can."

"I don't know how." My voice broke. "Please. Tell me how to give it to her."

"You share a bond," Grace said softly. "Its power is the only path that will let what you carry brush her heart without breaking it."

"This is what the chameleon fae never understood," she said. "A gift like this can never be taken. And it can only be used between those who share a bond."

"But my mother?" The word burned my throat.

"A mother's love is the purest bond," she murmured. "Some might say, even more than a mate."

I swallowed, trying and failing to process all Grace had shared. All that mattered now was that I could save Sav. "How?"

Grace closed the distance. She smiled at Sav, and my gaze dragged back to Sav's face. It was deathly pale, her lashes dark smudges against her cheeks. Her eyes had fallen closed. She was running out of time.

"Grace," I rasped.

She laid a hand on my shoulder and the other on Sav's chest, carefully avoiding the knife. "Close your eyes, Jacaranda, and find the tether."

I did as she instructed, and it flared to life almost immediately.

"Touch it with your mind."

I obeyed, running mental fingers along the silken strand that purred at my touch, taut and humming between us.

"Now," Grace said, "find the energy pulsing at the center of your soul. It will feel like home."

I exhaled a slow sigh, forcing my racing heart to steady, and, as I had done before, I turned the ability inward.

There.

Buried beneath my own magic, a kernel of deeper energy throbbed once, blazing hot.

I cupped the heat and coaxed it forward. A surge flared sharp and scorching against my mind's grip; I jerked as if burned. Panic gripped me. I couldn't do it. Sav was running out of time. I would fail her and live an eternity without her.

"Calm, Jack. Try again."

I breathed deeply.

"You cannot force it."

I nodded, eyes pressed firmly closed.

This time, I didn't tug. I held out an invisible hand and pleaded with the tiny, molten core. *Please. You must save her. Without her, I'm nothing.*

The kernel pulsed. Threads of heat uncoiled from it, tentative but alive, and crept along the tether like glowing vines beneath skin.

The bond tightened. Then one of the cords snapped.

My eyes flew open. "Sav!"

My heart seized in my chest. "She's not breathing." My grip tightened on her. "Sav. Sav!"

"Jack," Grace demanded, sharp for the first time. "Close your eyes and focus. She's running out of time."

Tears streamed down my cheeks, but I closed my eyes again, exhaling a shaky breath. Another cord snapped; I shuddered, but repeated the steps, faster this time, clinging to the feel of that ember in my core.

Heat raced along the bond, banding it in dim, molten gold. Broken strands fused in glowing seams until the whole tether thrummed, wrapped in a thin, ember-bright sheath. The tiny kernel inside me felt smaller, stretched thin, leaving a hollow ache under my ribs, as if I'd scraped myself hollow from the inside out.

I blinked, breath caught in my throat, and glanced back at Grace.

"Now," she said. "Remove the dagger."

Carefully, I laid Sav on stone and touched the handle of the wicked silver blade. The metal caught the candlelight. Memories rushed in. Every time I'd trusted Grace and almost lost Sav. Was I wrong again?

"She cannot wake with the poisoned blade in her heart."

My fingers were numb on the hilt. I wrapped them tighter around it and yanked.

SEVENTY-FIVE

SAV

Each breath burned, but my ribs hurt less than they should have. Jack's hands were under my head and the cavern steadied around his face. The bond between us was stronger now, humming in my mind, threaded so tightly through me it felt inseparable from my own heartbeat.

"What did you do?" I whispered.

"What I should have done all along," he said, voice rough. "Put you first."

Grace's golden eyes found mine. "He did more than that." She crouched beside us, gaze flicking between our faces. "The wound should have killed you. The poison still wants to. Jack drew a thread of his immortality along your bond and wound it around your heart. It's holding the blade's work at bay and caging the poison so it cannot spread."

My heart thudded hard against my ribs, each pulse echoing down the bond. A slow warmth unfurled in my chest, pressing deep and sore.

"I'm immortal now?" I breathed. I didn't feel that way. My lungs still hurt. My muscles ached.

"No." Grace's voice gentled, amusement glinting beneath it. "You're not unkillable, girl. You're just very stubbornly alive. Thank him for that."

Out of the corner of my eye, Jack flinched. His hand went briefly to his chest, fingers pressing over his sternum, then dropped. A muscle ticked in his jaw.

"Does it hurt him?" I asked.

Grace nodded. "The poison snaps at him now instead of you. It

357

cannot kill him. It will only sting." Her gaze softened. "A reminder of the choice he made."

Jack huffed a breath that might have been a laugh if it hadn't sounded so tired. "It was worth it," he said, grabbing my hand and lacing our fingers together.

My throat tightened. I was still here. Still breathing. His warmth thrummed through our connection, his grip firm, anchoring me.

For a heartbeat, it was only us.

Then the cavern rushed back in.

"Hazel," I breathed as he helped me sit up. The world tilted, but Jack's hold steadied me. He nodded once.

My gaze flew to Hazel's cell, her limp body just inside the bars, and I started toward her.

"Sav. Please." Larek's voice cracked. He was still trapped, knuckles white around the bars. I knew that sound now. The way a voice broke when someone you couldn't lose was slipping away.

I stopped at his door and traced a line over the metal with shaking fingers, my sliced palm smearing red as I completed the circuit. The cage shuddered and swung open.

Larek shoved past me, darting to Hazel's cell and gathering her into his arms.

"Hazel. I'm here."

He pressed a soft kiss to her temple, black eyes rimmed in green, holding her as if will alone could keep her breathing. Her lips were tinged blue.

I looked to Grace, but she'd already turned toward the boy at her side.

"Qaden," she said.

He stepped forward with more courage than I'd ever seen in a child, rolling up his sleeve and holding his arm out. Grace drew a nail over his tanned skin. He winced, but didn't cry as blood welled along his forearm.

"Let it touch her mouth," Grace said.

He knelt and carefully pressed his arm to Hazel's mouth, letting the blood smear across her lips. For an instant, I couldn't move. I couldn't breathe.

Hazel arched, gasping as air tore into her lungs. Her chest rose, fell, then steadied. Color crept back into her cheeks in thin, fragile streaks.

"Hazel," I whispered.

Jack released my hand and I dropped to my knees beside her.

Larek held her upright, cocooning her against his chest. She blinked, eyes unfocused at first, then found mine.

"How are you?" My voice came out raw.

She smiled through cracked lips and patted my knee. "I've been better," she rasped. "But I'm not dead."

Relief hit hard enough that I had to brace myself. I pressed my forehead lightly to hers, breathing her in. Too many friends had died. I wouldn't add Hazel to that list.

"Good," I managed. "Stay that way."

Larek made a sound that pulled my attention. Hazel's gaze lifted to his, something warm flickering between them. She looked at him as if nothing else existed. My chest warmed.

I pushed to my feet and felt Jack behind me before he touched me. He lifted my wrist, turning it gently. The skin there was whole again, the last of my smaller wounds closed. He brushed his lips over my pulse point. A shudder rolled through me and I let his mouth linger, the bond humming low and steady.

"We need to free the others," I said, tugging my hand from his grip.

Jack followed as I released Foxglove and Juniper. Murz was still missing, and Fero too. Even with Prim and Aegon dead, the not knowing clawed at me. Were they locked somewhere deeper, or already gone?

Now, at least, we had a chance to put things right.

Qaden tugged his sleeve back down, expression far too serious for a child. "Where is my father?"

"We'll find him," I said. "We'll find them all." My voice steadied as I met his gaze.

Grace lifted a hand and the room stilled. She studied Qaden's face before speaking. "There are many lives still in danger. You must find the scrolls first."

Qaden didn't argue. He tilted his head, listening to something distant, then shed his clothes. Bones shrank, fur rippling across skin until a black-and-white cat shook himself free and darted for the hidden door.

A tracker. *Rare.*

My gaze followed him as a group of fae stumbled into the room.

Jack moved in front of me and I stepped around him. "Since when am *I* the one who needs protecting?"

He grinned, bumping my shoulder, then turned back to the approaching folk.

From here, I couldn't tell who was mindless and who wasn't. My gaze flicked to the charred body on the floor. Prim. My friend, or so I'd thought. The true mastermind.

Betrayal curdled in my gut. I'd shared her anger once, her frustrations, never imagining how far she'd let them take her. The weight of it pressed down on me.

"Are you injured?" Grace asked, pulling me back.

359

Folk hugged the walls, blinking around as if waking from a nightmare. A fawn dropped to her knees at Grace's feet. Soon others followed, rail thin and bruised. A satyr cupped his hands in the stream and drank. Others followed, sobbing as water touched their lips.

"What is this place?" someone asked.

Foxglove started to answer, but Juniper stepped in, voice low and steady as she gave shape to the last few years.

Footsteps pounded back up the hidden stairs. Qaden burst through, a leather satchel clutched to his chest. He stumbled, silver tubes clattering across stone.

I dropped to gather them, hands shaking. Kaspar's bargains.

Prim. She must have taken them. How long had she been among us without our knowing?

Qaden's lip trembled. "My father."

Jack knelt beside him. "Where is he?"

Tears slid down Qaden's cheeks. "He's dead."

The room went still.

Grace held out her hand. "Take me to him, child."

Juniper and Foxglove followed. Larek lifted Hazel with infinite care. Grace nodded once.

We descended into darker halls, past rotted doors barely holding together. At the back, Qaden stopped. Grace lifted a hand and the wood crumbled.

The room beyond was small and lightless.

When my eyes adjusted, grief punched the air from my lungs. Fero lay bare, skin marked by dozens of blackened bites. His eyes were closed, just as they'd been before.

Grace shook her head.

Pain lodged beneath my ribs. He had held my name for years but never used it. In the end, he'd been my ally and he had died for it.

I wrapped my arms around Qaden. "Come. You'll stay with us and I will tell you about your father."

-•→(◡◆∩♦••-

We emerged into daylight, hundreds of folk spilling free. Cold air hit my lungs, sharp and clean after the damp underground. Ahead, Autumn stretched into an impossible distance. Where the ocean had crashed against jagged rocks just days ago, Faerie was restored, forest and cliff knitting together in rust and gold.

Juniper and Foxglove moved through the crowd with quiet authority, guiding the weakest, steadying those who stumbled, keeping everyone moving toward open sky.

"Sav!"

My heart clenched as I spun toward the voice.

"Sage?" I breathed.

She was there, half supporting a massive orc as they pushed through the crowd. Murz limped badly at her side, one arm slung over her shoulders, the other clutched tight to his ribs. His skin was mottled and torn, but his eyes were bright and clear.

"Thank Gaia," I breathed, relief leaving me weak as I hauled Sage into my arms.

I didn't know what came next, but we'd rebuild. And this time, we would make sure no one ever held that much power again.

SEVENTY-SIX

FOXGLOVE

I trailed a pace behind Sav and Sage as we stepped from the cave. Jack had fallen back, whispering to Grace as he held out a hand to Qaden. The boy glanced skeptically at Jack's blue-tipped fingers.

I'd never met Firethorn, but the rumors of his height had long survived him. Jack, no longer glamoured, was probably the tallest creature in Faerie, dryads and trolls excluded.

I understood the boy's hesitation. Jack was all strange angles and new power, too big for this world and too bright. But it wasn't just wariness tightening Qaden's jaw. Grief sat heavy in his eyes, years too old for his face, and that I understood even more.

Wind moved through the trees, sending leaves scattering across Autumn's carpet. It had been centuries since I'd been to this court, but the forest stretching out before me was as untouched as that missing pocket of Spring. It was true then. Faerie was restored.

Juniper fell into step beside me and I glanced at her. She hadn't slipped back into mindlessness since Grace helped her, and for that I would be forever grateful.

She glanced up, tucking a curl behind her ear, and a shy smile tugged at her lips. Warmth bloomed through my center. But even as my heart lifted, it dipped. Satyrs didn't mix with the high fae. She'd be expected to return to her clan now.

Still, a kernel of hope lived in my heart whether I wanted it or not.

Ahead, Sage leaned into Sav. Perfect ringlets fell down her back, the auburn curls somehow still mostly intact where others' hair hung limp or matted. Even as Prim and Aegon's captive, she'd managed to retain her regal air. Her dress, though dirty, wasn't torn to rags like so many others. No split seams, no blood stiff in the fabric.

It didn't match the bruises and hollow cheeks around us.

"You saved me," Sage said, and Sav squeezed her tightly.

Juniper's shoulder brushed mine and her hand swung close. My gaze dipped to her fingers as they grazed my knuckles, and my own moved reflexively, wanting to curl around hers.

Gullible as always.

The thought slammed into me, sharp and vicious. My attention snapped back to Sav and Sage. I hadn't caught their last words, but it wasn't what Sage had thought so much as the way she'd thought it. Cold. Cutting.

Sage glanced back at me and tried to clamp down on her thoughts. That only drew my interest. I rarely dug; it was a violation. But Sage was hiding something, and the dissonance between her tidy hair, intact skirts, and that ugly thought scratched at me.

Alder. Deserved death.

I stopped walking. Juniper halted beside me and nearly bumped my arm.

"Sage," I said, keeping my tone too even. "Where is Alder? He wasn't in the cells."

Sav slowed and turned to face her sister. Her thought brushed mine, quick and clear. *You see through glamour.* Aloud she said, "How did Prim fool you?"

For a breath, Sage froze. Then she lifted a hand to her throat. "I...I don't know. She fooled us all."

"She didn't," I said. "Not you."

Her thoughts tangled. *No... they can't know. Smile. Cry. Blame Prim.*

"She's working with them," I snapped. "Sav, look out."

Sage dropped all pretense and flung both hands wide. The ground bucked. Jagged stone teeth shot up around the twins. Dust and pebbles spat outward, forcing the rest of us to jump back or be knocked off our feet.

In moments, a solid ring of boulders walled the sisters off from view, leaving the rest of us outside, shut out.

"Sav!" Hazel yelled, yanking free of Larek's grasp.

She shifted effortlessly and jumped, claws scrabbling for purchase, but her weakened state and the height of Sage's prison were too much. She crashed to the ground and shook her head, dazed.

Jack reached the wall at the same moment as Larek. White sparks danced along his fingers. "Sav! We'll get you out!"

Larek placed both palms against the stone and it shifted a fraction under his touch. The inner voices of everyone around us rose in pitch and intensity until it was a shrieking chorus in my mind. I clapped my hands over my ears, as if that could muffle the sounds only I could hear.

I closed my eyes and forced my focus onto the only two minds that mattered.

"No!" Sav shouted from behind the rock wall. "Let me handle my sister."

Sav.

She growled in response to my internal nudge. *Someone could get hurt. Tell Jack to trust me.*

Sage's thoughts were rapid bursts of rage and triumph as she envisioned her sister's end, buried beneath the soil so deep none would find her. I'd known she harbored resentment and petty guilt, but this ran deeper.

I moved to where Jack was pressing sparking palms to the massive stone. "She doesn't want the others to be harmed," I said.

He flinched and kept pushing.

"Trust her, Jack. She can handle Sage."

Heat radiated off him in waves, but slowly bled away as he wrestled with himself. At last, he dropped his hands, leaving scorched, cracked rock in his wake. "You'll tell me if she needs me," he said.

I nodded. "The moment she does."

He eyed me, reasons he shouldn't trust me flickering through his mind, then those were swallowed by one blazing thread: *trust Sav.* He stepped back a fraction.

I pressed my head to the stone, leaning close to focus on the twins and block out everything else.

Won't kill her. Subdue.

The ground rumbled beneath our feet then stilled. Sav wasn't fighting with her elemental gift. She was using her innate one. Her will wrapped around Sage like a cage, squeezing, until Sage was forced to comply. Sav spat a series of commands. Ones that ensured her sister couldn't use her magic in any form to harm her or any of the rest of us.

"I should kill you," Sav said, voice loud enough for all of us to hear.

"Sav. Sister, please..."

Jack was grinning, hands fisted at his sides, and some bitter part of me hoped I never looked that foolish for love again.

Grace appeared by my side. "We must trap her," she said. "Sav can't hold her that way forever."

Larek moved to join Grace and she nodded. "Larek, stand beside the boy."

My gaze flicked to Qaden. He was a tracker and a shifter. Did he have yet another gift buried in his blood?

Sage pulled hard on her magic, trying and failing to break free of Sav's grip. Sav's commands dug into Sage's mind and bones. Sage was helpless. Even as Sav restrained her sister, memories of the coercion Kaspar had used against her surfaced and my stomach roiled at the thoughts tumbling in her head. The guilt she felt. She forced them down, thinking instead of us. Her friends. Her family. She would do anything for us, even the thing she hated most.

The walls shuddered, ready to topple in on them both, and Jack's grin faltered as he started forward. He couldn't hear the desperation in Sage's mind, but he didn't need to. Neither sister would survive if Sage managed to bury them beneath all that stone. Sav's hesitation might just give Sage the moment she needed to do it.

"When I tell you," Grace said to Larek and Qaden.

The wall of rock gave a low grinding groan and Sage began to beg in earnest behind the stone. Her thoughts and words tangled until I had to push mentally, dulling the cries so I could think.

Grace nodded. Larek placed one hand on Qaden's shoulder and the other on the rocks.

"The way we practiced," Grace said gently to the boy.

He nodded, clutching the leather satchel at his side as he squeezed his eyes shut.

Stone shivered under Larek's touch.

"Wait!" Jack's face had gone pale.

Grace cut him a sharp, warning look over her shoulder. The protest died on his tongue.

"He won't harm them, Jack," she said.

Jack swallowed hard but didn't argue.

The rocks gave a violent heave and, in moments, they crumbled into nothing. Jack rushed forward.

Sage stood rigidly several feet from Sav, glaring daggers at her sister. Her mind slung curse after hateful curse at the sister who had always defended her. Even now, when she could have ended her so easily.

"Hold her," Grace said.

Sav nodded. Sweat beaded on her brow. "She can't use her gift, but I can't keep her like this forever."

"We must bring her to the Easter Wood."

It hit me then. Grace's thoughts were blank. Not just calm, not simply disciplined. Blank. How had I missed it—that smooth, impenetrable nothing? Prim's soft violet eyes flashed in my memory and I shuddered. Grace's gaze swung to me, golden eyes meeting mine.

"I'm not the fae you believe me to be," she said. She looked around at all of us. "But neither am I a puca."

Hazel's tail twitched where she stood beside Larek. He leaned into her, and his thoughts steadied.

Grace stretched a hand out and vines answered her call, wrapping up her arms. Sunlight caught on the leaves, and for a moment, they gleamed gold instead of green.

Jack pressed a hand to Sav's back and whispered in her ear. His thoughts jittered, wary and rattled, but he remained pressed to her side.

Juniper's breath hitched. The leaves curling up Grace's arms shifted and glinted in the light, and Juniper dropped to her knees. "Mother," she whispered. Her mind fixed on that single word and then screamed it so loudly it drowned out everything else.

Mother. Creator. Gaia. The words pounded through my skull, thick with awe and terror and relief.

I went down without thinking, one knee hitting the earth. Larek did the same at my side. "Gaia," I breathed.

"Get up," she said. "I'm no fae royal to be bowed and scraped to."

"Grace?" Jack's voice cracked as he looked between her and the fae on their knees. His thoughts were a tangled rush.

She released her hold on the golden vines, letting them slip back into the soil. "Come," Gaia said. "My vessel needs our aid."

We stood. Our group crowded around Gaia, waiting for her next command.

"Spring," she said. "Can you move her?"

Sav nodded. Her thoughts flashed in quick, jagged images. Sage laughing in Spring's gardens. The two of them as children, their hands linked. Sage on a throne she'd always wanted. Fear threaded through all of it, but she stepped forward. "Sage Hawthorn, come with me."

It wasn't Sage's true name, the one she guarded even from those she loved, except her husband. But Sav didn't need true names to bend others to her will. Her innate gift was strong.

Sage walked stiffly beside Sav and try as she might to fight off the command, she was forced to obey. Sav nodded to Gaia, who turned, giving us her back, and marched into the forest.

Juniper walked in silence at my side, her thoughts locked on Gaia.

Gaia stopped at the edge of the Easter Wood. Black vines lay dead there, stretched in long snaking lines as if they'd tried to escape and failed. She raised both hands and spoke low in a tongue only the land knew.

The vines moved.

They uncoiled and slid, slow and purposeful, across the charred loam, climbing Sage's ankles, her calves, her hips. Sage was frozen in place, terror choking her thoughts as the ground caught her wrists and pinned them at her sides. The vines climbed higher.

"Grace," Sav gasped. "Don't kill her."

Sage's internal screams intensified as vines wrapped around her mouth and I winced, unable to block them out. My stomach twisted and I had to remind myself of all the terrible things she'd done, would continue to do, if she weren't imprisoned.

She tossed her head, eyes wide. The vines didn't care. They tightened around her.

"Grace!" Sav's strangled cry made Grace flinch and the vines halted as the last black tendrils curled around Sage's head.

Gaia lowered her hands. For a heartbeat, nothing moved. Only a light breeze brushed over cracked, dead leaves in a forest so inky it swallowed any signs of daylight. She beckoned Sav forward. "It will require more than poisoned earth to restrain her. You must encase her heart in an undying flame."

Sav's face paled and Jack was beside her again, a hand on her back. "I don't have that magic."

Gaia smiled. "Child, you wield my magic and nothing I possess may die."

Sav's eyes widened as she looked between Gaia and Jack. Her thoughts raced, settling on the question that mattered most to her. "Will it not kill her?"

"She'll remain in a form of stasis," Gaia said.

"But..." Sav's voice thinned. "How long?"

"A thousand years," Gaia said. "It's the only way to be certain."

Sav grabbed Jack's hand, squeezing. "Please," she whispered. "She's my sister. Give her a chance to change. A century."

Gaia regarded her for a long, unreadable moment. The land hummed under our feet. "One hundred is not enough," she said at last. "Three hundred years. No less."

Sav's throat worked as she swallowed. "Three hundred," she agreed.

Sage's fingers twitched inside the blackened vines, but the poison was still doing its job. For now, she couldn't call her magic.

Gaia nodded. "Come. When her heart has been entombed in flame, she'll remain in this state until we revisit her three hundred years hence."

Sav stepped forward and pressed a trembling palm to the clump of inky vines over Sage's heart. My stomach knotted as she moved closer to the line of black separating the Easter Wood from the Blood Wood.

Sav closed her eyes, and a soft humming filled the air. Jack stood rigidly beside our group, but he made no move toward her.

"Feel it," Gaia commanded. "Ask the land for what you want."

I watched as glittering golden flames the color of Gaia's eyes burst to life around the twins and began retracting, drawing in tight. It slid harmlessly over Sav and crept up the tightly coiled vines, wrapping itself around her fingers before disappearing beneath blackened leaves.

Sav gasped and stumbled back. Jack caught her, steadying her. She leaned into his hold, smiling up at him with an expression more of resignation than happiness.

Juniper's fingers found mine and squeezed. I glanced down, my heart pounding.

Fero's son stood alone, looking very small at the edge of the clearing. I started forward, but Jack held out a hand. The boy hesitated, eyes flicking from Jack's scarred knuckles to his face. His thoughts were a muddle of static and sharp edges, too jumbled to untangle. Slowly, he slid his smaller palm into Jack's.

Then a single clump of deadly nightshade pushed through the black tangle and burst wide, purple so vivid it glowed in the otherwise dark forest.

I let out a breath I hadn't realized I'd been holding. It was the first living color I'd seen in the Easter Wood since the Great War.

What did it mean?

An omen, Juniper thought.

SEVENTY-SEVEN

KASPAR

The shore received us without ceremony. Churning waves crashed against white sand and I knew none would bother us here. I'd seen the Prince of Summer and known he would be gone before the day was out. Summer's shores were no longer guarded. The Lady stood beside me, white and weightless against a slate horizon. She stepped into her element and the water brightened around her, sparkling aquamarine, clearing the deeper she waded.

I followed.

The trench opened like a mouth in the seafloor, rimmed with living coral that had gone the color of bone. We descended past forests of kelp, brown with too much salt and Mab's poisoned magic. The water grew colder as we descended, the pressure like a steady hand against the ribs. When we reached the shelf, coral parted in recognition, polyps retracting in neat, obedient ripples.

A pearl the size of a door sealed the cave. Not a tide-pearl. Something much larger and older, made of magic that pieced together the very fabric of our world. The Lady did not look at me. She lifted one pale hand and drew a point of light along her palm, cutting it open with a grace that made my own magic feel crude. Cerulean blood welled, kissed the pearl, and it shuddered. She spoke four words in the first tongue, older than courts, older than Mab and her long reign. The pearl rolled aside, a rush of freshwater surging out.

The chamber beyond was a cathedral grown rather than built. The walls were ribs of shell and mother-of-pearl, veined with bioluminescence. At its center waited a throne of glimmering light and coral, carved by time.

I had never been here. I would never belong here. This was a cave for the sea's oldest line. Not for a prince with blood too muddied to ever be enough.

She moved to the throne and sat. Hands crossed over her breast. Luminescent hair floated on the current, the sea's gentle lapping pull ever present even within this sacred place. Her eyes found mine. "I give it back," she said, voice carrying in the vast chamber. "My strength to the water, my years to the deep. When the sea is mended, I will sleep a long sleep. Let it take the time it needs."

"How long?" I asked.

Her mouth curved, not unkindly. "Until what is broken has been mended."

Pearl crept over her skin like frost on glass. The last of her breath left her in a ribbon of silver and the sea accepted her gift. Beneath her palms, blue light flared to life and a great sapphire stone in the shape of a heart thrummed once. Twice. A shockwave shot out. The magic clanged through the chamber and through me.

It tore outward, scouring everything it touched and leaving the water new.

I swam for the entrance to the cave, racing out into the open ocean.

Sea life scattered in every direction as the magic she'd held within so long exploded through the sea, restoring what Mab had destroyed all those centuries ago when she called down a dying star and poisoned Faerie. Silt leaped and danced and settled as something truer moved through it all. Far above, waves surged and crashed over land, reshaping the ocean. Coral colored itself in a breath. Brine-bent creatures straightened and bloomed with new life.

I followed the magic and the current to the great coral castle nestled at the center of the ocean.

I rose through clear water, calling wind into the depths where it did not belong until it learned the shape of my will. Aegon's castle was empty, the last of his creatures having fled when they felt my approach. Its walls were tattered and broken. A jagged blackened mockery of what it had once been. A reflection of Aegon's black heart.

I stripped it. Pillars straightened, halls cleared of dead seaweed and kelp in one blast as the sparkling light overhead pierced cleansed water and scoured the seafloor. In the throne room, I carved a new throne, demolishing the old and shaping it as a wave crashing against the shore. As I soon would.

Air burst from my fingertips, filling the space. Aegon never trusted shifters. In his court, they died the day they were birthed. Now, it would be my greatest weapon. As I worked to rebuild all, to merge our two folk into one, I would use his fear to my advantage.

On two legs, I climbed the steps to my new throne, spinning to face the empty room.

In time, they would come to trust me. Until then, I would rule with fear. Sitting, I raised both hands to my head, lifting the small crown of seashells and spikes.

This would not do. For a king.

There was work to be done. Paths to carve. Boundaries to redraw. Bargains to collect. The land would learn its outlines again, and who had drawn them.

I breathed once, slow and full, and the ocean breathed with me. Then I began.

SEVENTY-EIGHT

JACK

S av was shaking when I wrapped my free arm around her. It wasn't from cold or magic. Her whole body had gone too still against me.

"You did the right thing."

Sav stared at the blackened vines, eyes too wide, breaths too shallow. My chest swelled as I hugged her closer. She'd chosen mercy when death would have been easier.

She could have. The strange new fire coursing through her was enough to reduce Sage to ash. Instead, she'd dragged Sage to the poisoned forest and trapped her. I didn't think three hundred years bound in poisoned roots would be enough to change Sage. When I looked at her, I saw only pettiness and hate. A creature like that didn't have it in her to be redeemed.

An involuntary shudder ripped through Sav, and I squeezed her tighter, pressed my mouth to her temple, breathed her in. Rain and honeysuckle, even after all that power had roared through her veins. She shook only once more, then steadied.

"You showed mercy." I leaned back. "Savage. Look at me."

Her eyes cut to mine. Too bright. My feral girl.

"It's done," I told her. "It's over."

Her laugh cracked. "Not yet."

Of course not. She wouldn't let herself fall apart before she fixed the next thing.

She twisted in my arms to face the boy pale beside me, his hand still gripped in mine. He'd said nothing when we left the Autumn castle.

375

Nothing when Sage threw up her wall of stone. Even after Grace called on him to aid Larek, he'd remained silent.

I recognized that hollow look. Too well.

Soon, we'd need to help him begin the slow process of recovery. Losing his parents was no small thing. Nobody knew that better than I did.

Sav knelt, laying a hand on the boy's shoulder. "Will you give me the satchel?" Her voice was soft.

She held her hand out, stepping away from me, and Grace appeared beside us as though conjured from air. I knew I should think of her as Gaia now, but she would always be Grace to me. Qaden hefted the bag into Sav's arms and backed up. She undid the leather ties and unrolled the bundle across the mossy ground, then tugged another tube from her pocket to add to the pile.

Ions buzzed in the air, and I could taste Kaspar's magic. Weeks ago, I would've assumed rain was imminent. Now I knew it was the magic I sensed. Fero had taught me that.

"These," Sav whispered. "These are folks' lives. Their freedom." She lifted her chin. "Grace?"

Grace laid long fingers on Sav's wrist. "Spring," she murmured. "Do you know what you're asking?"

"Yes," Sav said. Her throat worked. "I'm asking you to tell me how."

A grin broke over my old friend's face. "That is the right answer, Fire Fae."

Grace's gaze slid to me. "You listen too, Jack. Your mother would want you to hear."

She brushed her thumb over the inside of Sav's wrist. "This land was mine," she said softly. "Before Mab cleaved it from my fingers and carved it to suit her whims. I welcomed her when she came, swollen with child. She was desperate to save her kind. I showed her kindness." Her mouth twisted. "But in Faerie, every bargain demands a price."

Grace looked up at me. "In exchange for one child, one most terrible and powerful child, to remain free, the other was given to me."

My stomach dropped.

"That child was Aconite," she said gently. "Your mother."

I forgot how to breathe.

"Aconite spent her first hundred years with me," Grace continued. "Raised in the wild forests of Faerie, among snow-peaked mountains and densely wooded groves. She learned to heal rather than harm."

Sav's fingers slid into mine, and I started.

"In time, Mab grew more powerful and more impatient," Grace said. "My true home, the source of my magic, resides north of the mountains."

Sav and Hazel held their breath in unison, and I glanced around, noting the group that had circled us. "Every century, I returned home to replenish my magic. After one hundred years, I left Aconite with her mother and began my trek over the mountain."

My mother hadn't lived with Mab, the creature who, by all accounts, sounded monstrous. She'd spent her time in Faerie learning to heal it. My heart expanded in my ribcage as Grace went on.

"It did not go to plan." Grace searched each of our faces, landing on mine last. "Mab's gift was a most terrible one. It worked not just on folk, but on the land. With a thing's true name, she could command it. Change the very fabric of our world."

Sav's fingers tightened in mine.

"I have been cut off from my magic, my home, for more than ten thousand years."

Juniper gasped.

"Without it, I was unable to undo what Mab had done."

"The seasons," Larek breathed.

Grace nodded. "But the land always finds a way." She looked to Sav, then to me. "In time, I was able to funnel my magic, the land's magic, to a wielder. But finding one whose heart was pure proved an impossible task. That much power was too great a temptation."

"Until Sav," Juniper whispered.

"Until Sav," Grace agreed, a gentle smile on her face. She patted Sav's hand, laced with mine. "Now we must right another wrong." Her gaze moved to the pile of scrolls lying in the grass.

"But Mab's gone. Can you not return home now?" Sav's eyes glittered in the dappled light peeking between the canopy. Once again, my chest squeezed. My mate. My perfect mate had been selected, after thousands of years and thousands of fae, as the first creature pure enough to hold such power. And even then, she wanted only for the magic to be restored to what it once was.

"Some things cannot be undone." Grace's voice was soft as she laid her other hand over Sav's. "Now. We must put this right."

Sav's voice was a whisper. "Tell me how."

Grace tilted her head. "We must burn them, just as you burned your bargains."

Several fae gasped, and I glanced around as Sav released my hand and laid both palms on the pile. "Will I need to open them?"

Grace laughed, a surprisingly throaty sound for such a small creature. "Mine is the land's magic of creation and decay. With it, a world can be shaped or shattered. Though you have access to a fraction of what belongs to me, I assure you it's more than sufficient to burn away a sea creature's magic."

Sav let out a shaking breath before golden flame burst from her fingertips.

Our party left the Blood Wood and pushed on, stopping for the night at the edge of Autumn. To our right, towering white peaks sparkled against the dying embers of the setting sun. Faerie hadn't seemed this big before. With my mother's magic gone, the missing pockets of our world were restored, seams stitched back together where they'd once been torn.

We chose Winter as our sanctuary. Autumn's castle was closer, but none of us had any desire to return to that putrid place again, not after what we found beneath it.

On our second day, a chill ghosted over my skin, and the air fogged as it left my lungs.

"Winter's stream was here. I'm sure." Hazel scratched her head, glancing back at us. I was lost, but Sav was shaking her head too.

"He has been hard at work," Grace said, stopping beside Qaden and wrapping her hand around his. "But we're getting close." She tugged the boy forward. He shivered, stumbling before catching up.

I reached for Sav's cold fingers, wrapping them in mine. "I don't miss this," she grumbled, and I grinned.

"I'll keep you warm."

I expected a sharp retort, but Sav only smiled, squeezing my fingers.

A roar scattered several creatures from the trees, and I yanked Sav against my chest, searching the forest for the owner of the sound. It came again, and Hazel groaned. I peered into the distance, seeing only a blanket of snow.

"Jack," Hazel said, looking back at me. "Your ride is here."

My brow furrowed as I puzzled over her words—then a massive shape broke over a snowy dune and barreled straight toward us.

Sav screeched, backing up.

A grin split my face. "Axallar." The beast who'd hauled me across Winter, and nearly died doing it, thundered closer.

He skidded to a stop, growling in my face. Hot breath caressed my cheek as black eyes met mine, glaring accusingly. "Hey, buddy. I missed you."

He squinted, then shoved his nose into my chest, rubbing it along my arm and shoulder. I laughed, throwing my arms around him. "It's good to see you've recovered."

He huffed into my ear. I looked up, spotting Sav several feet away. "Hey! Come on. He'll give us a ride."

"No thanks. I'd rather die of frostbite."

I rolled my eyes and gripped a fistful of his fur, pulling myself up his side. I could've sworn he was bigger the first time I met him, but maybe it was only that I'd grown once my mother's glamour fell away. "Suit yourself."

"Let's go," I said to Axallar, and had to bite the inside of my cheek to hold in my smile as we moved past Sav. Her shouts at my back became colorful curses, and I spun him around, circling back to the group.

Sav glared up at me, and Axallar growled when she approached. "I'm not getting on that beast."

"I'm not carrying you," Hazel said, and without another word, she shifted, nudging Grace—still holding Qaden's hand. They climbed onto the snow leopard and bounded away. Foxglove whispered something to Juniper, and she nodded. He shifted next, leaving his clothes in a pile in the snow, then darted after Hazel. Juniper ran after him, and I gawked at her speed. Clearly, the cold didn't bother her the way it did my mate.

Sav glanced around, finding only her and Larek left, and her cheeks reddened. "Fine." She reached for Axallar's fur, but he swung his head around, snapping at her.

"Easy," I coaxed. "I'm not leaving her, so unless you want to go at her glacial pace..."

A chuff of hot air burst from his nostrils, but he turned forward and let her pull herself up.

Larek glanced warily between us and the stretch of snow disappearing into the distance. He swallowed and slid a row of knives around to his back. "Is he... safe?"

I laughed again, never imagining I'd be the one less afraid of anything in Faerie than the others. Sav wrapped an arm around my back and leaned down, holding a hand out to Larek. "Come on. They have hot springs in the castle."

Her words were like magic, spurring Larek into motion. In moments, he climbed up, and Sav's other arm came around my waist. "Go." She shuddered at my back. Whether from the cold or the polar bear, I wasn't sure.

⋅•➔﴿⤸•♠♠♦•﴾⋅

We strode along familiar corridors lined with wolves, and a jolt of déjà vu struck me. I'd been here, it was true, but this time it wasn't just the place I remembered. It was the magic, waking as I moved, welcoming me home.

Robin Goodfellow hovered near the edge of the hall, half hidden behind a pillar, hair immaculate, eyes watching us warily. When he spotted me, he flinched, then tried to smooth his expression into something obedient.

My grip tightened on Sav's hand.

"Leave," I said flatly. "You're relieved of duty."

Robin dipped into a quick bow and slipped away without a word. Quiet satisfaction knotted in my chest. The last time I'd seen him, he'd made my mate feel small.

When we crossed an icy archway into the great hall, the wolves' heads swiveled toward me.

They watched me.

And then—one by one, like frost racing over water—their bodies rippled. The armor encasing them melted away as the creatures beneath changed. Faces broadened, jaws widening, fangs lengthening and turning black. Fur shifted from gray to white.

A pack of polar bears stared back at me.

Sav made a humming sound.

Behind us, Hazel whispered, "That's... normal."

Grace looked smug. Which, on a four-foot-tall creature with huge golden eyes and tufted ears, should not have been intimidating. It was.

I swallowed. "Hi," I greeted the bears.

Grace stretched a hand toward the nearest guard. He huffed, but didn't break position. "You are king now."

"King?" Sav gasped.

My breath escaped in a rush. King? No. I didn't want to be a ruler. Didn't think it was what the folk needed.

"Aconite knew this day would come. She hid you, kept you far away from Mab where, like her, you would learn kindness and be better than Mab ever was," Grace whispered. "Your mother knew you would be what Faerie needed."

I swallowed.

"I'm not a king."

"Good." Grace's ear twitched. "Be more."

I nodded. This land didn't need kings or queens or royal courts. It needed to heal.

Grace tipped her chin toward me, as though she'd seen past the words I hadn't said aloud. She turned as if to leave, but when I blinked, she was simply gone.

Mother Mahonia raced down the hall. "Jack! You're here." Qaden startled, as though the words roused him, and he ducked behind me as the female rushed for us, huffing by the time she reached the end of the long hall. A smile tilted my lips as I hurried to meet her. She wrapped wiry arms around my back, hugging me tight. "You've changed!"

I smiled at the healer. "So I have."

"Like your mother."

My heart cracked as I released her gently. She would've been my mother's healer too. Had she known all along who I was? *Yes.* She must have. I would have to tell her what happened. Pain sliced through my middle. Could I say the words out loud?

"And who do you have here?" she asked.

I glanced behind me. It wasn't Sav she saw, but Qaden, wide-eyed and trembling. I held a hand out. He stared at it, then at Mother Mahonia.

"Am I your prisoner?"

My lips flattened. "Of course not."

"I want to go to Summer."

They were his first words in days, and they were full of anger. He'd moved past shock and grief and was stranded in the one feeling that made him feel strong. "Qaden—"

"Summer is no place for a boy now," Mother Mahonia cut me off, leaning down to brush a lock of Qaden's dark hair from his forehead. "Let Mother Mahonia run you a warm bath and take you to the kitchens. We can talk more about it in the morning."

Some of Qaden's bravado fizzled at the promise of food and a bath. He took her hand, glaring over his shoulder at me.

I couldn't account for his misplaced anger, but we had time. Now, we'd all need it. As the pair left, I turned back to find Sav and Hazel already wrapped in a tight hug.

"I love you," Hazel said fiercely. "But if I stay right now, I'll never leave. I can already feel it. I'll chain myself here because you need me, and I'll call it a choice. But it won't be."

Sav said nothing, closing her eyes and nodding as they pressed their foreheads together.

Hazel swallowed. "Larek and Murz are coming with me," she added. "We're going to find Creig. Make him listen. Yolmar wasn't your fault."

Sav's voice was small. "I'll miss you."

Hazel huffed. "You'll have plenty to occupy your time." Her eyes slid to me, and I frowned.

Larek's gaze shot to me, and he gave me a once-over.

Sav made a soft, wounded sound. "You'll come back?"

Hazel's eyes shone. "Are you kidding?" She leaned back, searching Sav's face. "You're stuck with me."

Sav laughed a little hollowly.

Hazel swiped at her cheeks before backing up and turning from the room. Larek followed without a backward glance at any of us.

Sav watched them go, her mouth pressed into a tight line.

⸺◆→(ᴗ◆ʌ◆◆⸺

We left the great hall, and the strange guards didn't so much as blink as we passed. I felt the tug of my magic. Somehow they were part of it. Another of Mab's gifts? Were they bound? I would find out, and when I did, I would find a way to release them.

Foxglove was already waiting outside the great hall, Juniper's fingers hooked through his belt like she didn't trust the world not to take him if she let go.

"Will you leave us too?" Sav asked.

Foxglove straightened. "We're going to Spring," he said. "To find Juniper's clan."

"You're brave." Sav nudged Foxglove's shoulder.

Juniper searched Sav's face. "I'm sorry I didn't tell you."

Sav blinked back tears. My tough mate, who didn't cry for anyone's knife, was hurt that they were all leaving. I never would. I would be by her side to the end. "I understand. And I'm so sorry about your mother."

Juniper bared her teeth. "That debt is mine to claim, and no fault of yours."

"But my magic. Kaspar—"

Juniper wrapped a hand around Sav's wrist, twisting it to bare a strange mark I hadn't seen before. The memory of Grace running her thumb over Sav's wrist in the Blood Wood flashed in my mind. What was it? What did it mean? "You are blessed by the goddess. We should have protected you even then. It was never your fault."

Sav said nothing, staring down at the strange tree-shaped brand before looking back up. "Take care of them. I'll come back to Spring to help as soon as I can."

Juniper dipped her chin, glanced at me, then turned, tugging Foxglove out into the snow.

The hall went quiet.

It was just me and Sav now.

She let out a long, shaky breath. "We're alone," she whispered, eyes meeting mine.

My pulse jumped. "Are we?" I asked, trying to steady my erratic heartbeat.

"And there's no more contract." She stepped in, pressing against me, close enough that I felt every breath. One hand slid up my chest, the other brushed my arm, and my gaze snagged on her finger where the inky lines of Kaspar's bargain had once curled.

Bare skin. No brand tying her life to him.

The realization hit hard. No more magic waiting to tear her from my arms if we went too far. No more invisible line between us that ended in her death. The bargain she'd taken for me was gone, and for the first time since she married him, I could touch her without wondering if wanting her would kill her.

She was still my stubborn mate, but she was no longer bound to a prince who thought he owned her. She was here. With me.

Her hands slid into my hair, fingers curling as she tugged my head down. "Jack," she said, voice low and rough. "Kiss me like you mean it."

Just like that, the pain, torment, and death we'd crawled through faded to the edges of my mind. For this one moment, only this female, only this choice, mattered.

I leaned in, wrapped my arms around her waist, and tugged her closer.

Her mouth moved with mine, and it wasn't careful anymore. Before, we'd kissed like tomorrow might never come, like forever wasn't in our future. Now, anything was possible. Now, I claimed her.

I walked her backward until her spine hit cold stone. She arched into me like she'd been made to fit with me. Our bodies molded together, and some ruthless part of me swore I'd shield her from anything. From everything.

"Savage," I breathed.

"Yeah?" she rasped.

"Should we..."

She laughed, breathless and wicked, and slid her fingers deftly through my tattered, bloody tunic. Her hands were on me, greedily tracing the lines of my skin as though she'd been starving for it.

"Sav," I groaned. "Slow down."

"No," she said, and bit my lower lip.

She tugged at my clothes, desperate, unsteady, like we only had this moment, and realization struck.

"We're alive. We made it. I'm not going anywhere."

Hot tears slid down her cheeks, dripping onto my neck, but she pulled me closer, kissing me like she could consume me. She'd fought so hard to hold it together. To put on a brave face when we both might have died. When so many had. "Sav."

Abruptly, she shoved me, pushing me back, and searched my face. "Make a bargain with me."

I would've laughed, but she was crumbling, and my chest burned with the need to fix it.

"Name it," I managed, dropping to my knees. My hands slid up her thighs as I looked up into sparkling violet eyes. "Name it, Sav. Every piece of me is already yours."

Her breath caught. Her pupils blew wide. "Jack—"

"Tell me what you want," I said, forehead pressed to her stomach, bowing for my princess. "Tell me to stay. Tell me to worship. I'll do any of it. All of it. Just say it."

Her fingers slid into my hair and tightened. I felt the shiver run all the way through her.

"Stay," she whispered.

I almost broke.

"Yes," I said, voice low. "I'll stay. Forever."

I kissed my way up her body, sliding soft fabric up as I went. The sharp hitch of her breath when my mouth brushed high under her breast brought a smile to my lips. She swore, softly, and arched into me, her nails digging into my scalp.

"Jack," she gasped.

I slid my remaining scraps of clothes off as her hands fumbled at her own tunic. I tugged it over her head, pushed her back against the pillar, and she wrapped her legs around my waist.

I held her there, one hand braced under her thigh, the other fisted in her hair to bare her throat so I could watch her face when I finally—finally —slid into her without someone threatening to kill one of us for it.

She shattered.

Beautiful. Wild. Mine.

I hissed, forehead dropping to hers. "Savage," I groaned.

Her nails dragged down my back, and she screamed my name as we moved.

My name on her lips was my undoing. I groaned, moving slow and deep, because I would never give her less than everything. "I'm yours."

Her whole body jerked. "Again."

"I'm yours," I told her, panting against her mouth. "And I swear I'll never leave."

She broke apart under me, pulling me with her.

When we finished—together, sating our hunger and the bond's carnal need—we slid down the pillar in a graceless, satisfied tangle until we hit the cold stone, her curled in my lap, my face buried in her hair, both of us breathing hard.

We didn't speak on the walk to her room, but she looked back, double-checking I was still with her, that I would keep our bargain. I leaned down, scooped her into my arms, and she huffed, but didn't fight me as I carried her through the door to the room she'd stayed in the last time we were in

Winter. The last time I'd stood here, we'd shared our first kiss, and some reckless part of me had known it then: this was it. Not a flirtation. Mates. Forever, if the world had any mercy left.

I crossed the room, set her gently on the bed, and leaned over her, tipping my forehead to hers.

"I'm not better yet," I said, because I wanted to be. For her. But it would take time. "Not after my dad. Not after my mom died in my arms. I keep thinking I should be stronger by now. I'm trying, Sav. I am. Can you bear with me while I figure out how to be a person again?"

Her fingers slid into my hair as she tipped her head back to stare up at me. "I can bear anything," she said, eyes searching mine, "as long as you never leave me."

Something tight in my chest let go. I kissed her cheek, then her lips.

She pulled me down, and I fell beside her, legs tangling, laughter catching in our throats before dissolving into quiet.

Her hands were gentle at my shoulders, my jaw. Mine mapped the warmth at her waist, the line of her spine. Every touch was reassurance that neither of us would leave. That we were forever. When I cupped her face, she came closer, and the rest of the world faded.

I moved with her, following her lead when she wanted it, guiding when she asked without words. Our breath synced. This time, when she came apart in my arms, a part of me I'd never known existed flared to life. For the first time in my life, even with all I'd lost, I knew peace. If only in this moment.

The window spilled morning light across the sheets. It pooled at her throat, turned her eyes to amethyst. I pressed my lips to her thrumming pulse, felt it answer mine.

"Jack," she whispered, a prayer and a promise. She traced lazy circles on my chest. "I've never thought about a family," she whispered. "But..." She hesitated.

I went very, very still.

"With you," she said softly, "I can imagine it."

I hadn't ever thought of a family, a wife, a mate, until Sav. Now images swirled in my mind. Sav, a tiny precious baby that looked just like her, fiery red curls and freckles dotting her cheeks.

"Yeah?"

"Don't be smug," she muttered.

"Too late," I said, because smug didn't even begin to cover what I felt when I imagined a family with her. I kissed her hair. "How many?"

She barked a startled laugh. "What?"

"How many children?" I said, already smiling.

There was a beat. Then she huffed. "One. Maybe."

"Three," I said.

Her head lifted. She squinted at me. "Three?"

"Three's always been lucky for me." I kissed her nose. "Three feels right."

She stared.

"What," I said, suddenly defensive. "Why are you looking at me like that?"

Her face softened, and my chest expanded. "Nothing," she whispered. "Just remember you said that when you're surrounded by girls. I'm not having boys."

I grinned. "If it's girls you want, we can have seven."

She snorted. "Don't be absurd. Fae are lucky to have two. Three is rare. In the history of Faerie, no fae has ever had seven children."

"We have plenty of time to try," I teased.

Her breath hitched. "Yeah," she whispered. "Forever."

My throat tightened. "Forever."

I laid my head down on her chest, images of seven tiny creatures—a mix of Sav and me—running beneath our feet. The love we'd have for them. Would Faerie be a safe place for them to grow up? I would do my best to make sure it was, in this new world we'd help create.

"Jack?"

"Hmm?"

"I have to go talk to Kaspar."

All thoughts of family dissolved as ice slid down my spine. Of course she did. Of course. She'd never leave a wound open, even if it bled her out.

"I'll come with you."

She bit her lip. "He won't talk if you're there," she said quietly.

I ground my teeth. "He could kill you."

"He won't."

"I don't like it."

"I know."

I tipped her chin up so she had to meet my eyes. "Sav," I said softly. "If he hurts you, I'll burn him."

Her mouth twitched. "You can't burn a sea fae."

"Watch me."

She smiled and leaned in to kiss me slow and deep, sealing something. When she pulled back, her eyes were serious.

"I'll come back," she said.

I hated how much that helped.

"You better."

"Good," she said. "We agree."

She slid off the bed, wrapped a robe around her frame, and dragged her fingers through my hair, leaning in to capture my mouth in hers once more. "I love you."

"Me too," I breathed.

I watched her go.

Every instinct in me screamed to follow. But Sav was the strongest fae I knew. She wouldn't be cowed by him. Not when he had no more leverage. And if he tried to take her, I would come for him.

And I would end him.

SEVENTY-NINE

SAV

Kaspar's lake wasn't where it was supposed to be.

The place in Spring where it had always sat—clear water ringed in moss and old stones smooth from years of water lapping gently against them, reeds whispering, a place that had been safety back when I didn't have any—was raw churned earth now. Cracked mud. A hole in the world where someone had ripped the lake out by the roots and carried it off.

I'd been sure he would return to Spring now that Faerie was restored. Had he remained in Summer? Even now?

Leaves rustled at my ankles.

I glanced down, my mouth falling open, and knelt, holding out a hand. One small buttercup climbed into my palm.

"What are you doing here? So far from the Autumn border?"

A round face, rimmed in yellow, peered up at me. "Woe is me, the pretty flower, who with no water, has lost all power."

I exhaled. The poor things had relocated in search of water, only to find none where a lake had always been. But did that mean he'd taken the stream beside their home too? We'd all been shocked to see the ones bisecting Winter and Autumn were gone, but had he taken it all?

"I need to speak with him, the prince of Lakes and Streams," I whispered. My voice thick. "Where did he go?"

The tiny flower peered up at me, petals wilting. "He who was, is not. Seek him where the soil is hot."

"His lake is still in Summer?"

389

A chorus of wails erupted from the field of yellow. "Oh no. Oh no," they sang.

Not Summer? "The lake is not in Summer?"

"Not in lake nor leaf he stays; the sea now calls him to her ways."

I dipped my chin, lowering my hand to let the tiny fae crawl down as my mind worked to arrange their puzzle. "You have my gratitude, good folk, but will you also accept a bargain?" The field burst in sing-song delight. It was rare any paid the buttercups with a bargain, but they had not asked for payment. I knew it was because they were so thirsty.

My veins burned with the desire to set something on fire. How could he be so selfish? When all of Faerie depended on the lakes and streams to survive.

"Ice does not belong to Prince Kaspar. Make your way to Winter, and we will care for you. Tell the others."

Gasped wails and sobs swept over the field, and I stood, turning south to begin my long trek to the sea.

◆→◗ (◡ ◆ ◚ ◗◆◆

The seasons were already beginning to unwind without the influence of fae royals to sway them, but Summer was unlike the others. Here, it was still hot, the rise and fall of massive sand dunes stretching into a shimmering distance. Had Summer's reach grown since I'd last traveled here? Or was I misremembering its vastness?

Once, I would have called Kaspar and he would have answered. He would have carried me astride his back and the distance would not have felt so great.

Now, I trekked south in an unending line.

When the heat had burrowed under my skin, sweat staining my back, I arrived at the Summer palace. Memories of Fero's recent kindness, of the bargain he'd asked of us, surfaced and my chest tightened. A powerful prince had been struck down in the prime of his life. He should have had hundreds of years with his boy, but instead, they would never know one another.

I moved through the empty castle, glancing around. All was still and silent. Had they abandoned their court when their prince died? I owed it to them to help. To restore the land and its folk. Soon, I would help them all.

Now, I had another wrong to set right.

At the back steps leading to the beach, I stopped. Water lapped at the lowest stair. Where there'd once been a long stretch of sand, the sea pressed right up to the palace door.

But it wasn't the tide that stole my attention.

Kaspar stood less than a foot from me. His dark eyes held none of their usual apathy—only murder. And they were on me.

"Kaspar," I breathed.

"King Kaspar," he corrected, not moving an inch.

He didn't raise his voice. Didn't snarl. The title left his mouth stripped of any warmth, and that emptiness hurt worse than a shout. My oldest friend had never spoken to me with such contempt.

Heat drained from my face as I dipped my chin. I'd almost never felt the full force of his power. He'd always been cold on the surface, everything carefully bottled beneath. I saw now that it hadn't been indifference. It had been control.

And it was gone.

His magic bowled over me in waves, his control unmoored, his emotions loose and raging. Magic crashed through me again and again, soaked in fury. My stomach turned as I tried to lift my head.

"Kaspar... please." I gasped.

"King Kaspar," he shouted and the sound reverberated in my skull.

I touched the wetness at my lobe, wincing when it came away red.

Air vanished, yanked from my lungs at his command. I crashed to my knees, a hand at my throat as my chest dragged uselessly for breath.

My vision blackened at the edges. *He won't do it. He won't.*

Pain cracked through my ribs as my chest heaved and the world tunneled.

Air flooded back into my lungs all at once, and I was suddenly gulping, choking on it when there had been none a moment before. When my breathing finally evened out, I pushed unsteadily to my feet. "King," I rasped. "Will you not show mercy?"

His laugh was dry and brittle. "Have I not? You live though twice you mistook me."

Heat flared in my veins even as confusion muddled my thoughts. He thought I came to beg for my life? Mine? When he would kill us all? My jaw clenched as I straightened my shoulders. "I'm asking for the folk of Faerie."

His eyes, black with fury, clouded, lightening a fraction to a dark aquamarine. "Still crusading for your folk then, Salvia?"

The name scorched my insides. He wanted me to cower, to weep, to beg. I would not.

"You may have *my* name, *King*, but you cannot control them all. What will you do now that all your bargains are burned?" My smile was all teeth when I met his eyes.

He growled low in his throat and I thought I might just be seeing the cold prince the world knew. I'd heard the rumors all my life, but I had struggled to reconcile them with the creature I knew. He was cold, unfeeling, but never cruel. This was a monster I was only just meeting.

"I could just drown them all."

His words sent a chill down my spine. Kaspar didn't make jokes.

"What can I do to convince you?"

He tilted his head, giving me a once-over that made my skin feel hot and cold.

"You can't think I'd want anything you have *left* to offer." He bared his teeth in something that wasn't a smile.

Heat scorched my veins and I opened my mouth.

"Save your breath." He crossed his arms over his chest and I noticed the scales on his shoulders were darker. They still glittered in the sunlight, but the color wasn't as bright. I couldn't fathom what it meant. Didn't know enough about Kelpies. Had Aegon's scales once been bright? Had years deep under the ocean changed him? Or was it the blackness of his heart?

"You will deliver a message to your new *king*." He spat the word and I bristled, choosing not to correct him. "If any of your kind sets one foot in my water, their life is forfeit."

"But they'll—"

"One stream remains in all of Faerie. Redraw your lines, Princess. Because the sea isn't safe for your kind any longer."

My breath caught. So much of the land would be destroyed. It would change our world forever.

"Kas—"

Magic sliced through me, making me double over.

"That was your last warning," he seethed. "Tell your king if any blocks access to my stream, I will destroy you all."

My heart crashed against my ribs as I struggled against the weight of his magic and his words. One stream. One place in all of Faerie for the folk to survive. And this was all my fault. My spine bent as I crashed to the sandstone floor, pressing my palm against the gritty surface in an attempt to rise.

When the weight lifted an eternity later, I sat up, already knowing he would be gone.

-●→)(◡◆▲◆●●-

Jack paced outside Winter Castle's main doors, breaking into a run when he spied me.

We crashed into one another, a tangle of limbs and lips. He pressed his palms to either side of my face, tilting my head up to look at him. "Are you hurt?"

I shook my head and tears slid down my cheeks. "No."

"What is it?"

I squeezed my eyes shut, willing the tears to stop. They must have been red and puffy. I'd cried the entire trek back to Winter, my gaze cataloging every wilting leaf and forlorn creature. Some were already migrating across Faerie in search of water. I couldn't help them. Couldn't save them from the monster I'd unleashed.

We had survived Mab, Aegon, and Prim, only to learn my oldest friend would be the one to end us.

"Kaspar has redirected all the water in Faerie." I opened my eyes. "And... all land fae are banished."

Jack went very still. "Over my dead body."

I huffed a wet almost-laugh. "You can't stop him. No one can. No magic in Faerie is strong enough to overpower a sea king."

His jaw flexed. "Then we plan," he muttered. "Tell me exactly what he said. Hazel told us this wasn't the first time a sea king attempted to overthrow land. Then, Firethorn brought water from the mountain. We adapt."

Something inside me unclenched. Being near him, his words, brought clarity. All was not lost. "We need to find that book."

"Yes." Jack kissed me. Then he pulled back, eyes searching mine. "We'll deal with the angry seahorse later. Right now, you need a bath."

Despite everything, a laugh slipped out of me. "Are you saying I stink?"

"I would never say that to your face," he said, face utterly serious.

I snorted, which shouldn't have felt like relief and did.

-●→(∪◆∩◆●●-

I sank deeper into the hot spring bath, letting the heat soak into my bones. Muscles I hadn't realized were clenched finally loosened. Steam curled around my face, soft and hazy, muting the world and its worries.

For a while I floated, eyes half-closed. Jack was safe and so were Hazel, Juniper, and the others. The mountain's water lapped against my skin in a slow, constant rhythm, as if it had been doing this long before any of us existed and would go on long after we were gone.

The thought should have been comforting. Instead, something tugged at the back of my mind.

Kaspar had reached me here once, his voice rising from the water, claiming he had access to the hot springs. That they too were under his domain.

But... Realization broke over me. I bolted upright, sloshing water over the sides as I climbed out of the tub, heart pounding. Had Kaspar lied? One of his many lies to keep his secrets close?

"Jack!"

He was there instantly, like he'd been waiting just beyond the steam.

"The water," I said, breathless. "Kaspar said the hot springs were under his domain. But when he redirected the water, stripping everything down to a single stream, the mountain water didn't change." My pulse hammered. "It wasn't touched."

Jack's eyes sharpened. "Meaning he can't control it."

"Or he lied about having access," I whispered. "Or both."

Jack's brow furrowed as he held out a fluffy robe, and I took it. "We'll need to figure out why." He tugged my tangle of wet hair back, wrapping it in a high towel. I turned, facing myself in the mirror and laughed.

"What style is this meant to be?"

He leaned down and I watched in the mirror as he planted a kiss on my cheek. "It's meant to dry your hair so you don't catch cold..."

I rolled my eyes. "I won't die from wet hair."

"But you *can* catch cold." He laced our fingers and tugged me down a side hall I hadn't seen yet. Winter had a lot of those; narrow halls leading to a seemingly unending number of new wings of the castle with sparkling faelight overhead to light the way. A polar bear padded after us, and I glanced back, giving him a wary stare. "Come on. I want to show you something."

We stopped at a wall of smooth stone.

"There's something in there. I can feel it." Jack motioned me forward. "I was waiting for you to open it."

I grinned. "Scared?"

"Maybe a little." A dimple appeared in his lightly scarred cheek. I flinched at the reminder of his former mortality, but scrubbed the thought away. He would live. He would live forever.

I pushed the stone, but it didn't budge. "Are you sure this is a door?"

He stepped around me, pressing his palms to the stone, and the door clicked.

"Huh," I said.

Stone split down the middle. The halves slid apart with a low grinding groan, cold air washing out over us. The chamber beyond was lit by a pale, unnatural light.

At the center sat an altar of carved ice.

On it, a book.

It wasn't leather. It wasn't bark. It wasn't anything I knew. The cover was bone white and smooth, a constellation etched into it—one I didn't recognize. Something otherworldly buzzed in the air, and it seemed to be emanating from this odd book.

Up close, faint ornate letters curled over the cover. They reminded me, oddly, of Jack's back tattoo. *The Book of Winter.* A grin split my face. He'd found it! It would house the answers we needed to save Faerie from Kaspar's machinations.

Jack reached out. His hand shook as he laid his palm on the cover. The book glowed under his touch.

"Ready?" I whispered.

"No," he breathed.

I slid my hand over his. We opened it, staring down at the neatly written script. We leaned close, heads bumping together, and read:

My last desperate hope is that I find their father. The creature born of this strange place. He will know what to do. I have tried to raise him. To protect him as any mother would. But the heat that burns within him, the magic that cannot be consumed, is enough to unmake worlds.

Once, their father told me he was something other. Greater. But I, vain creature that I was, believed his words were meant only to seduce. I had never visited his world. Never seen how they feared him. Had I known, would I have created not one, but two, like him?

But it was far worse than I feared. His kind, those with the magic to bisect space and time, to melt the very core of a celestial body until they shaped it into their vision, their dream of paradise, are few indeed. And they have been unable to repopulate. One is enough to carve whole galaxies. Destroy entire solar systems. Melt suns. And I have made two.

But I have hope. My lover's sister is not so cruel as he. She told me of their weakness. The source of their magic, of all magic in the universe, exists beyond the mountains. Cut off from their source, they are weak. Even their immortality wanes.

For my son and my unborn babe, I must find a way to block it. To block them. Before my children grow too powerful. Before these beings of infinite power rewrite another world. Destroy a world as he did mine. I must stop Firethorn before he becomes as powerful as his father.

My stomach dropped.

Jack swore under his breath. "Sav," he whispered. "What the fuck am I?"

I stared down at the page, heart pounding.

"I don't know."

THE END

EPILOGUE

VEN

150 YEARS LATER

The problem with parties in Winter was that everyone pretended they weren't freezing.

It was August. Anywhere decent, that meant bare skin and ripe fruit and humidity. Here it meant forty degrees, and stone floors that bit into bare feet with a vengeance. Faelight burned in caged ice overhead and threw soft blue-white over a ballroom full of bodies.

Everyone in Faerie was here.

Not an exaggeration. Smugglers from the coast who smelled like fish. Autumn brutes in torn leathers. Spring healers with flora-stained hands. Pirates. High Fae and Low. Folk who'd kill each other any other night, spun under Winter arches like we were one happy, healed realm instead of a barely stitched-together cesspool.

Because my mother was four hundred and fifty, and we were all supposed to orbit her like she was the sun. I loved that for her. No, I did. Truly. I just didn't need to be in the room for it.

I was already in trouble. I'd shown up late, and one of my sisters had materialized in the doorway like judgment and said: *You're late. Do you own a brush. Is that what you're wearing.*

Yes. No. Absolutely.

If they wanted me here, they could have me here. They did not get to have me in curled and primped like a doll.

My dress was indigo, the darkest possible blue the seamstress had without it technically being black. Everyone else floated around in ice-silk and crystal and lace. I'd ripped the sleeves off as soon as I left my room and hadn't looked back. My mask was matte black, half-face, no filigree, no glitter. I'd cut it myself. It was almost ugly. I liked that.

If they wanted a princess, they shouldn't have banned royal titles. That's why I'd tattooed the word on my ass for my twenty-fifth birthday. Anyone who didn't like it could kiss it.

My hair hung loose down my back, a little gray from lack of washing. My lipstick, nails, liner: all violet to match my eyes. Rings on nearly every finger glittered, but hopefully didn't detract from my attitude. I just loved when things sparkled.

A slim vial the color of bruised plum hung on a chain at my throat. Tonight's stock was thick and purple and would buy me two months of silence from certain angry pirates who made it their business to stick their noses in mine.

Everyone kept saying "no crime tonight, Lavender, it's your mother's night," which was rude. Selling herbs wasn't a crime. Maybe mine couldn't be called herbs anymore—not after the number of times I'd cut them with magic.

I slipped through a knot of slow-dancing folk before someone's uncle could catch me, kiss my cheek, and call me "little Briar," ducked under crystal garland, and made for the drinks. It still made me laugh to think that Dad had taken Mom's maiden name.

Winter's ballroom had been repaired and re-charmed and polished a hundred times in the last century, but it still felt like a stone prison. Polar bears lounged at the curved edges of the room, huge white paws like dinner plates crossed, pretending to nap. You could always tell who'd never been north before by how fast they flinched when a bear huffed.

Music curled through the air, making my toes tap. Okay, I liked one thing about balls. Fae voices scattered up toward the ceiling and shattered there. I ignored all of it and went for the punch.

If you could call it punch.

"It's not even that strong," I muttered, mostly to myself, after my first swallow. "Stars. Did they water it down for the low fae?"

Henbane wine wasn't the standard drink in Winter. It was an homage to Mother's home court. Spring. Sweet, a little bitter on the back of the tongue, a comfortable float behind the eyes if you had two or three fast. Which meant: useless.

"You're supposed to sip it," someone said behind me.

The way he said it made me want to bare my teeth.

I didn't turn. "And you're supposed to mind your own business," I said sweetly, because I was in public.

He laughed. Closer. I caught his scent: candied fruit. *Spring Court*. He set his elbow on the table beside the punch bowl, crowding my space.

"Pretty mask," he said. "Too plain for Winter, though. They didn't give you anything nicer?"

I smiled. All teeth. "This is nicer," I said. "My other one has teeth."

He blinked.

Stars have mercy. Males were exhausting.

"I could—" he started.

"No," I cut him off and reached for the ladle again.

A shadow wrapped itself around wood before I could and poured for me. The spring court male backed up, bumping someone behind him. I ignored him, attention caught on the darkness pooling in the corner.

I felt it.

Not the way you "feel" a body come up behind you and your neck prickles because maybe they're bigger. This was older. Heavier. The sort of magic that commanded attention.

My limbs stilled. A predator. All my senses knew it.

The new voice—low, dark, not from here—said, "Henbane? At a Winter ball?" as a male stepped from the shadows, setting the ladle beside the bowl.

For one stupid second, I thought it might be Cais.

Tall, broad shoulders in black. Black velvet jacket cut to fit him perfectly. Black shirt open at the throat. Not one of the riffraff. A royal? Like me? My gaze trailed up, meeting dark eyes behind a darker mask and a moment of electricity danced between us.

Then I saw his mouth.

Not Cais.

Cais didn't have a mouth like that. And what a sinful mouth it was.

"I like henbane," I said. I didn't move back. I just angled my chin so I could see him through my mask. "Is that a problem?"

He looked at me and the air sizzled.

"Not a problem," he said after a beat. "Different."

I hated that my stomach flipped.

"You'll find I'm different in a lot of ways."

One corner of his blue lips tipped up. I tried and failed to catch his scent. To learn his court, but it was masked. The hairs on my neck rose. A spy? At my mother's party? *Brazen.*

"I don't doubt that," he murmured.

"You don't even know me," I said.

"Yet," he said.

I lifted my cup and swallowed what was left just to have something to do with my mouth. "You're not from here."

"No."

"Who brought you?" I let boredom drip from my tone.

"No one brought me."

So he'd slipped past Winter wards on my mother's birthday. Interesting.

"Everyone in Faerie is here tonight," I said. "I suppose that includes their spies."

"Everyone?" His quiet amusement had vanished and ice slid down my spine.

"Everyone." I cleared my throat.

"Somehow I doubt you comprehend the meaning of the word."

Another chill. It couldn't be. I'd heard of them. Spies from the sea court. But I'd never met one. How else could I explain his masked scent, his blue lips, the way he lurked in the shadows? They were the only creatures not invited to Mother's parties. My heart thundered in my chest.

"I'm sure they would be. If one only asked." I exhaled a shallow breath. I'd been searching for so long. Was this *finally* my lucky night?

"Mmm." His gaze dropped to my mouth, then back up, unhurried. "Are you?"

Starfire and damnation.

He wasn't playing the usual game. The part of the overexuberant male child looking for status from the great Sav and Jack Briar or a quick lay. He was just... watching me.

"Do you always lurk in corners and watch girls drink alone?" I asked.

"Only the interesting ones," he said, and made *interesting* sound like a sin.

My pulse ratcheted up.

I set my free hand on the table to steady myself. The faelight hit my rings—seven tonight, all shiny. Three harmless. Four with surprises. The purple vial at my throat flashed when I moved.

His attention flicked there.

"Poison rings," he murmured, like he was pleased.

My chin tipped up. "Protection."

"Mmm." He nodded. "Of course."

I watched his mouth form the words, delicious thoughts erupting in my mind. What was wrong with me?

"And you?" I asked. "Where do you keep your weapons?" Stars, I was playing with fire, but I found I wanted to play this game with the mystery male who had infiltrated my court.

He hummed. "Do you believe I need them to satisfy my dark cravings?"

Heat slid straight down my spine.

That wasn't fair. He didn't get to say that in that voice with that mouth and expect me to keep standing like I hadn't gone more than a hundred years without ever knowing what a creature like this could do with such a wicked tongue.

"I don't know you," I said. "I don't even know your name. How could I begin to know your cravings"

"No." That slow curl of his mouth again. "I suppose you would not."

"Are you going to tell your name then? Or your court?"

"No."

Rude.

"Fine." I tilted my chin. "Then I'll guess."

His brow tipped, up. "Very well. Guess my court and I will owe you a bargain."

I bit my lip. A bargain from a sea fae. A spy. The possibilities were limitless. But if I was wrong... I would chase this dark creature straight out of the castle and far from my bed.

"Oceans and—"

He hissed, cold shadow caressing my cheek as it wrapped around my mouth, cutting off my words.

Shadow magic. I'd known that's what it was. All the soft seduction in his mouth was gone now, replaced by fury. I had misjudged the situation. I'd never met a sea fae before. What if the stories were true? I grabbed a ring from my hand, moving quickly, and stabbed the shadow wrapped around my mouth.

A dark laugh erupted from the masked male and the shadows slid away.

"Good," he said softly. "Very good."

That voice should've been illegal.

"Am I correct?" I whispered.

He dipped his chin, that sensual grin back and I would have groaned if he wouldn't have heard it. "Very well. A bargain. What will it be?"

I should have calculated, should have considered all angles, but the words were free before I could stop myself. "I want access to the ocean."

Moisture in the air grew, my hair sticking to my face. Beside us the glasses rattled and I glanced down. Folk's gazes darted toward us and in moments we were enveloped in cool mist. I looked around, exhaling in wonder. All joy vanished when nearly black eyes met mine again.

"That is not yours to ask." Sharp teeth clicked as the words snapped out and the soft, seductive male who had so openly flirted with me a moment ago was gone.

I backed up, but a hand snaked out and clamped like a vice around my wrist. I reached for the vial at my neck, but he was faster, his other hand capturing and pinning my arm to my side. With calculated slowness, he brought my right hand to his mouth.

I watched, my heart hammering against my ribs as he bowed and soft cerulean lips brushed my knuckles.

"Princess, I bid you goodnight."

As quickly as we'd been surrounded by his shadows, he was gone and I was alone beside the punch table.

I ground my teeth even as my steps to the door grew light.

I'd just met my first sea fae... and he owed me a bargain.

Read Ven's story in *The Drowned Fae Realms*, Coming 2027

READ A PREVIEW OF WINTER

Scan here to read the first four chapters of Firethorn and Lorelai's story completely free:

Thank you for reading
Poison Amidst Blooms

If you enjoyed this book, please consider leaving an honest review.

Leave a review on Amazon:

Leave a review on Goodreads:

Acknowledgments

If you've made it this far, a special thank you to you. Readers like you are the reason I keep going!

To Brittni and my mom, for being the first people to read my horrible drafts and for reading it again and again as I worked through all the small details.

To Frankie, for sticking with me through another series. I appreciate all you do.

To my content team, for all your support throughout the series and for endlessly shouting about my stories to anyone who will listen.

To my son, who tells everyone he meets about my books, sometimes to my embarrassment. Thank you for being my biggest supporter. The cat is named for you. ;)

To Tivuel for creating such beautiful art and for inspiring me to write Kaspar's story. And to the other artists for creating gorgeous art of Sav, Jack, and the rest of the characters in the Deadly Fae series.

To Laura for creating the beautiful hardcover editions of the series.

To Nicole and Kelly, my editing ninjas. I appreciate all you do to help bring my stories to life. I think we're all Team Kaspar, for better or worse.

To Shelly, for formatting this beast.

Thank you.

ABOUT THE AUTHOR

Cassandra Aston grew up on a ranch just outside Austin, Texas. She's a lover of all things fantasy—especially the fae. Her dark portal romantasy series, the *Deadly Fae Duology*, takes readers deep into the world of Faerie. In 2027, she returns to the same realm with a new series set in that world. She will also release horrormance in 2026 under a new pen name.

She started writing in middle school when her obsession with *Goosebumps* inspired a project that consumed three years of her life and resulted in over sixty novella-length stories. When she isn't writing, she's dreaming of far away lands that only exist on the page. Cassandra lives in Houston, Texas with her family of five.

For more about Cassandra and her work, and to sign up for her newsletter, visit www.cassandraastonauthor.com or scan here:

ALSO BY CASSANDRA ASTON

Prophecies of Angels and Demons
Fated *(Sanura's Novella) – book 0.5*
Grave Secrets – *book 1*
Firefly *(Simon's Novella) book 1.5*
Grave Prophecies – *book 2*
Light (*Gabriel's Novella) – book 2.5*
Grave Revelations – *book 3*
Parable *(Peter's Novella) – book 3.5*

Deadly Fae Duology
Whispers Among Thorns – *book 1*
Spring – *book 1.5*
Poison Amidst Blooms – *book 2*
Winter – *book 2.5 (Coming 2026)*

The Drowned Fae Realms (Deadly Fae Continued)
Book 1 – *Coming 2027*

Vicious Villains: A Twisted Fairytale Reimagining Anthology Series
Book 1 – *Coming 2026*

STANDALONES BY C.ASTOR

A Treachery of Hearts – *Coming 2026*
Maladdiction – *Coming 2027*

CASSANDRA ASTON

dark fantasy author